AS L(

She followed the trail of candles and flowers to the second floor. A jazzy paino tune enticed her down the hall and toward the bathroom door. She nudged it open with her foot. A cloud of lavender hovered over the room.

Marek waited, dressed in a pair of black trousers and a white silk shirt. The sleeves were rolled away from his wrist and revealed arms covered with dark hair. A bottle of champagne and two fluted glasses sat on a small white table to his right.

Magnificent! He looked simply magnificent. His wickedly tempting smile made her melt like butter in a microwave oven. "Hey," he pointed to the old porcelain tub filled with bubbles and water. "I've got your bath ready."

Ohh! Every bone in her body liquefied while desire flared within her. It held her captive in the doorway. Just how far did he intend to take this? More to the point, how far did she plan to let him? Instantly, Cameron made her decision; she wanted him. She dropped the flowers on the floor next to the door and stepped inside the room. Drawn by an invisible string, Cameron floated to Marek.

With the elaborate flourish of a wine captain, he removed the bottle from the carafe and wrapped it in a white towel. He twisted off the metal cap and then uncorked the bottle. The effervescent wine ran from the top and into the carafe.

Marek poured champagne into both glasses and offered one to her. She took the glass and smiled her thanks.

"What are we celebrating?"

His eyebrows did a double lift and a gleam of sensual promise made her go weak. "To everything and nothing ..." he said, clicking their glasses together.

BOOK YOUR PLACE ON OUR WEBSITE AND MAKE THE ARABESQUE ROMANCE CONNECTION!

We've created a customized website just for our very special Arabesque readers, where you can get the inside scoop on everything that's going on with Arabesque romance novels.

When you come online, you'll have the exciting opportunity to:

- View covers of upcoming books
- Learn about our future publishing schedule (listed by publication month and author)
- Find out when your favorite authors will be visiting a city near you
- Search for and order backlist books
- Check out author bios and background information
- Send e-mail to your favorite authors
- Join us in weekly chats with authors, readers and other guests
- Get writing guidelines
- AND MUCH MORE!

Visit our website at
http://www.arabesquebooks.com

AS LONG AS THERE IS LOVE

Karen White-Owens

BET Publications, LLC
http://www.bet.com
http://www.arabesquebooks.com

ARABESQUE BOOKS are published by

BET Publications, LLC
c/o BET BOOKS
One BET Plaza
1900 W Place NE
Washington, DC 20018-1211

Copyright © 2002 by Karen White-Owens

All rights reserved. No part of this book may be reproduced, stored in a retrieval system, or transmitted in any form or by any means without the prior written consent of the Publisher.

If you purchased this book without a cover, you should be aware that this book is stolen property. It was reported as "unsold and destroyed" to the Publisher and neither the Author nor the Publisher has received any payment for this "stripped book."

All Kensington Titles, Imprints, and Distributed Lines are available at special quantity discounts for bulk purchases for sales promotions, premiums, fund-raising, and educational or institutional use. Special book excerpts or customized printings can also be created to fit specific needs. For details, write or phone the office of the Kensington special sales manager: Kensington Publishing Corp., 850 Third Avenue, New York, NY 10022, attn: Special Sales Department, Phone: 1-800-221-2647.

BET Books is a trademark of Black Entertainment Television, Inc. ARABESQUE, the ARABESQUE logo, and the BET BOOKS logo are trademarks and registered trademarks.

First Printing: October 2002
10 9 8 7 6 5 4 3 2 1

Printed in the United States of America

ACKNOWLEDGMENTS

There is an old African saying, it takes a village to raise a child. The same can be said for writing a book. My village includes a host of wonderfully talented people, starting with my editor, Chandra Sparks Taylor, and my critique group, Natalie Dunbar, Angela Patrick Wynn, and Aubrey Vaughan. Natalie, without your encouragement, I would have quit writing after our first meeting; thanks for insisting that I attend a second. Angela, thank you for goal, motivation, and conflict. You taught me well. Aubrey Vaughan, you taught me the wisdom and benefit of networking.

Darlene Bashore, Heather Buchanan, Sherry Dargen, Ellen Jones, Diane Perttola, Emita Odom-Shuler, Natalie Olsen, Sharon Stanford, Pam Weinstein, Kimberley White, Karen Williams, and Stephanie Worth, many thanks for your editorial input and support. I tip my hat to Jim Downey for helping me to understand the details of contracts.

Thanks to my husband, Gary, who never complained, always believed in me and encouraged me to continue to write. I will always be grateful to my nieces, Takisha, Kaon, Brittany, and China and my nephew, Kevin, who were the creative inspiration behind Jayla. To my brother, Clayton, and sister, Valerie, your never-ending belief that I could write a book, proved to be correct.

Thank you all for your help and support in raising this particular child to adulthood.

This book is dedicated to:

My mother, Helen Brown. You are missed.

Chapter One

Cameron Butler forced down the lump in her throat and glanced at the clock. How much longer would it take? She ran a hand over her face and relived the moments that had led her to Holland General Emergency Room.

After their afternoon nap, Cameron sent her students into the backyard to burn off a portion of their endless energy. Too late. Justin had shot past her, heading for the playground equipment. She'd dashed after him, ready to caution him against his latest stunt and found him posed like a diver at the top of the sliding board.

One of the children called his name and he turned. Justin tumbled off the edge and banged his arm along the way. Her heart almost burst through her chest when his body hit the ground. Horrified, she raced to his side while her staff hustled the remaining children inside the day care center. Cameron gathered Justin close, rushed to the van and used her cell phone to call his mother as she sped to the hospital.

If she'd told Justin once, she'd told him a hundred times

to be careful. It didn't matter. The fearless four-year-old ignored her every word of caution. Unfortunately, the incident could put the brakes on her plans to open an elementary school that fall.

Cameron nibbled on her bottom lip and glanced down the hospital corridor. Justin needed her and here she sat in Admissions with a pile of forms. Until his mother arrived, Justin remained her responsibility. And she took her obligations very seriously.

Standing, she dropped the clipboard onto a table, and barreled down the corridor toward the emergency room, swinging her long, brown arms with a "don't-mess-with-me" aggressiveness. In the ER, she inched her way through the triage and around the staff. At each drawn curtain, her ears were tuned for her charge's voice.

"Ouch," came Justin's harsh cry. Snatching back the curtain, she found him on the examining table with a tall, broad-shouldered man leaning over him.

"I'm sorry," the doctor said, pressing a white bandage to Justin's forehead. "I know this isn't easy. Just hold on. We'll get you X-rayed and then I'll set your arm. Okay?"

Braced for more pain, Justin's tear-smothered voice asked, "Will it hurt?"

"Some. Like when they position your arm to take pictures. Hold on a little longer and it'll all be over. I promise."

"Okay," Justin replied, brushing a tear away from his cheek with the back of his hand.

"Sarah? How long before we can get this little guy to X-ray?" he asked, glancing over his shoulders and straight into Cameron's eyes.

A soft cry escaped from her lips. Oh, Lord. Marek Redding. She stared across the confined space at her former love, feeling pain cut deep into her heart.

After four years, Marek still wore the air of confidence that belongs exclusively to the wealthy. A golden tan added color to his skin. Rich, chocolate-brown hair cropped short looked enticingly rumpled. A small bump marred his aquiline nose, but matured his hawkish good looks. Under his lab coat a Red Wings T-shirt hung over his green scrubs.

Marek's honey-gold eyes widened, and then widened a fraction more. He shook his head as if trying to clear her image from his mind. "Ronnie?" His use of her pet name sent ripples of awareness surging through her. "W—what? How?"

Tension held her in place. This couldn't be happening. She sucked in a steadying breath and asked, "Jus—Just—Justin? How is he?"

"He's okay." He moved so close that his fresh scent mingled with her own. "Are you related to him?"

"No. Justin fell off the sliding board in the backyard at my day care center. Mrs. O'Rourke said his pediatrician works here." Embarrassed, she stopped.

Marek tapped his chest with a finger. "That would be me. His mother phoned ahead and explained the situation. I assured her I'd handle things myself."

"Ms. Butler," the little boy whined, drawing their attention back to him.

"Yes, love. I'm here." She returned to Justin's side, blinking back tears. He looked so fragile. It hurt her to see him that way. "How're you doin'?"

"My arm hurts," Justin fretted. "I want my mama."

"Your mother will be here any minute," Cameron soothed.

"Dr. Marek said they're gonna ta—ta—take pictures of my arm." He turned to Marek, eyes glittering with hope. "Can Ms. Butler come too?"

"Sure." Marek's eyes slid over her, causing her insides to quiver. "But let's ask her first."

"Please, come with me. Please." Justin clutched her hand. "I'm scared."

"Oh, sweetie." Cameron folded his white hand between her brown ones. "You don't have to be afraid. I'll be right with you."

"Promise?"

"I promise." She felt Justin relax a little.

"Dr. Redding?" A nurse entered with a wheelchair. "X-ray's ready and this young man's mother is waiting." With a polite nod, the nurse dismissed Cameron and spoke to Justin, "Time for you to take a trip with me."

Relief washed over her. Thank goodness. Justin needed his mother.

"Here, let me help you." Frowning at the nurse, Marek brushed past Cameron and lifted the child off the examining table, causing a new set of tears to spring to Justin's eyes.

"I'm sorry, kiddo." Marek lowered the child into the chair. "It's almost over."

Cameron hunched down next to the wheelchair and brushed a few locks of blond hair from his eyes and whispered, "Sweetheart, your mom's going to meet you in X-ray. I'll wait in the lobby until you're done."

"Okay."

She dropped a kiss on his cheek and stood. "Don't worry. Dr. Redding will take good care of you."

"Dr. Redding, did you catch *All My Children* today?" Sarah asked, releasing the wheelchair lock.

All My Children? Cameron zeroed in on Marek. After all these years he still watched their show? Images flashed through her head like a video on fast-forward.

That show had played such a prominent role in the time they'd shared. Between Marek's fellowship and her student teaching, time together had been a precious commodity. But they always made time for a marathon session of All My Children. It had been a wonderful, magical period of her life.

Her senior year at the University of Michigan, when

Marek was off-duty, they'd snuggled in her bedroom to watch their "soap", kiss throughout the commercials, and make love after the show's conclusion.

"No. Too busy." Marek glanced at his silver Rolex and smirked at Sarah. "Oh well."

"Did you tape it today?" Sarah asked.

"Everyday," he answered with a smug double lift of his eyebrows. "The soap opera junkie always finds a way."

"So true." Sarah wheeled Justin through the curtain. "I'll be by your office after my shift to check it out."

"Ronnie, Justin's in good hands." He stripped the latex gloves from his hands and tossed them into the trash. "Why don't you come with me?" Before a word of protest left her lips, Marek cupped her elbow and steered her down the corridor. "It's more comfortable in my office. We can wait for X-ray to get done with him and catch up."

Justin went off with the nurse and left Cameron to cope with Marek and his disturbing plan to discuss old times. Worried, she brushed her sweaty palms along the thighs of her jeans. Her grandmother always said confession was good for the soul. Cameron hoped so.

With long purposeful strides, Marek pulled Cameron down a private hallway. He ushered her through an outer office and into his domain. Once the door shut behind them, his gaze slid over her appreciatively.

Her pulse accelerated to hyperspeed as his gaze cruised from her shoulder length bob to her battered Nike's. By the time he finished his inspection, there wasn't a spot his warm gaze had missed.

"You look wonderful," Marek pronounced, smiling broadly.

"Thank you," Cameron managed to reply.

"So, are you married?"

Her stomach lurched. Marek's directness caught her off-guard.

"Do you live in town?" he pressed. "Let's get together. Maybe have dinner? Before you leave, jot down your address and phone number."

Remaining silent, she moved aimlessly around his office. Instead of a traditional desk he'd opted for a computer workstation. The black, chrome and glass unit sat near an open window that allowed the April breeze into the room. The flat screen monitor flickered with a slide show composed of *Star Wars—Phantom Menace* scenes. A cinnamon-colored leather golf bag and clubs were displayed in the corner near the door. She smiled when she spotted a stack of *Mad* magazines mingled with a selection of medical journals on a wooden bookshelf.

"How long will it take before X-ray finishes with Justin?"

Marek frowned. His gaze swept over her once more, working to decipher her body language.

"Actually," he began, shrugging out of his lab coat, "the X-rays won't take too long. A half hour at the max."

She nodded, uncertain if she could hold out that long. Fishing through her short list of topics, she searched for a lead into a discussion that would take them to Jayla. But the proper words escaped her.

"So, you own a day care center." Marek grinned; even white teeth flashed against his tanned skin. "You mentioned something about the backyard. Where's your place located?"

"In my house."

"Mmmm. That makes things convenient," he muttered, waving a hand in her direction. "But the way you always loved kids, I'm not surprised to find you surrounded by little people."

"When you have three older brothers and you're the baby,

you've got to find somebody to boss around," she said flippantly.

"I'm sure it's more than that. You always had such love for any child that crossed your path. It's good to know you're involved in what you love."

A small portion of her brain reveled in his praise, while the rest of her mind tried to figure out a way to break the news that he had a daughter.

"Thank you." She gave him a small curtsy. "How about you? What happened to cardiology? Pediatrics is a far cry from the demands of heart patients."

"True. I practiced cardiology for a while." Marek perched on the edge of the workstation and stretched his long legs in front of him. "A short while," he emphasized with a self-mocking smirk. "My residency rotation in Peds always stayed with me. When it was time to decide on a specialty, I talked with the chief resident and some of my colleagues. They all agreed that I should stick with cardiology." Sadness flickered in his eyes. "It wasn't the right choice for me.

"Sometimes I'd lose patients within days of the initial consultation. That part bugged me. I found myself drawn to the kind of patients I could have a long association with. And, of course," he shrugged, then said, "children offer that. This is my place in the world. It's where I feel needed and complete."

"I know what you mean. Kids need so much. And I'm hoping my elementary school will help them, and prepare them for their futures. I want my students to have the tools they need to get on in life."

"You've always thrown yourself wholeheartedly into everything you do. I'm sure the school will be a success." Marek stood, headed toward a dorm-sized refrigerator parked next to the workstation and removed a soda. He popped the tab on a can of Pepsi and tipped it in her direction. "Want one?"

She wrinkled her nose and shook her head.

Fidgeting with the tab on the can, Marek's face turned serious. "Ronnie," he began, "about what happen—"

"How are your parents?" she interrupted, afraid of where he was going with the topic.

Irritation flickered across Marek's handsome face, but he answered, "It's been a few months, but Dad still spends two-thirds of his waking hours at the bank. And since Mom's conquered all the malls in Michigan, she's chosen California as her new target. She flies out there once a month or so and stays for about a week. Maybe two. Shopping junkets she calls them."

"Oh," Cameron muttered, unsure what to say. "So how did you end up here?"

Marek sipped the Pepsi, watching her from his perch on the edge of his workstation. "Being boarded in both cardiology and pediatrics gave me the leverage to do what I wanted. Remember how you begged me to take a weekend off and come to Holland?"

She nodded.

"Well, last spring I did. I was here just in time for that Tulip Festival you were always raving about and I fell in love with this tiny Michigan town. Then later that year, I was flipping through a medical journal when I saw an ad looking for a chief of pediatrics. That was my ticket." His wistful expression touched a chord inside her. "Life in a small community hospital appealed to me after the kick-ass pace of a large practice."

"You won't get rich here."

"Not a problem. I'm thirty-seven years old. My needs are different. I want a life. Not a career that supersedes everything else. I don't want to be alienated from my family like my dad." Marek's face twisted into a mask of distaste. "I plan to raise my kids. Not some nanny. This way I can have my career and go home at night."

She picked up an issue of *Mad* and flipped through the pages, pretending to scan it while digesting his comments. "When did you move to town?"

"About three months ago." Marek placed the Pepsi can on his workstation and strolled to within inches of her. Unnerved by his closeness, she took a step away. He removed the magazine from her hands and tossed it back onto the shelf, looking deeply into her eyes.

With a gentle finger, he combed the hair from her face. His touch sent a surge of conflicting emotions coursing through her.

"And you?" Marek asked, voice softening. "Why did you move to Holland? How long have you been here?"

"A couple of years. I have family here."

"What about my first question? Are you married?"

She grimaced, folding her arms across her chest. His eyes darkened as he followed her gesture. No ring. It didn't take a rocket scientist to figure it out.

"What about you? A—are you married?" Cameron stammered. Surprised that after four years, she still cringed at the notion. "Is there a Mrs. Redding or any baby Reddings running around town?"

"No." He shook his head. "I'm not married."

Longing touched every part of her as those words, spoken so softly, registered. Frantic, Cameron searched the room for another topic, any topic to break the tension. Her eyes returned to his golf clubs and she pointed to them.

"Is Wednesday still golf day?" she asked in what she prayed sounded like her normal voice.

"Not as often as I'd like. This job and finding a place to live makes free time pretty scarce. Do you still play?"

"Seldom. I'm in the same boat as you. Between work at Little Darlings and my master's degree, plus the elementary school, my schedule's pretty tight." *Add a three-year-old to the mix and there's no time.*

"Maybe we can tee off sometime," Marek suggested, taking an imaginary golf swing. "I miss playing," he paused and then added, "with you." The eagerness in his voice almost convinced her. Almost.

The urge to give in and be close to him again appealed to her. But just as quickly, she made a crash landing back to the real world. She swallowed hard then pushed away his provocative invitation. "I don't have time for much these days."

"Are you involved with anyone?" Marek returned to his prior topic. "Or living with anyone?" His eyes glowed with an inflexible light, which told her quite eloquently that he planned to learn all her secrets.

His questions also jolted her. Marek was the only man for her. Although, things like family and trust played a significant role in separating them.

Gazing into eyes so similar to her three-year-old daughter's, guilt made Cameron turn away. *Enough pussyfooting. Time to tell him.* Intent on that goal, she stepped closer. The air in the room thinned as cold hands closed around her lungs, squeezing.

How would Marek react? Would he want to see Jayla?

Perspiration dotted her forehead. Lips parted, the words refused to form. She couldn't do this. Not today. Maybe never.

She began, "Actual—"

The telephone's peal startled her. Perhaps he sensed her need to reveal something momentous, because his mouth tightened into a stubborn line as he ignored the persistent sound. After a half-dozen rings, duty won out.

"Excuse me," Marek snatched up the telephone and growled out his name. "Thanks. Be right there." Replacing the handset, he circled the workstation and stopped in front of her. "Got to go. X-ray's finished with Justin and I want to talk with the radiologist. No doubt Mrs. O'Rourke will demand an update. Perhaps you'd like me to speak to her for you?"

"No," Cameron vetoed, making her way to the door and twisting the knob. There were many things she needed from him, but she could handle her own business. "It's my responsibility. I'll put things right. Marek, it was good to see you. Good luck with everything."

"Ronnie?"

The odd note in his voice made her body stiffen. She faced him. "Yes?"

"Your phone number?"

"Oh, umm—umm. Let me give you one of my business cards." That was a joke. There weren't any business cards. But she needed to stall, give herself a moment to think things through. Until she told Marek about Jayla, she didn't want him making an unannounced visit to the house. "Hmm." She rummaged through her pockets. "I don't have any with me."

Returning to the workstation, Marek said, "That's okay. Here, take one of mine." He scribbled on the back of a business card. "My home number is on the back. And the office and pager numbers are printed on the front." Taking the card, she noted the telephone number before stuffing it into the breast pocket of her T-shirt. "Give me a call."

Marek's hands rested on her shoulders and dallied a moment longer than necessary. He felt so familiar, so male. Warm fingers traveled up her neck and cupped her face.

Cameron leaned into his touch; eyes drifted shut. This was madness, but she savored the bombardment of sensations. Gently, he touched her cheek with his warm lips.

A rap on the door brought her back to the sane world. Her eyes flew open and she stepped away.

"Yes?" he called.

A young blonde with acne stuck her head around the door. "Umm, Dr. Redding?" She giggled. "Excuse me."

"Hi, Wendy." Marek dropped his hands to his sides, but his eyes remained glued on Cameron's face. "What do you need?"

Cameron shoved clenched fists inside her pockets. There was a time when she had needed him too, but she had learned her lesson. Her dad was right; never trust a man.

Frowning, Wendy gaze shifted between Marek and Cameron as she stepped into the room and shut the door. "Umm, Sarah said I'd find Ms. Butler here. Hi." She giggled uncertainly, pushing a clipboard toward Cameron. "Is this yours?"

"My driver's license." She pulled her hands from her pockets and several scraps of paper fluttered to the floor. From behind her, Marek's amused chuckle filled the room.

Irritated, Cameron turned to him and snapped, "What's so funny?"

"After all this time you haven't changed." He shook his head, grinning. "You still carry zillions of notes on bits of paper."

Embarrassed, heat crept up her neck. "I can't help it." She dropped to her knees, gathered the pieces of paper and shoved them back into her pocket. "Where did you find my license?"

"In Admissions."

"Ahh, Wendy." Marek crooked a finger.

She changed directions. "Yes, Doctor?"

He plucked the license from Wendy's hand and examined it. "You live on Tulip Street. That's near I-31. Right?"

Damn. Frustration sizzled under the surface of her skin. *Marek thinks he's so smart.*

"Well," Wendy slipped through the door, adding, "my work is done. I'd better get back to my desk."

Cameron followed Wendy to the door. "Marek, thanks for taking such good care of Justin." She quickly shut the door after her and leaned against it. Her heart thumped wildly against her chest, before slowly returning to normal.

The damage was done. Her driver's license gave Marek all the information he needed. This forced her hand and made the need to talk with him her next priority.

For now, Marek and their personal problems belonged on the back burner. She needed to focus her energies on Tara O'Rourke.

When Little Darlings first opened, she and Tara had established a sort of camaraderie due in part to their mutual single parent status. But three and half years later, Tara's attitude had turned frosty.

A stream of complaints followed that left Little Darlings staff questioning why Tara had morphed from Dr. Jekyll to Ms. Hyde. Concerned for her employees, Cameron had morosely suggested Tara enroll Justin in another school. That idea had fallen on deaf ears.

Instead, each morning Tara dropped Justin off at Little Darlings. Every night, she drummed up a new set of complaints that tortured the staff.

Cameron concluded the redhead witch had no plan to leave Little Darlings. She wanted to make life miserable for everyone. And she got A's for effort. Cameron tolerated all of it because she loved Justin and had from the first day his mother placed the blue-eyed baby in her arms.

Starting down the corridor, she vowed to keep her cool, state the facts and make the other woman understand it was a terrible accident—if Tara would give her the opportunity.

"Where in the hell is the doctor?" Tara O'Rourke demanded. "He said he'd be out here to talk with me."

From the triage archway, she observed Tara terrorize a red-faced Wendy who was sitting at the Admissions' desk.

Cameron felt drained from the day's events, and wasn't up to Tara's Gestapo tactics.

"Page him." Tara pushed the telephone at Wendy.

"Ma'am," Wendy began, "Dr. Redding is with a patient and I can't disturb him. As soon as he's available, he'll be out to see you."

"Excuse me, did you hear what I said?" Tara tilted her head to the side and added a touch of force to her command, "Page him."

Annoyance crossed Wendy's face. Standing, she waved a hand toward the waiting area. "If you'd give Dr. Redding a few minutes, I'm sure he'll be right with you."

"You know, I've got an injured child here and I want some answers." Tara wagged a finger in the young woman's face. "Now!"

"When he's done, I'm sure he'll be happy to answer all your questions," Wendy soothed. "Please be patient."

"Don't talk to me like I'm the some kind of friggin' idiot. You're worthless." Tara flipped a hand in the air and glanced around the triage, asking, "Who's in charge here?"

Wendy picked up the receiver and began to dial. "I'll get the charge nurse."

"Hold on." Tara disconnected the call. "Is she with Dr. Redding?"

"No. But she'll be able—"

"Stop." Tara halted her with a raised hand. "I don't have time for this crap."

Wendy dropped the telephone in the cradle and shrugged helplessly.

"Let's try this again." Tara's features drew into a pinched mask. "I'd like to speak with the director of this department." She produced a packet of cigarettes from her purse, than thrust one between her lips, preparing to light it.

"I'm sorry, Mrs. O'Rourke, you can't light that in here."

Wendy pointed at the overhead no-smoking sign. "This is a smoke-free environment."

"Oh hell." Tara shoved the cigarette and lighter back into her purse and planted her hands on her hips.

Watching the whole performance from the triage doorway, Cameron felt incredible sympathy for the young clerk. Braced for similar treatment, she strolled toward the pair.

Meeting with Tara presented Cameron with an initial attempt at damage control. In Tara's present state, she would relish the opportunity to ruin the elementary school's reputation before the doors were open.

Drawing in a deep breath, she tapped the red-haired witch on the shoulder. "Tara?" The strong scent of hairspray mixed with a heavy dose of musk perfume assaulted Cameron's nostrils. She fought the urge to sneeze.

"Finally," Tara muttered, her emerald eyes narrowed suspiciously. "You've decided to show your face. I thought you'd left. Where did you sneak off to?"

Cameron glanced about, noting the curious glances directed at them. We're not going to be the main attraction today, she decided silently, guiding Tara to an empty section of the room. "Let's sit over here. The nurse told me you were in with Justin and suggested I wait out of the way."

"You know, I didn't see you when I came out here." She perched on the edge of a red plastic chair and examined her surroundings with a disparaging gleam. "Where were you?"

"Actually, I ended up in the doctor's office."

"Mmm." Tara crossed one knee over the other. "Let's get to the real deal. What happened?"

"First, I want you to know how sorry I am about this."

"Yeah, yeah, yeah." Tara waved aside Cameron's apology and said, "That's not important right now. I'm more concern with how Justin got hurt."

"He fell off the sliding board."

"Where was the staff?" Legs crossed, she cupped her hands around her knee. "Who was in the backyard with the kids?"

"I was," Cameron stated. "And so were Michelle, Linda and my grandmother."

A frown marred Tara's smooth, white skin. "If four adults were in the backyard, how come none of you stopped Justin?"

"Your son fancies himself an Olympic diver. Before I could reach him, he'd pulled another one of his stunts."

"Stunts?" Tara's voice rose above the hum in the room. "What are you talking about? Children don't just fall off of sliding boards."

Tara had just hit a nerve. "They do," she answered frostily. "Especially when they believe the slide can be used as a diving board. If you'll think back a couple of weeks ago I tried to talk with you about this. Remember, I encouraged you to talk with him?"

"Don't try to push this off on me. If you knew there was a problem, you should have been looking out for it."

"You're right. And we have. But he was too quick for us." Cameron ran a hand over her face. "Now that we're both aware there's a problem, why don't you stop by Little Darlings so that we can discuss ways to avoid a repeat of today's incident."

"You know," Tara answered in a non-committal tone. "I think I'll talk with Doc Redding first."

"What's he got to do with this?"

"He examined Justin." She slipped the purse strap over her shoulder. "He can explain more about Justin's injuries."

"If I can help in any way, please let me know."

Tara's eyes narrowed to green slits. "I think you've done enough. More," she added, one finely sculpted eyebrow rose, "than enough."

Cameron's nervous fingers busily rolled a section of her

AS LONG AS THERE IS LOVE   23

T-shirt. Suddenly, the hairs on the back of her neck rose. From across the room, her gaze met Marek's.

Strolling toward them, he said, "Mrs. O'Rourke. I'm sorry you had to wait. I was called in for an emergency." He took Tara's outstretched hand and helped her to her feet. "Your son's ready to go home. And I've got some instructions for you." He cupped her elbow and guided her toward the door.

"Thank you, Doc. I'm just so upset." Tara placed a hand on his arm. "Can we talk privately for a minute?"

"Sure." Marek led Tara away from the waiting area. "Let's go back to my office."

From the triage doorway, Cameron watched the pair disappear down the corridor with Tara's hand glued to Marek's arm.

Rage pulsed through Cameron as she left the hospital. She got behind the wheel of her Volkswagen van and slammed the door shut for good measure. The childish gesture made her feel better, but not much. Frustrated, she let out a pent-up moan and rested her head against the steering wheel.

This was the day from hell. Justin's accident, Marek, and now Tara. The combination made her brain hurt.

Justin's issues were resolvable. Keep him safe. No more backyard antics and he'd be fine.

His mother was a different story. Tara's inquiries about Justin's accident were justified and Cameron wanted to soothe her fears. But she sensed a deeper problem smoldering under the surface. This wasn't the end. Oh no. That redhead witch had a little extra jolt planned. It sizzled in the air like an electric storm.

They both needed a little cool down time. She would give

Tara a few days and an opportunity to look at the incident in a rational light.

Cameron glanced at the dashboard clock and noted the late hour. "Oh, Lord." Time to go home, she thought, adjusting the rearview mirror.

The reflection confirmed her suspicions: she'd survived, although at the moment Cameron felt each and every one of her twenty-six-years. A few additional stress lines edged her round, dark brown eyes and the disarray of her neat, sable-colored bob seemed to be the extent of the damage.

Her pecan-colored skin and high cheekbones were free of make-up, but covered by a fine sheen of perspiration. She pulled a tissue and her cherry lipstick from the glove box, patted the moisture away from her wide nose and applied a light coat of lipstick to her full, pouty lips.

Now, the question of Marek. "Marek . . ." his name slipped from her lips and conjured his image.

When her roommate had introduced them, Marek had literally awed her. After she had calmed down and closed her mouth, his unflappable approach to studying had relaxed her and helped her ace her teaching certification test in biology.

This same persuasive approach calmed her fears regarding dating Marek. Unfortunately, soon after intertwining her life with his, the fairytale ended and the nightmare began. When everything was said and done, Marek had proved that he couldn't be trusted.

Fear iced her skin when she thought of Jayla. One glimpse of her daughter's honey-gold eyes, aquiline nose and her riotous mop of chocolate hair, and Marek would know Jayla was his. Any fool with eyes would see the truth.

And Marek was no fool.

Chapter Two

Two weeks of playing telephone tag with Tara O'Rourke had propelled Cameron into action. Determined to get some answers, she and Jayla set out that Saturday afternoon for an unannounced visit to confront Tara.

"Honey?" Jayla used her pet name for her mother.

In the rearview mirror, Cameron examined her baby's crinkled brow. She answered, "Yes, Honeybunny."

"Who's house is this?" Jayla asked.

"Justin's," Cameron answered, parking the car and switching off the engine. She watched her daughter's eyes twinkle with happiness, filling Cameron's heart with love. "He'll be surprised to see us."

I'm doing all of this for you, little one. We won't ever have to ask my parents for anything, she promised silently. *We'll show them all. Your future will be set, stabile. I'll provide everything you need. All we need is each other. Just you and me.*

Cameron climbed from the car and opened the rear passenger door. "Come on, Honeybunny." She lifted the excited child from the car seat and nudged the door shut with her hip. Reaching for her daughter's small hand, they crossed the parking lot. "Jayla, we're here for a short visit. I want you to be very good while I talk with Justin's mother. Okay?"

"Yessss."

They entered the building and headed for the staircase. Jayla's slow progress on the steps increased Cameron's nervousness. At the top of the second flight, she whisked the little girl into her arms and carried her to the third floor, setting her on her feet in front of the O'Rourkes' door. Hand poised to knock, Cameron hesitated; Tara always required delicate treatment. Tapping lightly, she prayed this stunt wouldn't blow up in her face.

After a second knock, the chain rattled and the door opened a fraction. A tiny beam of light sliced across Cameron's face and bounced off the wall. Musk perfume followed by stale cigarette smoke drifted out the door.

Scowling, Tara demanded, "What do *you* want?"

"Hi," Cameron injected a sunny note into her voice. "I hope you don't mind my dropping by. I need to talk to you and I brought Jayla along so she could spend some time with Justin. She misses him."

"Aren't you supposed to be in school?"

"Not today. Winter term is over." She reached for Jayla's hand and drew her close. "May we come in for a few minutes? I promise we won't stay long."

Malicious intent danced in Tara's green eyes as she started to close the door. "No."

Acting instinctively, Cameron slipped her palm against the wood surface and held firm. This wasn't happening today. She hadn't come all this way for nothing.

"I promise we'll be just a few minutes." She kept the flat of her hand on the door, turning up the persuasive note in her voice a notch. "So much was happening at the hospital we couldn't talk properly. This is so much better, more comfortable and private."

Justin's blond head peeped through the crack in the door. Curious blue eyes rounded with surprise, then pleasure.

"Jayla!" Delight filled his voice. "Mama, let her in." The chain rattled as he tugged at the door. "Open the door, Mama."

Tara's lips snapped shut, but she removed the chain. Justin flew through the door and hugged Jayla.

"Jayla!" He cried. "Come see my room."

The children scurried inside while Cameron brought up the rear and shut the door. "Hey," she called. Jayla and Justin turned. "Wait a minute." She kneeled before Justin and caught him by the shoulders, drawing his small frame against hers. "How you doin'?" It felt wonderful to see him after two weeks.

Excited, he pranced from one foot to the other, giving her a toothy grin. "Hi, Ms. Butler."

She brushed a finger across his cast. "You okay?"

"Yeah." Justin raised his plaster-encased arm and confessed, "It itches. But I've got a Spiderman Band-Aid." He pointed at the patch on his forehead. "See?"

"Cool."

"Come on." Justin spun away, grabbed Jayla's hand and they raced down the hall together. "Mama bought me a Gameboy."

Standing, she caught sight of Tara in the hallway, dressed in a white silk blouse that showcased her amble bust, a tight, black leather skirt and three-inch black heels. Without a word, she turned and headed down the narrow hallway. Cameron followed.

Sunlight blazed through the floor-to-ceiling windows when they entered the living room filled with black leather furniture and red and gold accent pieces. Tara halted in the center of the room, facing Cameron.

"Make this quick." She snatched a pack of cigarettes from the glass-topped coffee table. "I'm expecting company."

Cameron drew in a deep breath and shoved her hands inside the back pockets of her jeans. *Well, here goes everything and nothing*, she thought, launching into her rehearsed speech.

"I want to reiterate how sorry I am about Justin's accident. Michelle, Linda and the complete staff want you to know how concerned we are. Tara, when we met at the hospital, you were justifiably upset," Cameron paused, offering her a chance to respond. The silence that followed left her worried. "Since then there's been some downtime for us both to consider the situation. I believe it's time to talk about Justin's accident and for me to put your fears to rest."

Tara's sullen expression heightened Cameron's discomfort. "First," she began, strumming the leg of her jeans with her fingers. "The children in my care take precedence over anything else. Every precaution is taken to protect them. They're never allowed outside without supervision." She waited for a response. None came. Reality crept in and her hopes for a quick resolution began to die. This little speech wasn't working. "That's my first rule. No child is left alone. Ever."

One arm wrapped around her waist while the other held a cigarette, Tara circled Cameron. The chilly gleam in the other woman's eyes flustered Cameron.

"You know, I did a lot of research before I brought Justin to you. Little Darlings came highly recommended. I wanted my baby to be in the best hands. But now I question that source. You were supposed to take care of him, keep him safe. Instead he ended up hurt."

Tara's accusation hit a raw nerve. "That was an accident. One that won't be repeated. Believe me, your son is safe with us. Give my staff and me the opportunity to show you how much and how well we care about him."

AS LONG AS THERE IS LOVE 29

"You want Justin back." Tara let out a bark of laughter and strolled back to the sofa. "That's precious. Just precious. Let me make this clear, you'll never get another chance to hurt him."

"Listen to yourself, you act as if we deliberately set out to hurt Justin. *It was an accident*."

"You know, there's no such thing as an accident," Tara lashed out. "Why are you here anyway? We're not buddies. You've never been to my place before." Red curls cascaded over her shoulder when she tilted her head in Cameron's direction. "Ohhh. Worried about that new little school, are we?"

"No," Cameron denied. "My business is just fine. I'm here to try and put things right between us. I love and miss Justin and I want him to come back."

"Don't love him too much," Tara taunted, sinking into the sofa. "I don't think he can survive too much more of your kind of love." Crossing her arms across her bosom, Tara stated, "Let's get down to the real reason you're here. You don't want any of the bad press to touch your new, little business. Am I right?" Her brow curved knowingly. "Too bad. Somethin' ain't right at Little Darlings and everybody's going to know when I'm done."

"I have nothing to hide. You're invited to come and check things out," Cameron countered confidently. "Matter-of-fact, why don't you? See for yourself. Ask all your questions, satisfy your concerns, then we can talk again."

"There's no need." Tara smashed out her cigarette in the odd-shaped clay ashtray Justin had made at Little Darlings. "I'm not interested."

"Of course you are," Cameron insisted. "This is about your son."

"No." Tara stood. Contempt flashed from her eyes and her voice rose. "This is about how you sent Justin into an unsafe environment. Don't think you're going to get out of it that easily. When the state finishes with you, you you won't have a place to hide."

"The state?"

"I've filed a complaint with the state." Tara grinned triumphantly. "I'm surprised you haven't been notified."

Cameron counted to ten. Then she did it a second time. For a third time she counted. This time she began at one hundred. How had this situation slipped from her hands? At ninety-seven, she turned on the other woman.

"What is wrong with you?" Cameron planted her hands on her hips and stalked across the floor to within inches of Tara. "Why didn't you give me the chance to explain? Justin's been with me since he was six weeks old. When you lost your job, I let you bring him to Little Darlings until you got back on your feet. Don't you think you owe me the benefit of the doubt?"

"Hell no," Tara shot back. "You didn't do me any favors. I paid you in full when I went back to work."

"That wasn't all about money." Frustrated, her arms flapping aimlessly at her sides, she stammered, "I—I—I—I helped you because I'm a single parent just like you. It's hard to make it alone."

"So what am I supposed to do?" She shuddered dramatically. "Kiss your feet?"

"Tara, this isn't a game," Cameron voice rose. "You're playing with my livelihood. My child's future." She stared at the redhead, holding her temper in check with superhuman strength. "Don't."

"And I'm supposed to care because?" Tara stood, crossed the living room and pointed to the hallway. "Get out!"

Standing rigid, Cameron eyed Tara. The urge to beat her down almost was strong. "I thought we could talk honestly. Obviously, I was wrong." Cameron turned toward the hallway. "Honeybunny," she softened her tone so she wouldn't alarm Jayla, "time to go."

"Mummie?" The kids emerged from the opposite end of the room. "Can't we staaay?" she whined. Her tiny plea broke Cameron's heart.

"Sorry, Honeybunny. Maybe another time. Come on." She wiggled fingers at Jayla.

Dejected, Jayla trudged toward her mother. Cameron plucked a stuffed animal from Jayla's hand and laid it on the sofa before lifting her daughter into her arms.

"Justin." Sadness gripped Cameron. "Be good."

At the door, she turned to Tara. "I don't know why you have this hatefest goin' on. But I'm asking you one final time to think about what I've said and reconsider." She drew in a deep breath. "Please remember, I've always treated Justin like he was my own, and deep down you know it."

Again, her words met with stony silence. Discouraged, Cameron pressed her lips together. Well, she'd known it wouldn't be easy. But she'd hoped for a chance to work things out. Swallowing her disappointment, she started through the door and barreled straight into a broad, solid chest. The male scent made her breath catch in her throat.

Marek!

Cameron eyes darted along the hallway as she searched for an escape route. Oh, why didn't the floor just open up and swallow them whole?

She tried to push past him, but he reached out and caught her arm. Frozen in the doorway, she waited, hugging Jayla closer to her chest.

"Hi," Marek greeted. Pleasure shined from his eyes. He touched a lock of Jayla's hair and asked, "Who's this?"

Jayla lifted her head and stared up at Marek. "Hi." She graced her father with one of her thousand-watt smiles.

Oh, Lord. Guilt forced her to look away.

"I thought I heard voices." Tara's suspicious gaze zipped back and forth between Marek and Cameron. "Hi, Doc."

She stepped aside and waved him toward the apartment. "Come on in."

"Give me a minute." Marek's eyes zeroed in on Jayla, then his jaw dropped opened.

He stared at Cameron. A question blazed from his eyes. The answer glittered from hers.

Oh, Lord!

A volley of unchecked emotions flashed across Marek's face. Shock, amazement and betrayal were there for her to see. Then his expression changed and he slashed her into bite-size morsels with a glare of such intense anger, that for a second she thought he might strike her.

Ignoring her, Marek concentrated on Jayla. "Hi yourself," he whispered. Stunned fascination held him glued to the spot. His fingers trembled as they stroked Jayla's cheek. Suddenly, Marek's hand dropped away and he brushed past Cameron.

Could this afternoon have gotten any worse? Cameron wondered as she secured Jayla into her car seat.

She climbed into the car, slammed her door and groped around the doorframe for her own seat belt. Life was full of irony. Marek. Of all the places they might have met, Tara's apartment was last on her list.

Why had he shown up here? First, he assured Tara that he would personally take care of Justin. Now he was at her house. What's up with that? Jealousy swept through her when she considered the provocative style of Tara's outfit. Pushing those thoughts to the back of her mind, she concentrated on the turn of events.

Things were screwed up. Big time. Now that he knew about Jayla, what would he do?

Marek wasn't her only concern. Tara continued to wear the crown as Ms. Queen B, and the title had nothing to do with insects. It still baffled her why the witch felt compelled to cause so much trouble. Her actions went way beyond a disgruntled customer. Nibbling on the edge of Cameron's consciousness was the conviction that Tara had some personal reason for kicking up so much dust. But why?

Justin provided the only bright spot to an otherwise dismal afternoon. That little boy was so precious to her.

Once more, her thoughts returned to Marek. Since their encounter at the hospital, she steered clear of him while she tried to figure out how to approach him about their daughter. But his shocked expression made her fear their next encounter.

Now she needed to convince Marek that she had intended to tell him all along.

Chapter Three

A daughter. Marek shook his head, unable to comprehend this twist in the tale, while he steered his Mercedes-Benz SUV along North I-31 to Cameron's house. When they met at the hospital, he'd imagined a boyfriend, maybe even a husband, and possibly a family. He laughed out loud. A daughter of his own was the last thing he had envisioned.

Euphoria dissipated and uncertainty knotted his insides. How could Cameron have maintained her silence for so long? Did she hate and distrust him so much that she would keep their child a secret?

Her motives were not his only concern. He needed to figure out how to approach her regarding their child. There was no doubt in his mind that Jayla was his child. Her eyes and hair. His daughter.

Marek parked behind Cameron's car, switched off the engine, and drained the last drops from his can of Pepsi before climbing from the SUV. There were lights on at the back of the house. He crossed the yard and rapped on the

AS LONG AS THERE IS LOVE 35

back door, fingering the coins in his pocket. A soft "come in" granted him entry; he turned the doorknob and entered.

The aroma of cinnamon and peaches greeted him when he stepped into the warmth of Cameron's kitchen. Marek spied a deep-dish pie cooling on the white range.

Luther Vandross's lyrics filled the air as he sang of secret loves. Instantly, Marek was transported back to happier times, when he and Ronnie had made love to Luther's ballads. That powerful image almost choked him with its intensity.

Still as stone, Cameron sat at the breakfast nook table. His eyes roamed over her delicate features. A mixture of sadness and suspicion glared back at him and tugged at his heart.

"I knew you'd come." She beckoned him with a wave of her hand. "Come in, Marek," her voice lacked emotion, but her hand shook as she pointed to the chair opposite hers. "Have a seat."

He moved across the kitchen floor and stopped in front of her. His gaze trailed over the smooth lines of her high cheekbones and full bottom lip. She looked so beautiful. A surge of longing assaulted him. It had been four long years since they'd been together, and he'd missed her. Ignoring those feelings, he glanced around the room and asked, "Where is she?"

"Napping."

With a curt nod, he sank into the chair and waited. The stereo hummed as the CD's shifted to a selection of Marvin Gaye tunes. They continued to sit there like strangers without a word to exchange as the silence stretched between them.

"Why didn't you tell me?" Marek attacked, tossing an exasperated hand in the air. "She's as much my child as she is yours. Hell, she looks just like me."

Cameron's lips twisted into something that resembled a smile, but wasn't. "Isn't it obvious?" Her fingers rolled a small corner of her T-shirt. "I didn't think you wanted this complication."

Marek frowned, not sure how to proceed. Cameron had never acted this way before, so detached. Full of life and fun-loving described her.

"You don't have a clue what I want," he snapped. "Why did you do this?"

She turned away and stared out the window into the backyard, but not before he caught sight of the tears that swam in her eyes. "You know why."

"You left me."

"Marek, you made the choice." She wiped away her tears with the back of her hand. "My baby and I went about our business and left you to yours."

His body sagged against the back of the chair as he came face-to-face with their unresolved issues. Would she listen if he tried to explain? She'd never listened to him in the past. Why would she start now? It was worth a try.

"Please, Ronnie," he cajoled. "It's time to talk about the past and work things out."

"No." She pouted like a small child. "I'm not going there with you. Our past is going to stay where it belongs, in the past. It's not a part of this. My daughter is the issue—"

"Our daughter," he corrected.

Her face tightened, but she didn't argue. His heart swelled with satisfaction. Good.

She ran her fingers back and forth across her forehead. "This has been a day from hell without adding you to the mix," her voice wobbled. She cleared her throat and began again, "I can't do this now. I thought I could. But I can't. Just go."

That's not going to happen, Marek promised silently. Settling in the chair, he crossed the ankle of one foot over the other knee. Not until things were straightened out.

AS LONG AS THERE IS LOVE 37

"Before we can make plans for our future, we need to clear up the past," Marek insisted. "It's time for you to hear the truth."

"What truth? The truth is, I found you in bed with my roommate."

Marek's face and voice hardened. "I didn't have sex with Nikki." He hid his disappointment behind a fierce denial. "I never gave you a reason to doubt me. Why won't you believe me?"

Contempt blazed like fire from her eyes. "Because I saw you both in my bed."

He expelled a harsh breath and ran his fingers through his hair. She was trying to bait him so the real issue would get muddled under a sea of other problems. *Stay focused.*

"Ronnie, we were set up."

"Yeah. Right." Sarcasm dripped from each word. "Or maybe one little black girl wasn't enough. Why not two?"

"No." He slapped the palm of his hand on the table. "That's not the way things happened."

"How could you do this to me? I trusted you."

He reached across the table and folded her fists within his hands. This conversation was upsetting her and he wanted to stop, draw her into his arms and comfort her. But the problems between them made it impossible. "And you can still trust me."

Pain flickered across her face. Again, he considered all that faced them. Was there a way for them to move past this? At the moment, he seriously doubted it.

No! His instincts shouted. They belonged together. Things would work out. No way would Jayla grow up like he had. A part-time father who felt more comfortable at the office than at home, and a shopaholic mother. No. Jayla deserved two fully committed parents. And she was going to have them if he had anything to do with it. First, he needed to get past Cameron, break down her wall of anger and distrust and get to the truth.

"I was dog-tired that night." He plunged ahead, hoping she'd let him finish. "I'd been on-call for close to thirty-one hours. When I got to your place, Nikki said you'd be home within the hour. So I went to your room to shut my eyes for a few minutes." She went rigid at the mention of Nikki and tried to tug her hand away. But he refused to release them. "I woke up when you turned on the light. Hell, Nikki shocked me as much as she did you."

"Oh, please," Cameron snatched her hands free. "After all these years that's the best you can do?"

"The truth doesn't change." Rage, sexual frustration and a sensation of complete powerlessness gripped him. "Nikki came between us. And we haven't been able to put the pieces back together. I'm sick and tired of taking the blame for her conniving ass."

"Then maybe you should have thought of that before you dropped your pants and crawled into bed with her!" Cameron yelled back.

Anger swirled out of control; he swung away from the table and drove his fist into the palm of the other hand. So far nothing he had said had sunk in. Maybe if he shook some sense into her beautiful head that might do the trick.

Lips curled away from his teeth, he ridiculed, "Same old Cameron. You don't trust anyone. Make up your mind and that's it. No one can change it. No blurred lines. Just black and white. Have you ever considered that Nikki might have been jealous of us?"

She switched off like a television. Her eyes dulled and she poked out her bottom lip. All emotions were replaced with this alluring, yet rebellious mask. Watching her, his frustration mounted.

"I see no reason to rewind the tape on our past," Cameron answered formally, then pulled her invisible armor tighter around her shoulders. "It's not very pretty. Our focus should be on Jayla."

"True." Marek felt the crushing anger drain from him. Although disappointment continued to flow freely within him. "One day you're going to realize the truth," he vowed.

"Jayla and I are fine." She laced her fingers together and placed them on the table. "We don't need anything from you."

"If you wanted nothing from me, why didn't you abort her?"

Cameron gasped, glaring at him as if he were a cockroach in her immaculate clean kitchen. And he felt like one, too.

"You sound like my father. This will ruin your life," she mimicked, her face contorted in pain. "Think about your future. You won't be able to make it alone." Her eyes flashed with protective fire. "I'd never hurt my baby! Never!"

Head bowed, he mumbled, "I'm sorry."

"You certainly are."

"You've thrown out your share of crap today. How much did you think I'd take before retaliating?"

"Be that as it may, I never thought you'd use my child to hurt me."

"Wait one damn minute," Marek lashed out as he grabbed her arm and hauled her up from the chair. "I didn't use Jayla. You started this. I put an end to it."

"The real deal is Jayla." She peeled his fingers away one by one, glaring at him defiantly. "She's *my* child. And you have absolutely nothing to do with her."

"Nothing to do with her?" he shouted, grabbing her shoulders and dragging her close to his chest, giving her a little shake. "I fathered her. Let me ask you this. Was I your private stud service? Your personal sperm donor that provided good genes, above-average intelligence and a specimen in prime condition? Is that how you used me?"

"I never used you." Stormy eyes raked over him and

seared him with their contempt. "You have a much higher opinion of yourself than I do."

"Is that right?"

All of the fight went out of her. "Stop." Cameron sagged against him. "Stop. We can snipe at each other all night, but believe me, I never planned to get pregnant. But it happened. Any expectations I had about you ended in that apartment four years ago. So you can just leave now." She pointed toward the door. "We won't bother you."

"Gee, thanks." He rolled his eyes. "That was on the top of my list of worries."

"Marek, I'm just trying to calm any fears you might have. I provide a good home for Jayla. Business is good. I give her the things she needs."

"How about the other things she needs?"

Her brow wrinkled over puzzled eyes. "Like what?"

"A father," he retorted, peeved at her naiveté. "How about a positive male figure? Or the benefit of two committed parents?"

"No," Cameron vetoed. She hurried to the cupboard and removed a glass. "Things are fine just the way they are."

"And for how long?" He followed her. "Jayla doesn't notice the differences now. Soon, she will. When you least expect it, some good neighbor Sam will take pleasure in explaining things to her." Frustrated, he snatched the glass from her hand and placed it on the counter. "Is that how you want her to learn about me? Or about her father?"

She turned toward the sink, switched on the tap and whispered, "No."

"Then we have to work together." He reached past her, switched the water off and turned her to face him. "We need to make her understand that she's unique and special."

"Marek, please just leave us alone," she begged, placing a hand on his arm. "If you don't plan to be here forever, you can hurt her."

AS LONG AS THERE IS LOVE 41

Cameron's lavender fragrance hung in the air. It thrust lustful memories to the forefront of his thoughts. Nights of tangled sheets, entwined bodies, and whispers of love brought him sharply to life when his eyes locked with hers. God, how he'd missed her. He wanted to hold her, taste her.

Again, he beat down those feelings. Instead, he concentrated on the real reason he was here. The true reason.

"I want to be her father." Marek stroked a finger across her soft cheek. "Jay ... Jay," he stammered, momentarily stunned by the electric jolt of sensations that shot through him. "She deserves the best from both of us. She needs me and should know that I haven't abandoned her. I want her to know that she has a father. A caring father."

"No," Cameron answered quietly, clenching her fists around the counter's edge. "You don't understand. Her life is calm, settled. Your presence will create new problems. We don't need this kind of drama in our lives."

"Well, you're going to get it. You don't have a choice," Marek reminded, looming over her. "If I have to, I'll take you to court. I don't want to. But I will. My first choice is to work with you."

"Don't." Cameron's eyes grew large. Alarm replaced all previous emotions. "Don't."

"DNA testing is very accurate." Feeling like a rat, he pushed on and watched fear take up residence in her eyes. But he needed to do this. Cameron's stubbornness eliminated all other options.

"Cameron, don't fight me on this." He caged her against the counter with his arms and body. "I'll ask for joint custody and I'll get it. I'm pretty sure you can't afford the long, expensive battle."

Her lips curled away from her teeth. "It always comes down to money. You don't even care about her."

"You don't know what I feel."

She gripped his arm and begged, "I want her to grow

up in a safe, comfortable environment. Your presence will confuse her. You've got your life. Leave us alone."

"That's not going to happen," he said with an arrogant tilt of his head. "You might as well get used to it. I'm here to stay."

Marek's gaze traveled over her face and focused on her lips. Something in him wanted to make her understand the tiny bud of love that blossomed inside him when he realized Jayla was his.

Her shoulders drooped. "Why would you want this kind of responsibility?"

"Because she's mine."

"I think . . ." Cameron stopped, an unreadable expression flickered across her face. "I think we've grown too far apart to work together. There's too much pain between us. It's time for us both to get on with life." She added, "I'm trying to."

"Are you?" He pulled Cameron close as her fragrance swirled around him. "I don't believe you. But this is a good time for me to find out."

Trembling, Cameron struggled against his chest, trying to break free. But he held her fast, wanting to shake her up and set free the passionate woman he remembered, and feel that blazing heat once more.

"Stop!" she yelled, twisting away from his hunting lips. "This won't solve anything."

"Is that right? What are you afraid of?" Marek cradled her face between his hands. "You've moved on. Remember?"

The first taste of her lips shook him to the soles of his shoes. God, how he'd missed her. She felt so right, he thought, feeling heat surging through him with the force of a summer storm. And maybe to her as well, because her fingers threaded through his hair and she began to kiss him back.

AS LONG AS THERE IS LOVE 43

"Sweet Peaches?" A voice pierced his passion-fogged brain. "Jayla? Where's everybody?"

Marek barely registered the unfamiliar voice before Cameron shoved at his chest and stumbled away. His hand shot out to steady her.

Wanting more, he gritted his teeth until it hurt. He moved to the window and pressed his heated forehead against the glass, allowing the coolness to seep into his limbs.

Through the windowpane, he watched a mature version of Cameron waltz through the door, bringing the fragrance of spring flowers with her. Marek smiled, turning away from the windowpane.

Her double-breasted strawberry pantsuit flattered her rounded figure and showcased her neatly fashioned French roll. Intelligence sparkled from a pair of lively brown eyes, and the soft lines in her face hinted at a life lived well.

"Sweet Peaches." Her excited voice refused to be contained. "The slots were good to your granny today. If you treat me right, maybe I'll give you some change for your pocket." She stopped just inside the room. Her gaze slid up and down the length of him with blatant interest. "Mmmm, hmmm. That's why you didn't answer."

She focused on his eyes and then chuckled. Cameron's grandmother recognized him. Good. He wanted people to know he was Jayla's father.

"Mmmm, hmmm," she muttered again.

"Granny, this is my friend, Marek Redding." Cameron moved forward and ran a hand over her hair, smoothing the wild tresses into place. "He went to U of M with me. Remember when Justin had his accident and I took him to the hospital? We ran into each other," she babbled. "Marek, this is my grandmother, Mrs. Butler."

A knowing smirk lifted one corner of her mouth. "Friends," Mrs. Butler repeated. "Mmmm, hmmm."

"Nice to meet you, Mrs. Butler." They shook hands,

Marek was surprised by the strength he felt in those tiny fingers. "I hope we'll see each other again."

"Maybe," she answered evasively. "We'll see."

Releasing her hand, he retreated to the door. There wasn't much more he could say or do in front of her grandmother. "Ronnie, it was good to see you." Disappointment cut a hole straight through his gut. "Let's get together soon. I'll call you."

"I'll walk you out," she offered.

"No need." Marek waved her away. He needed time to think and if Cameron followed him, they'd end up either kissing or fighting, maybe both. That was the last thing he needed right now. "I know my way," he assured, shutting the door behind him.

He wanted them both. Cameron and Jayla.

His family. Marek headed for his SUV, unlocked the door and climbed in.

Jayla needed him. She deserved both parents and he planned to make damn sure she got them.

The loneliness of his own childhood would never touch his daughter. Love would fill her life. His parents' interest had centered on financial success and empty achievement. Jayla would have more, much more. Love would be the key.

Too much of her life had already passed. No way would he miss anymore. They were going to be a family. He just needed to convince Cameron of that fact, and gain her trust. And he needed to make her understand about Nikki, and convince her to let him have a say in Jayla's life. And on, and on and on. There were probably a dozen "and's" to overcome.

He and Cameron hadn't come to any agreement. That bugged him. Instead, their history had exploded in their faces, opening old wounds and creating new problems.

His tongue swept across his lips, savoring the taste of Cameron. Her home was the worst place to try to talk. Mrs. Butler or Jayla might walk in or overhear something that wasn't meant for them. Besides, he couldn't keep his hands to himself.

It might be best to have their next meeting in a public place, maybe a restaurant. Would she accept? Yeah, for Jayla's sake, she'd come. He'd bet money on that. Plus, their surroundings would restrict and control his temper and libido.

Step one: He'd give Cameron a week to stew. Step two: He'd call and invite her to dinner. Step three: Until Cameron consented to joint custody he'd stay low-key.

Chapter Four

Cameron locked the door after Marek and eyed Granny. She'd be home free if she got out of the kitchen before the old girl started interrogating her.

"Where's Jayla?"

She edged toward the kitchen door, sensing escape within her grasp. "Napping."

"Marek is Jayla's father, isn't he?"

The interrogation had commenced. Cameron arranged her face into a bland mask and met Granny's question with silence.

Satisfaction twinkled from the old girl's eyes as she removed her jacket, rolled up the sleeves of her black silk blouse and headed for the range. Her floral scent lingered in her wake.

Cameron shook her head. What had she expected? Alice Butler missed nothing.

Granny chuckled. "Well, I guess that's my answer. What do you plan to do about him?"

Caught, Cameron returned to the breakfast nook and sank into a chair. "I don't know," she admitted. "That's the sixty-four thousand dollar question. He wants to be involved in Jayla's life."

"Mmmm, hmmm." Granny placed a kettle of water over the stove's flame. "Want some tea?"

"Sure. Thanks."

The old girl didn't fool her for a minute. Granny used the tea trick whenever she wanted information. And whether Cameron wanted it or not, she'd be the recipient of Granny's unsolicited advice. *Oh yeah.* She knew the drill, but there was no way out of this situation, so she might as well sit comfortably and let it happen.

Face drawn into a tight mask, Granny stood over Cameron, studying her. "When you asked if you could move in here, I could see you were hurtin' bad." She stroked Cameron's hair. "I knew there were some things goin' on between you and your folks. That's why you're so dead set on showin' them."

Cameron nodded, fighting the misery that gripped her. *Don't cry,* she warned herself silently, feeling tears slide down her cheeks.

"Sweet Peaches, I love you." With a gentle touch, Granny brushed away Cameron's tears. "Over the last four years, I've stood tall with you, helpin' you to prove to your folks that Jayla wasn't a mistake and that you could raise your baby and make somethin' of yourself without a husband. I've prayed over your loneliness and pain. It's your business and I've never pried. But now you can't keep your secrets anymore."

Touched by her words, Cameron swallowed hard and struggled to control her tears. "Oh, Granny, Granny. From the moment I moved in, you've always stuck your nose in my business," she corrected, albeit lovingly. "Why should today be any different?"

Granny's shoulders shook with laughter as she returned to the stove. "True. This is important. It involves you and my great-granddaughter. And I have to keep my eye on you, so you two won't end up in trouble."

Placing mugs, honey, and cream on the table, Granny took the opposite chair and studied Cameron with a practiced glare designed to make grown men squirm. The silence that followed tore at Cameron's nerves.

Finally, Granny spoke. "You still love him, don't you?"

All the blood drained from Cameron's face. "Yes."

"Sweet Peaches, if there's love between you, why can't you see your way through this?" A concerned frown marred her brown face. "You've got a baby to think about."

"No, Granny." She rolled up a small section of her T-shirt and answered firmly, "We can't."

"Girl, what kind of wild nothin' are you talkin' about?" Granny fired back. "You wouldn't have to work so hard and so much. He could give you everything you've been tryin' to show your folks. Stability, security."

"I don't tr ... tru ... trust him," she stammered. "I don't think I'll ever trust him again."

"Mmmm, hmmm." She leaned back in her chair, crossed her arms over her bosom and asked, "What happened? Come on, out with it."

Tears dotted Cameron's cheeks. "I came home from work and found him in bed with Nikki." This confession hurt like hell, but it felt good to unburden herself and share her agonizing memory with the one person who wouldn't take sides.

"That skinny black girl?"

"Yes." Cameron mopped away her tears with her hand, fighting for control.

Granny shook her head, reached into her purse and pulled out a personal-size packet of tissues. She tossed it to Cam-

AS LONG AS THERE IS LOVE 49

eron. "Mmmm. Not very pretty." The tea kettle whistled and the old girl hurried back to the range.

That's an understatement, Cameron thought, watching her grandmother pour boiling water into the teapot and return to the table with it. The delicious fragrance of peppermint filled the room. Granny settled in her chair once more, rummaged in the pocket of her jacket and produced a brown medicine bottle. She examined the white label then placed it on the table next to her mug.

"What's this?" Cameron lifted the bottle, cast a suspicious eye in Granny's direction, then read the label.

"New medicine." Granny snatched the bottle from Cameron's fingers and slammed it down next to her mug, spearing Cameron with a glare that dared her to say a word. "I'm sick of that doctor, Sweet Peaches. That boy can't even make up his mind about what medicine he wants me to take. This is the third pill I've tried this year."

"Granny, you have to be patient. Medicine isn't an exact science. Plus, it takes time and . . ." she stabbed Granny with a significant glare, "cooperation. Dr. Richardson will hit on the correct pill for you. But you have to do your part and follow his instructions."

"Hush, girl." The older woman shook an orange tablet from the bottle and popped it into her mouth; she followed it with a sip of tea. "Don't think I've forgotten about you. Did you ever talk to that man?"

"No. I couldn't." Cameron's fingers fluttered around her mug. She felt very much the coward. "I ran home."

"Sweet Peaches, that's part of the problem. But you'll have to work it out for yourself. I imagine you'll get it straight in your own good time. What about your baby? Why should her life be in limbo while you work out your problems?"

"I'm frightened for her," she blurted out, squirming under

Granny's relentless scrutiny. Cameron picked up her cup and sipped her tea. She felt like a specimen under a microscope.

"And for yourself I'd say," Granny added, with a certainty that sent shock waves through Cameron. "Why?"

"I don't think Marek will be satisfied with being Jayla's father. I think he'll want to stir up our relationship. Try to mold us into some sort of family," Cameron explained, as her fingers encircled the rim of the cup. "His own home life wasn't perfect. Mr. and Mrs. Redding had little time for kids. That's why Marek's so hell-bent on Jayla having everything she needs."

"Well, Sweet Peaches, you *are* a family, after a fashion. And always remember what I told you, money don't always mean happiness."

"I know. But he can't just walk back into my life and think we'll pick up where we left off," Cameron replied in a strained voice. "I'm sorry. It's not going to happen."

"That's what *you* think." Her chuckle of delight filled the room. "That boy's got that lean, hungry look about him."

"Maybe so. But that's his problem. I don't want him to use Jayla to get to me. He has the potential to cause a lot of trouble."

Lines of concentration wrinkled Granny's brows. "No." She smacked her lips. "That's not what he's after. He's not that kind of man."

Cameron laughed, and then asked, "How do you know? You met him five minutes ago."

"I know." She assumed a regal pose and stated, "And more than you do, I'd say."

Running her tongue over her lips, Cameron confessed yet another fear. "If he's not sincere, he'll hurt Jayla. I don't want my baby to get attached to him and then he leaves."

"If it's meant to be, it's meant to be." Granny reached for Cameron's hand. "Little girls love their daddies. When

AS LONG AS THERE IS LOVE 51

you were a child, we couldn't pry you away from yours. Remember?" She grinned at Cameron. "You trailed behind him like a second shadow. Everywhere he went, you followed."

"Yeah." Cameron smiled, raising her eyes heavenward. "I remember."

"Your daughter is a special little person who deserves both parents. Are you being fair to her? Or to him? Denyin' them the chance to draw comfort from one another?"

"That's what Marek said."

"Good." She leaned back in her chair. "Great minds think alike."

"Great minds?" Cameron laughed. Her heart filled with such love for this woman. "More like nosy, butting in, minding other people's business minds."

"I'm going to let that slide," she stated. "Now, you listen to me. I've never steered you wrong before and I don't intend to start now. He's Jayla's daddy and you had better find a way to live with that. From what I've seen here today, that man's serious, and not just about his child."

Embarrassed, Cameron lowered her head. Heat scorched her cheeks. "I know."

"If he wants to do the right thing by her, let 'im. You've carried that burden alone long enough. It's his turn for a taste of it." She wagged a finger at Cameron. "He can start next Saturday. Have him come by the house while I'm here and the two of them can visit for a while. Once Jayla gets used to him, they can go about their business and leave us to ours. After a while, you won't have to rush back. Come on home when you're ready."

Cameron swallowed a lump in her throat, and then admitted, "Granny, I'm scared."

"What kind of wild nothins' are you talkin' about?" She rose, circled the table, and hugged Cameron close. "Scared of what?"

"I'll lose her to him. He's this new person in her life, with lots of money." Cameron ducked her head into Granny's embrace, ashamed of the jealousy that gripped her.

"What's goin' on in that head of yours?"

"He can give Jayla almost anything she wants. Where does that leave me? I can't compete with him."

"Sweet Peaches, there's no need to be jealous." Granny hugged her close. "Jayla's your baby. Your place in her life is set, special, yours alone. Her father will make his own. And if it takes a few presents to get there, let 'im."

"I still don't trust him, though."

"Is it Marek you don't trust or yourself? I caught the tail end of that kiss. The kitchen sizzled and the temperature had nothin' to do with it. Is that what you're afraid of?"

"Noooo," she denied. "I don't want that with Marek."

"Mmmm, hmmm. I think you better let him know that. I don't doubt he's makin' big plans for your future." She returned to her chair and drained her mug, eyeing Cameron over the rim. "Now, I suggest you give him a call, set up some kind of meetin' and get yourself ready."

"Will you help me?" Cameron clutched the old girl's hand. "Run interference between Marek and me? Be here when he comes over?"

"Of course. Whatever you need, Sweet Peaches. You know I'll always be here for you."

"Thank you, Granny," Cameron muttered with a sigh of relief. "I'm tired of talking about me and my problems. Now," she gazed at Granny and asked, "the slots paid off, hmmm? How much did you win?"

The old girl gave her a coy smile. "That's for me to know and you to guess," she answered, strolling out of the kitchen with her purse on her arm.

Laughing, Cameron called after her, "Granny, you are soooo bad."

* * *

Standing over Jayla's bed, Cameron watched her softly snoring daughter. Jayla was adorable when she slept, lying in the bed with her rear end stuck in the air and the blanket bunched around her feet.

Cameron caressed her baby's cheek and tucked a lock of hair behind Jayla's ear. She grew up with the love of two parents, so why shouldn't her baby? If Marek wanted to be a parent, who was she to deny him or Jayla that right?

Could he handle a busy three-year-old? Sure he could. For goodness' sake, he was a pediatrician. If he hadn't mastered that fine art, shame on him. He'd learn.

She sent a prayer heavenward that it would work out. Saturdays were such busy days filled with classes for her Master's degree and she felt guilty expecting Granny to put her own interests on hold to baby-sit. If this plan succeeded, Jayla and Marek could spend Saturdays together leaving Granny free to head to the casinos with her friends.

This plan had merit. She could complete the final touches on the elementary school and spend more time in the library preparing her thesis.

Granny and her medicine also needed more of Cameron's attention. That really worried her. Her grandmother was a proud old girl who never gave an inch. Her blood pressure rollercoastered and the doctor still didn't have a clue which medicine would do the trick. Plus, Granny took matters into her own hands by only taking her medicine when the spirit hit her.

The only glitch in her plan lay with Marek. Keeping him out of her life might prove to be a problem. But she had to try. She planned to maintain a pleasant, if somewhat distant relationship with him and hopefully, he'd get the hint.

Marek was smart. He wouldn't rock the boat if she gave him access to their daughter. With Granny's help, everything could fall into place. Marek could return Jayla to Granny and minimize Cameron's contact with him and lessen any chance of a repeat of today's incident.

The thought of their kiss made her body grow hot. The moment their lips touched, they had both exploded like dynamite. Each time he was near, her heart sped up, not to mention how certain body parts warmed. Marek disturbed her in every way, and it was a continual battle to stay focused when faced with the memories of what they once shared.

She'd call Marek and arrange a date so they could discuss visitation and other issues related to his parental rights. But first, she'd call her attorney, Gregory Hunter. She might be able to kill two birds with one stone and get his take on the legal side of visitation and inform him of the possible complaint against Little Darlings.

Cameron tossed a lightweight blanket over Jayla's shoulders and kissed her cheek. She switched on the night-light and left the room. Monday morning she'd call Greg's office and schedule an appointment.

Chapter Five

Cameron looked up from the Little Darlings financial summary and took a sip of her watered-down Coke. Huddled in the corner booth at the Courthouse Bar and Grill, she glanced at her watch for the fourth time and came to a decision. If Greg didn't show up within ten minutes, she'd leave.

Telephoning Greg's law office early Monday morning had gained her zip, nada, nothing. His schedule was booked for weeks. By agreeing to meet him after hours, she had avoided going on the waiting list for the next cancellation.

Absently humming to Sade's sultry voice, Cameron watched a woman puff on a slim cigar. Yuck! Cigar breath. The woman blew smoke rings into the hazy cloud of smoke hovering above the bar.

A server whizzed by with a tray of food and Cameron's tummy rumbled, responding to the aroma of grilled beef. Greg better show up soon.

The door opened and a cool breeze forced its way into

the room. She looked up and found Greg filling the doorway, scanning the room. A warm smile curved his full lips once he spotted her.

Dodging bar patrons, he made steady progress through the crowded room. With each step, Greg's Armani suit caressed the lines of his tall frame. His bronze skin glowed with good health and dark brown, short-cropped hair framed his face.

Confidence faltering, Cameron scraped her hand over her face and shifted on the bench. Business was one thing, but sharing the intimate details of her private life made her uncomfortable.

He stopped at her booth and said, "Sorry, I'm late. Judge Chung called me into her chambers for a last minute consultation."

She waved a hand at the empty bench opposite hers and admitted, "I was getting worried."

"It's been a rough day." Greg dropped into the seat. "I need a minute to get myself together," he smoothed his already perfect hair into place and shot a disparaging gaze at her glass, "I think I need something a little stronger then what you're drinking." Signaling the server, he ordered, "Double Hennessey straight and nachos." Refocusing on Cameron, he asked, "What's up?"

Cameron circled the rim of the glass with a nervous finger and focused on her Coke. "I have a couple of problems I need to discuss."

"Go for it." He unbuttoned his suit jacket.

"You've met my daughter. Her father has ..." she paused, swirling the straw in her glass, "come back into the picture and he wants visitation. I need to know my rights as a single parent. Would I be giving up anything if I allowed him to see her? Are there any restrictions I can or should place on him?"

The silence that followed was full of tension. When she

looked at Greg, a muscle jerked unchecked at Greg's temple. *What was wrong?*

Suddenly, an invisible shudder covered his face and he became all business. The oddest sensation tickled her brain as she watched him. Had she imagined that tense moment? She didn't think so.

Greg fished a small spiral notepad and pen from his jacket pocket. He flipped through several pages until he came to a clean sheet.

In a professional tone, he asked, "You two aren't considering reconciling, are you?"

It was an appropriate inquiry, and one she had expected. But it was edged with something that disturbed her.

She shook her head.

"Are you certain?" he pressed.

Cameron lifted her chin a fraction, ready to check him on the subject. "Positive."

"Okay." He relaxed a little bit. "What do you want?"

She drew in a strong breath and plunged ahead, "He's welcome to see her. But no joint custody or any control over the way I raise my daughter. And I don't want him to leave town with Jayla without providing some detailed info, like address and a phone number. He could disappear with her."

"What about child support?" Greg sucked on the tip of his gold Cross pen. "I presume you want it?" Jotting notes on his pad, he asked, "Where does he work and what does he do?"

"He's a doctor at Holland General."

Greg's eyes glazed over as he internalized the information. After several seconds, he refocused on her. "How about his home life?" He began, firing one question after another. "How acceptable is it for a small child? Is he married? Does he have other children?"

"I've never been to his house." She frowned. "He's not

married. No other children. At least I don't know of any," she muttered. Hope pumped through her as an idea took shape in her head. "What if his home isn't satisfactory? Can we limit visitation?"

His lips pursed. "Doubtful."

"Why?"

"We don't have any negative information about him."

Cameron snorted and folded her arms across her chest. "Why should it matter? If I don't think his home is suitable, Jayla's not going there."

"His place may not meet your personal standards, but the court may disagree with you." Greg twirled his pen between his fingers. "Which brings up another point. How legal do you want to make this pact?"

She drained the last drops from her glass. "What do you mean?"

"The court system would be your best bet," he explained, wagging the pen in her direction. "A legal document would be binding. I can draw up an agreement that you and the father can sign and we'll work from that."

Cameron chewed on a fingernail, considering her options. "Your recommendation?"

"Go through the court," Greg encouraged. He took a long swig of his drink. "Everything would be set in stone and he can't back out. You'll have the court's support if there's a dispute."

She scrunched up her face. Horror stories from the single parents at Little Darlings pushed her toward a quick decision. "I don't want to go that route." A shudder of distaste iced her skin. "Besides, I have to think about Little Darlings. If I get into a long battle with Marek, Little Darlings could suffer," she rationalized. "I want to hit it and quit it."

Eyes narrowed, he tapped the end of his pen against the notepad. "You've never walked away from a challenge before. What's wrong with this picture?"

AS LONG AS THERE IS LOVE 59

Greg was no dummy. If she didn't tell him, he'd soon pick up on the bad vibes between her and Marek.

"I'm doing this under duress." Her fingers fluttered over the cutlery, straightening each piece just so on the paper napkin. "I have my doubts about him. I don't want Jayla to get attached to him, then he leaves her."

"Don't worry," he assured. "You don't have to give up a thing. We can keep him away if you prefer."

The temptation to do just that appealed to her, but Jayla's interest came first. Besides, Granny would have a conniption if she took too long to come to a decision.

"No," she answered. "It's best to let him see her. Jayla's growing up and asking questions, and I'm sort of caught between a rock and a hard place. I'm trying to protect her. Greg, I don't want her hurt."

"Don't worry, I won't let that happen." Greg reached across the table and cradled her hand between both of his, stroking her sensitive skin. "I promise."

Unsettled by his touch, she pulled away and placed her balled fist in her lap. "Thanks."

"This would be a perfect opportunity for me to take over the case," he suggested. "Any meetings scheduled?"

"No." She shook her head. "I'll talk to him first." At this point Greg's presence would complicate the situation. "Then we'll meet with you, if we have to."

"I can help." Greg leaned closer. "Why don't we meet in my office and discuss the particulars as a trio?"

"That's not necessary," she answered with quiet firmness. "I'll handle it."

"You should reconsider," Greg pressed. "I really believe I should be there to represent you."

She appreciated his concern, but this part was between her and Marek. "Thanks, but no thanks. I'll handle it."

"Cameron, I really don't think you should meet him

alone. What if he tries to change what we've discussed? What then?"

There was a warning edge to his voice that made her hackles rise. Instead of persuading her, she became more determined to do what she believed was right.

"Then I'll share his suggestions with you and arrange a new meeting." Impatience crept into her voice. "Until then, we'll stick with my plan and I'll pass along your number after we're done. It's all yours after that." She leaned back in her chair. "Now, next topic."

"Are you sure?"

His insistence irked her. "Positive. Next topic."

"Yes, ma'am." He held up his hands in a mock show of surrender. "You're the boss."

"Good."

"Anything else?"

"Oh yeah. More unpleasant business." Cameron wrinkled her nose, rummaged inside her briefcase and produced a yellow legal pad and blue-topped pen. "I'm warning you up front, Greg. I've got a laundry list of questions. A parent from Little Darlings has filed a negligence complaint with the state. Her son fell off the sliding board in the backyard. I need to know what comes next, and how I should proceed. What are my options?"

Greg scribbled on his notepad. "Go on."

She took a deep breath and plunged ahead. "What recourse do I have once the state contacts me? Will this affect my license for the elementary school? Should I continue to work on the school or wait until this is resolved? And what about my insurance? Will it affect my premiums? And finally, what's the worst that can happen?"

Greg whistled. One corner of his mouth curved into a smile. "That's quite a list." He reached across the table and turned the legal pad in his direction. "You've thought this through pretty thoroughly, haven't you?"

"I've tried to cover everything." She sighed. "This isn't easy."

"Why?"

"There are some personal problems between Justin's mother and me."

"Hold that thought." He took a long swig of his cognac. "We'll come back to it. First, how's the little boy?"

"Justin. His name is Justin. He had a real bad scare and a broken arm. Some stitches. A few bumps and bruises," she answered. "Jayla and I stopped by the O'Rourkes' last Saturday and he seemed okay. And happy to see us."

"Good." He nodded. "Have his parents filed any other lawsuits?"

"I haven't received anything. And it's only his mother." She slurped the last of her Coke through the straw. "Tara's the kind of person who'd wait until the complaint is resolved before she does anything else. What do you think?"

Nodding, he murmured, "Smart move."

"Tara's no dummy."

"Are you saying that from personal experience, or is that a guess?"

"Personal experience," she answered. "Much more than I care for."

"What happened between you two?"

"I don't know." Uneasy, Cameron rolled her shoulders, trying to relax her tense muscles. "For the last few months, Tara has been almost impossible to please, complaining about everything from the activity schedule to the lunch menu. Truthfully, I'd asked her to look for a new school for Justin. But she refused to consider it."

"Are you telling me that somewhere along the line, you've ticked the lady off, and this is her way of getting back at you?"

"Basically, yes." She shrugged. "There's cause for Tara to be upset about the accident. I'm not denying that. Unfortunately, there's something more going on. But I don't know what."

The ice cubes tinkled against the sides of the glass as Greg drained his cognac. "Tell me everything you know about the accident." He tipped the glass and caught a cube of ice with his tongue.

"Justin's a busy little person." She shuddered, reliving those horrible moments. "He likes to dive off the sliding board like a swimmer. I told his mother and asked her to speak with him. But I guess that didn't happen." Her mouth twitched. "This time he missed his mark and toppled over the edge. I took him to Holland General and he got immediate care. Tara thinks I should have done more to keep him safe."

"Did you miss anything?" he probed. "Was there something else you could have done?"

"Greg, I've gone over this for days. I've asked Tara to speak with Justin," she ticked the items off her fingers and said, "I cautioned him. My staff was aware of his antics and worked accordingly. I was on my way to stop him when he fell. I don't know what else I could have done, short of refusing to let him outside, or standing over him the whole time he's in the backyard. I'm certain Tara would have had a fit if I'd done either of those things."

"Anything in writing?"

"Sorry."

"Then that's what we'll work with."

"Thanks." She reached for a nacho from the wicker basket and dipped it into the chunky tomato salsa. "I need to believe someone's with me on this one."

"Don't worry, I've got your back. Until we receive notification from the state, there's not much we can do." A reassuring smile played at the corners of his mouth. "I suggest you have your staff provide me with a step-by-step account of the incident, in writing. And if possible I'd like to talk with the attending physician. It might help to get his opinion regarding the extent of Justin's injuries and how they occurred before we receive anything official from his mother's attorney. What's the doctor's name? I'll look him up."

"Ah, Greg?" she drawled, gripping her empty glass.

Eyes twinkling back at her, he teased, "Ah, Cameron."

"The attending physician is Marek Redding, Jayla's father."

"What?"

"You heard me," she answered, shifting around in her chair. "Couldn't there be an issue of privilege?"

"Let me think." Greg tapped his pen against the notepad. "Scratch that idea. I don't want to rock the boat until we absolutely have to. We'll wait until the state sends you a formal notice. Get in touch with me the minute that happens." He paused. "Wait, I've got a frat buddy who works for the state. I'll get in touch with him and find out what he knows. In the meantime, continue getting the school ready for September."

Her heart leaped in her chest. The school represented her future, stability and financial security. "Greg, are you sure?" she pressed. "I've come too far to lose everything."

"You won't. Think logically." He pointed at his forehead. "You've invested too much time, money and energy to stop things cold." He signaled the server with a wave of his hand. "Besides, this is your first complaint."

"What does that mean?" Concerned, her voice rose. "Will that make a difference?"

"I'm not sure," he hedged, pointing a finger at her glass. "Want another?"

"Thanks."

Greg ordered, "I'll have another double, and a Coke for the lady." Turning back to Cameron, he continued, "The state will probably send someone to inspect your facility, take a statement from Justin and your staff." He doodled on his notepad. "They'll check your procedures and pester you for a few days. Depending on what they find, you could be slapped with some type of warning."

"Warning!" Alarm raced through her. "What type of warning?"

"Don't have a hissy fit," he advised, patting her hand. "I'll find out all the details and get back with you."

She clutched his hand. "Does this warning stay in my file permanently? Will I have to pay a fine?"

"We'll worry about that when the time comes," he stated. "But for now, get your business papers in order. Procedures. Policies. Everything must be documented and in perfect order. Books, the building, everything."

"Now I am worried." Cameron twisted a lock of hair around her finger. "I can't afford any major setbacks, Greg. Too much is happening as it is."

"Calm down," he soothed. "Unless the state has overwhelming reasons to shut you down, everything will work out. Continue business as usual."

Yeah. Right. That was easy for him to say.

"What about my school?" The nagging thought in the back of her brain refused to be silent. "I haven't received the license for it yet. Could this complaint stall the license for the school?"

"Cameron, the day care center and the school are separate businesses. Don't worry. You'll get your license. I'll take care of that. I promise." Greg scribbled on his notepad. "I'll give them a call tomorrow to find out how much longer you need to wait."

"Good." She sank into her chair, choking down the fear clogging her throat. "I've invested all of my money and

Granny's refinanced her house to help me. I can't afford to lose it."

"Come on, Cameron, this is late April. Everything has to be ready by Labor Day. You've got plenty of time. So stop worrying. I'll take care of it." He flipped the notebook shut and slipped it inside his jacket. "That's what you pay me for." His pen followed the notepad. "It'll all work out. Okay?"

"Okay," she conceded, reaching for another nacho and pointing the tip in Greg's direction. "But if things don't come together soon, I'll be camping out on your doorstep."

"Trust me. You won't have to." Greg's tone turned seductive. "Now, are we through with business?"

Her stomach churned as she read the disturbing element in his gaze. "I think I've covered everything on my agenda."

"Good." A slow, sensuous smile spread across his face. "It's my turn." Determination glittered from his warm gaze. "I've got some issues of my own."

With mock bravado, Cameron challenged, "Such as?"

"When are we going to see each other socially?" He shifted the conversation smoothly from business to pleasure. His pleasure.

Oh, Lord. The signs were there, although she had chosen to ignore them. How did she get herself out of this one?

"I'm out with you now," she answered evasively.

"I mean a date." He toyed with his glass. "You and me, without business."

"Greg, I don't think dating is a good idea. Why can't we stay friends?"

His voice dropped, smooth but insistent. "Why can't we be more than friends?"

"Couldn't dating a client be," she hunched her shoulders, searching for the right word, "unethical?"

"Only if I continue to be your lawyer." His brows lifted.

"I've got a colleague who can pick up your case should we decide to get involved."

Sighing, she ran a hand over her face. "I'm not ready to get involved with *anyone*."

"Is it Jayla's father?" he sliced into her. "Are you still in love with him?"

"There's a lot of reasons," she hedged. "This complaint, the school, Jayla's father all have a piece of me right now. I feel as if I'm being pulled in three different directions. I can't take much more, Greg." Her tongue swished across her dry lips. "I don't want to see you hurt because I'm not ready."

"I can take care of my own emotions. I don't need you to safeguard them for me," Greg muttered, eyes dark with a spark of anger. "What I'm proposing is a chance to see where things might lead. Come on, take a chance. The next time I ask you out, just say yes and leave the rest to me. No pressure, just fun. What's so difficult about that?"

Cameron opened her mouth to respond, but shut it without muttering a word. She was so confused. "I don't know," she answered honestly. "My life is consumed with raising Jayla and keeping my business afloat. I stopped dating long before Jayla was born."

"That's commendable, Cameron. But what kind of life is that for a young woman? Here's the perfect opportunity to start over," Greg's voice persuaded softly. "We're both here together, sharing a drink. Let's finish the evening with dinner."

"Oh, no." Panicking, she grabbed her purse. "Maybe another time. I need to get home to Jayla."

Greg reached across the table and stopped her with a firm grip on her arm, holding her in place. "Don't run from me, Cameron. I'm not the enemy."

"I never said you were." Cameron shook off his hand and sank back onto the bench.

"What are you afraid of? I'm not going to bite." He flashed her a wolfish grin. "At least, not on the first date."

Afraid? She wasn't afraid of him. Her chin lifted a fraction and she met his gaze with icy calm.

"You're my attorney," she responded in a frosty tone. "I'm not sure I want to change that relationship. What if it doesn't work out? Can you imagine the tension it'll cause between us?"

Greg leaned back in his chair, tenting his fingers. "What makes you think it won't work?"

Cameron didn't share Greg's belief that there was a future for them. He was a wonderful family friend and an excellent attorney. On top of everything, she didn't want to hurt him. Turning away from his penetrating gaze, she feigned an interest in the barflies' antics while trying to think of a way out of this mess.

"You're always busy. No time. Jayla." He placed his hand over his heart. "If you want me to, I promise to have you home and in bed before nine-thirty."

Cameron groped for a new objection. "Well." She sighed. "Greg, I think of you as a friend. I'm not sure my feelings will change." There, she'd said it. Maybe now he would understand her reluctance.

His lips thinned. "You've never seriously considered anything more between us before now, have you?"

"No."

"So how can you know what you feel if you've never considered the possibilities?"

"I can't. I guess," she admitted. "But you're asking for things I'm not sure I can give you. We don't know if my feelings will grow. It might take a while for me to think of you as a potential boyfriend."

Irritation flashed across his handsome face. "How much time?"

"I don't know. If I agree to go out with you, we have to start real slow."

"I can live with that."

"Can you?" She stared doubtfully at him, adding, "No pressure. No sulking because I say no to things that I'm not ready for."

"Hey," Greg replied. "Scout's honor." He lifted three fingers in the Boy Scout salute. His overconfident attitude didn't fool her.

But why not? As long as they started out slow, she could relax and enjoy a friendship that could mature into something more. What harm would it do? She could escape from the day-to-day grind and have some fun. And if he pushed too hard, she'd just call the whole thing off and find herself a new lawyer. But she hoped things wouldn't come to that.

"Okay."

"It'll all be good, babe," he said before swallowing the last drops from his glass. "I promise."

Her gut told her Greg wasn't the man for her. She felt like such a fraud, letting him maneuver her into this evening. Greg was a friend, that was all. Besides, the drinking bothered her. That was an aspect of his personality she hadn't seen before.

When he walked her to her car, she'd turned down his suggestion of another date with a shake of her head, citing the problems plaguing her.

After all these years, Marek was still her love. Friendship was the stongest emotions she felt for Greg and nothing more. And no matter how much Greg tried to persuade her to the contrary, she felt this in her bones.

Locking her car door, she waved at Greg and started the car's engine. Pulling out of the parking lot, her concern shifted to Little Darlings. Far too much money and her

AS LONG AS THERE IS LOVE 69

dreams of security rode on the opening of the elementary school. Greg had advised her to relax and wait, give him a chance to earn his fee and sit tight until notification came from the state. Then act.

She'd give Greg a chance to settle things. If she didn't see any progress, she'd make inquires of her own.

Chapter Six

Cameron simmered over Greg's advice for several days before telephoning Marek. The satisfaction in his voice when she suggested they meet Saturday made her want to renege on her invitation.

Grand Haven Inn was located twenty odd miles outside of Holland and provided the privacy they needed. If her nerves held up, she planned to establish some workable visitation schedule and supersede Marek's threat to carry their personal disagreement into the public arena of the courts.

With visions of doom in her head, Cameron trotted alongside the waiter. God, she hoped she was making the right decision. The tuxedo-clad waiter stopped at an occupied table.

Marek ended his telephone call and slipped the phone into his belt holster. He rose, stepped around the table and captured her hands. "Sorry about that. I'm on-call tonight."

"Hey," she mumbled, withdrawing her hands.

"Hey yourself," he whispered, close to her ear.

Marek's warm breath caressed her cheek and kicked her pulse into first gear. His gaze lingered over the delicate scooped neckline of her violet two-piece silk dress and trailed over the soft fabric. Her body quivered, responding to the sensual promise in his eyes.

A slow smile of appreciation lit up his tanned face. "You look great."

"Thanks." She smiled, powerless to halt the ripple of excitement that surged through her. It felt good to know he still found her desirable.

Cameron glanced at him and did some drooling of her own. A rust, black and white striped shirt draped his torso while black linen trousers covered his sculptured frame. He looked so good she found it difficult to tear her eyes away from the handsome image in front of her.

Nodding at his glass, she asked. "Have you been here long?"

"No." He pulled her chair away from the table. "Just a few minutes." The sound of jiggling coins touched her ears.

She knew that sound, glancing at Marek's face. He's nervous. She hid a smile, remembering their first date and how he had fidgeted with the coins in his pocket all evening.

Marek had been so wonderful that night; tall, dark and handsome. The subtle scent of his cologne made her drool right there in her living room. That had been the start of one of the must blissful periods of her life.

With a jolt, she returned to the present, "Good," she muttered, then slid into the high-backed rattan chair. Beneath lowered lashes her eyes swept the restaurant.

"Let's have dinner and talk about our daughter. What do you say?" A wave of Marek's hand brought the waiter to their table. "What do you drink these days?"

"Chardonnay."

Silence settled between them as they browsed their menus

under the room's recessed lighting. Boney James's sax set the tone as the waiter returned with their drinks and took their orders.

The rattan chair creaked under Marek's weight. He studied her over his glass. "Your call surprised me."

Pleating the napkin in her lap, she said, "It's time we talked about Jayla."

"And?"

Cameron gripped the stem of her wineglass. *Just get the words out.* That's all she needed to do. "You're right. Jayla needs us both."

"What brought you to this great revelation?"

"My grandmother."

"Ahhh. I'll have to thank Mrs. Butler." The lines of concentration deepened along his brow. "What does all of this mean, exactly?"

"It means we need to come up with a workable visitation schedule." She fiddled with the fork. "Something agreeable to us both."

"Okay." Traces of skepticism glittered from the depths of his eyes. "Talk."

"How's your schedule on Saturdays?" She placed her hands in her lap as the waiter placed a Caesar salad in front of her.

He shrugged. "Fine. Empty."

"Good. Right now, I have classes on Saturday and Granny keeps Jayla. I thought that might be a good time for you to come by the house and visit." Pleased at how normal her voice sounded, she continued, "Does that work for you?"

Marek's lips drew together into a straight line. He placed his spoon next to his bowl of French onion soup and picked up his glass of water. The ice pinged against the glass as he drained the liquid.

"It sounds fine, should I agree." His stern tone suggested anything but. "Before I do, answer a few questions for me."

Questions? Her stomach twisted into knots. He should be thankful she planned to let him visit at all.

Cameron lifted her chin a fraction. "It's your turn at the podium."

"When do you expect all of this to commence?"

"Next Saturday, if you don't have other plans."

"Okay." He nodded. "Question number two. What do you plan to tell Jayla about me?"

Tell her? Her face scrunched up. *Tell her what?*

"Truthfully, I haven't considered it." She shrugged. "We've never discussed you."

His fingers strummed the tabletop impatiently.

"Why don't we say you're a friend?" She waved her hands wildly in the air. "No, no, I know. How about an uncle? Jayla has three uncles. One more wouldn't make a difference. Once she gets comfortable with you, the three of us can sit down and tell her who you really are."

"An uncle. Ummph." Several minutes of silence followed, then he pushed away his bowl of soup. "Have you thought about how Jayla's going to accept a total stranger?"

"Granny will be there to smooth the way."

"What about your grandmother? She doesn't know me from Adam and neither does Jayla. You're the person who knows both of us. How do you expect Jayla to learn to feel comfortable with me if the one person who provides continuity in her life isn't available?"

"Oh." Cameron's appetite died a quick death.

"That's right, oh," he stated in a tone that made her feel like an imbecile. "Don't you think she'll be afraid of me? A stranger thrust upon her without any warning? The least you could do is stick around for the first few visits. Or is *your* schedule *too* busy?"

Marek's belittling tone offended her. His criticism made light of her years of sacrifice and her temper flared. "I'm not the bad guy here," Cameron snapped. "I take my responsibility very seriously. I've done my duty as a parent for three years," she wiggled three fingers in his face. "And I've done it *alone*."

"Who decided that? No one consulted me," Marek snarled through clenched teeth. He drew in a deep breath and let it out in small increments, then resumed a calm front. "We'll save that discussion for another day. My question stands, can I depend on you?"

"Of course Jayla can count on me," she answered part of his question. "I don't see what's the big deal." Puzzled, she continued, "My grandmother met you. She'll be home to help."

"Cameron, you're the bridge that links the four of us. We need your help to make this a success, for our family to jell."

The truth of his words trapped her. Although Jayla was a happy, outgoing baby, sometimes strangers made her shy.

She felt helpless as the cage door locked behind her. "You're right," Cameron conceded. "Jayla won't know you and it's not fair to her. We need to rethink this."

"I have a solution," Marek piped in. "When I was a kid, I always wanted a day that was devoted to us. A family day." Sadness flickered unchecked across his face. "It didn't happen, but I always wanted it. Why don't we do this in increments? Start with a couple of visits with the three of us, maybe include your grandmother. Do lunch, the zoo or a drive. Jayla should start to feel relaxed by that time."

She shook her head and reached for her wineglass. "My Saturdays are full. I have obligations."

"Come on, Ronnie," he coaxed, waiting until the waiter had delivered their entrees. "Work with me here. How about Sundays?"

"Sundays are *my* day with Jayla."

"Good. Let's make it our family day." Marek brushed aside any additional discussion. "At least for a few weeks."

Slicing into his chicken breast, he added, "While we're at it, I want to discuss a name change for Jayla."

"Name change?"

"I asked Tara O'Rourke. Her name should be Redding." His expression dared her to challenge him. "My name is on her birth certificate, isn't it?"

Heat scorched her cheeks. She expected this topic would be a bone of contention between them. Her eyes darted away, but returned to find his steady gaze still latched upon her. "No."

A muscle jerked uncontrolled at Marek's temple; his lips tightened into a disapproving line. He placed his fork next to his plate.

"We'll get that corrected," he stated through clenched teeth. "She's my only child and I'd li—"

"You better check with Nikki before you make a declaration like that," she mumbled under her breath.

Fury blazed from Marek's eyes. He tossed his napkin on the table and rose. The unexpected gesture drew curious glances from other tables. "Maybe it would be better if we did this the lega—"

Cameron's heartbeat tripled.

"I'm sorry. I'm sorry," she whispered, groping for his arm. "That slipped out and it was totally uncalled for. Please. Sit down. I'm sorry. I guess . . ." Her voice trailed off. "I guess . . . I'm feeling the pressure of the situation."

Her eyes begged him to understand. For a second, she thought he might refuse. Instead, his mouth tightened a fraction more and without further comment he sank into his chair.

"Obviously, the skeletons in our closets are beating down the door. I think we need to clear some of the bones away." He reached across the table for her hand. "It might ease your mind."

"I was out of line," she stated. "It won't happen again."

"Cameron, I can handle your outburst." The hard glint in his eyes made a believer out of her. "But what bothers me more is what you think of me. We need to work on that. It's time to push past this and move ahead. Otherwise, our problems are going to flow into Jayla's life. I had enough of that growing up. Believe me, it's not the way to raise a healthy, stable child."

"Marek, let's forget this happened, okay?" She shook off his hand and picked up her fork, moving her food around her plate. "Now, what were we discussing?"

He ran an exasperated hand through his tousled hair. "Ronnie, work with me here. We don't have to be at odds."

"And we're not going to be." Her voice rose as her hand sliced through the air. "Now, let's get back to Jayla and then I can get home."

His eyes narrowed, grew hard. "If you don't change your attitude, someday it's going to bite you in the butt."

"Be that as it may," she stated, crossing her arms across her chest. "I won't worry about it until it happens. Now, about Jayla?"

Marek sighed and shook his head. "If something happens to me, I don't want her to do without anything." He folded the napkin and placed it next to his plate. "Plus, there's child support to discuss. Decide what you need and call my attorney." He withdrew a business card from his breast pocket and slid it across the table. The name of a prominent attorney blared back at her from the embossed card. "Alex has already established a trust fund for her education."

"My, my," she mocked, eyes opened wide. "You're forging right ahead. What about your parents? Have you told them?"

"I haven't talked to them in months. Don't worry about my parents," he responded. "When the time comes, I'll take care of things."

"How?" she persisted.

"Efficiently," he stated matter-of-factly. "Jayla is my family. Just as you are my family. And her needs take priority over everything else."

"Be honest," she taunted. "On the best of occasions, your parents won't be happy to find that they're the grandparents of a little baby out of wedlock."

"No one uses that phrase anymore. Besides, I don't care what my parents think," he dismissed. "I'm happy and that's what counts."

"I care. And you should, too, for Jayla's sake," she snapped. "Think about it. They are Jayla's grandparents. What if they come here? Or the two of you go there? How do you think that tight little community of Franklin will receive her? I don't want Jayla hurt, not by you or your parents."

"I admit there'll be problems. But my parents won't show up without an invitation." Abandoning any attempt to finish his meal, he shoved his plate aside. "I would never let them hurt her. Never! Oh, by the way, I'm not the only one with parent problems. How's your dad?"

Her father's red-faced prophecy popped into her head. *You'll never make it. A baby changes everything.*

"Have *your* parents truly accepted Jayla?" Marek asked.

"Yes, they have. They're disappointed by my choice..." Pain squeezed her heart as she realized how true those words were. "Not by Jayla. My parents wanted the best for me. When we were growing up, they helped my Aunt Jane in every way they could. She struggled for years with three kids and no husband. My mom and dad didn't want that for me. They knew how difficult life can be for a single parent."

"Obviously, it affected your relationship with them." He sipped his water. "Otherwise, you'd be in Ypsilanti."

"Where did you get that idea?"

"I know you. You're daddy's girl."

"Marek, we're getting off the subject," she reminded.

"But about the other stuff. I'll have my lawyer contact yours. Let them battle it out. That's what we pay them for."

"True," he said, with a dip of his head. "We still need to decide what we're going to tell Jayla about me. My vote is for honesty."

"Jayla needs time. She won't understand why you weren't around until now. There's no easy explanation. We need to move slowly. Offer her just what she asks us for, nothing more. Otherwise, we'll overwhelm and confuse her."

"Ronnie, I want to do this right. I want her to like me, to love me. I want to be the kind of father she can look up to. Better than what I had. And I don't want to start our relationship with a lie."

"Marek, she's three. Don't create problems where there aren't any."

"So, when can I come over?"

Cameron countered, "Are we in agreement about when and what we'll tell Jayla about you?"

Marek folded his arms across his chest and leaned back into the chair. "Is this Sunday okay?"

"We'll play it by ear and see how the first couple of visits go before we tell her?" she queried. "Okay?"

"Work with me here. What time Sunday?"

Brows arched, she asked again, "Are we clear on this thing about Jayla?"

"Dinner," he countered. "Sunday. Three o'clock?"

His persistence irked her. "Whatever."

Choking down the rest of her meal, she realized nothing had worked out the way she'd planned. This was supposed to be so easy. Walk in, eat dinner, inform Marek of the ground rules, and then head for the mountains.

Marek had fooled her, she realized, watching him stab a red-skin potato with his fork. Armed with his own laundry

AS LONG AS THERE IS LOVE 79

list of issues, he had swept away her concerns in favor of his own.

Disaster loomed large over the evening. What possessed her to believe meeting at a restaurant would reduce the tension? Make everything work out?

For Jayla's sake, she'd work with Marek. Play it cool, help her daughter over the rough spots and push them closer together. Sipping the last of her wine, she conceded that for the present, she'd go along with Marek's program.

Chapter Seven

"Excuse me." Cameron rose and plucked her purse from the vacant chair. "I'll be back in a minute." She dashed down the carpeted hallway to the ladies' room.

Entering the gray and mauve tiled room, Cameron hurried to the sink and dropped her purse on the marble vanity. Nerves frazzled, she pushed a paper towel under the tap, brought the saturated towel to her flushed cheek, then sank into the cushioned white wrought-iron chair.

The ladies' room door swung open and an influx of music and laughter filled the room. Aggressive steps echoed off the walls. Musk perfume preceded Tara O'Rourke's appearance.

Green eyes rounded with artificial surprise. "Well, hello." Tara's voice dripped with insincerity.

"Hello, Tara," Cameron answered in a "don't-bother-me" tone.

Ignoring the hint, Tara hopped onto the edge of the vanity and wiggled her bottom on the marble top. She sighed and drew a cigarette from her purse.

"Hey yourself. So, how's your evening going?"

Such a simple question, loaded with dynamite. "It's fine," Cameron replied, cautiously. What had Tara seen? Had she noticed Marek? "The food's good here."

"Really?" Her head tilted to one side. "I don't think food is the main attraction. Was that the handsome and eligible Doc Redding I saw you with?"

"I don't know if he's all that." She inclined her head. "But yes, I'm here with Dr. Redding."

"Interesting." Tara lit her cigarette.

"Why?"

"Come on." Tara snorted. "Can't you figure it out?"

"Maybe you should say what you mean."

Tara led with a left hook. "You know, the doc and you looked real cozy. I just know there's some fascinating history between you two." She followed with a right that almost knocked Cameron to the floor. "Maybe you guys are a little more than friends, hmm?"

Silence seemed to be the appropriate answer.

Tara jabbed the lit end of her cigarette in Cameron's direction. "You know, I've always wondered how you ended up in Holland. You landed on your grandmother's door, pregnant and alone." She inhaled the cigarette smoke deep into her lungs. "In the time I've known you, you've never mentioned a man. Now, here you sit with the best thing that's come to Holland in years. Why don't you share your secret?"

"There's nothing to tell," Cameron stated. "Marek and I have been friends for years. We went to school together."

"College buddy, huh?" She flicked the cigarette ashes into the sink. "Really? Did he know Jayla's father?"

Cameron's head shot up. "What gave you that idea?"

"Just curious," Tara answered on a cheery note. "You'd just finished college when you moved here, right?" She dropped her purse on the vanity, waiting for an answer.

Cameron's hopes plummeted. It didn't look as if Tara accepted her explanation. "I'm not going there with you today."

"Why? Is it some big secret?" Tara grinned. "You've never hidden the fact that you were a single parent. Come on, tell me," she coaxed. "Give it up."

One corner of Cameron's lip turned down. "What makes you think I'll tell you my business?" She zipped up her purse, turned on the stool, preparing to leave. " 'Night."

"You know the doc has the most unusual eyes." A sly gleam entered Tara's gaze. "Honey-golden. Just gorgeous. There's another person in town with eyes like those."

Oh, Lord. Cameron tried to swallow, but couldn't.

"Your child has them. The doc is Jayla's father, isn't he?" Triumphantly, Tara added, "Aren't you the dark horse."

Friends and neighbors would learn Jayla's parentage. It was inevitable. Holland's small-town atmosphere guaranteed that. But not yet. Not until Jayla and Marek bonded. Until she confirmed Tara's guess anything the redheaded witch said was pure speculation. Clutching the purse strap in her hand like it was her last dollar, Cameron debated and discarded several retorts.

"I'm not going to stand here and discuss my child with you," said Cameron. "Good night."

"Is that all you've got?" Tara taunted, then blew cigarette smoke toward the ceiling. "You've forgotten I've been around Jayla since she was a baby. Your daughter's a miniature Marek. Those eyes and hair are straight from his gene pool."

The temperature in the room rose. Perspiration trickled down the back of Cameron's neck. *Hold firm,* her inner voice counseled. *Don't confirm anything.*

"I'm a bit puzzled." Tara leaned closer and whispered as if they were cronies gossiping over the backyard fence.

"You've never talked about Jayla's father. You know, I just assumed he was a deadbeat dad you preferred to forget."

"None of this is your business."

"You know," Tara continued, ignoring Cameron's outburst. "He's not what I expected you to be involved with." Her head bobbed from side-to-side. "Marek's obviously well-off. The deadbeat dad profile doesn't fit." She crossed her legs at the ankles and swung them to and fro. "Jayla, your grandmother and Little Darlings are all that ever mattered to you. So, how did you squeeze in time for that cutiepie? I'd love to know the skinny on that."

This ain't happening. Not today. Cameron tossed the purse strap over her shoulder and sailed past Tara, giving the redhead an elaborate salute of farewell. "Enjoy."

"Come on, Cam. Don't be so sensitive." Tossing the cigarette butt into the sink, Tara hurried ahead and blocked the door with her body. "I'm just asking questions you'd get from anyone."

"Meaning?"

"What makes you think other people won't be curious, too? We live in a small town. You know, people talk. Gossip is a way of life." Tara leaned against the door. "You know, everyone at your precious Little Darlings will want to know all the dirty details. And they won't stop with you, either. When people want information, they're devious. They'll confront you and pump Jayla."

"Get out of my way."

"Oh, no." Tara shifted her body in front of the door handle. "I've just started."

"I'm warning you."

"You've always gotten your way," Tara snarled. Her lips curled away from her cigarette-stained teeth. "A home to raise your kid, family to help you, and now"—her eyes blazed with green fire—"Doc Redding can give your daughter all she could ever want."

"Are you finished?"

"One more thing." Tara bared her teeth in a sneer. "I thought filing the complaint would give me the satisfaction I wanted, but I see now that it won't help me get what I need for my son. Justin's welfare is far more important. I've found a better way."

"Good for you."

"My son needs a father," Tara shot back.

Baffled, Cameron muttered, "What's that got to do with me?"

Tara jabbed her thumb toward the door. "The doc will do just fine."

Anger and pity for the other woman warred within Cameron. "Good luck."

"A man like that needs a woman who knows what to do for him." Tara gave Cameron a thorough once-over, then snickered. "You ain't got what it takes."

Cameron stepped closer. Her voice lowered to a threatening growl. "This isn't a competition. My daughter is involved, and I won't tolerate your meddling."

Tara rolled her eyes. "Ask me if I care."

"If you know what's good for you, you'll learn to care. Quick."

"Ooh, I'm so scared." Tara pretended to tremble. "You know what? You don't have exclusive dibs on that cutiepie. I like what I see, and I'm going after him."

"You're grown. Do your thing. Just stay away from my family."

Tara planted her hands on her hips. "Oh. So, you plan to stop me?"

"I'm not fighting you over a man. Marek is an adult and he'll do whatever pleases him." Cameron came nose to nose with Tara. "He's made it clear to me he wants to play a role in our daughter's life and that's what's important to me."

Tara gloated.

Oh, damn. Cameron wanted to stamp her foot. How could she have been so careless? The damage was done. *Get this witch straight and get on with things.*

"If you want to mess with me, fine. Go for it. I'm an adult. And I can handle it. But my baby's innocent." She stuck a finger in Tara's face. "What's between you and me better stay that way. My daughter's off-limits. If any of this touches her, I'm coming after you." Cameron gave Tara a shove. "Understand?"

Fear extinguished the smug excitement in Tara's eyes. Her mouth dropped open as she fumbled for the door handle and tried to ease it open. Cameron backed Tara against the rest-room door.

Cameron felt her blood pressure soar. She needed fresh air. Badly. If she didn't get out of here . . .

"Now get out of my face." Cameron shoved her way past the redhead.

Chapter Eight

Man, Marek rotated his head from side to side, attempting to relieve some of the tension knotting his shoulders. *I'm nervous*, he thought, cruising along I-31.

The day was beautiful. A perfect Sunday afternoon to take his new family to dinner.

On the downside, storm clouds awaited him in the shape of Cameron Butler. In that arena, the odds were stacked against him. By refusing to tell Jayla about him, Cameron held all the cards.

Damn! He hit the steering wheel with the palm of his hand. All those years, wasted. Jayla's first step, her first words were lost to him.

If Cameron worked with him, this transition would be much easier. But no. Every time they were together, he spent all his time defending himself against something that hadn't happened.

He ran his fingers through his hair while considering his options. Cameron refused to give him an opportunity to explain. Maybe she'd listen to someone she trusted. Someone close.

Snapping his fingers, he muttered, "Mrs. Butler." It was obvious Cameron loved her grandmother and respected her wisdom. She had already admitted it was her grandmother who had convinced her to let him visit Jayla. Maybe Mrs. Butler would intervene on his behalf.

Parking behind a Volkswagen van, he jumped out of his SUV. His stomach knotted as he strolled up the walkway. Bouncing up the stairs two at a time, he covered his nervousness with a pleasant smile.

Marek's fingers shook as he stabbed the doorbell. He shoved an arm of his aviator gold-rimmed sunglasses inside the *v* of his shirt and waited, bracing for Cameron's scorn.

From the other side of the door the chain lock rattled. The door swung open and Mrs. Butler's petite frame blocked the entrance. He smiled, happy to have a moment's reprieve from Cameron's contempt.

Cool wariness greeted him. Mrs. Butler's eagle eyes studied him, from the top of his shower-dampened hair to the shoelaces of his Nike running shoes.

"Good afternoon," Mrs. Butler greeted formally, opening the storm door. The appetizing aroma of chocolate filled his nostrils. It enticed him inside with its wonderful scent.

His hand slipped inside his pocket and fingered the coins as he pondered Mrs. Butler's cool reception. Something was up. Stepping into the air-conditioned house, Jayla and Cameron's untutored voices floated down the steps as they sang the theme from *Beauty and the Beast*.

"My girls are upstairs." Mrs. Butler led him through the marble-floored vestibule, down a cream-colored hallway and through a set of carved sliding doors. "They'll be down in a minute."

His rubber soles squeaked on the marble floor as he followed Mrs. Butler into the living room. Rough waters lay ahead, if he'd correctly interpreted her less than enthusiastic greeting.

"Have a seat." Waving her hand in the direction of a three-pillow sofa, she stepped across an Oriental rug and settled into a worn recliner. The black leather groaned as Mrs. Butler shifted in her seat. "Let's talk before my girls come downstairs."

Her remark made him stop in his tracks. He knew it. Something was up.

Continuing across the room, Marek sank into the sofa's soft pillows, rested his hands on his knees and waited like a small child in the principal's office. Minutes ticked by. The only sound in the room came from the huge grandfather clock.

The pendulum swung from side to side in its wooden encasement. *Thump. Thump. Thump.* His nervousness grew with each tick of the clock and he felt he might break under the pressure. Marek ran a hand through his hair, shifted from one cheek to the other, and continued to wait.

Thump. Thump. Thump. This is just the beginning, it mocked. *This is just the beginning.*

Mrs. Butler linked her fingers together and rested them in her lap. She eyed him with unwavering calm.

He wanted to secure Mrs. Butler as an ally. Ignoring the tangled mass that had become his stomach, he maintained eye contact. She was a tough old bird, but he was tougher.

If he looked away, he'd forfeit everything. Moisture formed across his upper lip as he withstood Mrs. Butler's strong pull. Determined, he focused on her. Suddenly, her lips spread into a satisfied smile.

With a nod of approval she muttered, "Mmmm, hmmm."

He let out a sigh of relief. One hurdle down. He uncurled his damp fists and flexed his fingers.

"So where are you takin' my girls?"

"Dinner. Maybe ice cream on our way *home.*"

"Mmmm, hmmm." She nodded again. "Good. Jayla loves strawberry ice cream."

"I'll remember that," Marek promised. A touch of uneasiness settled in his bones.

Mrs. Butler rose from her chair. The expression on her face made Marek's heartbeat accelerate. With a sense of disquiet, he watched her cross the room, pausing at the archway before sliding the doors shut with a soft thump.

She stopped next to his chair, placed a manicured hand on his shoulder and glowered down at him. If it were possible, his stomach muscles tangled a wee bit more.

"I've got a few things to say to you before they come downstairs."

"Yes, ma'am," he whispered.

"Sweet Peaches has been shut-mouth about you from day one. Since you've come back into her life, she's made one thing real clear. She doesn't trust you or want you anywhere near her or Jayla." Mrs. Butler lifted one eyebrow. "Whatever happened between you two is still with her. It took a lot of convincin' to let you near Jay—"

"But I—"

"I'm not done yet."

His lips snapped shut.

"Sweet Peaches doesn't believe you're father material. My guess is, she saw somethin' that didn't sit well with her. But my instincts," she tapped her chest, "tell me a different story. That's why I stepped in. Now, it's your job to prove me right."

Marek shifted in his chair. He strummed his fingers against the thigh of his jeans.

"Whatever happened between the two of you happened." She placed a hand on his shoulder. "That's your business and I won't pry."

"Mrs. Butler, I can expla—" Mrs. Butler dug her nails

into the shirt's soft folds. He squirmed away from her touch, but she held firm.

"I'm talkin'." She gave his shoulder an additional squeeze.

"You and Sweet Peaches need to handle your business. And I know you'll get around to it. But I want you both to remember this. There's a child involved. Jayla's innocent of all of your problems. Now, if you forget that and she gets caught in your mess, I'll have to come out of my character and show you a side of me you won't like." Her nails dug into his shoulder and made him shift away once more. "Boy, I've put myself on the line for you because I believe Jayla needs her daddy. Don't mess things up, understand?" she warned. "Or, I promise you, I'll get real ugly."

"Yes, ma'am."

"Good. I want you to remember this. Sweet Peaches and Jayla are my family." Her eyes glowed with an inner light of love. "My heart." The light in her eyes snapped off like a lightbulb. A fierce, protective gleam replaced it. "You better not hurt them. Hurt them, you hurt me. Understand?"

"Yes."

"Good." She patted his shoulder. "Now, let me get this show on the road."

Chapter Nine

The doorbell echoed throughout the house. Cameron's heart fluttered like a bird's wings on its maiden flight. *Lord.* Her stomach churned. *I'm nervous.*

The sound of Marek's voice from below jolted her further. She shut her eyes and prayed for enormous amounts of finesse and tact for what came next.

She didn't want Jayla to learn about her father this way. Jayla needed time to adjust. But time was a precious commodity. Any additional delays would open the door to Tara's malicious tongue.

Needing a few minutes to pull herself together, Cameron pointed at the bathroom door. "Go on, Honeybunny. Wash your hands."

"Honey?" asked Jayla.

"What, sweetie?"

"I want to play," Jayla demanded. The stiff set of her baby's chin made Cameron's heart sink. *Oh, Honeybunny, not today.*

"Maybe later," she offered, stroking Jayla's hair. "We need to get ready."

"No."

"Now, Jayla," Cameron snapped, so keyed up the words slipped out before she could stop them. "I'm not going to argue with you. Now move!"

Jayla's head dropped and her lips quivered as she started down the hallway. Ashamed of her sharp words, Cameron hurried after her.

"Mummie's sorry." She gathered Jayla in her arms, rocking her back and forth. "Mummie's sorry. We'll play when we get back. I promise."

Fifteen minutes later, Cameron trailed her daughter down the stairs. Jayla looked adorable in blue jean overalls with Winnie the Pooh embroidery on the bib. A matching appliqué covered the sleeves of her pink short-sleeve T-shirt. Pink socks trimmed with white ruffles and white high-top Reeboks covered her tiny feet as she bounced down the steps.

Mmmm. Closed doors? She leaned closer and listened. Granny's soft murmurs were recognizable, although her words were not.

She tapped on the doors, then slid them open. Granny stood near Marek, waving them into the room. Jayla skipped past her mother and followed the old girl to her chair. Cameron brought up the rear, her gaze glued on Marek.

He jumped to his feet, hands clenching and unclenching at his sides. Awe, plus a dozen additional emotions flew across his face.

Guilt catapulted her out of her safe little world and forced her to admit her role in this situation. It had been wrong to keep them apart. She shoved her hands into the pockets of her dress and lowered her head. Tears pricked her eyes; she felt like a thief. A thief who had stolen three years of their daughter's life from him. From now on, she promised to help develop a strong bond between Marek and Jayla.

"Hi, babe." Granny opened her arms to Jayla. "How's my girl doin' today?"

"Fiiiiine." Jayla climbed onto Granny's lap.

"That's my girl."

Moving to Marek's side, Cameron stammered, "I—I need t—to see you outside."

"No," he rasped.

"Now." She tugged on his arm. "This is important."

Scowling, he followed her from the room, pausing inside the doorway to give Jayla one final glance.

"Granny, will you keep an eye on her for me? Marek and I need a few minutes." She smiled at her daughter and said, "Jayla? Mummie will be right back. Behave yourself. Okay?"

A long drawn out sigh escaped Jayla's lips. "I am being haved."

Marek stepped into the hallway with Cameron on his heels. She shut the sliding doors and then leaned against them to support her rubbery legs.

Folding his arms across his chest, Marek demanded, "Okay, talk." Suspicion glittered from his eyes like a new copper penny. "What's so important?"

Cameron wiped away the beads of perspiration dotting her forehead. "I need to talk to you about last Saturday night."

"Last Saturday?" He parroted, stepping away from the wall. "What about it?"

"While we were at the restaurant, I ran into Tara O'Rourke. She put two and two together and realized Jayla is yours." Her slender hands twisted together. "Tara plans to make it her mission to spread that information around town."

"Hmmm," he grunted. A thoughtful expression settled over his features. "Why? What business is it of hers?"

She tried to swallow, but couldn't. "Tara and I have

problems. She sees herself as my rival. I've tried to reason with her, but she won't listen." She struggled to control the tremor in her voice. "For myself, I don't care, but this involves Jayla and it's my job to protect her."

"Our job," he corrected. "Are you sure it wasn't a joke?"

"Oh, I'm sure," she answered frostily, stepping away from the door and touching his bare arm. "More importantly, this changes our plans. We have to tell Jayla today."

Marek's threw back his head and roared with laughter.

Shocked, Cameron flinched. She had expected a reaction, but nothing so elaborate. "What's so funny?"

"You," he answered on the edge of a chuckle, eyes dancing. "Saturday night, I listened to all your bull, but now we're back to my original suggestion." His shoulders shook as he laughed. "I love it."

Miffed, she answered, "Yeah, well. I'm still not sure this is the best idea, but I'm fresh out of options. How about you, Dr. Spock?"

"Wait a minute. You've known about this since Saturday? Why did you wait until today to tell me?"

"I thought I could handle it. Appeal to Tara's maternal instincts. I was wrong."

"Why didn't you call me? We could have put our heads together, discussed this like family. Who knows, I might have been able to convince her to leave things well enough alone."

"Yeah, maybe you could have," Cameron muttered. She was out of line, but she couldn't help herself.

"Was that a comment?" His inflexible glare prolonged the moment.

Embarrassed, she shook her head. "No."

"I didn't think so. At the very least, I should have been informed, Cameron." He sighed. "Either I'm part of this family or I'm not." His eyes turned frosty. "If you plan to make all the decisions, then I'll do the legal thing and force you to come clean."

She stiffened at the criticism in his voice. "Look." The tide of anger and fear made her reckless. "This is neither the time nor the place to go into this. Save it for another occasion, okay?"

"Oh, I will," he promised. "Don't think you'll be able to appease me with a few mmm-hmms."

"Let's get back to the issue at hand."

"So, what's your plan?"

"I can't stop Tara. So I thought we'd tell Jayla about you," she explained. "After dinner, maybe we can sit somewhere and see how it goes. If she's receptive, then we'll tell her."

He opened the door and answered, "Fine."

Marek's emphasis on that one word made her hackles rise. She searched his calm face, but found nothing. Brushing the feeling of apprehension off her shoulders, she followed him back into the living room.

"Honeybunny, come here so I can introduce you to my friend." Cameron wiggled her fingers, producing a high-energy smile. The room hummed with tension as Cameron led Jayla toward Marek.

Hand in hand, Jayla and Cameron stopped in front of Marek. Cameron's tongue stuck to the roof of her mouth as they waited for him to say something. Silently, she prayed everything would work out.

Finally. This was it; what he'd waited for since he first set eyes on his daughter. An incredible fireball of emotions surged through Marek. He searched his mind for the perfect thing to say.

"Honeybunny, this is Dr. Marek. Say hi." Cameron nudged the little girl forward. "Marek, this is Jayla."

He tried to get a handle on his emotions. They felt like confetti scattered in a New Year's Eve wind: love and happiness mixed together. Within seconds, the knot in the center of his gut started to dissolve as parental pride blossomed. The urge to draw Jayla close and hug her beckoned him. But not yet. There'd be plenty of time for that later. Right now, he needed to get to know her.

Marek's heart expanded with love when he gazed into his daughter's sweet face. He waited until Jayla completed her inspection of him, then went through a checklist of his own. *She's perfect*, he admired, dropping to one knee in front of her.

"Hi." He smiled. "You c—cc—c." He choked, then paused to clear his throat. *Great going*. More than ten years of advanced education, as well as a medical degree, yet the ability to string together a sentence vanished with the first tentative smile from his child. "Call me Marek." *For now*.

"Hi." She threw him a weak wrist wave of greeting, but remained glued to her mother's side.

She had his eyes. And nose. He grinned like a fool. It amazed him to see this miniature version of himself.

"How old are you?"

Four fingers wiggled at him. "Three," Jayla answered.

"How about?" Marek folded one finger into her palm, caressed Jayla's soft cheek, and then tickled her behind the ear. "Three." Giggling, she squirmed away from his touch.

Those brown curls beckoned him to touch and he responded. The lock curled around his finger. He ached to know more, but he didn't know where or how to begin. Instead, he settled for the obvious.

"Are you hungry?"

"Yesss."

"Your granny said you like ice cream. We'll have to stop and get some," he enticed, fascinated by the sparkle in her eyes. "What's your favorite restaurant?"

"McDonald's!" She bounced up and down.

"Ewww." Cameron placed a hand on Jayla's shoulder. "Honeybunny, maybe Dr. Marek would like to go someplace else." With a note of caution in her voice, she suggested, "He may not like McDonald's."

Jayla raised shocked eyes to her father. He wanted to laugh out loud.

"Don't worry," he brushed aside Cameron's objections. "McDonald's is fine. How about the McDonald's Playland?"

"Hallalula," Jayla yelled. Her smile disappeared and she darted a worried glance at her mother. "Can Honey come, too?"

"Honey?" Marek asked curiously.

"That's me," Cameron answered. "When she started to talk, Jayla tried to mimic my Honeybunny. But Honey was all she got out." She shrugged. "Honey stuck."

"Oh," he returned.

"Come on, Honey." Jayla took her mother's hand and pulled her toward the door.

Cameron turned to Marek and shook her head. "You don't know what you've just let yourself in for."

Marek shrugged. "I'll survive."

"Jayla, go upstairs and get your jacket." She strolled across the room. "I've got to talk with Granny."

"Okay." She raced from the room.

This meeting had taken a toll on Cameron. She looked drained. Her shoulders sagged and stress lines etched her face.

"Granny," she said. "Can I bring you anything? Sandwich? Soup?"

"Mrs. Butler, please join us," Marek added.

"No." Mrs. Butler shook her head. "You don't need me around. There's plenty of time for that later. Right now, you three go have some fun."

"What about dinner?" Cameron perched on the edge of the recliner and rested an arm around Mrs. Butler.

"I'm fine. Now go, go." She shooed them away with a wave of her hand. "Have a good time."

"Okay." She hugged Mrs. Butler. "Don't forget to take your medicine."

"Handle your own business." Mrs. Butler wagged a finger at her granddaughter.

"I don't think so." She grinned down at her grandmother and dropped a kiss on her cheek. "I learned the art of nosiness from a pro."

"Hmmmph." Mrs. Butler turned up her nose. "You must be thinkin' about your own self."

Fascinated, Marek watched the interplay between the two women. This was what he wanted for Jayla, and if he were honest, for himself. He wanted to be part of that closeness and love Cameron and Mrs. Butler shared with such ease.

He'd never had that kind of relationship with his parents. It seemed so natural, carefree, and he was going to find a way to get it. And he'd use everything available to him to insure he got the same thing for his family.

"Okay. We'll see you in a little bit." Kissing her grandmother on the forehead, Cameron rose and started toward him.

Chapter Ten

"Guess what, Honey?" Jayla bounced up to the McDonald's table and gazed expectantly at her mother. Excited, she pranced from foot-to-foot as if she needed to go to the potty.

Cameron smiled into her daughter's dancing eyes and countered, "Guess what, sweetie?"

Jayla cupped her hand to her lips and whispered, "I got a daddy."

The smile dropped from Cameron's lips. Shocked, her jaw fell open as her hand flew to her mouth.

They were supposed to tell Jayla together. Heart hammering, she searched the restaurant above Jayla's curls for Marek's dark head.

"Honeybunny," her tongue swept across her dry lips while she hunted for the right words. "Who told you that?"

"Dr. Marek."

"Where? When?"

She pointed to the glass-enclosed play area attached to the dining room and answered in a singsong tone, "In there."

Why would he make such a personal declaration in a public place like McDonald's? Before they left the house hadn't they agreed to tell her together? Cameron shook her head. Madaddy was right. Never trust a man. No. Never trust Marek Redding, she amended.

First, she needed to determine how Jayla had accepted the news. She cradled Jayla on her lap and finger-combed the curls away from her eyes. Inhaling deeply, she hugged Jayla closer; baby powder mixed with a faint hint of her father's cologne filled her nostrils. "Do you like your daddy?"

"Yeah." Her head bobbed up and down. Jayla's face brightened with hope. "Now I've got a daddy like everybody else. Is he going to come live with us?"

"Live with us?" Those words echoed inside Cameron's head. The thought of Marek's day-to-day life connected with theirs both thrilled and terrified her.

"Who's everybody else?"

"Kids."

"Your buddies, Eric and Rebecca?"

Jayla nodded solemnly.

Pain tugged at Cameron's heart. Children could be so heartless. How long had Jayla been curious about her father?

Since Jayla's birth, Cameron had dedicated her life to being a good single parent and proving to her parents that she could succeed. Maybe she'd been too preoccupied with success. Had she ignored Jayla's needs in favor of her own goals?

Jayla's brow furrowed over her eyes, flooring her mother with her next confession. "Sometimes they ask me where my daddy is and I tell them I don't know," she admitted. "Now I can show them I've got a daddy, too."

"Why didn't you ask me?"

AS LONG AS THERE IS LOVE 101

Jayla hunched her shoulders and her cheeks flushed pink. Cameron lifted Jayla's chin with a finger and gazed into her eyes. "Honeybunny, you can always come to me. I'm your mother, baby. I love you. You can ask me anything."

"Okay," Jayla answered, her eyes shifted away from her mother's face.

Cameron kissed Jayla's forehead. "When you see Eric and Rebecca, you tell them your daddy's a doctor and he lives in town and he'll be around for them to see."

Jayla's face brightened. "Hallaula!" Her infectious smile melted Cameron's heart and strengthened her vow to see Marek and Jayla together.

"W—w—what else did Dr. Marek tell you?" Cameron stammered.

"He said I didn't have to call him Dr. Marek," she answered. "I could call him daddy if I wanted."

"What did you say?"

"I said I had to ask you." Hope filled Jayla's voice. "Can I?"

"Of course you can." Her insides twisted with jealousy. If only it didn't hurt to share Jayla's precious love; a love that had been hers exclusively. Until now.

Over Jayla's head, Cameron searched for Marek. She spotted him crossing the restaurant. An amused twinkle winked back at her.

Lips thinning, she silently promised, *I'll get you for this.*

"Hi, Daddy," Jayla chirped as Marek approached them.

Stunned, Cameron bit the inside of her jaw. Jayla used that word so naturally.

"Hey, Pumpkin." Ruffling her hair, he smiled down at her.

Cameron stood; her baby slid off her lap. "Jayla told me what you did."

With a shameless grin, he shrugged. "So?"

Turning her back on him she said, "Honeybunny, why

don't you finish Mummie's drink while," she glanced over her shoulder at him, "D—D—Da—Dr. Marek and I talk." The word "daddy" choked her.

"Okay." Jayla slipped into her mother's chair and reached for the white plastic cup with golden arches printed on the front.

Facing him, "Why?" Cameron demanded, low in her throat. "I thought we agreed to tell her *together?*"

Insolently, he glared down at her. "That was your idea. And I never agreed to it."

"Be that as it may," she rasped. "We talked about it this afternoon at the house."

"No, we didn't," he corrected, sticking a finger in her face. "*You commanded.* Cameron has spoken." His cold gaze made goosebumps rise on her skin. "And everyone was supposed to do things your way."

"I—I," she began.

"Ronnie, this wasn't supposed to be a big deal." He stepped closer and his voice dropped a notch. "Jayla needed to know who I am. Nothing more. Instead you wanted to make a major production out of a situation that should have been private."

"Jayla's a baby, Marek," she scolded. "You know nothing about her."

"Whose fault is that?" he shot back. "If you'd listened to me four years ago, this wouldn't be a problem."

"That's not on the table for discussion right now." Cameron hissed, shooting a concerned glance at Jayla. Preoccupied with her drink, Jayla appeared not to notice the tension brewing between her parents.

"I know this isn't the best place to talk." He ran his fingers through his hair, further tousling the dark mane. "Maybe we should go someplace quiet and discuss this and get this whole sorry mess out in the open."

Alarmed, she blurted, "Oh no. I'm not going there with you today."

"Fine. When?" Marek challenged, shoving his hands into the pockets of his jeans. "Give me a date."

"Never," Cameron spit out and stepped back.

A look of disgust crossed his face. "That sounds just like you," he accused, lips turned down at the corner. "Don't you ever listen to anyone else? Trust a single soul? You think you have all the answers and go blindly about your business. No one else's opinion matters, only yours."

Cameron gazed away and tried not to cry. Marek's comments hurt. This wasn't the first time she'd been called stubborn or told that she had a problem with trust.

Silence lengthened between them, amplifying other senses. The aroma of frying meat was strong. The cash register drawer slammed at regular intervals, as orders were taken and money exchanged.

"Why didn't you wait?"

"It just happened. The time was right, so I told her."

"What about me? Don't you think I wanted to be with her when you told her?"

"Look at her." They turned and watched Jayla slurp the pink lemonade through a straw. "Jayla's not upset. She's fine."

Hands on her hips, Cameron stated, "I have a problem with you making decisions without cueing me in." Reproach filled her voice. "I don't appreciate being left out of the loop."

"Is that right?" He chuckled and looked down his nose at her. "I recall telling you something similar earlier today."

Stunned, Cameron opened her mouth, but Marek didn't give her time to speak.

"It's not fun, is it?" His faint smile held a touch of sadness. "Being left out of things."

"Is that why you told Jayla without me?" She barely

disguised the angry edge of her voice. "To get back at me? To prove a point?"

Jayla patted her mother's thigh, "Honey?" she whined, worry lines marring her young forehead. Her troubled eyes darted from one parent to the other.

"Hey, Honeybunny." Cameron forced a smile, softening her tone. "Did you finish Mummie's drink?"

Damn Marek. She didn't want her daughter upset. Jayla nodded and handed the empty cup to her mother.

"Why don't you toss that in the trash for Mummie?" Cameron suggested, pointing at the trash bin. This should give her just enough time to get Marek straightened out.

Uncertainty clouded Jayla's eyes as she searched her parents' faces. "Okay." Halfway to the bin, she turned and studied her parents.

Smiling, "It's all right," Cameron waved her away. "We'll be done in a minute."

Cameron ran her hand across her face. As soon as she could get him alone, she planned to share some choice words with Dr. Marek Redding.

The smile died the moment she turned to Marek. "We're going to establish some ground rules once I've put our G-rated audience to bed."

"You can talk all you want," he fished his keys from his pocket, "but I'm finished. Pumpkin."

Jayla skipped back to her father, slipped her hand into Marek's palm and followed him to the door. She looked over her shoulder and called, "Come on, Honey."

With a hand on the door, Marek turned to Cameron. "Yeah," he muttered sarcastically, leaving her to trail behind them. "Come on, Ronnie."

Chapter Eleven

"Looks like you've got company." Marek parked his Mercedes-Benz behind a silver Jaguar convertible. Facing Cameron, his brows creased. "Friend of yours?"

Cameron rolled her eyes and slipped out of the SUV. She took a second to admire the impressive piece of machinery. She didn't know anyone with this kind of car. Did Granny?

An image of Granny tooling around town in this silver beast with the top down and the wind blowing through her hair popped into Cameron's head. Laughing out loud, she opened the SUV's back passenger door and unbuckled Jayla from the car seat.

"Excuse me." Marek's warm hands molded around her waist. Her breath caught in her throat. Memories of warm oil and back massages flashed through her head, crowding out intelligent thought. Nudging her aside, Marek drew Jayla from the car and cradled her against his shoulder.

Jayla's little body arched and stiffened as straight as a ruler. Grumbling, she squirmed around in her sleep. Marek muttered in Jayla's ear, massaging her back. Their daughter quieted and snuggled into her father's embrace.

Marek's movements triggered recollections of his fingers soothing her tired muscles after a long day at the University's day care center. The image was so vivid she almost smelled the heated baby oil, felt its heaviness and warmth against her skin as his fingers meticulously worked it into her aching muscles.

An exaggerated cough snapped her from her private reverie only to find Marek and Jayla waiting at the front door. Embarrassed, she hurried to the porch, climbed the steps two at a time and pulled her keys from her purse.

Ray Charles's husky voice greeted them when Cameron opened the door. The aromas of cinnamon, sweet potatoes and freshly brewed coffee filled the air.

"Granny?"

"Hey, Sweet Peaches," she called from the kitchen. Her voice brimmed with mischief. "We'll be out in a moment."

We? Who's we? What was the old girl up to? Cameron started down the hall with Marek and Jayla in tow. She came up short when Granny emerged from the other end.

"Oh!" the old girl yelped, placing a hand to her chest. "You scared the mess out of me. I thought you'd gone upstairs."

A silent figure stood beyond Granny, and Cameron's eyes widened. *Greg!* What in the world was he doing here?

"I was looking for you," Cameron muttered, glancing from Marek to Greg and back again. Marek's eyes narrowed, sliding over her, then shifted to Greg. A speculative gleam lit up Marek's golden eyes.

"How was your day?" Granny strolled to Marek's side. "Did you have a good time?"

"Umm-hmm," Cameron replied. "It was nice."

"Good." Granny stroked Jayla's cheek. "It looks like she's knocked out."

AS LONG AS THERE IS LOVE 107

"She ran herself ragged in the McDonald's Playland," said Marek as he gazed lovingly at Jayla. "The excitement got to her. Jayla pooped out on the drive home."

"It's the motion from the car." Granny tucked a stray lock of hair behind Jayla's ear. "Puts her right out. Sweet Peaches is the same way. If you need company while you're on the road, she's not the one. Sweet Peaches doesn't get out of the state awake."

"Granny!" Cameron reproached.

The old girl strummed a finger in Cameron's direction. "Now you know I'm tellin' the truth."

"I know." Marek grinned.

Silent throughout their exchange, Greg leaned against the wall and rubbed one finger back and forth across his chin. His eyes run up and down Marek.

"Sweet Peaches? Where are your manners, girl?" Granny scolded. "Introduce your friends."

Marek leaned closer and whispered in Cameron's ear, "Yeah. Why don't you introduce us?" Smirking, his eyebrows arched. "Never mind, I'll do it myself."

Stepping around Cameron with an outstretched hand and a wicked spark in his eyes, he said, "Marek Redding."

"Gregory Hunter." He gripped Marek's hand in the shortest handshake on record.

Marek returned to Cameron's side, placed a possessive hand around Cameron's shoulder and drew her against his side. Greg's eyes narrowed to dark slits, focused on Marek's proprietary hand.

Marek was putting on quite a show, thought Cameron, as she shoved his hand off her shoulder and turned to Greg. She planted what she hoped was a convincing smile on her lips. "So. What brings you out on a Sunday evening?"

"I thought you might be home." He stood still as stone in front of her. "I got in touch with my buddy, and figured you'd like to know what he said."

News from the state. Her heart rate tripled. Maybe it was good news. She hoped so. Lord knew, she needed it.

"Thanks." Cameron turned and asked, "Granny, would you put Jayla to bed for me? I need to talk to Greg."

"Sure." Granny reached for the sleeping child.

Marek shifted away from Granny, his action stirring the child.

"Shh, Pumpkin. Daddy's here." Marek stroked her back until she quieted. "Daddy's here."

The dog! Cameron recognized Marek's gesture for what it was. She'd bet money Greg did too.

A muscle jerked unchecked at Greg's temple. His gaze shifted from Marek to Jayla and back again.

"Mrs. Butler, she's too heavy," Marek said. "I'll carry her upstairs for you."

"Thanks." Granny led him to the staircase. "She's quite a handful. Some mornings I look at her and it seems as if she's shot up overnight."

"Sometimes they do," Marek agreed.

"Have you noticed how tall she is?" Granny asked, stopping on the stairs. "Sweet Peaches is tiny. But not my Jayla. I think she's going to get her height from her father."

"Granny, Jayla needs to be in bed," Cameron called, moving down the hall with Greg. She pushed the sliding doors open and stepped inside the room. "Have a seat."

Greg pounced the moment the door slid shut, "He's Jayla's father?" His eyes were dark with suspicion. "Isn't he?" he demanded, coiled so tight he looked as if he was ready to pop.

No reason to deny the truth, she concluded. "Yes." She moved across the room and sat on the edge of the sofa. "There's no need for us to discuss it further, is there?"

He cut the distance between them. "Are you letting him see Jayla without a written agreement in place? Have you signed anything without my reviewing it?" Disapproval blazed from his eyes. "What happened to our plan to draft an agreement together?"

Cameron held up a hand to silence him. "Greg, Marek's in the house. And he could come downstairs any minute and hear us." She patted the cushion next to hers, and said, "Let's talk about this when I'm in your office. Okay?"

"This needs to be finished tonight."

Weary of the topic, she shook her head and replied, "No. I promise, the next time I'm in your office, we'll clear it all up."

Greg's eyes narrowed for an extra beat, then he answered reluctantly, "Okay. I won't push it." He moved toward the sofa and sat next to her. "But this isn't finished."

"Thank you. I promise, the next time I'm in your office I'll tell you everything." She tucked her legs under her. "So give? What did your friend tell you?"

"He hooked me up with someone from the licensing office."

"Cool."

"There is a formal complaint on file. We should be notified within the next few weeks." His eyes glazed over. "There is something he told me on the Q.T. If Mrs. O'Rourke can be persuaded to drop her complaint, we may be able to stop the investigation process."

"And how are we supposed to do that?"

"If we keep the lines of communication open maybe we can get this complaint resolved before the state comes to town." He tented his hands together and continued, "Say, for instance, we offer Mrs. O'Rourke something she needs and she accepts. What do you think?"

"I think this is a vendetta. The only thing I can do for her is present my head on a platter." Cameron slid her finger across her throat in a slicing motion. "I don't see anything else doing it for her. Besides, I didn't do anything wrong. And if it takes an investigation to prove that, bring it on."

"What if you lose your license?"

Her head shot up, "You told me I wouldn't." Panic crawled under her skin.

"I did." He patted her hand. "But this could be a drawn-out process. Do you want your business up in the air because of Mrs. O'Rourke?"

Greg had a point.

"No."

His eyes flared with the light of battle. "I'm a negotiator. Let me work with her and resolve this matter in an expedient manner."

"Say I agree. What will you use as bait?"

"Mrs. O'Rourke is a single parent. She must need something." Greg strummed his finger against his chin. "In addition to your head on a platter, that is. What about free child care for the next six months?"

"Greg, I'm in business to make money." She shook her head. "Besides, Justin hasn't been back since the accident."

"A little incentive might do the trick."

"It's too close to bribery for my taste." Cameron scrunched up her face. "Besides, Tara won't buy it." She unfolded her legs and turned to Greg. "If she really believes I was negligent, she won't bring Justin back to Little Darlings."

"Leave it to me." He folded his hand on top of Cameron's. "I'm the kid."

"Okay, kid. Go ahead and arrange a meeting, but don't be surprised if she doesn't show up."

"Think positively," Greg suggested, winking at her. "This might be the perfect thing to con—"

She turned at the light tap on the door. The doors slid open and Marek poked his head inside. He zeroed in on Greg's hand on Cameron's and his brows lifted.

"Sorry to interrupt," Marek said. The man looked more

smug than remorseful. "Jayla's asleep and I'm ready to leave."

"Let me see you out." Cameron rose. "Greg, give me a minute. I'll be right back."

"It's all good, babe." He smirked, stretching his legs in front of him and spreading his arms across the back of the sofa. "Don't rush. I've got plenty of time."

Cameron hurried from the room and slid the doors together, glancing around the hallway. "Where's Granny?"

"Mrs. Butler said she was tired and was headed for bed," Marek explained.

"I bet she was."

"So, what's going on between Mr. Jaguar and you?" His lips curled away from his teeth when he said the word *Jaguar*.

"He's my attorney."

Marek volleyed, "And what else?"

"None of your business."

Marek shoved his hands into his pockets. The faint jingle of coins touched her ears. "I'm Jayla's father, Cameron. If there's something between you and Mr. Jaguar, I have a right to know."

"If I decide you need to know, I'll tell you." She walked to the front door and opened it. "Good night."

"I'm not finished." Marek came up alongside her and shut the door. "I think Jayla's far from ready to go out alone with me. She needs a litt—"

Without warning, Marek's arms snaked around her waist, jerking her forward. Surprised, she landed hard against his chest.

His mouth covered hers in a kiss that spoke of passion, possession. It offered her a delicious invasion of the mind and body. She fought to control the emotions, but lost. Surrendering, she wrapped her arms around his neck and drew him closer, threading her fingers through his thick hair.

Lost in the taste and feel of Marek's kiss, Cameron barely heard the living room door open. She almost missed Greg's overexaggerated cough. But there was a slight hesitation in Marek before his moist lips recaptured hers, demanding more.

Finally, they broke apart and Cameron glanced into Marek's wickedly pleased face. She turned away from his self-satisfied expression.

The dirty dog! Cameron wiped her lips with the back of her hand.

"Excuse me," Greg muttered formally. "If you're through, I gotta go. I just got a page." He shook the electronic device at them. "Could you move your car?"

"Sure." Marek fished his keys from his pocket.

Cameron and Marek's hands collided when they both reached for the doorknob. She jerked away and rubbed her fingers against her skirt, trying to extinguish the electrical jolt that shot through her. Marek winked at her.

Opening the door, he leaned forward, brushed his lips across hers once more before slipping through the door. Greg followed. He stopped for a moment to spear her with a hard, accusing glare.

Chapter Twelve

"How long are we going to wait?" Cameron glanced at the clock on the corner of Greg's desk. "It's almost six and Tara still hasn't shown up. Don't forget, she's canceled three appointments this month."

"It's early May, we still have time to settle this situation," Greg answered. His eyes followed her movements back and forth across the room. "If you don't stop pacing, I'm going to bill you for the wear and tear on my carpet," he warned genially, waving a hand toward the sofa and suggested, "Why don't you have a seat?"

"I just want this to be over, Greg," Cameron confessed and brushed loose tendrils of hair from her eyes. "I'd feel more confident if I understood why Tara's doing this and how to put an end to it." She stopped in front of Greg's desk. "I feel so helpless."

"You're far from helpless. But worrying yourself into a frenzy won't accomplish anything," he remarked, with a touch of concern in his voice. "Leave it to me. That's what you pay me for. I'll take care of things. Now, have a seat."

"I can't help it." Cameron swallowed the knot in her throat. "Greg, I can't lose my business."

"You won't. I've told you that before. Why is this so important? What's going on?"

"My parents wanted me to have an abortion. Did I ever tell you that?"

"No."

She shrugged and continued, "Well, they did. They even suggested that I put my baby up for adoption. As if there aren't enough black babies in the system already." Once more the pain of betrayal stabbed at her heart.

"Madaddy kept telling me that I wouldn't be able to have the kind of life I wanted. That I would have to forfeit all my dreams. No master's degree, no school. Nothing. They beat me down with it."

Greg sat behind his desk, silent and watchful.

"There was never a chance that I'd abort Jayla. I made a promise to myself that I'd show them. I'd fulfill every dream I ever had and I'd never ask them for a damn thing. My life wouldn't fall apart because I made a mistake. I want my parents to see how far I've come. Jayla slowed me down a tad, but she didn't stop me from having the things I dreamed of. But this school is the icing on the cake. It's Jayla's future."

"Cameron, you don't have to prove anything."

"That's where you're wrong. I do have to."

She felt as if her legs might collapse from under her. So she obeyed Greg's earlier request and strolled to the cream leather sofa and sank into its smooth folds. Greg's subtle fragrance drifted under her nose as she passed his desk. The pleasant aroma complemented his expensive charcoal gray suit, white shirt and gray striped tie.

"We've got to win this," she continued in a strong,

determined voice. "Get things straight so that it doesn't affect the school. I won't let Tara beat me. I won't."

"It's time for a pep talk." The teasing smile dropped from Greg's face and a serious light entered his eyes. "Relax," he stated, smoothing his tie into place. "Remember, you said it yourself, you did nothing wrong. The worst that can happen is Mrs. O'Rourke doesn't agree. This is one of the avenues we're pursuing. If it doesn't work, we'll try something different."

Cameron snorted, rose from the sofa and began to pace again. "Yeah. Right. This is my life on the line." Greg sounded so reasonable. Then why did she feel so powerless? "Besides, you haven't met Tara." She toyed with the handle of her purse. "I bet your tune will change once you've had that pleasure."

"I'm a litigator." He flashed her a confident smile. "I negotiate with difficult people all the time. Your Tara O'Rourke is no different."

"That's what you think," Cameron replied, offering him a sad little smile. His overconfidence was in for a shake-up. "And pleasssee,"—she rolled her eyes heavenward—"don't refer to her as *my* Tara O'Rourke. She's not *my* anything. And I want to keep it that way. She's not yours either," Cameron warned. "You won't be able to use your persuasive talent to win her over."

"We'll see."

She stopped in front of his desk, laid a hand on its smooth surface. "It's six o'clock. Tara's thirty minutes late. I'm ready to go home."

"No. Let's give her fifteen minutes more then we'll call it a ni—" The telephone began to ring and he snatched up the receiver. "Yes? Good. Is she alone? Mmm?" His brows drew together in a surprised frown. "Send her in." He stood and replaced the handset. "She's here." Greg straightened his tie, buttoned his jacket and strolled across the room.

Tara stood posed in the entrance when he opened the door. The heavy fragrance of musk perfume wafted into the room.

This was it. Cameron wet her lips with her tongue and beat down her attack of nerves. Here was her chance to clear the air. Tara had put in an appearance. *That was a good thing, right?*

Cameron drew in a deep breath, straightened her cream suit jacket and ran a hand over the wrinkles in her linen skirt.

"Well, I'm here," Tara announced.

"Mrs. O'Rourke, I'm Gregory Hunter, Ms. Butler's attorney." He shook her hand and glanced out the door beyond her. "Will your attorney be joining us?"

"No," Tara answered curtly and cut across the office on legs encased in black leggings.

"Liz," he nodded at his administrative assistant, "Why don't you call it a night? Don't walk alone; get security to accompany you. Thanks for staying."

Greg escorted Tara across the room to a chair before he rounded the desk and slipped into his own chair. Once they were seated, Cameron perched on the arm of the sofa and waited for Greg's opening remark.

Tara reached under the collar of her blouse and lifted her hair. The red mane tumbled free over her shoulders. She unzipped her black leather bag, rummaged through it and produced a pack of cigarettes and a gold lighter, then shook out a cigarette. Flipping her lighter open, she touched the cigarette tip to the flame and asked in a challenging tone, "Mind if I smoke?"

Greg's face tightened as he watched Tara draw on the cigarette. Cameron cringed. The game had begun. First point to Tara.

Icy contempt blazed from Greg's eyes as he weighed his options. A muscle jerked unchecked at his temple. He hated cigarette smoke.

"Help yourself," he offered in a frigid voice.

Ashes dangled from the tip of Tara's cigarette, threatening to fall. Her eyes searched his desk. "Your ashtray?"

Irritation flashed across Greg's face. He reached inside his desk drawer, produced a metal ashtray imprinted with "Las Vegas" in thick, red letters and shoved it across the desk.

Waving away her cigarette smoke, Greg opened a drawer and removed a thick green folder. "I strongly recommend you contact your attorney." With a slight tilt of his head, he settled back in his chair and continued, "If you'd prefer to reschedule when your attorney can join us, I'd understand."

"I don't need counsel. I won't be here that long, you know."

"All right then." Greg pulled a document from the folder. "Mrs. O'Rourke, as I indicated in my letter, Ms. Butler and I would like to discuss your complaint against Little Darlings. I've called this meeting, with the hope that we might skip some of the legal entanglements and financial burdens that a long, drawn-out court case would create. I'm proposing we try to resolve the situation here and now."

Tensing, Cameron rose and stepped closer to Greg, waiting. This was his show.

Tara looked up as Cameron approached. She studied Cameron for a beat, and then refocused on Greg.

"Our objective is to work toward an amicable resolution," Greg paused. Silence followed. "And to that end, I've invited you here to air your concerns and grievances. But," he smiled at Tara, "before we get into that, how's Justin?" He grabbed a pen from the cup on his desk and lightly tapped the pen against the desktop.

"Fine." Tara stamped out her cigarette.

"Good," he stated. "I understand he has a broken arm. How's it mending?"

"Justin's fine," she muttered evasively.

Satisfied, he smiled. "Good. Glad to hear it."

Greg sifted through the papers in his file and picked up a sheet. He scanned its contents. "Let's start with the accident. As far as I can tell, Justin fell from the sliding board. What do you believe happened?" He placed the paper on top of the pile and gave Tara his full attention. "How do you believe Ms. Butler was liable? Tell me what we can do to correct this situation to your satisfaction."

Tara scooted closer to the desk and tipped the chair forward, balancing on the front two legs. "What else do you have on your list?"

"Your complaint states you believe Little Darlings lacked the proper staff when the accident occurred." He read from a page with the state of Michigan logo at the top.

"Yeah," she muttered.

"Mrs. O'Rourke," he said, linking his fingers together on top of the pile. "Are you aware that the full complement of employees required by the state were present when Justin fell?"

Voice heavy with disbelief, Tara queried, "How do you know?"

"I compared the requirements of the state with Ms. Butler's employee timesheets. She exceeded the state's guidelines." He handed Tara a blue pamphlet. "If you'll refer to the highlighted areas on page thirty-eight."

Tara took the pamphlet, glanced at it for half a second then tossed it back onto his desk. "What about supervisors?"

"Two supervisors, a total of four staff people on duty. Three of which were in the backyard. Michelle, Linda," he pointed at Cameron, "And, of course, Ms. Butler were in the backyard when the incident occurred."

Tara turned cold eyes on Cameron and pointed a finger in her direction. "How's Jayla?"

Surprised, Cameron's mind shut down for a minute. Tara had never showed the slightest concern for any of the children at Little Darlings, least of all Jayla. Something wasn't right here.

"Jayla's great, thanks," Cameron answered evenly, while her insides burned with caution. "She misses Justin."

"Oh, really?" Tara's dry bark of laughter filled the room. "How sweet."

"They're best buds," Cameron said. "Of course, she misses him."

"And the doc?" She crossed one leg over the other. "How's he?" Tara's eyes slid up and down Cameron.

"I don't know. He doesn't live in my pocket."

"Mrs. O'Rourke, can we get back to the matter at hand?" Greg injected.

Tara fixed him with a frigid glare. "You know, I'm going to put my cards on the table. You can't change my mind. Your client," the word took on all the emphasis of a four-letter word, "was negligent. And in all of this crap nothing has changed my opinion. These are my final words on the subject." Her acid tone tore through the quiet room. "Don't bug me! No more letters. No more phone calls. And don't leave messages with my landlord! Understand? The state investigation will bring everything to light and resolve it all."

Returning the documents to its file, Greg tried to regain control over the situation. "Well, Mrs. O'Rourke, perhaps we ca—"

"No! Perhaps we can't," Tara tossed the straps of her purse over her shoulder. "Don't you speak English?" she gestured wildly. "*This* is the end of the discussion. *Period!*"

"And as for you," Tara snarled at Cameron. "I warned you. Did you think I was kidding?" Her face reddened as her voice rose to a furious pitch. "You can't have it all."

"Mrs. O'Rourke," Greg called sternly. "We're here to discuss your complaint."

"Fine." She threw her hands in the air and pointed an

accusing finger at Cameron. "We're done for now," she promised. "But it's not over." With a careless twist of her hand in the air, Tara sailed out of the room.

Cameron checked her watch, and then shook her head. Six-fifteen. Tara had come, conquered and whipped them, all in the space of fifteen minutes. She'd warned Greg that Tara couldn't be persuaded to do anything she didn't want to.

Resolving the complaint had been the furthest issue from Tara's mind. As far as Cameron could tell, Tara wanted the state's validation, nothing more.

Under lowered lashes, she watched Greg as he finished making notes on a legal pad. He ripped the sheet from the pad's binding and slipped it into a green folder.

Maybe it would be best for the investigation to go forward. Have the state do their thing and when the dust settled, Little Darlings would be vindicated. Any attempts by Tara to file a lawsuit would end in sudden death.

Chapter Thirteen

"Okay. You were right. That was a fiasco." Greg flipped the file shut and shoved it into his overstuffed outbox. "But what I don't understand is the animosity." He stood, opened the credenza behind his desk and removed a bottle of cognac and two glasses. "Cameron, you've got to give me the real deal."

"I told you." Her voice broke. She collected herself, wanting to run for the mountains and forget all of this. "This is all a vendetta."

"I can see that."

He poured cognac into one glass, lifted the bottle in Cameron's direction. "Want one?"

She shook her head. How long had Greg been drinking?

He swallowed half the glass's content in one gulp and caught the expression in her eyes. "It's all good, babe," Greg said.

"So you keep telling me," she answered in a dubious

tone. Maybe she should mind her own business, but his drinking disturbed her.

"You should believe the kid."

"Well, kid." Weary, she brushed her hands along the thighs of her skirt. "Tara has the crazy notion I'm coming between her and Marek. She's got him pegged for Justin's new daddy."

"Because?"

"I don't know," she said, baffled. "Whatever it is, the complaint is wrapped up in it."

"From my position, Marek knows what he wants, and it's not Mrs. O'Rourke," he stated with complete certainty. "So what's the deal with Marek?"

Cameron was so tired of holding things together, pretending she could handle it all. She was going to have to answer Greg's questions at some point anyway. Why not now?

"I want to help," his soft tone, persuaded. "Talking might put the incident in a different perspective."

"What do you want to know?"

"Anything you want to tell me." With a serious gleam in his eyes, he said, "The beginning makes a good place to start."

"I met Marek my senior year at the University of Michigan." She fidgeted with the button of her suit jacket. "It was time for me to take the teaching certification exam in biology and I wanted a really high score, so my roommate suggested I get a tutor. And she knew the perfect person." Cameron rolled her eyes heavenward. "Nikki ... Nikki knew Marek from the hospital where she worked and she convinced him to take me on. Marek was great. Calm, patient. The only down side was his hours. Because he was a doctor, his schedule was pretty hectic. He came to the house whenever he could arrange it," she explained, "which made him a fixture around our apartment. It didn't take long for him to go from being my tutor to something more."

She was unable to read him. Greg had his lawyer's stoic face in place. "How long were you two together?"

"Little over a year. He was on the last leg of his fellowship in cardiology and studying for the boards." Under Greg's steady gaze Cameron squirmed in her chair. She twisted the strap of her purse around her hand. "We were pretty tight, though we had a couple of rough spots."

"Rough spots?" Greg prompted, his brows knitted together. "That boy looks like a rich kid. Is he?"

"Marek's dad owns a bank in Franklin," Cameron said. "I could tell his parents weren't pleased. But I expected that." Her lips twisted into a cynical smile. "I think they thought it was a phase he'd outgrow. I suppose that's why they didn't kick up much dust about us."

"What about your folks?" Greg rose from his chair, stepped around the desk and perched along its edge in front of her. "How did they take it?"

"You've been to our house with my brother." She chuckled without humor. "I'm sure David told you about our father."

Cameron stood and lifted a crystal paperweight from Greg's desk. She tossed it from hand-to-hand, pacing the room. "The first time they met, Madaddy wasn't pleased, but he didn't say much. Believe me, when he learned I was pregnant, Marek's stock plummeted."

"Okay. Problems on both sides of the family. Is that what happened to you guys?"

"No. I wish it was. Oh, how I wish it was. A couple of days after graduation I came home from work and ... and ..." The words trembled on the tip of her tongue. "I found him in bed with my roommate."

"Hell!" Greg's whistled. "You've got to be kidding?"

"Not this time."

"What did you do?" Greg prodded, his eyes dark with concern.

"I got out," she gulped. Once more betrayal churned inside her. "Turned around and left the apartment without a word and headed straight back to my folks' place."

"What about Marek?" he questioned. "You just left him there? You didn't confront him?"

She turned away and answered, "No."

He stormed over to her, grabbed her shoulders and turned her to face him. "Let me get this straight. You left without finding out the truth?" He stared down at her as if he'd never seen her before. "I don't believe this. I've seen you fight like a maniac for anything Jayla needed. To get that school going, you've worked seven days, without one word of complaint. And there's nothing you wouldn't do for your grandmother." He shook her. "So, why didn't you fight for your own happiness?"

"So much," she paused. "So much was going through my head." Her knuckles clenched white around the paperweight. "You know my dad's a cop."

He nodded.

"Growing up with a cop and three older brothers wasn't easy. Daddy monitored every thing I did. Every boy that came into the house had to get pass my brothers and my father's inspection."

A look of confusion crossed Greg's face as he let her go. "Where is this leading?"

"I got lectures whenever I went out." Preoccupied, she tossed the paperweight from hand-to-hand. "So you can imagine how it was drummed into my head to be careful, not to trust men. Don't let my guard down."

This trip down memory lane was painful. There were far too many potholes on this particular road.

She sucked in a deep breath and noted somewhat abstractly that her hands were shaking. "When I opened the door and saw Marek and Nikki in my bed, every lecture Madaddy ever gave me zipped through my head." She shut her eyes against the image of her so-called friend and lover together. "For a second, I heard my father's voice saying 'See I told you that you can't trust a man.'" A dull ache gnawed at her insides. "The room suffocated me. I had to get out. I ran to the only place I knew was safe."

"And to top it off, I came home pregnant. You can't possibly know the fireworks I went through after I told my parents." Her stomach twisted into knots. "Oh my God, it was terrible. Right then and there, I promised myself that I'd show them. I'd make a success of my life and I'd never ask them for anything."

Greg caught her hands, retrieved the paperweight and placed it on the desk. He drew her to the sofa and forced her down next to him. Their shoulders brushed as they sank into the soft leather and Greg's warmth penetrated her jacket as they sat shoulder-to-shoulder.

"Okay, now I understand why you're so driven. Your need to have everything perfect. But I can't believe you let the situation with Marek ride all these years."

"What was I supposed to do?" Tears pricked her eyes. "I saw them."

"What about confronting him?" Greg snapped. "What if you're wrong and there's more to the story than you know?"

"What do you mean more to the story?" A dubious note crept into her voice. "Greg, they played me for a fool. Marek used me."

He sighed and tapped the tip of her nose with his finger. "You, my dear, need to learn how to question and listen with more than your ears. Emotions can distort."

Could Greg be right? The possibility made her heart leap, then settle into its normal rhythm. No. Her eyes worked just fine.

"Believe me, I know," Greg continued. "I've seen it happen in court. You have to see with all of your senses."

"I can't go back to it, Greg. I want to leave that stuff in the past." Cameron tried to block out the pain. "It hurts so much. Too much. I won't go through it again."

"Have you guys cleared the air since he moved here?" Greg pressed. "Is that why you've allowed him to visit Jayla without a legal document in place?"

"No." She shut her eyes, drew in a deep breath, then opened them. "I want him to see Jayla. My baby made me see how much she needs her father. It's not fair to keep them apart."

"But what about your needs?" He studied her for a beat then asked, "Don't you think you need to know the truth? You have to have closure so that you can move on with your life. If you don't get things straight with this incident, it'll eat you alive. It's already started to."

"I don't need closure," she denied. "Marek and I understand each other just fine."

Greg threw back his head and laughed. "Sure you do. But it's not about that incident. I'm a man. I know what he is thinking. And trust me, Marek didn't try to hide it." He tipped her chin up, met her glare. "And you, my girl, are no better."

"You're wrong," she answered, halfheartedly.

Greg snapped his fingers in front of her face, "Cameron, wake up. You can barely put together a sentence when he's in the room. And don't think I didn't pick up on his warning." He paused long enough for the significance of his words to sink in.

Embarrassed, heat crawled up her neck.

"You forget I'm an attorney. I make my living reading faces. And baby, you're easy to make out," he stated. "Whatever your feelings, it's time for you to own up to them. Get on with it, or get gone."

AS LONG AS THERE IS LOVE   127

She frowned, then asked in a confused tone. "Why are you defending him?"

"Because you won't see me as anything more than a friend until you clear this up." He smiled sadly back at her. "I'm not going to spend the rest of my life as your bud. After you've ended that part of your life, there may be room for me. But until that time comes, I'm going to back off and give you a little space to get yourself together." Greg inhaled and added, "Even if what you saw was correct, confirm it. Plus, you need to hear Marek's side of the story. His apology. Whatever he has to say. Because you won't be able to move on until that's happened. And you know what else? You need to say your piece. Get it out of your system. Spit on him. Whatever."

Greg was so good to her. Why couldn't she care for him?

"There's something else you need to know. I'm not trying to get into Heaven by doing a good turn. This is completely selfish. If we're going to be together at some point there can't be any what ifs. Understand?" He tilted her chin to look at him. "Until you clear up this mess with that rich kid, there can't be a you and me, an us." He squeezed her hand. "Whatever happens, I promise, I'm here for you."

"Do you think we can still work together?" Worried, she asked. "Should I find another attorney?"

"Oh yeah, we can still work together," he said. "I told you before, I can take care of my emotions. Besides, I've been your attorney far too long to let someone else take over. I'll see this case through."

She bit her bottom lip and muttered, "Thanks."

"You're welcome. Understand me, this has nothing to do with *him*. This is for you, and I'm gambling on it being for me. I won't play second fiddle to any man, especially some rich boy with the easy life." His lips curled nastily. "The truth of the matter is, he's been convicted without a trial."

"You sound just like Granny." Cameron smiled weakly. "Have you two been conspiring against me?"

"No. But Mrs. Butler is very intelligent," he grinned. "You should listen to her."

Her doubts resurfaced. "What if you're wrong and things are exactly the way I remembered them?"

"Then you'll know. And you can move on. And I'll be waiting for you." He linked their fingers. "If things turn out to be the way you believe, then I'll be expecting that real date we talked about. I have a lot of faith that you'll do right." His touch was comforting. "Don't let me down."

Cameron considered all Greg had said as she left his office. Could he be right? Did Marek deserve to have his own day in court? She buttoned her jacket and headed down the corridor.

The elevator doors opened, she stepped inside and punched the button for the lobby. Smiling, she shook her head. Men were so unpredictable. Greg as Marek's champion was almost too much to believe.

The years since their break up had been hard. But like so much of that pain, she'd stored it away in a place that couldn't hurt her.

Greg was right. Time to start living. A plan began to solidify in her mind as she left the building.

Sunday, after Marek arrived for his visit, she'd send Jayla in the house with Granny. Then she'd ask him for his side of the story. She prayed Marek wouldn't disappoint her.

Chapter Fourteen

Marek cruised up Cameron's block and rolled to a stop near her driveway. He cut the engine and folded his arms over the SUV's open window frame. The warm June sun caressed his skin as he enjoyed Cameron and Jayla's front lawn antics.

His confidence soared when he eyed the plastic bag in his passenger seat. Maybe this would shake her up, make her realize how important she was to him, how much he wanted to regain her trust.

Cameron stood several yards away, facing the SUV with an orange Nerf ball in her hand. Jayla was closer, but her back was to him. Chuckling, his heart swelled with love as he watched her lunge a giant green Nerf bat. The bat was almost taller than she was.

Then Cameron drew his full attention. For a woman who'd had a baby, her small frame showed few, if any, after-effects of pregnancy. Of course, so far she had refused to let him get close enough to do a thorough examination. But it would happen.

Sensual hunger nibbled at the pit of his belly while he admired the beautiful picture she presented in a pair of knee-length shorts and matching blouse of green splashed with blue and yellow. He turned his attention to her face and watched her pink tongue dart across her lips. That unconscious gesture created an inferno in a different area of his anatomy.

The orange ball sailed through the air and past Jayla. Dejected, she dropped the bat and let out a gigantic sigh. "Aww, Honey."

"Come on, Honeybunny," Cameron's voice grew stronger as she crossed the yard. "You can do this. But you have to practice," she coaxed. "Remember, concentrate, watch the ball, then swing when it gets near you."

"Mummie, I can't."

"Yes, you can." Marek caught the persuasive note in Cameron's voice. "Here, let Mummie show you." With a slight nod in his direction, Cameron dropped to her knees and covered Jayla's fingers with hers. "Now, you hold it like this and then swing when the ball comes near you. Okay? Just take your time. You can do it."

"What if I miss?"

"That's okay." Cameron hugged Jayla close, then stood. "We'll just try it again. Now lift the bat and hit that ball way over Mummie's head." She scooped up the ball and returned to her previous position.

"Ready?"

Uncertain, Jayla answered, "Yesss."

"Okay. Now watch." Cameron aimed the ball, then released it. "Here it comes."

Posed, Jayla stood ready to strike.

Come on, Pumpkin, Marek cheered, pressed against the doorframe. *You can do it.*

Jayla stepped into her swing and the bat connected with the ball, sending the ball sailing through the air. The bat hit the ground and her arms shot straight up into the air.

"I did it!" Jayla exclaimed, bouncing around like a boxer who'd just gotten his first TKO. Her mouth formed a perfect "O" and jubilation spread across her face. "Did you see me, Honey? I did it!" Jayla said. "Mummie, are you proud of me?"

"Yes, I am, Honeybunny." Cameron raced to Jayla and lifted her high in the air, swinging her around in a circle. "Mummie's so proud of you."

Unable to restrain himself, Marek let out a hoot of delight. He climbed from the Mercedes, pulling the gaily-colored plastic bag along with him, and slammed the door shut. Jayla wriggled out of her mother's embrace, ran toward Marek and launched herself into his arms.

"Daddy. Did you see me?"

"I sure did, Pumpkin." He hugged her close. She smelt of the great outdoors. Grass and dirt, with a dash of baby powder. "Give Daddy a kiss."

She wrapped her arms around his neck and gave him a juicy smack on the cheek. "Daddy, where've you been?" Her little face scrunched into a frown. "We've been waiting for you."

"I'm sorry I'm late, Pumpkin. I had to see your friend Justin. I took his cast off today."

Cameron strolled across the lawn toward them. She looked more beautiful up close, he thought, enjoying the natural sway of her hips when she walked. Nostrils flaring, Marek inhaled the lavender fragrance that danced around him as she moved closer, kicking his heartbeat into overdrive.

"Hey," Cameron flashed him a bright smile that didn't quite reach her eyes. Her eyes were large and she caught her bottom lip between her teeth.

"Hey, yourself."

"Did I hear you say you saw Justin?" she asked eagerly. "How is he?"

"Good. Arm's mended." He motioned toward the front lawn and asked, "What was that about?"

"Jayla, tell your father." Cameron grinned.

"Eric wouldn't let me play on his team." Jayla lifted her chin a fraction and said, "He said I was too little. I'll show him," she muttered, with a determined nod of her head. "I can do it."

"You sure can, Pumpkin."

The bag rattled in his other hand. Jayla spied it and asked, "What's that?"

Show time. The inner voice inside his head cautioned him that this stunt might blow up in his face, but he ignored it. Instead, he held up the bag for them to see.

"This is a present for you." Marek set her on the ground, dropped to one knee and opened the bag. Jayla's eyes grew large as he withdrew a white teddy bear dressed in a red and green velvet dress and red hat.

"Woooow!" Jayla exclaimed.

Out the corner of his eye Marek saw Cameron go stiff. A twinge of guilt and doubt hit him like twin fists in the gut when he saw the mist of confusion sweep across her face.

"She's called a Santabear." Marek held Cameron's gaze over Jayla's head. "I want you to have her. Your Mummie gave her to me before you were born. And your grandfather gave it to her." He smiled, spying Jayla stroking the velvety fur. "When I get sad or miss you and your Mummie, the bear always makes me feel close to you."

"Daddy, don't you need it anymore?"

"No." Marek's eyes clung to Cameron's, begging her to understand, give a little.

"I'm not sad anymore." Disappointment filled his heart as he watched Cameron's uncompromising expression.

"You and your mummie are close now and I can see you both anytime I want. So, I want you to take good care of Santabear for me. Okay?"

Solemnly, Jayla stroked the bear's fur. "Okay." She tucked the bear under her arm like a football and touched his cheek. "Thank you, Daddy."

"You're welcome, Pumpkin." Marek rose to his feet and searched Cameron's face for signs of life. She stood so still he wondered whether she'd tuned in to his words.

"Mummie, look what Daddy brought me." Jayla displayed the bear for her mother's inspection. "He said you gave it to him."

For one unguarded moment, Marek saw pain cloud Cameron's eyes before she switched off her emotions. Her attention shifted to the stuffed animal in Jayla's hands.

It was obvious the bear had made an impact on Cameron. But the question remained, would she open up and question him about why he had kept it all these years?

"It's nice, Honeybunny." She laid her hands on Jayla's shoulders. "Why don't you show your grandmother your present?"

"Okay." Jayla scurried up the stairs to the front door.

Cameron wrapped her arms around herself and stared into the silent street. "You kept it."

"Yes."

She dropped her arms to her sides, turned to him. "Why?"

"I had to. It kept me close to you."

Her teeth sank into her bottom lip, but she remained silent. Suddenly, she whirled away and headed for the porch. He fell into step beside her.

"Each time I looked at the bear I remembered something special about us. Like when I—or rather we were—studying for my boards," he amended. "Remember how you helped me cram for my exams?" His words came out in a rush as he fought to make her listen with her heart. "You never complained. When I look back, I think you studied harder then I did. No matter how tired you were, when I asked for help, you willingly gave it," his tone was filled with respect. "Or should I say, lovingly."

His comments met with more silence, but he didn't stop. He needed to hammer home his point and make her see that whatever their problems, they belonged together.

Stepping into her path, he stopped her and forced her to face him. "How about the time I got the measles?" She stood in front of him with her eyes glued to his chest.

"Ronnie. Please. Look at me. What I'm saying is important." His fingers tipped her face to meet his gaze. "No man should suffer those indignities in the presence of his woman. You were so good to me. I always marveled at how, after classes and work, you'd come home and take care of me. I've never forgotten that. That's when I realized what an important part of my life you were."

Cameron dodged to the right. He followed and continued to block her way. "I'd never allow another woman to see me in such a vulnerable state." She stood for a moment, then volleyed left, but again he followed. "When I was sick, you just bulldozed your way into my home and took charge." He ached to touch her, but knew this was not the time. It would cheapen his words and add to her insurmountable doubts. "I remember how you wiped my brow, gently forced fluids into my system and whispered encouragement." His whole being seemed to be filled with waiting, waiting for her to let him in, to open up a bit. "Every day when you left for school, I felt a void that cut deep. And I was always so impatient for your return." His voice lowered to a soft purr. "No one had ever cared for me the way you did. And I've never forgotten. You brought light to a place in my life where there had never been before."

It troubled him to hound her this way, but he pressed on. She was so stubborn, imprisoned in her ignorance.

"There are so many reasons why you're important to me." He cupped her face and caressed her cheek with his thumb as he gazed into her confused eyes. Her skin felt like warm velvet and he wanted to taste her again. But not yet.

Finally, she spoke, "I don't want to think about any of that." She stepped around him and continued up the walkway.

Miffed, he watched her climb the stairs and sit on the top step.

Following her up the walkway, disappointment weighed heavily on his shoulders. Cameron hadn't given an inch.

He slipped into the space next to hers and waited. For a short time, neither spoke.

"Marek?" The tip of her pink tongue slid across her lips.

"Hmmm?"

"I've got a question." Cameron remained motionless. But she couldn't hide the fear in her eyes.

"Sure." *What's going through that beautiful head of yours?* He wondered. "What's up? Jayla okay?"

"She's fine," she dismissed. "It's about us."

"Now I'm really intrigued." He smiled and took one of her busy hands between both of his. "Talk."

"About the nigh—"

"Hi, Marek," Mrs. Butler greeted, stepping from the house. The storm door banged behind her. "How you doin'?"

Damn. He looked from Cameron to Alice. Whatever Cameron wanted to ask must be important. He felt the tension in her hand. *What's the deal?* She was far too keyed up.

"Fine. And you?"

"We'll talk later," Cameron whispered and snatched her hand away. "Can you stay after Jayla goes to bed?"

"Sure."

Behind them Alice started across the porch and stumbled. She pitched forward, straight for the edge of the stairs.

"Granny!" Cameron jumped to her feet and tried to use her body to break her grandmother's fall.

The womens' combined weight hit Cameron hard and they pitched closer to the porch's edge. Alice's arms flailed wildly as she tried without success to grab the railing.

Marek rose and scooped Alice off her feet and deposited her in a wooden chair near the front door. She fell heavily into the chair, head rocking back and forth.

A frown marred Cameron's features as she examined her grandmother. "You don't look so good. Did you take your medicine?"

"Of course I did," Alice snapped, fanning herself with her hand. "I just felt a little dizzy, that's all. When I get back in the house, I'll take some aspirin."

Marek nudged Cameron aside and touched his fingers to the pulse at the side of Alice's neck. Her skin felt feverish and her pulse pounded. Things weren't quite right. But he couldn't call her on it.

"What are you doing?" Alice's voice rose a bit.

He took her hand and flexed her fingers. "Do you still feel dizzy?"

"No."

"Any double vision?" he asked. "Headache? Tingling in your hands or face? Ringing in your ears?"

"No. No. No. And no." Alice jerked her hand away. "It was just a senior moment."

"Senior moment?" He threw back his head and howled. "Alice, there's no way you're a senior. Last time I looked, you were as active as a spring chicken."

"Damn right."

Cameron dropped to her knees next to the chair and touched Alice's hand. "Granny, I don't like this." Her face was shadowed with uneasiness. "I don't like this at all. Your skin is clammy. Maybe I'll stay home with you and let Marek and Jayla go visit."

"No, you won't." Alice's lips drew into a stubborn line. "You three go on about your business. I'll be fine."

"We shouldn't leave you alone, Alice," Marek stated. The minute the words were out, he wanted to bite off his tongue.

Alice's lips thinned and her eyes flashed.

"It's no problem for us to order take-out and rent some videos," he amended, placing a hand on her shoulder and muttering suggestively, "I'd love to spend the night with you."

"Oh you." Mrs. Butler blushed and waved him away. "Go on about your business and leave me to mine." She crossed her arms over her chest and speared them with a cool stare. "Go enjoy your day."

"Only if you promise to rest while we're away," Cameron bartered. "And we'll be home early. I'll bring you dinner."

"I don't need you to get me dinner." Irritation was etched into her brown face. "I'll fix my own."

"No, you won't," Cameron snapped. "I'm going to bring you dinner. That's final. You just get on back inside the house." Cameron shooed her away. "Rest until we get back."

Alice snorted and rose unsteadily from her chair. "Hmmph," she lifted her shoulders. "Mind you curb that bossy streak."

It didn't feel right, Marek realized as he backed out of the driveway with Cameron and Jayla. He couldn't shake the sensation that Alice shouldn't be left alone. But what could he do? He wasn't her doctor and she'd insisted they leave.

Alice didn't look well. When he had checked her pulse, it was racing out of control. And her skin felt clammy. Although she denied having any pain, her wrinkled brow and soft groans suggested something more than a senior moment.

He stopped the SUV in front of Cameron's house and studied it for an additional beat. There was nothing he could do without Alice's consent. Damn. He hated this. Alice was part of his family and he wanted her safe.

His frustration mounted when he glanced at Cameron. Nothing worked out the way he planned. The bear represented happy memories. He had hoped to plant a kernel of trust. Instead, he'd gotten the silent treatment. If she wouldn't bend, how would they get their relationship back on track?

Marek shifted into first, let up on the clutch and caught sight of Cameron rolling the edge of her blouse. Oh yeah. Something was definitely eating at her. But what?

And as soon as they got back and he checked on Alice, he'd force the truth from Cameron regarding what had caused that look of panic in her eyes.

Chapter Fifteen

Like a snake, a creepy sensation sizzled along Cameron's spine when Marek pulled into the driveway. *Where are the lights?* she wondered, checking the clock on the dashboard. Nine o'clock. Granny never went to bed without leaving a lamp burning in the living room. Her insides quivered. Where was Granny?

Marek glanced down at her fingers plucking at the seat beat. His forehead wrinkled. "Everything okay?"

"Mmm. The house is dark," she replied, worried. "Granny always leaves a light on for us."

He patted her hand. "Maybe she went to bed early and didn't feel like coming back downstairs."

"But she always—"

"Don't worry," he cut in. "I'm sure everything's fine."

The instant the SUV stopped, she hopped out and headed for the front door. She needed to see for herself. Marek followed her up the walkway with a sleeping Jayla in his arms. In her haste to open the door, the keys slipped through her nervous fingers. He scooped them up, completed the task and fumbled for the light switch.

There was a moment of stunned silence.

"Call 911!" Marek handed Jayla to Cameron and dashed into the house.

Fright swept through her as she followed. Her heart slammed against her chest when she saw Granny's unconscious body stretched out on the hallway floor. He kneeled next to her, pressing two fingers against the pulse at her neck.

"Granny?" Cameron stood over them. The sleeping child stirred in her arms. She hurried to the living room to deposit Jayla on the sofa.

On her return, she dropped to her knees at Granny's side. Why had she gone out with Marek? Tears blinded Cameron when she lifted the old girl's hand to her cheek.

"Is she? Is she?" Cameron rejected the ugly word and tried again. "What's wrong with her?"

Marek's doctor's mask dropped into place. "I can't say."

Fear inched up a notch. "I shouldn't have left her," she muttered.

"Cameron," his voice barely registered against the misery gripping her. "CAMERON," Marek's commanding tone forced its way through her fog of guilt and dread. "Call 911, then get my bag from the car. Move!"

His tone worked. Cameron responded like a computer to a programming command. She leaped to her feet and rushed down the hall to the telephone. After placing the call, she hurried out the front door.

Not Granny. She prayed. *Please God, not her.* Within seconds, she burst through the door with Marek's medical bag under her arm.

"Get me a pillow and a blanket." He unzipped the bag and removed the stethoscope. "We have to keep her warm to fight off shock."

AS LONG AS THERE IS LOVE 141

Again, she responded to Marek's brisk command. She dashed to the linen closet at the end of the hall.

This can be fixed. She just needed to keep her wits and get Granny to the hospital. Just get her there. Returning, she tossed the pillow in his direction and spread the blanket over Granny.

"Her heartbeat is irregular." He lifted the disc-shaped instrument from Granny's chest. "Sweetheart? Where does Alice keep her medicine?"

"In her room."

"Good. Gather everything," he advised. "When we get to the hospital, the doctors will want to know what she takes."

"Okay," she called over her shoulder climbing the steps two at a time.

In Granny's bathroom, Cameron scooped her medicine into the first bag her fingers touched. Out of breath, she returned to the hallway and handed Marek the plastic bag. "Is she," Cameron tried to shut down her overactive thoughts, "is there any change?"

"I can't lie to you. This isn't good." His lips drew into a thin line. But the words that followed were gentle. "But I swear I'll do everything I can to make her better. Did the medics tell you how long they'd be?"

She forced the word past the lump in her throat, "No."

"We have to do something with Jayla." He muttered, reading the labels on Granny's medicine. "Is there somebody close who'll keep her while we're at the hospital?"

Cameron blinked as she tried to comprehend his shift in topics. *Somebody to keep Jayla.* "Nancy. She'll keep her."

"Nancy who?"

"One of the supervisors at Little Darlings."

"Call her," he ordered tensely. "Get her here before the medics arrive. I don't want Jayla in the middle of that chaos."

She didn't want to leave Granny's side. Indecision made Cameron hesitate. Her eyes shifted from Granny's unresponsive face to Marek's stern features.

"I'll watch her. I promise." Marek waved her away with a sweeping motion of his hand. "Now go."

On the third try, she got the telephone number correct. Cameron almost wept with relief when Nancy answered the phone. She arrived within minutes to collect Jayla before the emergency van pulled into the driveway.

The distinct sound of emergency sirens filled the air and seconds later the medics hustled into the house. Without delay, they lifted Granny onto a stretcher and were out the door.

Cameron rushed behind them. "Where are you taking her?"

"Holland Community."

"Do I need to call her doctor?"

"Yes, ma'am."

"What about her medicine?" She lifted the bag. "Do you need them?"

"Thank you." He grabbed the bag from her hands and climbed into the white van. Cameron attempted to follow him, but the medic stopped her.

"Why can't I go with her?" she shouted, near hysterics.

Marek slipped his arm around Cameron's shoulders and tried to steer her away. "Come on, sweetheart, you don't want to delay them."

Her nostrils flared. "No." She shoved Marek's arm away, shooting the evil eye straight at the van. "I want to go with Granny."

"You can't. How are you going to get home?" Marek linked their fingers, tipped his head toward his SUV. "Come on."

"No," she whispered in a lost voice. "I don't want her to be alone."

AS LONG AS THERE IS LOVE   143

"She's not alone. The medics are with her." A red strobe light swirled and the siren again disturbed the quiet night as they pulled away from the curb. "I'll take you to the hospital." Marek offered, gently guiding her toward his SUV.

"I—I—I can drive myself."

"Oh yeah. That's sounds really logical," he censored. "Look at yourself. You're upset. I'll drive. Now get in." He slammed the door behind her. "Stop wasting time. There's plenty of paperwork to be completed and you need to get your head clear, so that you can give Alice's medical history."

Oh, Lord. Cameron plucked at her seat belt as they raced through the quiet streets. This was all her fault. She should have followed her first thought and stayed at home and let Marek and Jayla visit together. Instead, she had let herself be convinced that everything was fine. She shook her head, unable to get the image of Granny's unconscious body out of her head.

Guilt surged through her like an electrical current. She should have realized something was wrong.

Granny, hang on. Just hang on.

For the first time since the van had driven away, Cameron took a hard look at Marek. She gave him big brownie points for his actions tonight. When all of this was over, she planned to thank him.

Her parents needed to be called. Madaddy would probably blow a gasket when he heard the news.

Marek turned into the circular drive and stopped at the hospital's emergency entrance. He leaned across her, opened the door and she climbed out. She didn't want to do this alone. The SUV pulled away from the curb and it took every ounce of her willpower not to call him back.

She needed Marek beside her. Holland Community Hospital's red brick building loomed before her as she hurried toward the emergency room door.

"They're gone! Where?" Cameron snapped into the pay phone. "When did they leave?"

Marek tapped her on the shoulder.

She turned.

"Shhh." He placed a finger to his lips.

Cameron wriggled her fingers in his direction and presented her back to him. Her voice dropped, but it still vibrated with the same degree of irritation.

"David," she spoke into the telephone. "Granny's in the hospital. I need you to get in touch with the cruise line and get a message to Madaddy. I'm sorry it's their anniversary trip, but don't you think he'd want to know that his mother's in the hospital?"

She rubbed the palm of her hand across her forehead and tried again. "Fine. If you reach them, I'm at Holland Community. Have them page me. I'll be here. Okay? Thanks." Cameron leaned her forehead against the telephone receiver and reached deep within for the strength to get through this.

Three older brothers, yet sometimes she felt more like the oldest child, taking charge of the family crisis. She loved her brothers. But they were far too willing to let others take over in a crunch.

Cameron headed back to the waiting area with Marek at her side. Despair hit her when she entered the room filled with uncomfortable red plastic chairs, loud television monitors suspended from the ceiling and the worried faces of significant others.

She sank into a chair in an empty section and shut her eyes. Again, Marek followed. He took her hand, cradled it between both of his and stroked it from the wrist to her fingertips. The sensation spread through her veins like wine.

"Did you hear anything while I was on the phone?" she asked, opening her eyes.

"No. Sorry."

Irritated, she tried again. "How much longer do you think we're going to have to wait?"

"Don't know."

"So, what good are you?"

Marek smiled regretfully. "Right now, not much."

"I'm sorry." Cameron squeezed his hand. "I don't mean to act like this. You've been great. I'm just worried."

"Sweetheart, it'll be okay. Why don't you come back to my office with me?" he coaxed. "It's more comfortable."

She shook her head and said, "No, thanks. I want to wait here. If you need to go, don't worry. I'm okay."

"No. I'm here with you and I'll leave when you do." He stroked her cheek. "Just have faith. Alice will be fine."

"Marek, I left her," she cried, in a voice filled with self-loathing. "I should have stayed home."

He pulled her into his arms, held her close. "Sweetheart, Alice didn't want you to stay. She almost pushed us out the door."

"But she was sick."

"I know. It was her decision. Not yours. Stop beating yourself up." He brushed the renegade locks of hair from her face and kissed her forehead. "You did what your grandmother wanted you to do. Now come on." Marek shifted closer, nestling her against his chest. His male scent rose from his shirt and she sniffed appreciatively. "Lean against me and relax," he ordered in a gentle voice. "I promise I'll wake you the moment the doctor comes out."

"Marek," she muttered, drifting to sleep. "I don't know how to thank you."

Cameron had barely shut her eyes when her comfortable

pillow gently nudged her awake. Slowly waking, she blinked at the bright lights in the waiting area and focused on Marek's face.

"Wake up, Ronnie," he helped her into a sitting position. "The doctor wants to talk with you."

Instantly alert, she started to stand, but stumbled over her feet.

"Hold on," Marek's arm slipped around her waist and steadied her. "Give yourself a minute to wake up."

The triage's double doors swung opened. A tall, thin African American woman dressed in red scrubs approached them.

"Ms. Butler?"

Prepared for the worst, Cameron tensed. "Yes," she answered, edging closer to Marek.

"Easy," he whispered in her ear.

"I'm Dr. Washington." The woman pushed her glasses up the bridge of her nose.

"Dr. Washington." Marek offered his hand. "I'm Dr. Redding, Chief of Pediatrics." The two shook hands.

"Ms. Butler, I'm sorry to say that your grandmother has had a stroke."

"Stroke?" *Oh, Granny. Stroke.* Cameron staggered under the force of everything that word represented.

"Is she paralyzed?" she asked, rolling a section of her blouse. "Ho—how severe is it?"

The doctor hesitated.

Cameron's fears grew.

Dr. Washington continued, "Ms. Butler, we've found that your grandmother has some weakness on her right side. But we really won't be able to assess the damage properly until all the test results are in."

"What does that mean?" Cameron drew away from Marek, looking at the doctor for clarification. "Will she be able to walk? Go back to work? Get on with her life?"

"She doesn't have complete control over her limbs." The doctor removed her glasses and rubbed the bridge of her nose. "Brain functions are slower than normal. But she's conscious."

"You didn't answer my question. Will she be able to walk?"

"Ms. Butler, it's too early to tell." The doctor reached out and squeezed Cameron's hand. "Don't borrow trouble. Many times with rehabilitation, stroke patients regain partial and/or full mobility."

"What are her chances?"

"Again, once all the tests are in, we'll develop a treatment plan for her. For now, your grandmother needs your support and love." Dr. Washington polished her lenses with the shirttail of her scrubs before returning them to her face. "Let's concentrate on that. Mrs. Butler needs to know that you're here for her."

"Can I see her?"

"Certainly." Dr. Washington led them out of the waiting room and down a corridor. She stopped outside a hospital room. "Just remember, she's weak and her speech is slurred. But she understands."

"Thank you." Cameron squared her shoulders.

"Don't stay too long." Dr. Washington patted Cameron's shoulder reassuringly. "It's been a long day for her. Rest is important."

Cameron opened the door, but shook her head when Marek tried to follow. "I won't be long." This she needed to do alone.

The room was so still, silent. Green shadows from the monitors cast silhouettes on the walls.

Braced for whatever might come next, she moved across the room. Granny looked so tiny in the narrow bed. With cautious movements she lifted the old girl's hand and rested it against her cheek.

"Granny?"

"Hey, Sweet Peaches." The words came out slow and slurred. "I'm sorry I caused so much trouble," she mumbled as her eyes drooped.

"If you wanted some attention, all you had to do was tell me," Cameron teased. "I've always got time for you."

Granny's eyes closed. But a smile remained on her lips.

"I can only stay a minute. I wanted to see you before I go home." Cameron tucked the blanket securely around Granny. "We have big plans for our future, and I can't have you out of commission."

Granny opened her eyes and tears spilled down her cheeks, confessing, "I think I messed up this time."

"You just stop thinking like that." Cameron blinked repeatedly, fighting back her own tears. "Whatever happens, we're together on this.

Brushing away her tears, Cameron placed Granny's hand under the blanket. She leaned over the older woman and hugged her close, then kissed her cheek. "Granny, it's you and me. Doesn't matter how long things take. We'll deal with this as a family. Just like we've always done. I love you. You know that, don't you? I'll always be here for you."

"I know, Sweet Peaches, and I love you."

"I'm going now. Okay? Get some rest. I'll be back tomorrow."

Granny's eyes fluttered as she fought the urge to sleep. Within seconds she lost that battle and dozed. Cameron kissed the old girl's cheek and tiptoed from the room.

Leaning against the hospital room door, she felt the last of her energy ebb away. Thank God. Granny was alive. A stroke was no small thing, but she was alive.

Rehabilitation. The word sent the fear of God racing through her. There were some difficult days ahead of them.

Marek led a numb Cameron from the hospital. Barely able to put one foot in front of the other, she stumbled her way to his SUV. Once he'd buckled her into her seat belt, she leaned against the headrest and shut her eyes, willing her body to relax.

He drove through the quiet streets without comment, sensing her need for silence. Now that the initial crisis had ended, fatigue nipped at her diminished strength. All she wanted to do was crawl into her bed and let sleep overtake her.

Chapter Sixteen

Marek pulled into Cameron's driveway and turned off the engine. Before she realized it, she'd opened her mouth and let out a colossal yawn.

"Ohhh, my!" *Where are my manners?* She straightened in her seat and mumbled, "Excuse me." Fatigue made her voice wobble. "Needless to say, I'm jumping into bed the minute I get in the house."

An understanding smile came and went on Marek's lips. He reached across the seat, squeezed her hand. "After a night like this, you deserve it." Sensations shot through her like a spark to newspaper, stirring her blood.

"That's for sure." She smiled tiredly. "I got my miracle. Granny's going to be okay."

"She sure is," Marek agreed and then frowned. "What about Little Darlings? Who's opening tomorrow? You?"

"Nooo! Not after tonight." Little Darlings was the last thing on her mind. "Nancy," she explained on the edge of another yawn, "the woman who took Jayla. She's opening tomorrow."

"Good." He wiped an imaginary row of sweat from his brow. "I really didn't relish the idea of opening the door to a group of screaming three-year-olds."

She laughed out loud at the image of him surrounded by a herd of monster babies. "I wouldn't do that to you. Besides, you'll be turning over for the second time when I'm dealing with them."

Cameron unclipped her seat belt, ready to leave the SUV, but something held her in place, something she needed to say to him. With one hand curled around the door handle, she focused on him.

"Marek?"

He snapped off the radio and faced her. "Hmmm?"

"I want to thank you."

A spasm of irritation crossed his face. "Stop." He placed a finger over her lips. "You don't have to do this."

Removing his finger, she continued, "No. Let me. Please. I need to tell you."

For a brief moment she hesitated, shuddered at the sensations that bombarded her. Heat flushed her neck, filled her cheek and her voice quivered. "Tonight, I really needed your help and you were there for me. Thank you." Those were the only words she got out. It was time for her to move on before she embarrassed herself further.

Cameron headed to the front door and unlocked it. Marek followed. She switched on the hall light and spun around to face him. He caught her around the waist as she swayed on her tiptoes. Rebalancing herself with a hand on his shoulder, her lips grazed his cheek.

Oh, be careful. This could be dangerous. Emotions were far too high.

"Thanks again." She said as his delicious scent filled her nostrils. "I'll see you."

A crooked smile touched his lips. "You're welcome." He stepped into the hallway and with a flick of his wrist, the door shut and the lock slid home. "We need to talk."

Oh, Lord. Her eyes widened as she searched his face. Had he picked up on her feelings? She shut her eyes, seeking some level of calm. Opening them, she tried to concentrate.

"Marek." Her arms sagged at her sides. "I'm really tired. Can't this wait?"

Determination blazed from his eyes. "No." He shoved his hands into the pockets of his jeans and fingered the coins. The gesture drew her attention to the front of his trousers. *Oh, my.* She looked away, disturbed by what she saw, the emotions he stirred. Instead, Cameron concentrated on the threads of his conversation.

"Until things settle down with Alice, you'll need help." He removed his hands from his pockets. "I'm volunteering my services."

Oh, he wants to help. That's sweet. She smiled as her heart returned to its normal rate. This was manageable.

"Oh, Marek, you have helped," her voice was filled with gratitude. "It's sweet of you to want to do more, but I can't accept anything else. You've got patients. I've imposed enough."

He ushered her into the living room and guided her to the sofa. "It's not an imposition," he dismissed. "Hear me out before you decide. Alice's illness will require a great deal of your time."

Alarm bells rang in her head, sending her blood pressure soaring. She shot to her feet and began to pace.

Marek stepped into her path and placed his hands on her shoulders. "Calm down. I'm not saying things will get worse. But she does play a major role in your daily life. Who's going to hold up her end? You?" He pointed a finger at her. "That means more time away from Jayła."

For a minute, she thought he was criticizing her. Her

head shot up and she searched Marek's face for signs of disapproval. All she saw was concern. Tension eased from her body.

"So what do you suggest?"

"You need me." He answered quietly, as he massaged the tightness from her shoulders. "I'm pretty flexible. I can rearrange my schedule to suit my needs. Why don't I move in and help with Jayla? Get her up in the morning, dropped at Little Darlings before I go to the hospital. That'll free up your time, so you can open."

Moving in! She chewed on her bottom lip, allowing the idea to dance around in her head.

Her life was peppered with mistakes. She didn't want to make any more. Plus, there was Jayla to consider. What would she give up if she opened her home to him? "I ... don't ... know."

"What don't you know?"

Cameron arms flapped aimlessly. "This is so extreme."

"Is that right?" He dropped his arms to his sides as he took a step closer. "I'm Jayla's father. If anyone should be available for her, it's me."

"But to move in here?" Her nose wrinkled and she waved a hand around the room. "Why can't you just help when I need you?"

"What happens if you need to go to the hospital in the middle of the night?" he questioned matter-of-factly. "Who are you going to call? Nancy? My guess is she'll be closing each night. She's out. That leaves me."

Score one for him. But the battle wasn't over. What was his angle? She wondered, eyeing him suspiciously.

He seemed sincere, but she felt uncertain.

Marek's nostrils flared. Her expression must have betrayed her thoughts. His face flushed dull red as he grabbed her arms, brought her close.

"Damn, woman!" he hissed, eyes blazed. "You're not

superwoman. It's okay to need help. Bend. Let me help you. You're exhausted and we have a small child to care for."

"I'm sorry." She shoved against his chest. It felt like a wall of warm bricks. "I'm sorry. It's just . . . just I'm not one to ask for help. I do it all. Accepting help is hard for me."

"Jayla's mine. And I want to help."

"I understand. But people always disappoint me," she admitted, glancing away, thinking of her parents. "And I'm the one who ends up hurt. So I've learned not to expect or accept anything."

Marek remained silent, but his eyes clung to hers, analyzing her words.

"You're right. It's not fair to wake her at the crack of dawn," she admitted. "Thank you. I'll take you up on your offer."

"Good." He headed out the room and down the hallway toward the kitchen, instructing, "You should get ready for bed. Tomorrow's gonna be a busy day."

She followed him. "Excuse me."

Marek faced her. "Yes?" Eyebrows arched over curious eyes.

"What are you doing?"

"I'm going to the kitchen," he answered as if talking to the town idiot.

"I can see that. Why?"

"I'm going to make you some hot tea to help you relax."

"That's not necessary," Cameron stated. "I'm tired. Please go home so I can get to bed." She pointed toward the door. "Gooood night."

"No problem," he continued into the kitchen, than flipped on the light. "Good night. I'll lock up."

Was she speaking Greek? She marched into the kitchen and waved a hand in the air. "Hello. That was me being polite. Now I'm not. Go home. Come back tomorrow."

"I'm not leaving."

"What?"

"You heard me." He filled the teakettle. "If the hospital calls, you'll need me."

"Marek, Jayla's with Nancy." Weary, she ran a hand through her hair. "I can manage."

"I have no doubt that you can." A clinical eye slid over her. "But you just told me that you were exhausted."

"I am. And I'll be fine." Her eyes slid over him. "Besides, you don't have a change of clothes. Can't we start this a little later in the week?"

"Clothes are no problem. I'll just throw them in your washer." He shrugged. "No biggie."

A mental image of him sorting through the laundry made her smile. "Marek, please. I'm so tired." Fatigued, her shoulders slumped. "Can't we discuss this tomorrow?"

"Sure." He waved her away. "Sweet dreams."

"No." Cameron shook her head. "You don't seem to understand what I'm saying. Go home."

"Look," he retraced his steps to where she stood in the doorway. "I'm here for the duration. Period. End of discussion."

"I . . . I . . ." she began. Marek laid a finger against her lips. She fought the urge to draw it into her mouth, taste it.

Shaken by her thoughts, she turned aside.

What's the point? Let him stay. If Granny needed her during the night, she'd probably wreck the car trying to get to the hospital.

"You're right," she called over her shoulder, moving toward the stairs. "I'll see you in the morning."

Chapter Seventeen

Alarm swept through Cameron like a lit match through autumn leaves. She had to find her baby.

"Jayla?" Cameron burst through her daughter's bedroom door. Her heart lurched in her chest when she saw the empty bed. Where was her baby?

Cameron examined the dark, empty room for clues. Her bare toes curled into the carpet, fighting off the cold that settled in her veins as she debated her next move. Maybe Jayla had climbed into bed with Granny. Retreating from the room, she slammed the door with a sound of finality and shot down the corridor to Granny's room, the hem of her white silky nightgown flirting around her ankles. Flinging the door open with one hand, she stopped and examined the room for signs of life.

Chilled, she wrapped her arms around her. The room felt cold, sterile without a trace of life in it. She sniffed the air then shuddered in revulsion. A musky, unused stench assaulted her nostrils. The room smelled of abandonment. A flurry of tears pricked her eyes.

With a strangled cry, Cameron bolted straight up into a sitting position in her bed. Sweat drenched the neck of her nightshirt. She struggled for air, greedily snatching quick, shallow breaths, willing her pounding heart to slow down and return to normal.

The door burst open. The tall, broad-shouldered silhouette of a man filled the doorway. She gasped and scrambled toward the center of the mattress.

"Ronnie, Ronnie. It's me." Marek rushed across the room and sat on the edge of her bed. "It's okay." The mattress sank under his weight. "It's okay," he chanted. "It's me, Marek."

Panting, Cameron whispered, "Marek?" Relief knifed through her as she reached for him.

He gathered her shaking form in his arms. She wrapped her arms around his neck and clung to him. Warmth seeped into her cold limbs as she buried her face in the hollow of his neck.

Marek was here. Each time she felt alone and lost, he made her feel safe.

"What happened, sweetheart?" His soothing voice probed as he stroked her back. Fear receded inch by inch under his gentle ministry.

She drew in a ragged breath. "I—I, I'm sorry." Embarrassed, she buried her face further into his neck and rubbed her cheek against his smooth flesh. "I didn't mean to wake you."

"Don't worry about it," he dismissed. "I heard you at the other end of the hall. Bad dream?"

"No," she corrected in a weak whisper. "Nightmare."

"Okay, nightmare." He cupped her face between his hands and kissed her forehead. "Want to tell me about it?"

"Oh, Marek." She drew away, looking into his eyes. "I

went to Jayla's room and she was gone." Cameron shivered, reliving those moments. Marek drew her closer. "She wasn't in the house. I searched everywhere. Even Granny's room, but it was empty." Tears sprang to her eyes and quivered on the edge of her lashes, then spilled down her cheeks. "The bed didn't have any sheets on it. Granny's sweet fragrance was missing. It didn't look like Granny or Jayla lived here anymore. It was awful."

Marek brushed her tears away with the pads of his thumbs. "Shh, sweetheart. It was only a dream. A nightmare," he amended. "That's all. Jayla's safe with Nancy, and Alice is holding her own. I spoke with the nurses' station before I came upstairs." His voice lowered to a dusty rumble as he cradled her in his arms. "It's natural for you to be upset. You're the strength behind the family." Kissing her softly on the lips, he suggested. "Relax. I'm here. If it'll make you feel better, I'll call the hospital again."

Heat surged into her cheeks. She didn't want to cause a greater stir. "No." Lowering her lashes to conceal her embarrassment, Cameron fidgeted with the tail of the sheet. "Thanks for checking on Granny."

Fear subsided, replaced by more disturbing emotions. Her hand rested on his smooth skin. Oh, Lord. She'd been stroking his bare chest for the past ten minutes.

The desire to run her fingers through the thick mat of dark hair on his chest zipped through her like an electrical current. Everyplace their flesh touched tingled with sensual promise. She found it hard to stay focused on their conversation.

Pulling away, her eyes slipped lower, pausing to admire the lean, hard muscles of his stomach before moving even lower. Immediately, she looked away. *Oh, my.* Although he had on a pair of jeans, he hadn't bothered to zip them in his haste to reach her. She could see a pair of blue, silk jockey shorts through the zipper opening.

AS LONG AS THERE IS LOVE

"It's been a hellava day." Eyes blazing, Marek ran his hands up and down her arms. "You need your rest." He released her, stepped away from the bed. "Try and get some sleep, okay?"

His husky, bedroom voice spread through her like cognac. It forged a warm path through her veins and touched her core. She needed him.

Marek's face was a mask of conflicting emotions. Need and desire sparkled openly from his eyes. He backed away from the bed and bumped into the wall.

"Don't leave," she cried. Fear returned with the impact of a car crash.

Obviously torn, Marek hesitated.

"I need you." She beckoned him with an outstretched hand. "Please stay."

"Sweetheart." His eyes darted toward the door as if he contemplated his escape route. "Th—there's nothing to be afraid of. I'm right down the hall. If you need me, give a holler."

A hot ache grew inside her. "But I don't want you to go." She allowed the fear and longing in her voice to reach out to him.

Rotating his head as if it hurt, he rubbed the back of his neck. "This isn't a good idea."

"Why not?"

"You're upset," Marek reminded. "I don't want you to say I took advantage of you."

"That's not where my head is."

"Ronnie, you've gotta understand." He held her gaze with his own. "If I stay, we're going to make love."

"That's what I want." She opened her arms, welcoming him.

Marek stood motionless then took the first tentative step toward the bed. It dipped under his weight while his fingers tenderly stroked Cameron's cheek.

Leaning into his touch, her eyes drifted shut. This was what she wanted, needed. Marek's hand slipped under the hem of her nightshirt and glided up her back. Each stroke of his hand fueled her need for him. She quivered, encouraging him with feather light kisses along his jaw, cheeks and lips.

"Ronnie," he pulled away. His velvety tone made her tremble with hunger. "Are you sure?"

"Yes," she whispered, ignoring all the reasons why she should put a halt to this. "Oh, yes!"

Her lips parted, her eyes shut as she waited for the feel of Marek's firm lips against hers. He held her close and trailed a series of light, feathery kisses over her cheeks, neck and shoulder. She quivered at the sweet tenderness of his lips.

"Marek," she moaned. His tongue moved between her lips, danced with hers, bewitching her. Cameron's busy hands greedily roamed over his broad shoulders and skated over the soft mass of hair on his chest.

She wanted to die and go to heaven with his wonderful taste on her lips. But she had more important things brewing, like kissing Marek back with all the passion in her heart. He tasted wickedly addictive.

Suddenly, the tempo of his kiss changed. He slid the nightshirt along her body, over her head and tossed the garment to the floor without a second glance. She rubbed her bare breasts against his chest, awed by the warmth of Marek's skin, which felt like smooth fire. She wanted to burn in his flame.

Marek's tongue traced a path of fire along her neck pressing her back against the cotton sheets. The fabric felt cool against her skin. His hands sought her breasts and kneaded her flesh.

Her blood pounded. Hunger flamed within her. Marek flicked his tongue across the tight nipples.

Examining his handiwork, he muttered, "Exquisite."

The desire to give and take pleasure was keen. Reciprocating, she ran her tongue across his nipple, circled the dark orb, and marveled at his immediate response to her touch. It gave her a hearty sense of power. Under her sensual assault, he was as vulnerable as she was.

Marek stood, pushed his jeans and shorts to his ankles in one fluid motion and kicked them off. He returned to the bed.

"Wait!" Cameron cried. "I can't. Not without some protection. I want to. But, I can't."

Nodding, he rolled to the edge of the bed and retrieved his jeans, fishing in the back pocket for his wallet. He removed a foil package and tore it open with his teeth, quickly rolling the condom into place.

"Just like a Boy Scout," she muttered.

"Better protected, then not. Where were we?" he asked in a husky voice, pulling her back into his arms and kissing her until she couldn't remember her name. He leaned close and nudged her legs apart with his knee, then arranged her thighs around his hips.

With an arm around her hips he lifted her, guiding himself into her warm, moist heat. He sank into her velvety sheath inch by delicious inch. They sighed in unison.

"Marek," she moaned against the pulse at his throat.

He withdrew, than sank into her wet passage. His hips thrust steadily and she met each downward thrust with an upward movement of her own. Her world narrowed until he was the only clear focal point. He was all she could feel, see.

"Marek."

"Come with me, baby," he urged in a voice rough with passion, thrusting deeply into her. "Let it happen."

They moved together. Her body strained against his. One

final thrust sent Cameron over the edge. Her climax rocked her. Dazed, she fought to catch her breath.

His body began to shudder within her and his harsh cry was muffled against her neck. Spent, he slumped over her.

"Thank you." He rolled onto his back, taking her with him. Gently, Marek kissed her throat, ears and finally her lips. "Thank you."

Resting on her elbows, Cameron gazed down into her lover's eyes. "You're welcome." She smiled back at him, muttering, "Again," in a provocative tone, tracing a finger along his broad chest, past his narrow waist and slim hips. His flesh leapt to life when she touched him.

"Again," she whispered.

Cameron stretched in the deliciously contented afterglow of lovemaking, enjoying the view of the sun peeking through her bedroom curtains. Stifling a yawn, she gently turned to face the still-sleeping Marek. For several minutes, she admired how peacefully he slept.

Last night had been incredible. Although she really shouldn't have let it happen, she wasn't sorry.

Her contented smile faded. Guilt and distrust came back to her with the force of a gun blast. How could she have made love with a man she didn't trust? Because she loved him and had never stopped, came the truthful answer.

Turning away from his body, she threw her legs over the side of the bed and sat on the edge of the mattress. Marek would demand answers. Unfortunately, she didn't have any.

Easing from the bed, she grabbed her jeans from the rocking chair and shoved her legs into them before snatching up her T-shirt. She needed some time alone to pull herself together and decide how to deal with all that had happened.

At the door, she halted. Her gaze lingered over Marek.

How ironic. This was her room, yet she was the one running away. She needed to think, sort things out in her mind. And she couldn't do that with him so close. So enticing.

Chapter Eighteen

"Coward." Cameron slammed Little Darlings's door with more force than necessary. She had behaved like a damn coward. After making love with Marek, she'd slipped out of her bedroom before dawn like a vampire escaping the sunlight.

Throughout the day, she relived their night of passion. Heck, each time she thought of him, she became more confused.

Coward. She switched off the lights and locked the doors throughout the day care center. All of that would be remedied tonight. She planned to put the ground rules on the table. Period. End of discussion. If Marek didn't like it, out the door he'd go.

Frying meat permeated the air as she secured the door that separated the day care from the rest of the house. Cameron sniffed the air and grinned. Beef. Jayla loved cheeseburgers.

Like a beacon, father and daughter's playful chatter led Cameron to the kitchen. She stopped inside the entrance and found the pair dancing to Phil Collins's lyrics. Marek scooped Jayla into his arms and performed elaborate dance steps. Jayla giggled in return.

"Hey, Honeybunny!" Cameron spread her arms wide.

"Mummie!" Jayla wiggled from her daddy's embrace, ran across the floor and launched herself at her mother. Cameron hugged Jayla close and kissed her soft cheek. She swung Jayla high in the air and playfully gnawed on her daughter's neck. Marek's fresh scent clung to her baby's clothes and filled Cameron's nostrils.

Marek's eyes glided over her, causing a spark of excitement to zip through her. Her body quivered, responding to the sensual suggestion in his eyes.

"Hey," she drawled.

"Hey yourself." His face broke into an easy grin that confused her even more.

"Mummie," Jayla patted Cameron's shoulder, "Daddy needs a kiss, too."

"Yeah, Daddy needs a kiss very badly."

Marek wasn't above using every situation to his advantage. If she said no, Jayla would have lots of questions that Cameron wasn't prepared to answer. So, she had no choice. For the moment, she'd play along. *Smirk all you want,* she thought, *things are about to change.*

Creeping across the room with Jayla on her hip, she leaned close to Marek, intent on a quick peck on his cheek. A split second before her lips touched his skin, he turned his head and her lips grazed his.

You dirty dog! Cameron screamed silently, drawing away and settling Jayla on her feet.

"Thanks." He winked. "I really needed that."

Unnerved, she turned away and Jayla slid to the floor. "Ohhh." She noticed the breakfast nook table was set for dinner.

"Dinner is served," Marek announced in his best English butler voice, then bowed from the waist.

Little hands patted her leg. "I set the table, Mummie," Jayla declared. "Daddy let me help."

"Good. I'm proud of you, Honeybunny."

"Jayla folded the napkins and put the silverware on the table," he explained as he placed two fluted wineglasses on the table. "Ronnie, have a seat." He pulled out a chair, than deposited their daughter in her high chair. A plate filled with potato chips and a ketchup-coated cheeseburger was placed in front of Jayla. "She begged for cheeseburgers."

Without preamble, Jayla attacked her cheeseburger. She lifted her ketchup-streaked face and grinned. "Mummie, it's good."

A flash of humor crossed Marek's face and she laughed as Jayla devoured her cheeseburger.

"She needs a bib."

"I hear you. Hold on, Pumpkin." Marek grabbed a floral kitchen towel and tied it around Jayla's neck. "Go for it." He ruffled her curls. "I thought your palate might appreciate something a bit less G-rated. We're having Caesar salad with grilled chicken, Ronnie."

Mmmm! Her mouth watered like Pavlov's dog. Caesar salad. She liked this home cooked meal thing.

He positioned a glass bowl of tossed salad sprinkled with grilled chicken in the center of the table and tossed a pair of salad tongs into the bowl. From the refrigerator, he placed an open bottle of Piesporter wine next to the salad.

"I'm impressed."

"I'm here to help. But don't be too impressed." Shamefaced, Marek turned away, concentrating on pouring the wine. "There's a unique little gourmet shop near the hospital."

"Ahhh," she shook out her napkin and dropped it across her lap, "I see. I'll give you ten points for your presentation."

"Well, thank you, Madame. You have to make life easy

when and where you can," he explained, filling her plate with salad. "Tell me about your day."

"Things went pretty well although we're without . . ." For a beat, Cameron studied a cheeseburger-absorbed Jayla. "G-R-A-N-N-Y," she whispered.

"You don't have to worry about that." Marek slipped into the chair across from her and placed his napkin in his lap. "I've already talked to her about Alice. She's okay with it."

Her heart pounded as she stared across the table. Less then twenty-four hours in her house and he had managed to override her authority with her child.

Anger flared. It wrapped its way around Cameron like a boa constrictor. Who did he think he was? She laid her fork down next to her plate. Jayla was her child and he had no right to take charge without consulting her.

"Jayla asked me," Marek said matter-of-factly, hunching his shoulders. "Actually, she demanded to know where her Granny was. Her fears needed to be alleviated. If I left things unsaid, I would have upset her more. This way, it's done and she's fine with things.

"You may have controlled everything up to this point. But I'm part of this family now. We're partners. Look at it from Jayla's point of view." Marek shoved his chair back and rounded the table to tower over Cameron. "When she left home yesterday, everything was fine." Hunching down in front of Cameron's chair, Marek placed a finger under her chin and forced her to meet his gaze. "This morning, part of her family was gone. She a bright kid, Ronnie. Did you think she wouldn't notice?"

The sincerity in his eyes melted the tight ball of anger in her chest and the fight went right out of her, leaving her limp. As usual, his explanation made sense.

Humbled, Cameron picked up her fork and returned to her salad. "You're right. I'm sorry."

With that said, Marek returned to his chair and they concentrated on their meals. Throughout dinner, she debated ways to broach the subject of their night together. But none seemed appropriate. Dinner concluded and their plates were secure in the dishwasher, but still no opening gambit struck her. They sipped their wine and watched Jayla inhale a bowl of ice cream.

Cameron placed her napkin on the table and plunged ahead. "Marek?" she whispered, aware of Jayla's presence.

An amused gleam danced in his eyes. "Go ahead."

"What?"

"Say your piece," Marek prompted. "It's been on your face all night. Go for it."

He wanted it. Well, here it was. "Fine," she blurted. "While you're in this house, what happened last night can't happen again."

"Is that right?" Marek leaned back in his chair and folded his arms across his chest. "Why?"

"Because it was a mistake." Her voice rose a tad. She stopped and brought it under control before continuing in a raspy whisper. "I was upset, confused. Things got out of hand."

"That may be true," he conceded, "the first time." His voice lowered to a husky rumble. "What's your excuse for the fourth? By the third time, you seemed to have your wits about you."

The blood began to pound in her temples. "That was low." She wrapped her arms tightly around her middle, shifting away from the table.

"Not really," he leaned back in his chair. "Just on the mark."

"All I'm saying is you're here to help. Period," she answered. "Please remember that."

"I haven't forgotten anything. Least of all how you felt in my arms," he purred. Her heart leapt in response to the

AS LONG AS THERE IS LOVE 169

sensuous note in his voice. "You're not going to turn our evening into something dirty. You feel guilty? Too bad." He flicked a finger in her direction. "That's your problem. Not mine. As far as I'm concerned, it *was* the most beautiful experience I've had in years." Fire smoldered in his gold-flecked years. "And I'm looking forward to repeating it."

"No!" She went hot, then grasped at anything to relieve the suffocating tension. "It was ..." her eyes shifted to Jayla and her voice lowered further. "... S-E-X. That's all."

"S-E-X." The peanut gallery piped up. "Sex," Jayla recited with an innocent tilt of her head. "Right, Mummie?"

Startled, Cameron's eyes almost popped out of her head when she heard that word. "How do you know that?"

"Eric," Jayla answered. "He knows how to spell lots of words," she wiggled in her chair. Puzzled, her brows drew together and she gazed at her mother with a curious expression. "What does sex mean?"

Oh, Lord. *I'm not ready for this.* Cameron let out a weak moan. There should have been years before this topic came up.

"Well, ahh ..." Cameron rubbed her damp palms along the legs of her jeans. *Where do I go with a question like that?*

"You know, sex can be divided into two types," Marek's confident voice stepped in. He moved between Cameron and Jayla and lifted the child from the high chair. "Boys," he tapped his chest, "and girls." He tickled Jayla behind her ear. She giggled and squirmed around in her father's arms.

"Your mom and you are girls, and Eric and me are boys."

"Mummie's a big girl."

"Exactly right. One day, you'll be a big girl, too. And from now on, if you have any questions about sex, come see your mother or me. Okay?"

"Okay."

"That's my Pumpkin!" He kissed her cheek. "Ronnie, you better get going if you plan to see Alice tonight. Visiting hours end at eight."

"Can you give this card to Granny?" Jayla presented a yellow sheet of construction paper. Orange, green and red flowers along with stars embellished the handmade card.

"Sure," Cameron took the card, impressed by her daughter's thoughtfulness. "It's beautiful, Honeybunny." She hugged Jayla close. "Granny will love it."

"Tell Granny I want her to come home."

"I sure will. Maybe tomorrow we can call her and you can talk for a bit. Okay?"

"Yesss."

Marek took Jayla's hand. "It's time for your bath and bed, young lady."

"Ahhh," she pouted, "I'm not sleepy."

"That's okay. You will be by the time we're done."

Jayla slipped her fingers into her father's hand. Cameron watched the pair, feeling a twinge of jealousy. Bath time usually represented a special time for her and Jayla.

Cameron opened the front door and stepped onto the porch. Marek and Jayla followed her to the car and waited while she unlocked the car door and climbed inside.

"Be careful." He hoisted their daughter on his hip.

Jayla leaned through the window and kissed her mother. "Be careful, Mummie."

"I will, Honeybunny."

"Give Alice my love." Marek leaned through the car window and touched his lips to hers, then stepped away.

Chapter Nineteen

Relief swept through Cameron when she stepped into Granny's hospital room.

"Hey you," she called cheerfully. The sight of her grandmother propped up in bed made Cameron feel as if she'd just won the lottery.

Granted, several large white pillows supported the old girl and an IV tube snaked up her arm and into the sleeve of her blue and white hospital gown. Someone had taken the time to arrange Granny's hair into an orderly style. Today, she looked far from marvelous, but more like herself. Oh yes, she definitely looked better.

The old girl's face brightened at the sight of Cameron. "H—i—i Swe—ee—t Peaches."

Cameron hugged her close and planted a kiss on her cheek. The faintest hint of rubbing alcohol lingered on Granny's skin.

"You look better than when I last saw you." Cameron dropped her purse on the chair next to the bed and covered

Granny's hand with her own. Her warm hand lay limp within Cameron's. "How are you today?"

"So-so."

"Just so-so?"

"Bet—ter."

"I like the sound of that." Cameron grinned, opening her purse and produced the card. "Jayla made you a get-well card." Pride puffed out her chest as she displayed her daughter's artistic contribution.

"Well! Ni—ce." Granny jerked her head in the direction of the nightstand filled with cards and flowers. "There."

Cameron shifted Granny's get-well wishes around on the nightstand and added Jayla's card. Her eyes widened when she recognized Marek's bold signature on a card stuffed in a large basket of violets. The floral arrangement added a cheery note to the room.

"Jayla told me to tell you to get well because she misses you. I promised her we'd call you tomorrow so that she could talk to you."

"Good." One edge of Granny's lips tipped up in a half-smile.

"I tried to reach Madaddy." Cameron sat on the bed. "They're on a cruise. I thought I'd try David again to see if he's heard from them."

"No," Granny dismissed. "Let 'em e'joy."

Puzzled, Cameron questioned further, "Don't you want Madaddy with you?"

"W—ait."

"Are you sure? I can still try to reach them."

"Co—me soon." Granny's jaw clenched. Frustration made her bite her lip. "Don't," she paused and tried again, "stop va—va—" The word quivered on her lips, but she couldn't push them out. "Tr—tr—trip."

"Are you sure?" Cameron asked once more. "You've been very ill."

"Www—ait."

Resigned, Cameron shrugged. "Okay." Unless there was a critical change in Granny's condition, she'd respect the old girl's wishes.

"Did the doctor talk to you?" she asked. "Have they run any tests?"

A haunted expression crossed Granny's face. She nodded. It broke Cameron's heart to see her grandmother that way. She felt so helpless. "And?"

"Test. Test. Re—hab."

"How do you feel about that?"

Granny shrugged, but couldn't hide the flash of fear in her eyes.

Tears of concern pooled in Cameron's eyes. *Lord, this is difficult.* She blinked rapidly to prevent them from falling. "I'm here for you. The whole deal, rehab, everything," Cameron pledged, then swallowed the lump in her throat. "I'll be your coach or partner or whatever you need. We'll get through this together. Right?"

"You," Granny lips trembled. Her left hand pleated the sheet. "Lots," her tongue moved across her lips, "to . . . do."

For a split second, a lie seemed the best answer to calm Granny's fears. But she refused to do that. A lie would cause a new set of problems. Besides, Granny always sniffed out the truth in a nanosecond.

"Little Darlings will be just fine. We made it work today and we'll find ways to continue until you're ready to come back." Cameron squeezed Granny's hand. "There's no hurry. A little creative scheduling, plus an agency cook and a childcare aide are starting tomorrow. That should take the edge off," she reassured. "Don't worry about that stuff. Just concentrate on getting better."

"Jay—la?"

Maybe a little white lie wouldn't hurt. Guilt kicked in.

She couldn't do that to Granny. Their relationship demanded honesty.

Cameron shifted away from Granny. She stared out the window and pretended to be fascinated with the moonlight. Underneath that façade, she evaluated the right words to tell her about Marek. There weren't any, so she just spit it out. "Marek's at the house with us."

For the first time, a sly grin spread across Granny's lips. "Mmmm, hmmm."

Cameron's lips pursed. "Don't mmm, hmmm me, old girl." She jabbed a finger in Granny's direction. "It's not what you think."

Granny chuckled. Her shoulders shook as laughter grew. "Mmm, hmmm?"

"Oh, you're so bad." Cameron stabbed Granny with a severe glare, then dissolved into a fit of giggles.

A rap on the door drew their attention. " 'Night, ladies." The aide entered the room, placed a tray on an overbed table, rolled it within Granny's reach and lifted the lid. "Supper's ready."

For hospital food, it looked tasty. The aroma of roasted chicken filled the room. Fresh parsley flakes dressed a golden chicken breast. White, fluffy potatoes and bright green peas completed the dinner. All in all, it looked like a pretty decent meal.

Cameron unwrapped the plastic cutlery, napkin and arranged it all within Granny's reach, then sat back, waiting for her to pick up the fork and dig in. Nothing happened.

A worried frown pleated Cameron's brow as her gaze swung from the food to her grandmother. "Granny?" she probed. "You need to eat."

"No!" Her poked-out bottom lip looked similar to Jayla's. Cameron almost laughed.

She softened her voice to a persuasive purr. "Do you

need something else?" Only the soft rumble of Granny's tummy answered her.

Granny's lashes lowered over her eyes and she shook her head.

"Care to tell me what's wrong?"

Red color crept across Granny's cheeks. Her eyes flashed with angry brown flecks. "Ca—n't hold." She confessed then clamped her lips together.

Oh, Lord. Cameron looked away. *Granny can't hold the fork.* The words swirled in her head.

"I'm here to help you," she encouraged. "I told you, we're in this together. And I meant it."

A scowl marred Granny's features. Cameron understood her grandmother's sense of pride and the frustration this situation caused. She chewed on her bottom lip, searching for some way to keep Granny's pride intact while helping.

"I love you too much to let your illness beat us." Cameron's voice trembled as she spoke. "I want you home with Jayla and me." She lifted a forkful of potatoes to Granny's lips. "Please, let me help you."

The expression on Granny's face made Cameron cringe. Granny's lips remained defiantly shut while she shot an angry glare straight at Cameron.

The old girl's body slumped against the pillows. Wearily, she opened her mouth and allowed Cameron to place a forkful of mashed potatoes between her lips.

For Cameron's part, she felt low, really low. At this point, Granny's pride came in a poor second to her need to regain her strength.

"More?" Cameron prompted gently.

The barest trace of a nod gave her permission to continue. "Try the chicken." Cameron sliced a piece of poultry. "It smells heavenly." The aroma of lemon herbs filled the air when she cut into the white meat.

Granny opened her mouth and took a bite. Pleased, Cameron cut another piece. "We'll have you back home in no time."

"Hmmm," the older woman snorted.

To keep Granny occupied, Cameron recounted the chaos that had transpired in the kitchen at Little Darlings. With each story, she worked her way through the meal until Granny had finished almost half of it. Pleased with her progress, Cameron offered the old girl a paper napkin. She took it and wiped her mouth awkwardly. Granny gave the table a pitiful shove and asked, "Jay—la?"

"She's with her father." Now was the time to tell Granny about Marek and their arrangement. "He's moved in to help." *With an agenda of his own,* she thought. But Granny didn't need to know that.

The old girl's eyebrow rose and she tilted her head to one side. All she needed to add was the word, "Well!"

"He's there to help," Cameron repeated. "Period. He gets Jayla dressed and fed in the mornings. That frees up my time to open and close Little Darlings."

"My—my." She smirked. For a woman with limited verbal functions, the old girl got her point across. Thank goodness she didn't know the whole story; she'd have much more to say.

"He's there to help. That's all."

"Mmm, hmmm."

She was messing this up. "Jayla's happy with this arrangement. It's nice to have dinner ready when I get home," Cameron babbled. "I wash my hands and sit down to a meal. I like it."

Granny's smug expression slipped a bit. "You?"

Images of her and Marek locked in each other's arms popped into Cameron's head and made her blush. *Keep cool.* That part Granny didn't need to know.

"Marek helps around the house." She answered slowly, tiptoeing through this particular minefield. "Last night, he did the laundry. I couldn't believe it. Today he picked up Jayla. She went with him without a backward look at me. I think they'll do fine."

The question came a second time with more force. "You?"

Should she confide in Granny how left out she felt when Marek and Jayla were together? Or about the jealousy she felt when they entered the house hand in hand and left her in the car? No. Her personal confessions could wait.

"I'm okay."

The faint light in Granny's eyes made Cameron uneasy. "Oh?" Granny's eyebrows slanted in a frown and her expression became even more questioning.

Cameron shifted on the bed and drew in a nervous breath. "Marek's great. It's just," she nibbled on her bottom lip, "he's there. In our house. Invading my space. I'm finding everything hard to adjust to."

Granny laughed. Her shoulders rose and fell as she gave Cameron an I-know-what's-going-on look.

"What's so funny?"

Amused, the old girl strummed a finger at Cameron, "Jea—lous?"

"No, I'm not," she denied huffily. "I just feel left out. That's all. It'll work itself out."

"Mmmm, hmmm."

"Really," Cameron insisted.

The lines of concern deepened along Granny's brows as she weighed Cameron's words.

Feeling very foolish, Cameron examined her fingernails. "I know. I'm Jayla's mother. But it's different when he's around twenty-four/seven," she admitted. "It's difficult to be objective with so much unfinished business between us."

Granny smiled slyly. "Fin—ish it."

Okay, old girl, you've got me.

"Lo—ve him?"

"Yes," she admitted. Wearily, she covered her face with her hands.

Granny drew Cameron's hands away from her face. "Make . . . wo—wo—rk."

"Oh, Granny. I'm so afraid. Afraid I'll get hurt again," she spoke in a broken whisper. "No matter how I try, I can't make myself trust him. There's this part of me that can't get the image of him and Nikki together out of my head."

"Ask."

"No." Cameron shook her head. "I'm not ready to deal with those questions, or the answers."

"Ask!"

"You never let me back away from a fight, do you? I'll think about it. I won't promise I'll change my mind. But I will think about it." She glanced at her watch, brushing her hair away from her eyes. "Oh, Lord. Look at the time. I've got to get home." Cameron grabbed her purse, hopped off the bed and kissed Granny's cheek. "I'll be back tomorrow."

Cameron kept her calm façade in place as she traveled through the hospital. Inside the elevator, through the lobby and until she slipped into the driver's seat of her car. The tears fell seconds after the car door slammed behind her. *Tissues*, she thought, rummaging frantically through her purse. She needed tissues.

Helplessness swept through Cameron as she mopped away her tears. She saw Granny's proud resolve shattered by her need for help.

How was she going to handle this development? She couldn't let Granny be humiliated or bullied by the hospital staff. Leaning her head against the headrest, she considered her options. If Marek took on more responsibility for Jayla, that would free up her time to get to the hospital and feed Granny.

That also meant more time away from Jayla. Maybe it was a blessing that Marek offered his help.

First, she needed to talk with Marek and the staff at Little Darlings. Next, call an agency and add a couple of temporary employees to cover her absence. Then a lunchtime escape to the hospital would be easier. Regardless, Granny needed her and she intended to be available as long as the old girl wanted her.

She swept a shaky hand through her tousled hair. Now that that was resolved, Granny's words came back to haunt her. Was she being unfair to herself and Marek by refusing to listen to Marek's explanation? Maybe.

Flipping the sun visor down, she checked her reflection in the mirror and brushed away the loose particles of tissue from her cheeks. Sometimes Granny's advice was the best. Then, all the fear and distrust rushed back and frightened the hell out of Cameron.

There was already too much drama in their life. She'd let Granny's advice roll around in her head for a few days, then she'd act on it.

Chapter Twenty

Cameron shoved the transmission into park and turned off the engine. Far too weary to get out of the car, she leaned her head against the headrest and massaged her temples.

Boy, was she tired. A week of twice-a-day visits to the hospital, work at Little Darlings, plus preparations for the inspection had drained all of her energy. She felt like a soggy dishcloth.

Today's misadventures topped the list. When the alarm clock went off that morning, she hit the floor in hyperdrive. Interviews with applicants for the elementary school and her trek across town to the hospital delivered on its promise for a stressful day.

Now came the real test of her abilities: Marek. Her groan floated through the car. *Get out of the car,* she advised silently before grabbing her purse and briefcase from the passenger's seat. *You can't avoid him forever.* Since they had made love, stepping into her house felt like taking a trip to hell number two.

AS LONG AS THERE IS LOVE 181

Her steps slowed as she moved up the walkway. *What's up with the lights?* The lights were on, but dimmer, like a brown-out.

Maybe Marek had gone to bed and left a light burning in the hallway instead of the living room. Good! A little time without his disturbing presence would go a long way to saving her sanity.

Since he had moved in, Cameron found herself listening for the purr of his SUV at the end of each day or the deep, sensual rumble of his laugh when he played Uno with Jayla. If things ended there, she'd be fine. But there was more. Much, much more. Each time he looked at her with that naked hunger, she shuddered and her resolve to be just friends crumbled a little bit more.

Cameron moaned. Marek's eyes promised bliss. And she wanted it so badly. But too much unpleasant history crammed their lives.

She stepped into the hallway and shut the door behind her. "Oh my!" The briefcase and purse slipped from her hands and hit the carpeted floor with a muffled thump.

"Marek," she muttered, feeling as if she'd wandered into her own fantasy. Candles, tall, short, white, red, pink and lavender lit an aromatic path to the staircase.

Another jolt greeted her when she reached the stairs.

On the bottom step a single white long-stemmed rose beckoned her. "For friendship," she whispered, plucking the flower from the stair. She stroked the flower across her cheek, moved by Marek's thoughtfulness.

Another rose waited on the second step. Red. "Passion," she muttered. *We have plenty of that.* She glanced up the stairs and delight filled her heart. A rose beckoned on each step, one red, the next white.

Her heart did a rat-a-tat in her chest. It looked as if Marek had big plans for them tonight. Was she ready? *Oh yeah.*

She followed the trail of candles and flowers to the second

floor. A jazzy piano tune enticed her down the hall and toward the bathroom door. She nudged it open with her foot. A cloud of lavender hovered over the room.

Marek waited, dressed in a pair of black trousers and a white silk shirt. The sleeves were rolled away from his wrist and revealed arms covered with dark hair. A bottle of champagne and two fluted glasses sat on a small white table to his right.

Magnificent! He looked simply magnificent. His wickedly tempting smile made her melt like butter in a microwave oven. "Hey," he pointed to the old porcelain tub filled with bubbles and water. "I've got your bath ready."

Ohh! Every bone in her body liquefied while desire flared within her. It held her captive in the doorway. Just how far did he intend to take this? More to the point, how far did she plan to let him? Instantly, Cameron made her decision; she wanted him. She dropped the flowers on the floor next to the door and stepped inside the room. Drawn by an invisible string, Cameron floated to Marek.

With the elaborate flourish of a wine captain, he removed the bottle from the carafe and wrapped it in a white towel. He twisted off the metal cap and then uncorked the bottle. The effervescent wine ran from the top and into the carafe.

Marek poured champagne into both glasses and offered one to her. She took the glass and smiled her thanks.

"What are we celebrating?"

His eyebrows did a double lift and a gleam of sensual promise made her go weak. "To everything and nothing," he clicked their glasses together then lifted the glass to his lips.

She followed suit, enjoying the full-bodied taste of the champagne. Marek moved closer nibbling on her lips. He placed her glass on the table.

"Where's Jayla?"

"Nancy's."

"Oh."

Marek's eyes slid over her. She felt beautiful, desirable.

He helped her out of her jacket and tossed it to the floor. She grabbed at his busy hands. "What are you doing?" The zipper slid down. Steam, warm and moist caressed her skin as his hands parted the skirt.

"Undressing you," he muttered, intent on his task. "I don't want your bath water to get cold."

"Bath?" she repeated stupidly.

"Yeah." He wrapped his arms around her waist and lifted her in the air. Her shoes hit the floor and he stripped the skirt and hosiery from her body in one fluid motion. The garments dropped to the floor in a tangled mass of colors and fabric. Marek kicked the heap out of his way. Her near-naked flesh slid along the length of his body.

Oh, Lord. Her breath came out in short gasps while every muscle tightened. This was happening way too fast.

Marek swept her into his arms, then lowered her into the scented water. Cameron sank deep into the water and sighed.

The CD player hummed and hissed before Luther Vandross's voice cooed, promising love forever, for always. Cameron's eyes drifted shut, enjoying the warm water. This felt like heaven.

Marek hooked a foot around the leg of the stool and pulled it close. Smiling, he dropped onto the seat.

He scooped up a handful of water and let it cascade over the swell of her breasts. Cameron gasped and shifted restlessly. He removed the cap from her shower gel and worked the wet pouf into a rich lather. The fragrance of lavender filled the room.

His lips glided along the side of her neck then she felt the saturated pouf move along her skin like a caress. It stroked the swell of her slick breasts and brown taut nipples. She quivered, wanting everything he had to give. Inch by inch his fingers drew closer to her heated core. He stopped short. Heart pounding, she waited, positive there was more to come.

Sinking further into the water, Cameron said, "Your clothes will get wet."

His smiled broadened. "You're right." Standing, Marek pulled the shirt from his trousers. "How's this?" The first button on his shirt popped open. Button by button, he continued until the shirt hung open. His muscles rippled as he shrugged out of his shirt. Mesmerized, Cameron's eyes remained glued on him.

The shirt slid off his shoulders and landed in a heap on the floor. He kicked it toward the pile in the corner. Resuming his position on the stool, he bent close, licking and nibbling Cameron's earlobe. Restless, she moaned and shifted.

Marek's rich chuckle filled the air. His laughter made her all too aware of how vulnerable she felt.

With long sensuous strokes, he began to wash every part of her body. Her breasts tingled from his detailed ministry. No spot missed his attention.

By the time Marek lifted her from the tub, she was a quivering mess of soaked flesh. She stood in the center of the room, wet and slick as he wrapped her in a towel and rubbed her dry.

Marek's lips covered hers. His hot tongue snaked between her lips and dueled with hers. She lifted her arms and wrapped them around his neck.

Scooping her off the floor, Marek strolled down the hall to her bedroom. He nudged the door open with his foot and ripped the comforter from the bed with one hand before he laid her among the cool sheets.

He stripped off his trousers and stood before her, hard and erect. Her eyes trailed along the mat of hair on his chest to his erected flesh.

Marek dropped down next to her on the mattress. "You're so beautiful," he praised. His fingers skimmed over her

An important message from the ARABESQUE Editor

Dear Arabesque Reader,

Because you've chosen to read one of our Arabesque romance novels, we'd like to say "thank you"! And, as a special way to thank you, we've selected four more of the books you love so well to send you for FREE!

Please enjoy them with our compliments, and thank you for continuing to enjoy Arabesque...the soul of romance.

Karen Thomas
Senior Editor,
Arabesque Romance Novels

Check out our website at
www.arabesquebooks.com

**SPECIAL OFFER!
4 FREE BOOKS**

ARABESQUE®

A PRODUCT OF

BET BOOKS

3 QUICK STEPS TO RECEIVE YOUR "THANK YOU" GIFT FROM THE EDITOR

Send this card back and you'll receive 4 FREE Arabesque novels! The introductory shipment of 4 Arabesque novels – a $23.96 value – is yours absolutely FREE!

There's no catch. You're under no obligation to buy anything. You'll receive your introductory shipment of 4 Arabesque novels absolutely FREE (plus $1.99 to offset the costs of shipping & handling). And you don't have to make any minimum number of purchases—not even one!

We hope that after receiving your books you'll want to remain an Arabesque subscriber. But the choice is yours to continue or cancel, anytime at all! So why not take us up on our invitation to receive 4 Arabesque Romance Novels, with no risk of any kind. You'll be glad you did!

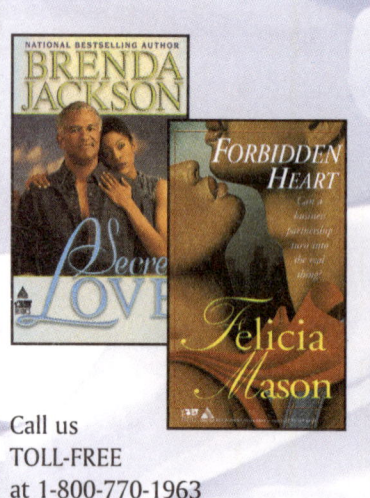

Call us TOLL-FREE at 1-800-770-1963

THE EDITOR'S "THANK YOU" GIFT INCLUDES:

- 4 books absolutely FREE (plus $1.99 for shipping and handling)
- A FREE newsletter, *Arabesque Romance News*, filled with author interviews, book previews, special offers, and more!
- No risks or obligations. You're free to cancel whenever you wish... with no questions asked.

BOOK CERTIFICATE

Yes! Please send me 4 FREE Arabesque novels (plus $1.99 for shipping & handling). I understand I am under no obligation to purchase any books, as explained on the back of this card.

Name _____

Address _____ Apt. _____

City _____ State _____ Zip _____

Telephone ( ) _____

Signature _____

Offer limited to one per household and not valid to current subscribers. All orders subject to approval. Terms, offer, & price subject to change. Offer valid only in the U.S.

Thank you!

AN102A

Accepting the four introductory books for FREE (plus $1.99 to offset the cost of shipping & handling) places you under no obligation to buy anything. You may keep the books and return the shipping statement marked "cancelled". If you do not cancel, about a month later we will send 4 additional Arabesque novels, and you will be billed the preferred subscriber's price of just $4.00 per title. That's $16.00 for all 4 books for a savings of 33% off the cover price (Plus $1.99 for shipping and handling). You may cancel at any time, but if you choose to continue, every month we'll send you 4 more books, which you may either purchase at the preferred discount price. . . or return to us and cancel your subscription.

THE ARABESQUE ROMANCE CLUB: HERE'S HOW IT WORKS

ARABESQUE ROMANCE BOOK CLUB
P.O. Box 5214
Clifton NJ 07015-5214

PLACE
STAMP
HERE

breasts and brought then sharply to life. Everywhere he touched tingled, responded and begged for more.

His kisses were soft, enticed. His lips moved to her breast and took one swollen nipple between his lips and sucked. Cameron's breath caught in her throat and her fingers ran through his hair. Nipping at her skin with his teeth, he moved lower, trailing a moist path from her breast to her navel. His tongue circled the indention, then nibbled lower. Through a haze of passion, Cameron panicked. This was too much. Far too much!

Cameron grabbed a handful of dark hair and pulled. His smoldering gaze met hers.

"No!" she pleaded.

Marek smiled. "Yes!" he insisted, lowering his head.

With the first sweep of his tongue, her breath caught in her throat. She bucked when his tongue swept along the vertical seam, licking the flesh that covered her wet, heated core.

"Yes!" came his muffled response. Cameron's hips rose off the bed, but Marek held her fast. He cupped her and brought her closer, while his tongue repeatedly flicked across the sensitive nub. Heat pumped through her like an electrical surge.

Cameron shuddered at the intensity of the pleasure and surrendered to every sensation. She'd never felt anything like this. Higher and higher she flew as his tongue worked its magic.

Unable to hold back, Cameron shattered into a hundred pieces. Her body seemed to hover above the mattress as her cry of completeness filled the air. She felt drained, satisfied, and thoroughly loved.

Marek kissed the inside of her thigh, then crawled up her body. "You taste so sweet."

With one powerful thrust, he slid inside her. A new set of exquisite sensation made them groan in harmony. He flexed and she shattered a second time. Instinctively, Cameron opened herself, wanting all of him inside her.

A fierce growl broke from Marek's heated lips as his breath warmed the side of her neck. With the first stroke, he set the pace for their lovemaking. Each thrust came harder, more powerful and deeper than the last. Cameron met his body with her own and ran her finger over his back and shoulders slick with perspiration.

She sailed away on a sea of passion. Erotic sensations touched her nude flesh like pinpricks on her skin until she shattered for the third time. A split second later, Marek groaned, following her into the mind-bending abyss of passion.

Snuggling up against Marek's chest, Cameron shut her eyes. Contentment blanketed her.

Later, Marek would insist that they talk about things and that she wouldn't have any choice. Rubbing her cheek across his chest, she decided, *I'm going to go with the flow and worry about the rest later.*

Chapter Twenty-one

Cameron woke to the pungent scent of sex as Luther Vandross's "Forever, For Always, For Love" swirled in her head. She snuggled against Marek's warm flesh, enjoying the feel of his fingers as he drew circles on her responsive skin.

Images flashed in her head like a movie. Every detail of their night together came to her with crystal clarity. Last night, their relationship had reached a new plateau.

No matter how hard she denied the fact, what they shared refused to be swept under the bed. She went to Marek, aware of his intentions, accepted his challenge without hesitation. Without a doubt, she welcomed it.

No excuses. It happened. Their bodies expressed the emotions each refused to put into words.

So, where does that leave us? Cameron wondered, tracing his stubble jaw line with a finger, thrilled to touch him.

Marek's eyes drifted open. He reached out and pulled her close, feathering soft kisses over her cheek.

"Good morning," Marek flipped on his back and took her with him, fitting her along the length of his body.

Embarrassed, she focused on a point above his shoulder. "Morning," she responded. After last night, she couldn't believe she still felt shy.

"So," his husky voice rumbled against her chest. "Do you plan to tell me this was another mistake?"

Her gaze flew to his face, than shifted away. Heat spiraled up her neck and warmed both sets of cheeks. Score one for Marek.

"No," she mumbled.

"Aah?" He cupped his ear and asked, "What did you say? I didn't quite catch it."

"No!" she answered loudly.

Satisfied, he nodded. "Ahh, progress." His hand caressed her buttock. "Good." Marek's hoarse whisper broke the silence. "Ronnie, look at me."

His serious expression made her stomach flip-flop.

"Last night brought one point home. We're still good together," Marek stated as his hand glided along her spine. "But I want more. I want you and Jayla in my life. You're my family. And we belong together. So the only question left is what do I need to do to make things right between us?"

Her heart leapt with joy, then terror washed over her. What about their past? How did he expect her to ignore something as fundamental to a relationship as fidelity?

Cameron lowered her lashes over her eyes, shielding her expression. This time, she planned to thoroughly examine the situation before ruling on their fate. No more impulsive decisions that led to misery and loneliness. She intended to study the facts and decide according to what worked best for her and Jayla.

Which brought her to the next issue. Was their love strong enough to overcome their past? Trust? Was it possible?

Cameron swallowed hard as the bitter taste of fear took hold. And that wasn't their only problem. Would he forgive her for keeping Jayla from him?

"Marek," her voice shook as she watched him, "there are so many problems. Do you really believe we can fix things?"

"Honestly, I don't know," he answered, holding her close. "I know I don't want to go back to that old life without you." With a gentle hand, Marek smoothed the creases from her brow. "For the second time, what do I need to do to make things work between us?"

Love me. The voice in her head screamed. *Don't hurt me again. Be faithful.*

She couldn't say those words, so she settled for, "I'm afraid we won't be able to get it together. Then I'll be alone again."

"It's possible that we can't fix things," he conceded. "Maybe there's no way for us to find our way back to each other. But what type of person would I be if I didn't fight for want I want?" Marek cupped her face in his hands and asked, "What about you? Am I worth fighting for?"

Uncertain, she asked, "I'm the reason you missed the first three years of Jayla's life," she said in a regretful whisper. "Can you forgive me?"

Marek shifted away and threw his legs over the side of the bed. "I'd be lying if I said I don't resent losing that time with Jayla." He fell silent for several tense moments. "But I think I can live with it. I know I plan to try to give it my best." Studying her over his shoulder, he said, "It's my turn. Why didn't you at least call me and tell me you were pregnant?"

She threw her legs over the side of the mattress, stood and wrapped the sheet around her, sarong-style. It was a fair question and he deserved an honest answer. But Marek's question stood between them like a volcano ready to erupt.

She wasn't sure he'd appreciate her answer, but it was all she had.

Cameron sank into her rocking chair, drew her knees up, and rested her head on her knees. "It took a couple of months to realize I was pregnant," she confessed. "We'd always been so careful. It just never occurred to me. Once I confirmed it, I did try to reach you at school. Nobody knew where you'd gone."

"I took a fellowship in Washington."

Ice spread through her veins as she remembered. "Oh, Marek, you have no idea what I went through with my parents, especially my father." Tears slipped down her cheeks unnoticed. "His disapproval and insistence that I take care of my problem nearly did me in. The constant whispers behind my back. I was miserable and had to get away. So I tried to reach you again. Only this time I called your parents' house."

His head snapped up. "My parents? When?"

"That August after I graduated. Your sister answered the phone."

"Paige?"

Cameron nodded. "I didn't tell her about Jayla. I felt that was our business. But I did ask for your phone number. Paige told me you were out of the country, but would be back in a couple of weeks. She took my number and promised—"

Shocked, Marek wailed, "I never knew you called." He jumped off the bed and stalked around the room. "Paige never said a word. This sounds like one of my parents' stunts, not Paige's. Why would she do that?"

Marek's expression was too sincere to be fake. *Which meant . . . oh, Lord!* Their whole relationship seemed destined to fail from the start. But Cameron wasn't finished. There was more.

"I waited three weeks for you to call. When that didn't happen, I tried one more time. I got your mother this time."

Cameron worked hard to control the trembling note in her voice, but failed. "She confirmed Paige's explanation." Marek stopped and moved across the room to kneel down in front of her chair. "Your mom was so sincere. She promised to get my message to you and suggested I call back if I didn't hear from you. Frankly, the whole situation embarrassed me. I figured we were through, so I thanked her and hung up."

"Oh, babe, I'm sorry," he took her cold hand within his. "So sorry." He drew her close and kissed her lips. "I don't know why Paige did that. Yes, I do know. I'm sure my parents were behind the whole sorry mess. Nothing would have kept me away. Nothing."

The sincerity in his voice touched her and she began to believe. Those words healed a portion of the raw wounds in her heart.

Their roles reversed, Cameron began to comfort him. "I understand. It's okay," she muttered. Arms around each other, they rocked to and fro. "That's all in the past. I just knew that I was on my own."

"It seems we didn't have a chance, any way you look at it." Agitated, he shook his head. "My family, your dad, and Nikki. How the hell do we get back to one another?"

"Marek—"

"This isn't the time to pussyfoot. How do we fix things?"

How indeed? she wondered. Each time she thought they had conquered their final demon, some new problem cropped up.

"Give me an answer," he demanded, caging her in the chair with his hands. "Come on, Ronnie, it's time to take a stand."

"I choose us," Cameron announced, stroking his cheek.

"Thank you."

"I want Jayla and I to be with you."

"Thank you." Marek kissed the palm of her hand. "More

progress. There are still issues we haven't discussed. And you know what I'm talking about."

"No," Cameron hushed him with a finger against his lips. "I don't want to talk about Nikki. She has no place in our lives anymore. Let's leave her in the past."

Defiance flashed across Marek's face. He ran his fingers through his tousled hair. "I thought you wanted to move ahead."

"I do. But going over the past won't enrich our future."

"I don't understand."

"That's over," she said. "Gone. Let's move forward."

"Don't you want to hear any of it?" He persisted.

"No," she answered, linking their hands together. "I have to take the blame for some of what happened. I never felt secure with our relationship. So it was easy for me to think that you took us lightly."

"I never knew you felt that way."

Sadness covered her face. "I hid it well," she admitted embarrassed. "It always puzzled me why you chose me. I'm nothing special. What made me different from the rest? As far as I could tell, those leggy brunettes were more your style."

Stunned, he stared her. "Didn't you hear what I said to you that day Alice took sick?" He kissed her lips. "You're a major part of my life."

"So you said."

"You're all I need. There will always be beautiful women. But I want you," he shook her. "You! What we have goes beyond looks," he stroked her arm. "You've been with me in the good times as well as the bad. It's about Jayla being raised with two parents who care about one another. Us. Our family."

"I know you care about me. But we have very different backgrounds. Sometimes," she drew in a shaky breath, "sometimes, I feel so lost about where I belong in your life," she confessed. "It's hard to know how I fit in."

"You fit in all the places in my life and in my heart. Let me show you," he drew her from the chair. "In my arms," he whispered, walking her to the bed. Marek gave her a little shove and she landed in the center of the bed. "In my bed," he dropped down beside her. "And in my life. All the places in my life."

Unwrapping the sheet as if she were a precious Christmas present, Marek proceeded to show her all the places in his life that she fit.

For the second time, Cameron woke wrapped within Marek's embrace. After baring their souls, she still had doubts. Her fears hadn't been silenced, just put on the back burner.

She couldn't let Marek know the truth. After preaching loud and sure about how important it was for them to put the past behind them, how could she explain the fear that gripped her each time she considered their past?

She wanted their lives to come together. To make that happen, she needed to hide her uncertainty until she found a way to deal with them. Maybe trust would come with time.

Until that happened, she had to bury those fears deep, where he'd never find them.

Chapter Twenty-two

Cameron stretched, then snuggled deeper into the cushions on her living room sofa. The aroma of sausage and blueberry pancakes still lingered in the air. Stuffed, she patted her tummy and exhaled a long sigh of contentment.

Her world was perfect on this Saturday afternoon. Granny's rehab progress had surpassed the therapist's expectation. Yesterday, the old girl mustered up enough energy to feed herself. A firm date for the state inspection had been established and Cameron believed she was ready.

Life was good. Real good.

Jayla's happiness capped everything. The little girl glowed. And Cameron planned to keep it that way. She and Marek had struggled to get to this point, and no one was going to come between them.

Cameron grabbed a throw pillow from the opposite end of the sofa and anchored it behind her head, draping her nightshirt-clad frame along the sofa. Tickled, she watched

Marek and Jayla clown around. They circled the living room, singing and dancing to the perky lyrics of the Spice Girls.

"If you wanna be my lover." Jayla swayed from side-to-side, using a tall white candlestick as her microphone. Wry humor glittered from Marek's eyes as he worked to keep a straight face regarding their daughter's off-key and outrageous lyrics.

"So, where did she learn this?" he whispered into Cameron's ear, lifting her legs from the sofa and sinking into the cushion next to her. Marek's hand glided along her brown legs causing her senses to leap to life.

"Trust me. I don't encourage it," Cameron confessed. "Our daughter is a regular Spice Girls groupie. She loves them."

"I think we need to keep a closer eye on what she watches on television." His hand stroked up and down her legs. With each stroke, heat radiated from her core. "It looks as if we're raising the next generation of Spice Girls."

Cameron rolled her eyes to the ceiling. "God forbid."

Jayla bounced over to the sofa and grabbed her father's hand. "Come on, Daddy."

Marek's eyes slid over Cameron like a caress and her heart rate accelerated. He dropped her feet to the floor, stood and kissed her hair, allowing Jayla to pull him away.

"Duty calls."

"You love it and you know it." Cameron waved them away.

Marek's bare shoulders flexed as he spun Jayla in a circle. Cameron covered her lips with her hand and smirked.

Her family. Cameron grinned. She felt blessed that they were together, finally.

On the positive side, it amazed her to see how she and Marek had resumed their previous life. Even with the addition of Jayla, things jelled. They fit together perfectly. Everything about their relationship felt cozy.

Except there were times she looked into Marek's face and felt so dishonest.

Mistrust made it impossible for her to put the past behind them. Their future seemed uncertain if she didn't control her emotions. Honestly, Cameron had never completely believed Marek's declaration of innocence, although she worked hard to accept it. Each day, she tried to put those negative emotions behind her and to make the best of the opportunity for them to live together as a family. Now if only she had the power to keep the outside world from intruding, things would be perfect.

Long, male fingers eased around her ankle and pulled. Cameron slipped off the sofa and landed in a heap on the floor. Her nightshirt slid up her thighs and a generous portion of brown flesh was revealed.

"Hey!" She untangled her legs and folded them under her as she shot Marek a dirty look. "I was minding my own business," she muttered with a pretend scowl. Unable to maintain this pretense, her face broke into a smile as she smoothed the hem of her cotton nightshirt over her thighs.

Jayla ran over to her mother's side, her nightgown flounced around her feet. Excited, the little girl pranced around them. "Daddy, dance with Mummie."

"Well?" His eyebrows lifted.

Marek's bare chest and low riding cut-off jeans gave flight to a series of X-rated fantasies. "Fine with me." She wanted to be in Marek's arms, all she needed was a reason.

"Good." He offered her a hand. "It's been hours since I've held you in my arms." *Oh, this man definitely knows the right things to say.*

Without hesitation, she placed her hand within Marek's and he pulled her to her feet. She stepped straight into his embrace and nuzzled against the warmth of his body. Content, her eyes drifted shut as the essence of Marek filled her nostrils.

They swayed to the saxophone music of Najee.

"I love you, Ronnie," he breathed into her ear. His words shimmered over her skin like a gentle spring rain.

Her heart leapt with joy. Astonished, Cameron halted in the middle of their dance.

This was the first time he's said those words. Elated, she drew him close and their lips touched gently.

"I've never stopped," Marek confessed, drawing away with an expectant expression on his face.

Cameron opened her mouth to return the words and hesitated. Lack of trust kept her from making a declaration of her own.

Things were pretty good the way they were. Was she ready to take the final step while mistrust held a piece of her heart? She gazed into his love-filled eyes, certain of what he wanted, but unsure whether she could give it to him.

Her tongue snaked out and moistened her lips. "I—I—" she clasped her fingers together. Marek's gaze shifted from her fidgeting fingers back to her face while his brows formed a straight line across his puzzled eyes.

The words quivered on her lips, "I . . . lo . . ." She did love him, but she wasn't sure if this was the right time to say the words.

The doorbell rang. Her shoulders drooped. Relieved, she started for the door. "I'll get that."

"Ah, sweetheart." Marek gazed at her white nightshirt. "Maybe I should do it."

Cameron glanced down and muttered, "Oh."

"Jayla?" he called.

She bounced up to her father and answered, "Yesss?"

"Go upstairs and find your mother's robe." Marek buttoned the top button of his jeans and walked out of the living room.

Cameron heard his bare feet slap against the floor as he

made his way to the door. The chain rattled and the door creaked on its hinges as it swung open.

"What the hell are you doing here?" came the angry question.

"Lower your voice," Marek snapped back.

Oh, Lord. "Madaddy!" Cameron rushed toward the sliding doors, then stopped, calculating the distance between the living room door and the staircase. It might be better if she avoided this whole scene until things cooled down.

"Don't tell me to lower my voice," her father's voice boomed. "I'll do any damn thing I want."

"You might think about your granddaughter," Marek reminded.

Cameron slipped out of the living room door and tiptoed toward the stairs, intent on making it to the confines of her bedroom unnoticed. As she tried to slip past, she found her father nose-to-nose with Marek. She stood transfixed in the hallway.

Mom's petite form stepped between the two men. "Excuse me." She studied Marek for thirty seconds and dismissed him with a twist of her wrist, then speared Madaddy with a warning look. "Honestly, Robert. Have you forgotten why we're here?" She brushed a lock of auburn hair away from her tea-colored cheek.

"He," Mom gave Marek another swift glance, "can wait."

Her father puffed up like a balloon, but remained silent. For dramatic effect, he snatched off his jacket and revealed his service revolver in the shoulder holster.

With a small portion of her mind, she examined her parents. She hadn't seen them since Christmas. They both looked good. A healthy golden tan kissed Madaddy's caramel skin and highlighted the gray strands in his light brown hair.

Mom turned to Cameron, and studied her with eyes the

same shade of brown. She placed a hand on her hip and asked, "How's your grandmother?"

"She had a stroke."

Mrs. Butler gasped and her hand flew to her lips. "Oh no!"

"Are you sure?" Her father's voice shook.

"Her doctor confirmed it," Cameron nodded. "They started rehab last Wednesday."

"Why didn't you get in touch with us earlier?" his angry voice demanded.

"I tried," Cameron cried, stepping away from the fierce anger in Madaddy's expression. "David said you were on a cruise. Besides, Granny stabilized the next day and she told me not to bother you."

Tears pricked Cameron's eyes. Maybe she hadn't made the right decision, but she'd been trying to comply with Granny's wishes. "Granny said you'd be around soon enough and to not disturb you."

"Babygirl, you know better than that," Madaddy stepped forward and said. "Let's get this straight now, if there's ever an emergency, I want to know right away."

Mom searched the room with curious eyes. "Where's Jayla?"

Cameron tipped her head toward the stairs. "Upstairs. She'll be down in a moment."

"Do you believe this girl?" Madaddy raged to Mom. Disgust blazed from his eyes. "That piece of trash opened the door to *my* Mama's house. I don't care how we try, we can't get rid of him."

His words threw her back to the time she had told them that she was pregnant. All the pain and disappointment spiraled around her and made her feel like a fifteen-year-old instead of a twenty-six-year-old mother.

"You haven't had enough, girl?" he bellowed. "Do you like stepping back into crap?"

"Dad—"

"Wait one minute." Irate, Marek stabbed a finger in Madaddy's direction.

Mom stroked Madaddy's arm. "Robert, calm down."

"Grandma!" Jayla skipped down the stairs, hurried to Cameron's side and handed her the robe. Cameron shoved her arms into the robe, tied and knotted the sash. Although her baby seemed oblivious to the tension, Cameron didn't want her to get caught up in this adult situation.

"Poppy!" Jayla hurled herself at her grandfather. He caught her in midair and swung her around.

"There's my big girl. Give Poppy a kiss," he commanded, as the little girl wrapped her arms around his neck and gave him a big juicy smack. Madaddy's glare crucified Cameron over the top of Jayla's head. Cameron got the message clearly. It brought tears to her eyes. But she refused to let them fall. Under the layers of disapproval, hurt shone from Madaddy's eyes, then died.

"Poppy! Poppy!"

"What, little one?"

"I got a daddy." She pointed a finger at Marek. "See?"

A loud silence hovered over the little group. He stroked Jayla's hair. "So I see." The frosty expression in Madaddy's eyes ground Marek into dog meat.

"What about me, little one, where's my kiss?" Mom gathered Jayla in her arms. "We haven't seen you since Christmas. Look at you."

"Granny's sick," Jayla explained. "She's in the hopsital."

"Hospital, sweetie," Cameron corrected softly.

"Yes, she is," Mom confirmed. "And that's why we're here. So, where's my kiss?"

"I've got a computer and my daddy put some games on it." Jayla wriggled out of her grandmother's arms and ran ahead to the steps. "Come see?"

"Okay. I'll be right there," Mom promised. Everyone watched as Jayla rounded the corner at the top of the landing and raced down the hall to her room. "Robert," Mom said as she followed Jayla up the stairs, "don't say or do anything you'll regret. And please remember, there's a child in the house."

Madaddy snorted and muttered under his breath, "Doesn't look as if they've been too concerned."

"Robert," her mother called from the staircase. "Why don't you come see Jayla's computer?"

"Be there in a second," Madaddy answered, facing Cameron. "Don't you have any respect for yourself? Here you are with this piece of trash, while your grandmother lies in a hospital bed!"

Marek moved toward Madaddy. Oh, Lord. She had to stop Marek before war broke out between them.

"No!" Cameron maneuvered between the two men. She pleaded. "Don't!"

"Look at him." Madaddy's lips curled away from his teeth as he wagged a hand in Marek's direction. His eyes ran over Marek's bare chest and jeans, then returned to her. "Look at you!"

"Mr. Butler."

Madaddy's belligerent gaze swung to Marek. "I don't remember calling your name."

Mom's shoulders slumped. She stepped off the bottom stair and returned to the group. "Robert." She shook his arm, pulling him toward the stairs. "Come on."

"I've told you all your life that you can't trust men. Especially him. Didn't you learn your lesson the last time?" Madaddy stated. "Have you forgotten how he left you with that load?"

"Dad, you can't talk to us that way. This is my house."

Madaddy stalked back to where Cameron stood and regarded her with cold deliberation. "This is *my* mother's home. I can do whatever I please." He jabbed a finger at the stairs. "Now get upstairs and put some clothes on." He folded his arms across his chest and waited at the bottom of the stairs.

Eyes blazing and his jaw clenched, Marek looked ready to kill. Oh, Lord. Fear surged through her. If things got too far out of hand, nothing would ever be the same. Everything she had worked so hard for would be lost. Sorry just wouldn't cut it.

"Don't," she begged, holding Marek's arm in a death grip. "He's my father."

"Father!" Marek recoiled from her. "Who am I?" he asked in a harsh undertone. "Who the hell am I?" Disbelief was written all over his face. "What do I mean to you?"

"Madaddy's upset," she whispered, cutting a nervous gaze at her father. "Give him a little time and things will smooth over."

Marek's expression turned grim. "I don't care how upset he is, he's not going to talk to me that way."

"Please, don't." Her eyes darted between the two men. "Don't. Give me a little time to handle this."

"No. It's time for us to come to an understanding."

"Not now!" she rasped between clenched teeth. "Go upstairs and get dressed while I get this settled." He stepped toward her father. "Please, Marek, please." She blocked Marek's path. "I can't let you do this. Madaddy needs a little time. He'll come around."

Eyes narrowing, Marek stared at Cameron as if he'd never seen her before. "You're telling me to walk away from this, aren't you?"

"No," she retorted sharply. "I'm asking you to leave him to me."

"Cameron, you're not daddy's little girl anymore," he reminded. Although his voice was quiet, it carried an ominous quality. "You're a grown woman. It's your life. You have to stand up for it."

"Don't," she warned, "tell me what to do. I'm trying to get this problem resolved and I don't need you creating new ones."

Marek nodded, turning away. "Okay," he muttered, climbing the steps two at a time.

How had her beautiful morning turned into such a nightmare? Everything had been right with the world until Marek opened the front door.

Cameron stomped up the stairs. At the landing, Madaddy watched her from the bottom of the staircase. His brown eyes sparkled with satisfaction.

She shot Madaddy a glare of disgust and stormed down the hallway. As far as she could tell, her displeasure dropped off his shoulders like rain off an umbrella.

A portion of her anger ebbed as she slammed her bedroom door. The sound gave her a measure of satisfaction. The distinct odor of sex lingered in the air and she hurried to open a window.

All Madaddy needed was a little space and time to think. Once he cooled down, things would work out. She planned to make good use of that downtime to talk with Marek and make him understand how her family operated.

Cameron sank into her rocking chair and rocked back and forth as the high-voltage emotions that sizzled through her earlier began to ease.

Madaddy had always treated her like a child. Hell, she was a grown woman now, with a child of her own. Who did he think he was, barging into her house and upsetting her family?

Her father's behavior was ugly and downright offensive.

Right now, Marek was her priority. A little personal attention would put him in a better mood.

Marek's declaration of love forced its way to the forefront of her thoughts. How could she not respond in kind to those life-affirming words? Cameron knew the answer. She didn't quite trust him.

Chapter Twenty-three

Cameron sank onto the edge of the mattress and scraped her hair away from her face. Peace was a limited commodity in this house, especially when Madaddy visited.

No time to think about that, she decided. Right now, Marek needed her reassurances.

She rushed to her dresser, plucking a pair of jean overalls off the bed along the way and jerked open a drawer, searching for a blouse. Mentally rehearsing her speech, she pulled a white T-shirt over her head, then stepped into her overalls.

There was a sharp rap on the door and Marek slipped inside the room. Her heart leapt with pleasure. Marek.

With hooded eyes he watched her. A chill scurried along her spine as she stared at his unreadable mask.

"Hey," she muttered, running damp palms against her jeans.

A nod was his only response.

Her eyes slid over his tall frame and frowned. A pair of trousers and a silk shirt and tie replaced his cut-offs. His smooth-shaven chin and the subtle aroma of soap pointed to something different.

Had the hospital called him? No. The phone hadn't rung. Maybe his pager had gone off, or his cell phone.

"Did you get a page?" she asked. For some unexplainable reason she feared his answer.

"No."

"Oh?" Her frown deepened. "What's up?"

"I'm leaving."

"Yo—you mean to go to work?" Cramps twisted her stomach into knots. "Right?"

"No."

That one word plunged a knife into her heart. Her hand flew to her lips. *No!* She cried silently, willing herself to stay calm and find out what was going on. *This can be fixed,* she decided, lowering her hand to her side. She needed to learn the facts.

Marek really didn't want to leave. She believed that with every cell of her being. His anger had gotten the best of him. That's all.

"Don't let Madaddy get to you."

He laughed. The harsh sound caused goose bumps to rise on her skin. "I'm not concerned with your father."

"Oh?" Puzzled, her face scrunched up and she stared at him. "Sooo, what's the what?"

"You."

Her head snapped back. "Me!" Cameron squeaked out. "What are you talking about?"

His mouth tightened into a straight line. "You! The way you acted when your father showed up. Daddy's girl!" he sneered, tossing a hand in the air.

Panic was only a second away. Her sweaty palms brushed against the hips of her overalls. She drew in a breath and let it out in tiny increments. Her mind frantically worked on a way to fix this.

AS LONG AS THERE IS LOVE

"Madaddy is a delicate matter," she explained, drawing closer, pleading for understanding. "You have to calm him down before anything will sink into his big brain."

His stony mask remained locked in place. "I don't think your father is as much of a problem as you are."

"Marek, let's not fight," Cameron pleaded. "Madaddy will only be here a few days. Things can go back to the way they were. Just hold on," she advised. "It'll all work itself out. Believe it."

"You don't get it, do you?"

Her temples throbbed as she tried to reason with Marek. "I know you're angry with me. But don't condemn me just yet. You'll see I'm right. I bet you by the time we have dinner, Madaddy will be a different man. You'll see."

Disgust flashed across his face. "Sometimes you are truly unbelievable."

Taken aback, she asked, "What are you talking about?"

Marek snorted and shook his head. "Let me spell it out." His quiet tone frightened her. "I don't care what your father thinks about me."

Cameron touched Marek's arm and he jerked it away.

Gasping, she looked at her hand. He acted as if he hated her touch. Tears burned her eyes, but pride kept them from falling.

His smile was sad. "Doesn't feel good, does it?"

The large lump in her throat made speech impossible. She turned toward the window, seeing nothing, but intensely aware of his presence.

"You let me down, Ronnie." She turned back to him when he called her name. "We've gone through so much." Marek's voice shook and he raked his fingers through his hair. "When the time came to stand together, you blew it. How do you think that made me feel?"

Cameron knew things hadn't gone well, but she expected

Marek to understand. He had always understood. Why was this time any different?

"Regardless of what your father says or does, we're supposed to be family. He can't change that. But you did," he lowered his head, eyes fixed on the floor. "Your father needed to hear it from you." Marek lifted his head. "Instead, you stepped away and shook me off like a roach. I won't take that."

Cameron stood with her head bowed, frantically searching for a way out of this mess. There must be a way to fix things.

"I'm not stupid. Loving you doesn't make me blind." Marek's voice lacked any emotion. It was dead. "Did you think I wouldn't notice that you didn't say you loved me?"

Oh, Lord! This was bad. Terror ate away at her insides.

"That's not true," she denied. "I . . . I . . . I didn't want my father upsetting everyone with his tantrum. I was trying to protect you."

Marek's hands dropped to his sides. "In case you've forgotten, I'm the man in this family." He sighed and she heard the distinct sound of coins jiggling. "Ronnie, I love you. And I want you and Jayla in my life. But you have to make a choice. It's either me or your father. You can't have it both ways."

Oh, Lord! She didn't know how to fix this. Right now, Marek was serious enough to end things between them. She read it in his face.

"You still don't see it, do you? I saw that look of terror in your eyes when I said I loved you. Your father offered an easy out. An excuse."

"Marek, please," she whispered. "Stop and think about what you're doing."

"I have thought about it. I can't think about anything else," he shook his head. "I can't do this anymore. You're not going to hurt me anymore than you already have. So I'm going to protect myself and move back home."

Panic seized her. What would she do without Marek? He was the single most important person in her life, after Jayla.

"Wow! No! That's not going to happen," she balled her hand into a fist. "Nobody is leaving this house. We—we—we're going to sit down like adults and talk until we work this out."

"Adults," he rasped. A humorless smile came and went on his face. "Hah! That's interesting coming from Daddy's girl."

Reason with him, her mind shouted. "Marek, you know how much I care about you."

"That's all you can say to me? Care!" Marek's harsh chuckle made her cringe. "Care." He shook his head. "Thanks for clarifying that for me. Multiply your caring thirty times, maybe than you'll understand how much I love you."

Cameron stood in front of him, totally lost as to what to say.

He faced her and said in a tired, almost unrecognizable voice, "I need to clear my head and you need to think," he sounded tired. "Maybe then you can come to terms with our relationship."

Cameron ached to touch him. But she was afraid he might reject her yet again.

"The way I see things, you've got a couple of options. One," he lifted one finger, "accept our relationship with everything that goes with it, be a family with me and Jayla or two," Marek added a second finger to the first hand, "be daddy's girl and live under his rules. But I'm warning you. It'll be the end of us. I'll always be Jayla's father. That's my right. But that's all. No you and me."

"Marek, don't!"

"I'll be back tomorrow to pick Jayla up. I promised her

we'd go to the zoo." He swallowed. "And I'll be here Monday morning to get her off to school. I will keep my promises. I said I'd help you and I will."

Marek stepped through the door and then glanced back at her over his shoulder. "If . . ." His voice shook. He stopped, cleared his throat, and then said, "If you need anything, just call or page me." The door shut behind him with a final click.

Oh, Lord! He's left me!

Stunned, Cameron sank into the rocking chair. Her body felt numb.

How had things gone so terribly wrong? Why didn't he understand?

Her morning had been filled with bright happiness. Marek's confession of love made her life almost complete. The only wrinkle came when she refused to return the words.

What did Marek expect of her? Granted, Madaddy irritated everyone. But, he was still her father.

She pushed those turbulent thoughts away. Going over those events wouldn't change a thing. It was time to think about Marek and how to get him back. She needed a plan.

Think, Cameron, think. She picked up a notepad and pen, dropped onto the edge of the bed and jotted a few ideas on the notepad.

Madaddy! She circled his name. He presented the greatest obstacle. She needed to find a way to make her father see Marek in a better light.

Mom! Cameron drew an arrow between the two names. Mom held the key to it all. If Mom could be convinced to talk to Madaddy, that was a step in the right direction.

Cameron tore the sheet from the pad and stuffed it inside her pocket. She moved toward the door.

Standing in front of the mirror, she examined her face.

AS LONG AS THERE IS LOVE 211

No way would her parents get the satisfaction of seeing her upset over Marek. Oh no! She snatched up a tissue and blew her nose. Time to pull herself together she thought as she dabbed at her eyes.

After dinner, she'd dazzle Mom with a list of Marek's finer points, then hit her with the big one.

Whatever came next, she refused to let Marek walk out of her life. Oh no! She'd find a way to pull things together again. It was only a matter of time before she convinced him how much she cared.

Chapter Twenty-four

Cameron heard the soft purr of her father's car as he pulled into the driveway. Her parents were back from the hospital.

She gave her chest a pat of reassurance as she fought the wild hammering of her heart. It was time to put her plan into action.

For a moment, she entertained thoughts of escape. No, that wasn't an option. She couldn't chicken out now.

On cue, Mom waltzed through the door on a cloud of Red perfume. Her penny loafers clicked against the white ceramic tile. Cameron paused in the act of loading the dishwasher, waiting.

"Your grandmother asked about you," Mom announced, before she opened the refrigerator door. A cool breeze scampered out the door, swirled around Cameron and sent chill bumps up her arms. Mom removed a can of Coke, closed the door and leaned against it, popping the tab.

"I'm not surprised," Cameron said. "Granny expects me

AS LONG AS THERE IS LOVE 213

to visit every day. I thought I'd step back and give you guys a chance to catch up." She switched on the hot water and held a plate under the spray. Covertly, she studied her mother. "How is she?"

"Alice looks good." Mom toyed with her soda can. "It's hard to believe that she had a stroke." She placed a manicured hand on Cameron's arm. "Oh, guess what?"

"What?"

Mom slid her soda can on the counter and wrapped both hands around Cameron's arm. "She had on makeup."

Happiness surged. "No!" Cameron jumped up and down.

"Yes."

Finally, a major step toward recovery. Cameron grinned like a fool. If Granny left the hospital tomorrow under her own steam, she couldn't be more excited.

The old girl was on the mend. Before her stroke, she never got dressed without putting on her "face." Her vanity had offered the perfect form of therapy. Cameron had brought her makeup bag to the hospital and suggested Granny apply a little lipstick and color to her cheeks. But her lack of hand coordination had forced her to shun this daily ritual, until today.

"Does Granny need anything?" Cameron loaded the last plate in the dishwasher and shut the door.

"Not that I know of."

She hit the start button and turned to her mother. "Ma, would you keep Jayla tomorrow while I go to the hospital?" The dishwasher hummed, swished, and began its cycle.

"Sure." Mom looked around the room. "By the way, where is your monster baby?"

"Bed," Cameron replied with a sigh of relief.

"Good." Mom picked up her Coke. Her petite frame whisked across the room at superspeed and dropped into a chair at the breakfast nook table.

Cameron wiped her damp hands on a paper towel, following her mother's movements with her eyes.

"Why don't you take a break and come over here so we can talk?" She patted the chair next to hers.

A knot tightened in the pit on Cameron's stomach. *Well, you wanted to talk, didn't you?* No time like the present. Far from calm, Cameron strolled into the breakfast nook and sank into the chair opposite her mother.

"So, Ma, how's Mr. Aronson?" she asked, stalling.

"Fine. He's got retirement on his brain."

Cameron's mouth fell open. "No! Where does that leave you?"

"There are other VP's I can work for. Or, I might retire when Mr. Aronson does." Mom shrugged. "Ford's retirement plan is pretty good. Maybe I'll work for a temp agency a couple of days each week."

"That's a far cry from executive assistant to a VP at Ford Motor Company. Are you sure you want to do that?"

"It's an option. That's enough chitchat, young lady." She placed her Coke can on the table and gave Cameron one of her lets-get-down-to-business glare. "We have more important matters to discuss."

Oh, Lord. Cameron's heart performed a swift rat-a-tat-tat in her chest. *That we do,* she conceded and ran a shaky hand over her face.

"Okay, Ma, ask your questions."

"Are you sure you know what you're doing?" Mom inquired in her direct, authoritarian tone.

Under attack, Cameron shifted in her seat. "I believe so."

"Remember, you're not alone anymore." Mom strummed the tabletop with professionally manicured fingernails. "There's a child involved."

"I know."

"Before Jayla, I didn't like the fact you were involved with *him*." That term made Cameron's stomach churn. "But, I believed in your right to make your own decisions and mistakes. So I let it go. Besides," a little smile came and went on Mom's face, "you refused to listen to us. So there wasn't much we could tell you. Now, there's Jayla. I'm going to say my piece because someone has to protect my grandbaby. It looks as if that *man's* got your nose open, again, and it falls to me to point out the obvious."

Cameron's face tightened. This little soiree resembled the mother-daughter chats she'd endured during adolescence. "Ma, Jayla is always my first priority."

"Your emotions are on front street and you're ignoring the pitfalls." Mom wagged a finger at her. "Have you considered how your actions will affect your child?"

"Of course I have."

Mom sighed, then said, "I know you mean that. You may even believe it. But, young lady, what we walked into makes me question whose priorities come first. What did your father and I see this morning? You and," Mom snipped, "that *man*, all hugged up when we walked in."

Embarrassed, Cameron fiddled with the hem of her overalls. "Marek's here to help me with Jayla while Granny's in the hospital." *Be calm,* she cautioned silently. *Don't let her rattle you.* "Once Granny comes home, he goes back to his place. End of story."

"And?" Mom prompted.

Her mother was not a fool. She detected a lie quicker than a polygraph machine. Cameron held her mother's gaze for a beat. "We're working out our problems."

Disapproval glared back at her.

"Does this mean you've forgotten that you gave birth to Jayla alone?" Mom's eyes flashed with fury, but her voice remained reasonable and calm. "That *man* couldn't be found when you needed him. And where has he been for the last three years?" She cupped her knee and asked, "Have you questioned him about any of that while you were all hugged up and courtin'?"

Cameron rose, this wasn't going to work. Mom's attitude made it almost impossible to explain.

But Marek's last remark about trust and standing together swirled around in her head. She wanted him back and in the quickest possible way, and that meant courting Mom's assistance.

"Contrary to what you believe, I'm not a complete fool." Cameron folded her arms across her chest, returning to her chair. She fixed her mother with a tough glare of her own. "I'm satisfied with his answers."

"Hmm," Mom snorted. "What kind of excuse did he come up with to explain his absence when you were nine months pregnant?"

"You've already made up your mind," Cameron retorted. "Why should I bother talking to you?"

"Because you want something." Mom gave Cameron an I've-got-your-number smile. Her eyebrows lifted. "So go on. Explain it to me."

"After I realized I was pregnant, I tried to reach Marek at his parents' house. There was a mix-up with the message." The explanation left her drained. She took an extra moment to compose herself. "Anyway, he recently confessed that he never knew I had called."

Mom ran a hand over her perfectly styled hair. "Sounds pretty convenient to me."

"Nothing about this situation has or ever will be convenient."

Worry lines crinkled Mom's brow and she touched Cameron's hand. "You're my child and I don't want to hurt you. But use the brain God gave you. Are you truly buying into his garbage because you want to believe him? No matter how farfetched the explanation?"

"Ma, I know you think I don't know my own mind. But I do." She squeezed her mother's hand. "Marek would never hurt Jayla. You should see him with her. He's so gentle and loving."

With a skeptical lift of her arched eyebrow, Mom asked, "He loves your child?"

"*His baby,*" Cameron corrected. "I'd never let him get close to her if I suspected anything else." Her tone dared her mother to contradict her. "Jayla's everything to me. No one, and I mean no one, hurts her."

"I'm still not convinced."

"What can I say that will make you understand?" Cameron questioned. "Marek's far from perfect. I'm no perfect chickie, either. But we're committed to our child and to dealing with our problems so that she'll have a strong, solid home. We've both made mistakes and we've both forgiven each other so that we can get on with our lives."

"I don't like it."

"Sorry." Cameron hunched her shoulders. "That's the way things are. Marek is Jayla's father. That will never change," she stated in a firm tone. "You're also a part of our lives and I'm asking you to treat him fairly. You don't have to be his best bud. Just be civil, polite when you meet."

"I don't understand you." Disappointment flashed, then faded from her eyes. "I thought I raised you with a clearer head. With more sense." Mom fidgeted with the empty soda can. "Why would you believe his lies?"

Hurt by her mom's lack of faith in her abilities, Cameron drew away. "You did raise me well. But his explanation rang true. And after almost four years, I want us to work this out. Which means I have to put the past behind me."

"Oh, Babygirl." Her mother's voice was filled with concern. "What's going to happen to you?"

"I'm fine, Ma." She ignored the butterflies dancing the tango in her belly. "But you and Madaddy can make life easier by getting along with Marek."

Mom shrugged. "You know your father."

"Yes, I do. So I'm asking you to please talk to Madaddy. Convince him to give Marek a chance."

Sadly, Mom shook her head. "When your father makes up his mind . . ."

"Please, Ma."

"You might convince me by explaining what happened between you and him."

"I can't." Cameron went stiff. "That's private."

"Then no." Mom pursed her lip. "This is your battle. And I'm not taking sides. Just like you came to me, you need to do the same with your father. It's not my job to convince him. That's up to you and that *man*. If you plan to pull your father's coattail, you better do it soon."

"Okay," she muttered as her hopes sank into the sea. "Your help would go a long way into validating things."

"That's too bad," Mom answered in a definitive tone. "This is your fight. Talk to your father. Plead your case. I can't and I won't do it for you."

Cameron groaned.

"You're the adult," Mom reminded. "It's time for you to stand tall."

"Ma, don't blame Marek," she pleaded. "He's not the villain you think he is."

"I'm sorry," regret peppered her words. "I do want you to be happy. But I don't trust him and I won't help him hurt you."

"You'd have to understand the situation. And Marek's family," Cameron persisted, feeling as if she'd fired the last bullet, but she felt compelled to continue to pull the trigger. "As you probably guessed, they weren't happy with our relationship."

"Are you sure you want those people involved in your daughter's life? Have you thought that part through?"

"No," Cameron answered. "I'm not sure how Marek's parents will react. But they're Jayla's grandparents and if they want that job, it's theirs."

Mom frowned. "How did you guys get back together anyway? Is he paying child support?"

Cameron nodded. "We met at the hospital and once Marek found out about Jayla, we set up child support through our lawyers."

"Well, at least he's owned up to his financial responsibility." She smoothed her T-shirt and studied Cameron. "But can you trust him? You were listless and barely got a drop of food down you when you graduated from U of M. It frightened me to think that you might not recover. You're my daughter and I love you. I don't want to ever see you like that again."

Ashamed, Cameron avoided her mother's gaze. This was a touchy subject for her. Each time her family brought that up, her embarrassment grew. "It won't happen again. I'm stronger now. I have Jayla to consider."

"What about Jayla?"

"Ma, what are you saying?" Hadn't they discussed every option related to her baby?

"What if it doesn't work between you guys and Jayla gets attached to that *man*?"

"Marek will always be her father."

"Lots of men are great fathers when they're with the mother," she pointed out. "The moment the couple separates, the child's forgotten."

"Marek won't do that."

Her mother leaned closer. "How do you know?"

"He loves Jayla." Cameron leaned toward her mother. "He won't leave her."

Mom sighed and sank back into her chair. "I hope you're

right. It's your call. But you need to think hard and long about who'll be hurt if you and that *man* don't make it."

"Ma, his name is Marek. Ma-rek. Not 'that *man*.' "

"Fine. Ma-rek," she spat out. "It's still '*man*' to me."

"Okay." Cameron raised a hand in her mother's direction. "I'm not going there with you today."

"You want everyone to accept your relationship with him? Then you'll have to handle your business. Talk to your father." Mom pushed her chair away from the table and stood. "I suggest you have that talk real soon." She rinsed out her Coke can and stored it under the kitchen sink.

Cameron folded the damp dishtowel and hung it on the white rack near the sink. She glanced out the window into the dark backyard.

Marek would never come back if she didn't straighten things out with Madaddy. Her first attempt to handle her business had fallen flat.

There must be another way to pull things together. Her mother's suggestion that she bare her heart to her father about a man he hated seemed wrong.

Her initial plan to have someone talk to Madaddy on Marek's behalf was still a good one. She needed to find another ally.

That ally must be someone who's authority Madaddy didn't question.

Granny! She represented the key to the solution. After all, without Marek's help, Granny might not be here today. That should be worth a couple of brownie points.

It might work. Madaddy wouldn't dare contradict his mother. Granny had the power to force him to sit and listen. Cameron smirked; she wanted to be a fly on the wall for that conversation.

She planned to go to the hospital tomorrow. Perfect opportunity to ask for help. With a gleeful nod, she gave the kitchen a final check, then switched off the lights. This twist in the tale might put Marek within her reach.

Chapter Twenty-five

The powerful odor of hospital disinfectant made Cameron's nose twitch when the elevator doors opened. She dodged a yellow and black wet-floor sign and made her way to Granny's room.

When she had arrived earlier, Granny had pointed a finger in Cameron's direction before giving explicit instructions. First, go to the cashier and pay the television and telephone bills. It didn't matter that Cameron had to wait twenty minutes for the line to thin out. Second, head to the cafeteria and pick up ice for her orange juice.

Cameron glanced at her watch and quickened her pace. She wanted to make it home before Marek picked up Jayla. She planned to talk some sense into him before they completely lost their way back to each other.

Also, she wanted to plead her case to Granny before her parents showed up. With her hand on the doorknob to Granny's room, a distinct male voice drifted out into the corridor.

AS LONG AS THERE IS LOVE 223

Madaddy! She wanted to stamp her foot. *There goes my window of opportunity,* she thought. Maybe she should head for the mountains and come back later.

Coward, she chastised herself, but spun away from the door anyway. Cowards lived to sneak away another day.

"Mama, I can't believe Babygirl had that trash living in our house."

Pausing, Cameron turned back to the door. Okay, eavesdroppers rarely heard good things about themselves. But heck, she needed to know what was brewing in Madaddy's head.

A chair scraped against the Formica floor. Her father's sneakers squeaked as he moved around the room.

"After the way he treated her, you'd think she'd run a hundred miles." His voice sounded gruff. "But noooo." Cameron could almost see the cynical twist of Madaddy's lips. "Not my daughter. Babygirl opened the door and gave him the run of the place."

"Sweet Peaches said he was at the house," Granny confirmed. "She needed help while I'm in this prison."

"Trust me. That's not the only thing he's doing. Mama, they were playing house when we got there. And I'm positive, your welfare wasn't part of the deal."

"Bobby, what kind of wild nothin's are you talkin' about?" Granny let out a sigh. "Sit down. Your bouncin' back and forth is wearin' me out."

Cameron heard the chair scrap the floor and vinyl groaned as her father returned to the chair.

"Good," Granny said. "Now, we can talk."

"I can't believe that girl." Frustration oozed from each word. "He's wormed his way back into her life. Here, the Chief and I thought she was back on track."

"What do you want from her, Bobby? Sweet Peaches's life is her own. Her business is goin' good. And the new school is gonna open in September. She'll finish school at the end of the summer. Jayla is a happy three-year-old. I think she's doin' pretty good for herself."

"I want her to leave him alone."

"Bobby, that's not your business."

"Why can't she find somebody better? Somebody who'll treat her right."

"Marek treats her just fine. He pays child support. Babysits when she needs it. They go out every weekend. I'd say he's a good father. Sweet Peaches wants for nothin', and he makes sure Jayla gets everything she needs."

"Hmmpf." He let out a short snort.

"Tell me, Bobby. Is it Marek you dislike so much or any man that comes between you and your Babygirl?"

"I—I just want the best for her," he blustered. "And he ain't it."

"How do you know?" she questioned. "Have you ever taken the time to talk with him? Or really given him a chance?"

"He had his chance. He split after he got Babygirl pregnant. That doesn't make me like him any better," his voice boomed. "It makes me want to hurt him."

"Well, that ain't going to happen," Granny stated. "But I'll say this. There's more than one side to this situation. Until you sit down with Sweet Peaches and find out what happened, you've only got your own opinion. I bet you've never asked her about him. Have you?"

"Once," he admitted grudgingly. "But she told me to mind my own business."

Granny chuckled.

"What's so funny?" he asked.

"You and your daughter are just alike."

"What's that supposed to mean?"

"She keeps things all inside. Just like you."

"Hmmpf," he grunted.

"Mmmm, hmmm. Bobby, you can't keep this up. I know

AS LONG AS THERE IS LOVE

she's your Babygirl. But she's a grown woman with a family of her own. It's time you accepted that."

"But why does it have to be him? I hate the fact that she's back with him," Madaddy burst out. "Damn, I hate it."

"Say what you want. The bottom line is you're jealous."

"I—I—I," he stammered. "No, I'm not."

"Robert Cameron Butler." Granny's voice rose. "Yes, you are. Pure and simple. You want her to be your baby forever. You hate any man that comes between you two."

"No. Maybe. I don't know," Madaddy admitted in a barely audible voice. He sounded like a defiant child. "I want her to be happy. But not with him."

Cameron felt a sense of astonishment at his admission. Madaddy never admitted to any mistake.

"I repeat. It's not your business. Your daughter's grown. Accept it."

"I know," he answered. "But she's still my Babygirl."

"Always will be," Granny agreed. "But you've got to let her go. It's time."

"When she was little, she'd listen to me. Hell, I can remember watching cartoons on Saturday mornings with her," he said gently. "My Babygirl. I never wanted her to grow up."

Cameron's heart softened as she relived those memories. Madaddy and her in front of the television with bowls of Captain Crunch cereal, while the Road Runner and Bugs Bunny battled on the screen. The family room was all theirs as the rest of the family slept late. God, it was one of her precious moments that never faded.

"Bobby, Sweet Peaches will always be your little girl. Just like you'll always be my baby boy. But she's twenty-six-years-old. It's time for you to let her handle her business. If you force her to choose, you might find yourself on the wrong end."

That's enough. Cameron moved from behind the door. If she listened much longer, they'd start discussing her sex life. Lord knows, Granny offered her opinion on any and all topics.

Plastering a smile on her face, Cameron stepped into the room. "Hi." She wiggled her fingers in Granny's direction.

"Hey, Sweet Peaches." She waved her toward the bed. "Your Dad's here."

Her smile slipped a tad, but she nodded in her father's direction. "Hey, Daddy."

"Hi, Babygirl."

With anxious steps, Cameron moved toward the bed. She dropped the receipts for Granny's phone and television on the nightstand. All the while, Madaddy's disapproval sliced into her back as she poured orange juice over the ice. But she refused to allow his cop's intimidation methods to rattle her. Instead, she completed her task before facing him.

"Well," Madaddy rose from the chair. "I think I'll get on home and check on the Chief." He stopped next to the bed, leaned over and kissed Granny's cheek.

He turned to Cameron. She held her breath, eagerly anticipating their long established ritual. Since she was a small child, he had always said good-bye with a kiss to her forehead.

The second seemed to go on forever. But that kiss never came. She glanced into her father's face and her heart sank. No encouraging words or kisses were coming from that closed expression. Madaddy spun on his heels, headed toward the door.

Disappointed, she released the air from her lungs and watched him cross the room.

"Mom, I'll be back later," he promised over his shoulder. "Babygirl, I'll see you at the house."

Hurt, Cameron busied herself, straightening the blankets.

" 'Bye, Daddy." The sun's rays floated through the window

AS LONG AS THERE IS LOVE

and touched her face like a heated caress when she sat on the edge of Granny's bed. "Your IV's gone." Cameron stroked Granny's arm.

"Mmmm, hmmm." Granny displayed her arm, free of IV tubing. The only remnant was a Band-Aid in the spot where the IV had sunk into her skin. "They took it out this morning."

"Good!" Cameron smiled. "How's rehab?"

"Comin' along." Her head tilted to one side, eyes narrowed. "You heard us, didn't you?"

Red-faced, Cameron shrugged. " 'Little bit."

"Sweet Peaches, I didn't say anything I wouldn't say to your face."

Head lowered, Cameron muttered, "I know."

"Neither did your father." She laid a hand on Cameron's hand. "He's concerned."

"I know."

"Do you understand me?" Granny squeezed Cameron's hand.

Cameron bit her lip and nodded.

"Mmmm, hmmm." Granny watched her. "What's wrong?"

"Nothing."

"Mmmm, hmmm." Granny sat up straight. "Somethin'." She waited. "Tell your Granny."

"Marek left."

"What do you mean 'left?' " Granny sank into the pillows propped against the headboard. "I thought he was stayin' until I come home."

"He was supposed to," she muttered, "but when Madaddy came, things went crazy." *Boy, was that an understatement.* "And he left."

"What happened?"

"He thinks I was taking Ma and Madaddy's side over

his." She plucked at the lint balls on the blanket. "I have to admit, the first words out of my mouth weren't the best."

"Cameron, he's a man," Granny reminded, wagging a finger at Cameron. "And he has his pride. You'd better remember that. How did you expect him to react?"

She dropped the edge of the blanket and raised her hands in a helpless gesture. "I don't know," Cameron admitted, like a little girl caught talking in class. "I thought he'd understand." Her hands fell to her sides. "What was I supposed to say? Guess what, Daddy? We're living together."

"Honesty might have helped to keep Marek with you."

"You know how Madaddy gets. I didn't want him flying off the handle."

"Who are you trying to convince? Me or yourself?" Granny shook her head. "Mmm. You've hurt that man. Now, how do you plan to fix things?"

"I don't know," Cameron admitted in a slight voice. "Maybe I can talk to him."

"Ain't that nice of you," Granny retorted. "Sweet Peaches, your father didn't cause the problems. He added fuel to the flame, but trouble was there before he walked through the door." Granny sat quiet for a moment. "What else did Marek say?"

Granny wasn't going to like this one. Cameron's voice trembled. "He told me he loves me."

"Good." Approval beamed from Granny's eyes. The hint of a smile touched her strawberry colored lips. Her smile faded as she studied her granddaughter. Her brow formed a straight line over her eyes, than asked, "And what did *you* say?"

"Nothing."

"What?" Shocked, Granny yelped. "Nothing? No wonder the man left!"

"I couldn't say it back. Lord knows, I tried," she cried. "I just couldn't."

"Why not?"

"I don't know. Yes, I do. I'm afraid. He hurt me so bad before," Cameron defended, shoulders slumped. "Deep down, I don't think I'll ever trust him again. Marek wasn't pleased. He said I had a couple of options. Stand with him and prove that I believe in our relationship or we can stick to being parents. After everything we've gone through, how could he even think anything else?"

"He's right." Granny folded her arms across her small bust and shook her head. "How do you expect to have a relationship without trust?"

"Granny," she whined. "How can you say that?"

"Easily. That man loves you and he's never hidden it. But he's no doormat. You better watch yourself. It's past time for him to demand his respect." She unfolded her arms and speared Cameron with a disapproving frown. "If you can't love him, then leave him be."

Tears dotted Cameron's cheeks. Now more than ever, she needed Granny's support, not this cold reprimand.

"Madaddy shocked me when he showed up." Cameron touched Granny's hand, searching the old girl's face for sympathy. "I wanted to keep things together."

"Well, you didn't do a good job," Granny dismissed. "Sweet Peaches, if you love that man, give him his propers."

Cameron's heart sank. It didn't look as if she'd find an ally in this corner.

"I told you before that you can't run away from your problems. You have to face them straight up. It looks as if you're going to have to do somethin' sooner than you expected. It's not fair to treat Marek this way. If you can't love him the way he needs, I don't want you messin' with him. Leave him alone."

Cameron took the criticism without comment.

"Not many people get second chances. You better wake up before yours is gone. If you don't do something pretty quick, you're going to lose him. I'm tired," she dismissed, leaning against the pillows. "Maybe you should get on home and think about what I've said."

Cameron punched the hospital elevator button and waited. Why was her life so screwed up? If she had her way, she'd head for the mountains and leave the whole sorry mess behind.

First, Mom had refused to help. Now Granny shoved criticism down her throat. And it hurt. Big time.

The elevator doors opened, she stepped inside and stabbed the button for the lobby. How was she supposed to fix things if she didn't have any backup?

She loved Marek. There was no denying that. But she still had doubts. It didn't matter what Granny or anyone said, until she knew he was trustworthy, she refused to say the words.

She glanced at her watch. Marek had probably come and gone. Maybe she could catch him when he returned with Jayla. She would force him to sit down with her and discuss how they could repair their relationship, iron out their problems and get on even ground.

If she could keep Madaddy out of the mix long enough to be alone with Marek, she felt confident she could fix things. If she could just get past her father.

Chapter Twenty-six

What now? Cameron wondered, parking her car in the driveway and moaned. All she wanted to do was get home and talk to Marek. From the look of things, she'd missed her mark.

Her father's roar of anger carried through the car's open window. Clipped words swirled through the air, offering everyone within earshot an audio version of their family problems.

Great! She hit the steering wheel with the palm of her hand. Her neighbors were probably enjoying the show.

Oh, Lord. Her heart rate accelerated when she noted Marek's expression. He looked ready to pop. If she didn't stop them, an appearance by the police might be in order.

Cautiously, Cameron approached the pair. Why couldn't she have an ordinary life like everyone else? Instead, she suffered through this twisted existence.

"You're not taking my granddaughter out of this house," Madaddy stated arrogantly.

"You can't stop me. Jayla's my daughter."

"Hmmmpf. Don't bet on getting in here."

"Cameron and I have an agreement," Marek challenged. "I will see my child whenever I choose."

Oh, Lord. The air crackled like a live wire.

"Hmmmpf!" Madaddy rocked back on his heels. Contempt blazed from his eyes. "It amazes me that you can turn your lips up and say those words. You know nothing about being a father."

"You don't know what the hell you're talking about. My advice to you is to stay out of my business. Now, call my daughter," Marek demanded through the screen door. "We have plans."

From the bottom step, Marek's anger entangled Cameron in their conflict. She shook her head. Madaddy's flushed skin and blazing eyes made her suspect that he'd have a stroke at any minute. If he didn't calm down, her next trip to the hospital would be to visit him.

"Making a baby doesn't make you a father," Madaddy ranted. "Where were you when Jayla needed you?"

"Well, this is nice," Cameron stated.

Both men whipped around, facing her. With raised eyebrows, she glanced from one man to the other.

Guiltily, Marek glanced away. Her father scraped a hand over his face, then shoved his hands into the pockets of his jeans.

Cameron nodded at her father, taking an extra moment to glare her disapproval at him. "Daddy." She swung to the younger man. "Marek. While you two are entertaining the neighbors, can either of you tell me where's my baby?"

"The Chief took her shopping."

Her tolerance level dropped a notch. Madaddy was showing his natural butt. Boy, did she want to wipe that smug expression right off his face.

A muscle jerked at Marek's jaw. His pager went off and

he glanced at the illuminated face, then silenced it with a tap of his finger. "Excuse me," he said, pulling his cell phone from its holster.

Hitting Madaddy with another warning glare, Cameron suggested, "Why don't we *all* go inside and close the door? Let's keep some of the family secrets private, hmm?" She tugged on the door handle and when it didn't open, she asked, "Do you mind?"

Cameron strummed her fingers along the thigh of her dress and prayed Madaddy would let them inside. After a moment of silence, he unhooked the latch and moved away. *Thank goodness.*

Marek slipped his cell phone back into its belt holder and followed her inside. For a moment, his scent captivated her, rattled her and made it impossible to think.

Then, the screen door slammed shut and Madaddy began his verbal assault. "Have you lost your mind, girl?"

She faced him. This was one of the ways he used to gain the advantage over an opponent. Today, she refused to buy it. "I'm pretty sure my faculties are working."

Madaddy's eyes narrowed and he thrust a finger in Marek's direction. "We know absolutely nothing about him. How could you let him see Jayla? Let alone take her away from this house without supervision?"

Marek's frame went rigid beside her. "Cameron knows everything she needs to know."

She turned to Madaddy. "Daddy, please ca—"

"Don't 'daddy please' me." His face turned even redder. "What were you thinking?"

"Calm down," she placed a hand on his arm and felt anger radiate from him. "Marek and I have an agreement. My lawyer drew it up."

Madaddy's head shot up. He speared her with a surprised look. "What lawyer?"

"Gregory Hunter, David's college buddy."

"His roommate?" His brows formed a straight line over his eyes. "Why didn't you let your brother do it? Then I'd know that your interests were secure. David would find a way to keep him," his eyes spliced into Marek, "out of our lives."

"I have my own lawyer," Cameron pointed out. "And I do things my way."

"Hmmmpf," he snorted. "I can't protect you if you go off and do things behind my back."

"Daddy, I don't need you to protect me."

"Babygirl, you need my help." Madaddy placed his hands on her shoulders. "You just don't realize it."

Marek's pager went off a second time and Cameron and Madaddy turned to him. Irritation marred his features when he checked the number. "I've got to go. Something's going on at the hospital."

Marek and Madaddy stared at each other like adversaries. "We're not done," her father promised.

Marek's icy glare showed no fear. "Count on it, Mr. Butler," Marek warned, but anything else was cut off when his pager beeped a third time. Glancing at the face of the pager, he hurried toward the door. "Ronnie, I'm sorry. I'll talk to you later. Explain to Jayla what happened and we'll do the zoo next week," he said and shut the door behind him.

The explosive silence that followed Marek's departure was deafening. Madaddy's eyes blazed with hatred.

"I remember what he did to you when you came home from school." The rage in his voice chilled her soul. "He changed you. You weren't my Babygirl anymore."

Okay, it was common knowledge that she had been a basket case when she had gotten home. But couldn't they let it alone?

"That was bound to happen," Cameron said. "But that's all in the past."

"It tore me apart to see you that way," Madaddy confessed, pacing the hallway. "And I thought you would wither away in front of me. We couldn't reach you." His expression hardened as determination glittered from his sad eyes. "I won't give him a chance to finish the job."

"Daddy," she searched her mind for the right words. "That happened a long time ago. Things are different now." She tapped her chest. "I'm different."

His features softened. "Babygirl, I know the Chief and I sheltered you from much of the real world. Maybe too many things. I think that's why you're so naive and gullible."

Gullible! Gullible! How could he say that about her? Madaddy didn't know her at all.

"I'm far from gullible." Cameron fired back. "And," she straightened to her full 5'2" height, "I resent your saying it. Since I left your house have I asked you for anything?"

"No."

"Then how can you toot your lips up to call me gullible? I take care of my child, run a business and provide everything my child needs. Take off the blinders and look at me. I'm an adult. A responsible parent."

"You call bringing that trash back into our lives responsible?"

"That's not *your* business," she stressed. "It's my choice and you have to accept it."

"No, I don't. I have to protect you." Something dangerous sparkled in his eyes. "I'll bet he doesn't care anything about you. He's just here to see what he can get."

Cameron gasped, turning away, fighting back tears. Is that what Madaddy thought of her? That she allowed men to use her? It hurt to think she rated so low on his good sense scale.

She couldn't allow him to get away with this. "Listen to

yourself," she advised. "Do you think I'm an idiot who doesn't know her own mind?"

"No, Babygirl," he patted her arm. "I think you're naïve and can't see the bad guys coming."

"I know what I'm doing. I don't need your help," Cameron pointed an angry finger at him. "What Marek and I choose to do for Jayla is our business. Not yours."

"That's where you're wrong," voice hardening, he dismissed. "Everything that happens to my grandchild and you concerns me."

"Maybe so, but the decisions are mine to make," she answered. "And you owe me an apology."

"Apology," he snorted and crossed his arms over his chest. "Hmmmpf! You just keep waitin', Babygirl."

"Okay. Let me lay the facts out to you. This is my home. You have no control here. If you can't accept that, maybe you should find a hotel." Cameron tapped her chest. "I make the decisions here. Oh yeah, you're going to have to accept Marek as part of Jayla's life. He's not going away," she stated. "Jayla adores him and I won't destroy that relationship."

"I can't accept him." His unrelenting expression frightened her.

She didn't want to lose her father. She loved him, but he left her no choice. It was time to stand tall.

"Daddy, I'm warning you. Don't make me choose between you two. I have to think about what's best for my daughter," she explained, holding his gaze with her own. "I'm not going to push Marek out of our lives to please you."

"There is no choice." Madaddy stepped closer, dwarfing her. "I'm her grandfather and your father."

"And Marek is Jayla's father," she countered, standing

AS LONG AS THERE IS LOVE 237

firm. "My baby needs her father. Just like I needed you when I was growing up. Can't you see that?"

"How can she need someone who's just appeared without warning in her life?"

"At first, I felt that way, too." She felt calmness dissipate her razor sharp anger. "But Jayla told me different. She wanted to have her own father, just like the other kids. She's lost so much. I won't take anything else from her."

"Jayla has me," he declared.

"But you're not her father," she pointed out. "You're her grandfather. Poppy. You've raised your children. Let me raise mine."

Cameron stumbled outside, gasping for air. Her heart pounded against her ribcage and her hand shook as she wrapped it around the pillar for support.

What had she been thinking, talking to Madaddy that way? She'd never been very good at confrontations, and especially not against her parents.

She leaned her head against the pillar and cooled her heated skin. The roar of a ravenous lawnmower mingled with the excited screams of the children down the block. Both faded as she concentrated on her problems and a way out of them.

Things hadn't gone the way she wanted. Things had turned out pretty lousy.

So far, she'd fought with her parents and her grandmother. And what good had it done? After all of this ballyhoo, had she accomplished anything?

Her head buzzed as she tried to think. She needed time to collect her thoughts and decide her next course of action. Once she cooled down, she'd come up with another plan to convince Madaddy that Marek was a good man. This time, she'd find a different route. No more direct confrontation.

The porch swing zigzagged out of control for a second before settling under Cameron's weight. With a slight nudge of her foot, she sent it swaying back and forth. All she needed was a little time to collect herself.

The screen door slammed and Madaddy stepped onto the porch. *There goes my quiet time,* she thought, watching him stride across the porch and sit down on the top step.

Bracing his back against the pillar, Madaddy stretched his long legs across the step, and gazed out at the residential street. He withdrew a cigarette and green plastic lighter from his pocket and stuck the filtered end between his lips. They sat that way for several minutes while he smoked his cigarette.

"Your grandmother suggested we talk," Madaddy injected into the silence. "She said we need to clear the air. No more secrets." He shifted on the step to face her, folding one leg under him. "What do you think?"

What did she think? As usual, Granny knew her stuff.

It was well past time for them to talk. Madaddy needed to hear the truth from her, although she cringed at the thought of baring her soul. Instead, she gave herself precious seconds to sort out her emotions and determine how much of the truth she wanted to reveal.

"I think Ma's going to kill you when she finds out you're smoking again," Cameron replied. "Didn't you quit?"

"Yeah." He winked at her. "Don't tell the Chief. She'll get me for this one."

That was an understatement. Ma had done everything but hold his hand to get him through withdrawal. She'd lose her mind if she knew he'd started this nasty habit again.

Cameron grinned back at him. All of their earlier animosity vanished as they shared this moment.

"Besides, I only smoke when I'm stressed out."

Sobered by his words, her smile evaporated.

"Daddy." She drew in a deep breath. The odor of fresh-cut grass filled her nostrils. "You're wrong about Marek."

"Really?" He examined her with an all-seeing glare. "Tell me more."

She drew her legs up and wrapped her arms around her knees. "He didn't leave me," she answered, watching children playing hopscotch down the street.

Inhaling his cigarette, Madaddy's face remained impassive. Regardless, she planned to press on until she made some headway.

"Cameron, each one of my children is special to me. Junior, the twins and you. From the minute you came into the world, I promised to protect you." He got to his feet and strolled across the porch to stand in front of the swing. "My Babygirl." His fingers stroked her hair.

"On the streets I see so much tragedy. Sometimes it sickens me to think people can do such horrific things to one another." Revulsion made him shudder. She could only imagine what he had seen in that world. He'd always made a point to separate his family from his career as a cop. "Because I know the danger, I've always tried to protect my family from the darker, uglier side of life." Pointing a finger in her direction, he said, "You especially."

"I know." Cameron reached out to catch his hand in hers. "When I was growing up, you worried about everything I did." She swung his hand a little. "Where I went. Who I went out with. Remember Tim? I thought you'd give him a heart attack when he came to see me the first time."

"Nahh," he dismissed, waving away her reference to her first boyfriend. "I didn't do anything to him. He just didn't have any backbone."

"Daddy," Cameron cried, "Tim was only fourteen." She grinned back at her father. "His backbone was still growing."

Madaddy's face turned serious. "Your mother and I disagreed all the time about how much freedom you should have. I wanted you to stay at home and go to Eastern, where I could keep a watchful eye, instead of the University of Michigan. The Chief vetoed that idea. She informed me that it was time for you to leave the nest. So I shut up and off you went to Ann Arbor."

He pointed at his temple and asked, "See these gray hairs? Your freshman year damn near drove me insane. Every time I got into the car to go and check on you, the Chief made me mind my own business." He dropped his hand and looked into the street. "Maybe that's why you got into trouble. I listened to your mother and let you live your own life. I should have followed my own mind."

"I did fine," she reminded. "My grades were good."

Facing her, "Yeah, you did good in school. But I was worried about you." His lips thinned. "I knew eventually some dirty dog would come sniffing after your coattail. And I couldn't stop it from happening. I expected you'd bring home some trash that we'd have to deal with. And you did. But I never thought you'd bring *that* kind of trash home. I could have lived with him if he hadn't left you with that load."

Flinching away from his harsh words, she bit her lip. He'd never been this raw with her. She wasn't sure she wanted him to continue. But proclaiming her adult status meant dealing with unpleasant matters.

"I've already told you that wasn't planned. And he didn't leave me. I left him."

"Whatever." He tossed a resigned hand in the air. "Once we found out about Jayla, I wanted to kill that bastard. String

AS LONG AS THERE IS LOVE 241

him up and shoot off his private parts. But he disappeared. Vanished. And you wouldn't give us a clue."

"I didn't know where he was."

He continued as if she hadn't spoken, "I promised myself that I'd hurt that bastard if he ever showed up again." She heard the bitter edge of hatred in his tone.

"Daddy, I admit I made mistakes." It wasn't her father's fault that her life had turned out the way it had. She didn't want him to carry the blame. "But my mistakes are not your responsibility. I made the choices. I had to pay the consequences."

"Yes, it was, Babygirl. It was my responsibility to protect you. I should have stood my ground. When you came home, I didn't know who you were. We watched you wither away before our eyes." He stroked her cheek. "I never forgave myself for letting you go away to school."

"Daddy, I'd mapped out my future before I left home. Believe me, getting pregnant was *not* on the agenda. I planned to come home and teach while I finished my Masters." She rested her chin on her knee. "Then I was going to do what I'm doing now . . . open my own school. Having Jayla slowed me down, but it didn't stop me."

"Hmmmpf. The Chief said that yesterday." He gave a snort of laughter. "She won't say much, because she thinks you have a right to your life, whether she likes it or not. But I've got to say my piece. I can't let it go."

"Dad, look at me. I've built a life for me and Jayla. It's time for you to accept it."

"And I'm proud of you. What you've accomplished on your own. You think I didn't know how you felt. But I did. I know why you refused to take anything from us."

"Dad, I . . . I . . ."

"That's all right," he muttered, patting her hand. He ran a hand over his face and asked, "Are you sure this is what you want? Have you thought about everything?"

"Yes. I'm sure."

He sighed, shaking his head. "From everything you've told me, his family sounds like they're really stuck up. We're not rich. You work for a living. Those stuck-up people can make life real hard for you."

"I know."

"This may be a new millennium, but people are still the same. They're cruel." He squeezed her hand. "They'll say hurtful things to you and Jayla, then turn their noses up. I don't want that for you."

"I don't want it, either. But I believe when you take the man, you take everything that comes with him."

"There's a rough road ahead. Think very carefully because you don't have to do this."

She knew all of these things. Had thought endlessly about where their relationship was headed. And she had a lot of fear and reservations. Each of Madaddy's points made her fears increase. But she had to stand firm and give their relationship everything she had.

"Daddy, you're right. It's not going to be easy and it scares me. Not just for me, but for Jayla," she admitted. "But I want my life to be with Marek."

He leaned closer and said, "Let me ask you a question. What if it doesn't work? How are you going to feel after putting years of your life into a marriage that falls apart?"

"That can happen in any marriage." Cameron snorted. "What makes you think I haven't thought of that?" She stared at the planks in the floor, than whispered, "I'm scared. I'm scared for Jayla. I'm scared for me. And I don't want to be hurt again." Her voice shook and she felt her insides go haywire. "But as long as I have Marek standing with me, we can make things work."

Oh my God! Her hand flew to her mouth. *That's what Marek was trying to make me understand yesterday. We have to stand together. How could I have been so stupid? I've got to talk to him. Apologize.*

"Well, if what I've said doesn't make you think, there's not much more I can say. But I have one more question. What happened?" he asked. "I got to know why he didn't help you."

She lifted her chin, meeting his eyes with a frosty gaze. "I can't tell you that."

"That won't do this time." His face hardened. "If you want me to play nice with him, then give me a reason."

"I'll tell you this much, we were both duped by someone we trusted. She manipulated us both and caused all types of trouble," she confessed. "But that's all been settled now and we're working things out."

"He didn't leave you once you got pregnant?" Madaddy's skeptical voice persisted.

"No." She shook her head. "I know I should have talked to you guys. But I was so crushed, I couldn't."

He studied her. After a moment, he slipped into the empty place beside her.

"I can't make you tell me the details. So, I leave that alone." He linked his fingers with hers. "Count on this, I'm your father and I will always love and try to protect you. You and Jayla."

"Daddy, Jayla has a father. And like you, he'll protect her. I don't expect you to stop being my dad. But I'm asking you to give Marek the chance to be a father to his daughter." She placed her hand against her heart. "I was wrong to keep them apart."

"You're grown." Madaddy smiled when he noted the disbelief on her face. "Yes, I do know it. I just hate to admit it. But I want you to know that as long as I'm alive, I will be here for you. All you have to do is tell me what you need and I'll do my best to get it."

"I need you to be fair to Marek. Give him a chance."

Sighing, "I'll *try*," Madaddy rolled his eyes to the heavens, "to be civil when I see him. But I'm warning you now, don't push him in my face too much or too soon. Give me some breathing room, than maybe I'll adjust."

She grinned. "For you, that's a lot. I'll take it."

"I don't want to be his friend." His scowled. "I'll try to be reasonable for your sake. That's all I can guarantee. I need some time to put everything together. If you don't give me my space, I can't say what might come out of my mouth."

"That's for sure."

"Hey," he stuck a finger in her face, "watch it, young lady. I'm still your father."

"Thank you," she leaned close and kissed his cheek. "I know this isn't easy for you."

"Let's get one thing straight. I'm never going to stop caring about what happens to you and wanting the best for you. That's just not going to happen. But I do understand that you have to live your own life. It'll just kill me to see you wasting your time on him. I don't see any way to convince you, so I'll leave it alone."

She heard a "but" coming and waited for him to throw a boot into the soup pot.

"Let's make an agreement. I'm not promising that I won't say my piece when I think it's necessary, *but* I'll try to keep my comments to a minimum. Deal?" He held out his hand to her.

Cameron wrapped her arms around his neck and hugged him. "Deal."

Chapter Twenty-seven

Cameron peeled Marek's address from the scraps of paper in her pocket and checked the black numbers on the door against the address in her hand.

"This is the place," she declared and replaced her nervous expression with a serene, calm mask. Parking in front of Marek's condo, she rubbed her sweaty palms along the hip of her floral, sleeveless dress, then climbed from the car.

From the walkway she surveyed Marek's condo. Although he'd invited her to visit several times, she had always declined. Until today she had always felt reluctant to invade his personal space.

The two-story Georgian-styled structure stood among a half-dozen attached units. White wood trim framed the red brick dwelling. A welcome wreath hung from the deep-green door. She prayed Marek would be as welcoming.

Climbing the concrete stairs, Cameron admired the spray of multi-colored flowers and green potted plants that lined the railings of the miniature porch, filling the air with the sweet fragrance of azaleas.

Tense, she rang the doorbell, then took a step away from the door, pressing a nervous hand over her belly to calm the dancing creepy crawlers. She wasn't sure what she'd do if he refused to let her in.

The door swung open and Marek stood on the threshold wrapped in a black toweling robe. An identical piece of fabric draped his shoulders and caught the droplets of water dangling from his wet hair.

Oh, my! Her mouth went dry as her eyes roamed over the attractive picture he presented. Pleasure surged through her at the sight of his broad, bare chest visible in the *v* of his robe. Marek looked so wonderful, he took her breath away.

All traces of welcome vanished as his handsome face hardened. His nose twitched as if he'd smelled something foul.

An enormous lump swelled in her throat as she tried to smile. *Great!* Things were getting off to a terrific start. Stiff, she mumbled, "Hi."

Marek stuck his head out the door and checked the street. Confused, she stood on the porch and watched him. What in the heck was he looking for? He stepped aside and waved his hand in the general vicinity of what she suspected led to the living room. Once inside, the coolness of the house showered her as she followed a pair of male voices into the living room.

With undisguised interest, Cameron checked out his place. The hallway opened into a dark-beamed, cathedral-ceiling living room.

The front door shut and she spun around in time to see Marek baring down on her. Suspicion blazed from his eyes, making her mouth go dry.

"Where's your father?" Marek asked in a frosty tone,

yanking the towel from his shoulders and running it over his hair.

She stared back stupidly. Of all the things she expected him to say that was the absolute last.

"Madaddy's at home."

"Did you ask him if you could come here?" he taunted, slinging the towel around his shoulders. "I didn't think he'd let you out of the house without his permission."

Cameron cringed. *Okay, so that's how he wanted to play things.* "I don't need his permission," she answered. "I'm grown and I make my own decisions."

"Really?" Marek's mouth quirked, but his eyes glittered coldly back at her. "What's so important that you ran over here without daddy's permission?"

His dig sent her skittish heart into a gallop. But she refused to let him see it. They had things to discuss and she planned to stay focused. "I wanted to talk with you."

Chilled, she ran her hand over her arms. It looked as if Marek intended to make this as difficult as possible. She'd eat humble pie if it made things better between them. After she had made her explanations, the ball was back in Marek's court. Should he choose to kick her to the curb then she'd switch to Plan B. As soon as she figured out Plan B.

From somewhere within the house Marek's pager went off. "Give me a minute." He picked up the remote, tapped a button and the Detroit Tigers disappeared from the television screen. The gadget landed on top of an open copy of *The New England Journal of Medicine* as he left the room.

Perspiration beaded on her neck as she prowled the living room, twisting her nerves to the breaking point. *You can do this,* she coaxed herself, taking a good look around the place.

An oriental rug of cream splashed with blue and tan lay under the coffee brown, leather modular unit dominating the room. A large wooden curio sat near the sliding door that led to the patio.

Marek returned to the doorway and leaned against the doorframe. His cold glare sent chills nipping at her bare arm.

"Talk," he ordered in a silky purr.

"I came here to apologize," she explained, rubbing the goosebumps from her arms.

That got his attention. Marek's head shot up and he stared back at her as if she'd just declared war on the United States. There was silence for a moment, then he asked, "What brought that about?"

Cameron groped for the right words. "You hit it on the head." She met his glare of disbelief with a confident gaze of her own. "You're right. I am daddy's girl. Measuring up to his expectations has always, always, been important to me." She paced around the room. "Coupled with the fact that in our family, Madaddy ruled. Period." A little smile came and went. "End of discussion. My brothers and I have all been conditioned to accept that."

He folded his arms across his chest and leaned against the doorframe. "That doesn't mean he's always right."

"I never said it did. I'm stating how my family operated. That's all."

"Haven't you figured out that you can't live your life for your father?"

"Be that as it may, sometimes life can beat you up a bit and it's easier to take a back seat and leave the driving to someone else."

Marek stepped further into the room. "And sometimes you have to pull yourself out of those situations, once you recognize them."

"True. I've done that in the past. When my parents found out I was pregnant, Madaddy's ever-present disapproval forced me to leave. I refused to raise my baby in that environment. That's when I moved to Holland. But that's only part of it. And although I have my own life, whenever my parents come to visit, I revert to their little girl all over again. It doesn't matter that I have a child of my own and I run a business." She flapped her arms helplessly. "I'm their Babygirl."

Marek looked down his straight aristocratic nose at her. His handsome face was expressionless. Another shiver tore through her. He appeared so remote, she wondered if her admission had touched him.

"I've been the Babygirl of my family since day one. I've never been able to break that image. You have no idea how difficult it is to hold your own against three older brothers and a dominating father. Over the years, I've learned to choose my battles with extreme care." Her voice shook. "Everyone thinks they know what's best for you. Sometimes it's easier to keep the peace by giving in." She shrugged. "I'm not proud of it, but I've done it."

Cameron's shaky fingers smoothed her hair into place. "That's why things got so out of hand yesterday. I just wanted to stop the bickering before you got hurt." She took a tiny, tentative step closer and whispered, "There's no other excuse. Despite my best efforts, you still got hurt, and for that, I'm deeply sorry."

His expression remained unchanged.

Several feet still separated them. The crisp, clean scent of him wrapped around her like tentacles, drawing her closer. "While I've sat on the fence accepting everything and giving nothing, you completely committed yourself to Jayla and me. I'm not a user, at least that's not how I see myself," her voice dropped a persuasive octave. "I want you to see that there's much more to me and forgive me."

Pleading brown eyes held his. "Cameron, it's hard to believe that you've allowed this situation to continue after leaving your parents' home." Lips pursed, his eyes swept over her. "When are you going to cut that cord and live your own life?"

"Now."

His dry chuckle of disbelief grated against her already taut nerves. "Oh, yeah."

"I know you don't believe me. But I can show you."

"How?"

Cameron's hand ran over her face. "Granny's getting out of the hospital Thursday."

"Good!" A genuine spark of pleasure spread across his face. "I'm glad to hear it."

"Me too," Cameron confessed. "We're going to have a welcome home thing at the house. Mom, Madaddy, Jayla," she gathered her courage, "and you."

He stared at her in amazement. "Are you kidding?"

"No."

"What do you expect to achieve beyond pissing off everyone?"

"I expect them to understand that you are part of my life and family," she insisted softly.

"And if they can't?"

"That's their problem," she shrugged. "I stand with you. Besides, you're responsible for getting Granny to the hospital in the first place. You deserve to celebrate with her, with us," she added. "And I want you there."

"What about your father?"

"What about him?" She stood her ground and maintained steady, unfaltering eye contact. "This has nothing to do with my father. This is about us."

"That sounds incredible on paper," he muttered and shoved his hands inside the pockets of his robe. "But it's time to come back to earth. How do you think he'll react?"

She grinned as a mental image of her father popped into her head. "Like he always does. He'll rant and rave and lose his mind. But I'm not going to let it get to me," she promised. Marek's warmth beckoned her and she moved within a hairsbreadth of him. "You, me and Jayla are a family. We're going to stay that way until *we* change the rules."

"We've talked about everything but the most important thing. We've fought this battle far too long and I'm tired of pussyfooting around what I need to know," Marek held her gaze. "I'm going to ask you straight out. Do you love me?"

Her legs turned to noodles. Time for the truth. She moistened her lips with the tip of her tongue and met the full force of his consuming gaze. "Yes."

"Then say the words," he demanded. "I need to hear them."

"I love you," Cameron whispered without hesitation, anxious to please him. Afraid of rejection, she reached out timidly and stroked his smooth cheek with her fingers. Her eyes drifted shut as she enjoyed the feel of his warm skin against her palm. It felt so good.

Marek held her hand against his cheek and kissed her palm. "Thank you." He pulled her close and feathered tender kisses over her mouth. His tongue slipped between her lips, deepening the kiss. It felt like heaven to have him close, to be in his arms again.

Marek swept her up, laid her on the carpet and followed her down. She felt the accelerated beat of his heart against her breast and reveled in it.

"I love you forever," he promised in his velvety voice that sent shivers dancing along her spine. "I love you."

Later, Cameron leaned over Marek and asked, "I see you brought another box. What made you do that? I've never been here. I've never even mentioned coming to your house."

Marek gave her a wicked little smile, "Are you kidding? This was my fantasy. I had to be prepared."

"Well, I hope it was worth the wait."

"Yes." He answered in a husky voice. "Yes, it was. You've always been worth the wait."

A little awed by his statement, she muttered, "Thank you."

"You're welcome." Marek framed Cameron's face between his hands and asked, "Did you mean it?" There was a touch of eagerness in his voice that he failed to hide.

"Mean what?" Cameron queried, outlining his sensual lips with the tip of her tongue. He tasted warm and seductive.

"About the party?" His hand smoothed over her sensitive back and down to caress the round curve of her rear end.

"Yes. You're invited. Without you, there wouldn't be a celebration."

Thursday should prove to be an eventful day. Especially once Marek arrived. She hoped that Madaddy kept his word about getting along with Marek.

The shrill of the telephone interrupted them. Groaning, Marek rolled Cameron onto her back and got to his feet. He winked back at her, then strolled along the hallway into the kitchen. Flipping onto her stomach, she admired the glorious sight of his tight butt as he moved down the hall with sleek animal grace. A shiver of delight surged through her as she watched Marek. Once more, her body flushed with desire.

She rose from the floor and stretched. Whining, she moved gingerly about, acknowledging the aches and pains that went hand in hand with making love on the floor. A hardwood floor.

Finally, she felt some level of security in their relationship. Maybe now they could put the past behind them.

Chilled, she ran her hands up and down her arms, searching around the room for Marek's black robe. Spotting it on the floor next to the curio, she retrieved it. *Now, how did that end up way over there?* A mischievous little smile formed on her lips, as she shoved her arms into the robe.

AS LONG AS THERE IS LOVE 253

The curio's interior light drew her. Curious, she peeped inside and found a couple of dozen photographs.

Jayla's smile beamed back at her as she sat, jumped and entertained her Daddy. Their afternoon at the zoo and trip to Six Flags were among many photographic memories.

Her gaze touched photograph after photograph until she reached one particular shot. Stunned, she opened the curio door and removed the print. Tears burned her eyes and blurred her vision.

They stood in her small apartment, wrapped in an embrace. She in her cap and gown and he in his lab coat stared lovingly into each other's eyes. Pain shot through her when she thought about what had followed a few days later. Turning away, she searched the room for Marek.

He'd kept their picture all these years. Why?

Oblivious to his nudity, Marek lounged in the doorway and watched her while sipping on a can of Pepsi. She eyed the can in his hand and lifted an eyebrow.

"Better than a cigarette." He tipped the can in her direction. She took it and drained the last of the sugary drink, then placed the empty can on the end table.

"I love that picture," Marek slipped his arms around her waist and dragged her against his warm, semi-aroused flesh. The strong odor of sex clung to his skin. "It always reminds me of how carefree and in love we were back then." He removed the photo from her fingers and placed it on the table next to the empty can. "I want that again. I've missed it and you."

How had he read her feelings with such little effort? She wanted the same thing so badly it scared her to hope they could obtain that kind of happiness once more. On edge, she waited for him to continue.

Turning her to face him, he said, "We screwed up big time. I lost my daughter and you for almost four years," Marek whispered between kisses. "I'm never going through that again. Right here and now, we're going to agree to talk things out. And if there's something we can't agree on, we're going to agree to disagree."

Cameron laid her head against his chest and listened to the steady beat of his heart. It offered comfort and hope.

"You won't get an argument from me," she said. "I want us together from now on."

"Good." Marek drew her close and covered her lips with his.

Chapter Twenty-eight

Preparations for Granny's homecoming were in full bloom as Cameron hurried around the kitchen. The old girl had worked hard to get released from the hospital and Cameron wanted to celebrate her accomplishment.

A stainless steel colander filled with freshly cleaned shrimp sat in the sink, ready for Cameron's special stir-fry. The unmistakable aroma of fresh chopped scallions and red onions filled the kitchen.

"Mummie," Jayla burst into the kitchen, ran up to her mother and tugged on the leg of Cameron's black shorts. "Poppy's here!" The little girl trumpeted, dancing around the tile floor. "Granny's home!"

"Good!" Cameron removed a floral decorated cake from its white box. Happiness bubbled up inside her.

"Honeybunny, wait!" She turned toward the countertop. "Mummie has to put the cake down."

Jayla's animated features boosted Cameron's already jubilant spirit. Her emotions pretty much mirrored her baby's.

She wanted to join Jayla in a jig around the room. But first things first. They needed to help Granny out of the car, into the house and get this party into full swing.

"Come on, Honeybunny," Cameron slid the cake onto the counter and wiggled her fingers at Jayla. "Let's go help Granny."

She needed one final check of everything; Cameron dug into the pocket of her shorts and scanned the bits of paper. Strip after strip was returned to her pocket until she found her list.

Banner? They stopped in the hallway to admire the welcome home banner hanging from the ceiling. Check. Cake? Check. And stir-fry? Check.

Everything was ready. Time to party.

Jayla ran ahead and out the door. Through the screen, Cameron watched her daughter prance around. Coming up beside Jayla, she wrapped her arm loosely around her baby's shoulders; anticipation soared the moment the car pulled into the drive.

Madaddy slipped from behind the wheel of his shiny gray Impala and rushed around the hood to the passenger door. Mom climbed from the back seat and waited as he unlocked the passenger door.

It swung open; an aluminum three-prong cane hit the ground and Granny shooed away Madaddy's outstretched hand. Awkwardly, she scooted from the front seat, stood and swayed on her feet.

A wealth of emotions hit Cameron. *Granny's home!* Cameron breathed a sigh of relief. *Finally, my best friend is home!*

Granny turned toward the house. Madaddy, Mom, even Jayla faded from her consciousness.

A brilliant smile of appreciation spread across Granny's face once her gaze locked with Cameron's. "Thank you," she mouthed.

Cameron grinned back at her. "You're welcome."

"Mummie," Jayla patted her mother's leg. "Can I go to the car?" She asked. Through all of the excitement, she had remembered the rule against playing in the driveway.

Cameron nodded, ruffling Jayla's soft curls.

Jayla scurried down the stairs and across the lawn. Her baby moved so quickly, her little feet seemed to glide across the lawn. Cameron trailed behind her at a more dignified pace.

"Granny!" Jayla threw her arms around Granny's legs.

"Hey, Babe," Granny greeted and planted a kiss on Jayla's forehead.

Cameron moved across the lawn and paused several feet from the small group as the old girl released Jayla. Cameron took a step closer and somehow found herself wrapped within Granny's embrace. Tears sprang to her eyes and ran down her cheeks. They hugged and swayed together.

"Welcome home." She kissed Granny's cheek and hugged her as if she'd never let her go. "Welcome home," Cameron whispered. "I've missed you. Welcome home." Arms wrapped around each other, they rocked together for a minute that lasted forever. Slowly, reluctantly, they released each other when Marek's black SUV roared into the driveway.

Long, blue-jean clad legs climbed from his SUV followed by a white short sleeve T-shirt. Dark aviator sunglasses hid his eyes from the small group.

"Daddy!" Jayla skirted the group, hurried toward her father and launched herself at him. He caught her and swung her in a circle.

"Hey, Pumpkin." He ruffled her hair. "Give Daddy some sugar."

She wrapped her arms around his neck and gave him a loud, juicy smack on the cheek. Marek settled Jayla on his hip and approached Granny.

Silence hovered over the little group.

"Welcome home, Alice." Marek smiled at Granny, then nodded hello at each member of the Butler clan.

"Hi, Marek." Granny opened her arms and he walked into her embrace. She folded him within her huge bear hug. "Thanks for everything."

"Don't do this to us again." Releasing her, Marek strummed a finger at the old girl. "My heart can't take it."

Tears dotted Cameron's cheeks. She brushed them away with the back of her head.

Madaddy puffed up and started toward Marek. Her mother detained him with a touch of her hand and shake of her head. If Madaddy thought this was bad, boy, did he have a surprise coming. Things were going to get hotter.

Cameron strolled to Marek's side and slipped her arm around his waist. He drew her close and kissed her lips as his large fingers danced over her bare arm. As always, his nearness excited her.

They laced their fingers and turned to her parents, presenting a united family.

Smiling sweetly, Cameron said. "I hope you don't mind." A note of challenge crept into her words. "Marek played such an instrumental role in getting Granny to the hospital," she shrugged. "I just felt he should be here."

Braced for fireworks, Cameron held her breath. Oh, Lord. Her spirits plummeted at the peeved expression on her parents' face.

"More the merrier," Granny said, moving with slow deliberation across the lawn. "Let's get in the house."

Take your time, Cameron cautioned silently. *Don't rush.* Cameron rubbed sweaty palms along the legs of her shorts. Help her make the stairs, please, God.

The old girl took the first step and paused. Madaddy

hovered behind his mother, dogging her every step. His hands fluttered around her as she scaled the steps one by one. Perspiration beaded her forehead. Granny's breathing accelerated and she rubbed a couple of fingers across her forehead. At the slightest hint of a problem, his outstretched arms were posed to steady her.

Madaddy grabbed Granny's elbow firmly and steered her up the stairs. She smacked his hand away.

"I can do this," Granny stated.

Cameron wiped the grin from her face before her father saw her. Madaddy may rule their home in Ypsilanti. But in Holland, Granny was the Queen.

By the time the old girl made the top step, perspiration trickled down her face and neck. "Wow." Gasping for air, she dropped into a wooden porch chairs. "I need a minute." She fanned her face with a shaky hand.

Cameron touched the old girl's hand. "How about a glass of water?"

"Yeah," she panted, "thanks."

Marek bounced up the steps and squatted down next to her chair. Cameron noticed how his clinical eye swept over Granny. He smiled at the older woman and sandwiched her hand between both of his.

"You know, Alice," he began. "You're one of my favorite ladies. It would be my pleasure to escort you into the living room."

Chest heaving, Granny studied Marek for a minute. Then she gave a quick nod of consent.

"I need a minute to regroup," Granny muttered. "How about you?"

He sat down next to her and waited. "I've got plenty of time."

Cameron hurried into the house, down the hall to the

kitchen and opened the cupboard for a glass. She turned toward the refrigerator and found her mother in the doorway.

"Oh!" Cameron tightened her fingers around the glass. "I didn't hear you."

Brows arched and lips set in a disapproving line, Mom stepped into the room. "What game are you playing at?"

"What do you mean?" she replied innocently.

"Don't play coy with me," Mom's voice rose. "Why did you invite him here?"

"Because he has a right to be here. He's part of my family and he helped when Granny took sick."

"Young lady," Mom stepped further into the room. "Do you have any idea how much you've upset your father?"

"I'm sorry," Cameron admitted honestly. "But it's time he accepted how things are."

Mom's eyes narrowed and she warned, "This is your father you're taking about."

Cameron snorted. How could she ever forget? "Yes, it is." She opened the freezer door and dropped ice cubes into the glass. "But, this is my home, too, Ma. I pay bills here and my daughter and I live here. It's my right to invite whoever I please."

"We don't want him here."

"Ma, I'm asking you to give Marek a chance." Cameron put the glass on the counter and faced her mother. "If not for my sake, then for Jayla's. She loves her father."

"Mmm-mmm," Mom dismissed with a wave of her hand. "I'm not sure I can do. There's too much unpleasantness between us."

Cameron shook her head. This wasn't the conversation she wanted to have. At least, not right now. "Please, Ma," she persisted, "it's important to me."

"Why should we?" Mom challenged. "That man has been a pain since you brought him home the first time."

"I see." Disappointment sank its teeth into Cameron's

heart. "Thanks for your understanding." She turned on the tap and let the cold water run. "But he's here to stay."

"Just like the last time, hmmm?"

"No." Cameron faced her mother. "Very different from the last time."

"Are you two planning to make this legal?"

"We haven't discussed it."

Smirking, Mom folded her arms across her chest. "Well, young lady, I would say things really aren't different. The only change is you have a child who might get caught in the middle of your mistakes. Are you willing to take that risk?"

Cameron felt anger bubble to the surface. Her lips tightened a fraction. "It's Jayla's happiness that I'm concerned with."

"This big display of togetherness is only a small part of things," Mom paused, than asked. "What are you really trying to tell me?"

"I don't want to have to make a choice," Cameron answered. "Don't force me."

"Oh," Mom drew herself up to her full height. "There's no choice. Your family should always come first."

"Ma, I mean it," her voice rose a bit. "Don't do this. I'm not giving up Marek." She stuck the glass under the running tap and filled the glass. "You guys better figure out a way to live together, because I'm not giving up Marek or you."

Headed toward the door, Cameron faced her mother. Eyes narrowed, Mom hit her with that glare she used to reduce her and her brothers to five-year-olds. Today, it wasn't happening.

Heart pounding, Cameron stood in front of her mother. "Excuse me," she waited. After a minutes that seemed like days, Ma moved aside.

Cameron ran a shaky hand through her hair. Jesus! She

knew things would be difficult. Boy, this was hard. She hadn't expected things to be this difficult.

By the time she made it to the hallway, Marek and Granny were just stepping through the front door. The pair labored down the hall and into the living room. Cameron followed. With a deep sigh of relief, Granny sank into her chair as Marek continued to examine her with that clinical eye.

Granny drank thirstily from the glass. She handed the glass back to Cameron and requested a refill.

In the kitchen, Cameron switched off the oven and removed the wingdings, adding the appetizer to the silver serving tray. Granny's homecoming hadn't hit the proper note, but they still had time to make things work.

Forget all the fanfare, the real thrill of the day came when Granny stepped from the car. She was home!

A handful of napkins found their place on the tray. Cameron tried to put a name to the emotions she felt when Madaddy had pulled into the drive. One word couldn't describe it. Elation, happiness and anticipation filled her while she waited for Granny to make her appearance.

Rummaging through the cupboard for condiments, she considered her parents' reaction to Marek's arrival. That hadn't gone very well. She really hoped seeing Jayla and Marek together would make her parents consider their granddaughter's needs.

Her family was very important to her and so was Marek. She hadn't made an idle threat when she had told them to find a way to get along. Somewhere along the line, her parents would have to come to terms with her relationship with Marek.

Until she came up with a new plan, she needed to keep Marek and Madaddy separated. And that was going to be difficult with the party going on. Lord knew what would happen if they were left to their own devices. She lifted the tray and started for the door.

Granny's party could still be a success. All they had to do was get along for a few hours, enjoy the food and drink the tea.

Chapter Twenty-nine

Groaning, Cameron hesitated in the doorway with the tray in her hands. Tension hovered overhead like stale cigarette smoke. Her hand shook and the dishes rattled when she glanced at Madaddy's expression. Oh, Lord. If this little party made it through the afternoon without bloodshed, she'd declare the day a major success.

"Honey—" Jayla hopped off her daddy's knee and raced across the room, yelling—"I'll help!" She tugged on the leg of Cameron's shorts with eager hands. "Sometimes Daddy lets me help him."

"Wait," Cameron warned. "Let Mummie set this on the table." She lifted the tray high above her baby's head. "Stop, Honeybunny!" she cried, swaying as Jayla raced around her.

"No, baby, stop!" Cameron shooed Jayla away with a tilt of her head "Don't!"

Cameron took a step forward; Jayla tripped over her feet, slammed against Cameron's leg and knocked her off-balance.

AS LONG AS THERE IS LOVE 265

"NO!" Cameron groped for the teapot, fighting with every ounce of strength to untangle herself. The hot tea would scald Jayla.

Fear knotted Cameron's insides and she gasped. "Baby move," she pleaded as the teapot slid off the edge of the tray.

Without warning, Marek was beside her. He plucked their daughter from harm's way while wrapping the other arm around Cameron's waist, lifting her away from the spraying liquid. The tray crashed to the floor and tea flowed away from the trio, filling the room with the aroma of apple cinnamon.

Her parents surrounded them. Madaddy snatched Jayla from Marek's arms; Mom ran a light hand over Jayla while her father held her high for a thorough inspection. Satisfied that Jayla was okay, Madaddy turned, running a critical eye over Cameron. "Babygirl, you okay?" he asked.

"I'm okay."

Granny leaned forward in her chair, trying to see the goings-on. "Everybody all right?" Her worried tone added another level of panic to the pandemonium.

"Everybody's okay, Mama," Madaddy assured. "Jayla had a little accident."

Cameron slid along the length of Marek until her feet touched the ground. "Thank you," she muttered.

"You're welcome."

"It's okay, sweetiepie," Madaddy soothed. "It wasn't your fault. It was just an accident."

"Excuse me," Marek appeared and extracted Jayla from Madaddy's arms. Oblivious to Madaddy's red-faced expression, Marek set Jayla on her feet and stooped down in front of her.

"Things," Marek began, "are not okay. Do you realize you could have been hurt?" He spoke in a soft, yet stern voice. "Your mother told you to wait, but you didn't listen."

"Sorry." Jayla's bottom lip quivered and she looked at the floor. "I made a mistake. Everybody makes mistakes."

"Yes, they do." With a finger under her chin, he tilted Jayla's head to meet his gaze. "But this was a mistake that could have been avoided."

Cameron's heart bled for them both. Generally, Marek shied away from disciplining their daughter. Instead, he left it to Cameron's discretion. As much as she'd like to step in on Jayla's behalf, she couldn't this time. Jayla needed to understand the danger her eagerness had caused. This situation could have ended very differently.

"You have to think," Marek pointed at her head, "before you act. When your mother talks to you, listen," he stated. A slight tremor entered his voice. "Pumpkin, I don't want to see you hurt. Do you understand me?"

Jayla nodded, then burst into tears. Marek's eyes softened as he drew Jayla into his arms.

"Daddy's sorry he had to do this. But I love you and want to keep you safe." Ruffling her hair, he continued, "I know you wanted to help Mummie, but you have to be careful. Listen to us when we tell you to stop." He pulled away and brushed her tears away with a finger. "Okay?"

Jayla nodded, "Okay." An almost inaudible, "I'm sorry."

"I know, Pumpkin." He hugged her close.

Tears made it impossible for Cameron to see. But she heard her father loud and clear.

"Hmmmpf!" Madaddy snorted. His contemptuous tone mocked Marek. "Now he acts like a father."

Everyone halted for a beat. The soft hum of the central air screamed in the quiet of the room. All eyes remained focused on Marek.

Oh, Lord. Cameron's hands clenched at her sides.

"Robert," Mom warned, gripping Madaddy's upper arm.

"This isn't our business." She led him toward the sofa. "Come on. Come on."

Cameron turned to Marek and found his eyes spiked with anger while red heat colored his cheeks. Her stomach muscles tightened.

Marek headed across the room toward her parents. Fear swept through her. *No!* She raced after him and grabbed his arm. The look of implacable determination on his face made her falter, but just for a moment.

Mouthing the words, "Please, for Granny," Cameron ran a soothing hand up and down his arm.

His eyes drifted shut and she heard the distinct sound of coins. Marek ran a shaky hand through his hair. Marek opened his eyes and returned to the doorway, dropped to one knee and began to collect the pieces of china from the floor.

"Why don't you like my daddy?"

Cameron whipped around. Out of the mouths of babes! That old cliché swirled around in Cameron's head as hysterical laughter bubbled up inside her. Jayla stood in front of Mom and Madaddy, like a teacher reprimanding unruly children. Her small hands were planted on her hips, as she demanded an explanation.

"Well, ahh, ahh," Madaddy sputtered, squirming under the tiny tot's interrogation. "I, I don't . . ."

"Sweetiepie," Mom smoothed a lock of her hair into place. "Poppy wasn't talking about your father."

Jayla's head tilted. A puzzled expression seized her sweet face. "Who?"

"Just someone we know," Mom dismissed the whole issue. "Someone from home."

Cameron rushed to Jayla's side, placed her hands on her daughter's shoulders and pivoted her away from her parents. "Come on, Honeybunny. Help Mummie clean up the mess on the floor."

"Mummie," Jayla said, raising confused eyes to Cameron, "why are Grandma and Poppy mean to my daddy?"

"They're not mean, Honeybunny." Cameron shot her parents a "see-what-you-started" glare. "They just have a lot on their minds, that's all."

"Then why does Poppy look like that?"

"Like what?"

Her little fingers wiggled near her cheeks and a snarl transformed her features into a scowl. "Poppy's face turned all different colors and it squashed up."

Cameron bit the inside of her jaw, fighting the urge to laugh. "Sometimes he gets excited."

She steered Jayla away from her parents. Marek's normally pleasant features were rock-hard and his eyes glittered with suppressed rage as he moved past them. A black chill enveloped her when she realized his destination.

"Marek?" Cameron whispered, hoping to draw his attention.

"Give me a minute." He continued across the room and stopped in front of Madaddy. Legs braced apart and fingers linked behind his back, he said, "Mr. Butler, it's time we talked."

Tension swirled around them like a windstorm, lifting higher with each pass it made around the room. Oh, Lord.

Her father rose from the sofa. He drew within inches of Marek, bared his teeth in a snarl and jabbed a finger at the door. "Let's go."

Making one final attempt to defuse the situation, Cameron called, "Ma?"

"I'm not getting in this." Mom shook her head and waved them away. "Not my business."

"Bobby," Granny called. "What kind of wild nothin's are you up to?"

"This doesn't concern you," Madaddy answered, continuing to the door. "We'll be back in a minute."

Madaddy marched from the room with Marek on his heels. Cameron trotted behind them. At the door Marek halted, resting his hands on her shoulders. He smiled down into her face, kissed her forehead then followed Madaddy out the front door.

Rushing across the room, she peeped out the window. The pair stood like adversaries on the porch. Marek's rigid stance and Madaddy's red face and wild hand gestures pointed to a charged discussion.

"Mummie," Jayla called. "Help!"

Reluctantly, Cameron moved away from the window and found Jayla in the center of the spilled tea, wiping at the mess with a saturated paper napkin.

"I tried to fix it." She showed Cameron the napkin.

Caressing Jayla's cheek, Cameron dropped to her knees. "Thank you, Honeybunny. Let me help you." She wrapped the soggy napkin in a clean napkin. "Hold the tray for me."

All the while she cleared up the mess her thoughts drifted back to the porch where the two most important men in her life stood. What were they saying?

That hard expression on Marek's face made chills run down her spine. If she and Marek were going to have any chance at happiness, her parents must accept his place in her life.

Once they were done, Cameron resumed her vigil at the window. Her eyes darted between the men, trying to decipher their body language.

"Sweet Peaches, come away from the window."

Sparing a glance at Granny, she answered, "Okay, Granny, in a minute."

"Now," she insisted.

"I just want to—"

Shaking her head, Granny stated, "Come over here. You have no part in that."

Returning to the couch with a sullen pout, Cameron stated, "It involves me. Why shouldn't I see what's going on?"

"What those men say out there is between them."

"I understand that, but this is about my family," she reminded. "I should be out there with them."

"Not this time," Granny corrected. "This is a man's thing and you keep your nose out of it. There are things that need to be said without you sittin' in the middle."

"But I—"

"No back lip. When this is all said and done, you keep your mouth shut and mind your own business."

The front door opened. A car's horn honked and the excited voices of children drifted into the house and then went silent. Cameron broke for the hallway, halting in front of the men. They stood shoulder to shoulder. Examining their faces, she found nothing. Expressionless brown and golden eyes met her anxious gaze.

Okay, so what happened? she wondered. *Did they clear the air?*

"Babygirl," Madaddy reentered the living room followed by Marek. He stepped around her without a touch or word.

Her lips pursed. Mmm. She folded her arms across her chest. *Marek Redding, you wait until I get you alone,* she promised, retreating to the kitchen to start dinner and to think.

"Dinner's ready," Cameron announced from the living room doorway. Her gaze skirted across the small group.

Mom rose from the sofa and smoothed the non-existent wrinkles from her top. "I'll give you a hand."

"Thanks, Ma," she said, returning to the kitchen.

Cameron was placing the final serving bowl on the table when the last of their small party entered the dining room.

AS LONG AS THERE IS LOVE 271

The family surrounded the dinner table, waiting for Granny to take her position at the head of the table.

"Ohhh!" Granny fingered the white linen tablecloth. "This is nice!" She ambled to her spot with the aid of her cane.

"What do you expect?" Cameron looked around the table, admiring her handiwork. The good china and gold-edged silverware sparkled. "This is a celebration." The sweet aroma of onions and garlic seeped from under the lids of the serving bowls. "Your homecoming."

Granny slipped into chair, demanding, "Bobby." She pushed the chair to her left away from the table with her cane. "Have a seat."

"Yes, Mama." He skirted the edge of the room and took the chair to Granny's left.

"Marek? Marek?"

"Yeah, ma'am."

"You sit there," she pointed to the chair at her right.

Madaddy glanced across the table at Marek. A wry smile of understanding passed between them. Marek responded with a slight dip of his head. One corner of his sensual mouth turned up into a smile.

The tight ball of tension in Cameron's chest eased. Good. Maybe there was hope for them.

Glancing around the room at her family, Granny demanded, "What you waitin' for?" And the rest of the clan scurried around the room to their places.

"How about grace?" Madaddy suggested, spreading a lace napkin over his lap.

"Mmm, hmmm." Granny stretched out her hands and grabbed Madaddy's and Marek's. The rest of the small group followed. "I'm thankful to God to still be here," she said, a slight catch in her voice.

"So are we," Madaddy added.

"I know it was my own fault that I ended up in the

hospital. I should have taken my medicine." Stains of red heat stroked her cheeks. "And I want to thank all of you for not remindin' me of that. Sweet Peaches, I love you. You promised you'd be there every step of the way and you were. You worked so hard to get me home. Tears shimmered in her eyes. "Thank you."

"Bobby and Helen, I appreciate your support too." Her voice trembled. "Thanks to you both." She stopped, wiped her eyes with the edge of her napkin. "Marek, thanks for making sure I got good care while I stayed in the hospital. Now, I've said my piece. Time for the blessing, then let's eat."

A collective *yes* echoed around the table. Soon afterward, serving bowls and trays passed from hand to hand, followed by silence as everyone got down to the business of eating.

"Everything looks so good, Babygirl," Mom praised.

Halfway through the their meal, "Sweet Peaches," Granny laid her fork down next to her plate. "How are things going for the inspection?"

"Fine," Cameron answered, concentrating on her meal.

"Do you have a date?"

"Granny, this is your first day home," Cameron reminded. "Let me worry about the inspection."

"Sweet Peaches?"

"Oh, there's no more rice." She stood up and collected up the serving bowl. "I'll be right back."

"Sweet Peaches."

Hurrying from the room, she tossed the answer over her shoulder. "It's next Tuesday."

"Thank you."

Marek followed Cameron from the room. "I'll give you a hand," he offered. "What's up with that?"

"It's just that Granny's such a stubborn old girl. I'm trying to protect her."

"Ronnie, this may come as a surprise to you." Marek

AS LONG AS THERE IS LOVE 273

drew her against him, nibbling on her ear. "She's a grown woman. And a pretty tenacious one at that."

"Tell me something I don't know." She wrapped her arms around his neck. "I want to keep her life stress-free."

Marek planted swift kisses on her cheek, moved along her jaw to her lips. "Sweetheart, you can't do that for her. It's Alice's life and her decision. I know you love her, but you can't control her life. I suggest you quit trying, before you have the next stroke or heart attack. All you're doing is making yourself crazy."

"I know. I know." She fiddled with a lock of his hair. "I can't help it. She's my grandmother. We look out for each other."

"That's good. But in the meantime, why don't you concentrate on me for a few minutes?"

"Mmm," Cameron muttered, pretending to consider his request. "That's a challenge I like." She drew his head down for a kiss.

"Thank you," he muttered, capturing her lips.

A cough from the doorway penetrated Cameron's fuzzy brain. She glanced over Marek's shoulder and stiffened. Madaddy stood in the doorway. Eyes alert. His expression passive and calm.

Embarrassed, she stepped away.

"More rice?" Madaddy asked.

"Ohhh." She moved to the counter and scooped rice from the steamer into the dish.

"Thanks." He lifted the bowl and headed for the door.

The moment Madaddy left the room, she turned to Marek. "Well! That was different." She gave Marek a speculative look. "Are you the responsible party?"

Smiling coyly at her, he answered, "Maybe."

"If you had anything to do with it, I'll thank you later." She kissed his lips.

Chapter Thirty

"Are you ready?" Greg asked as Cameron stepped inside his office.

Her stomach knotted in response to his question. Was she ready?

Hunching her shoulders, "I think so," she forced the words past the gigantic lump in her throat. "Can I have a week to think about it and get back with you?"

He rubbed a finger back and forth across his forehead with a big pretense of seriously considering her request. "Nope."

"Some friend you are," she muttered wryly, checking her appearance in the mirror behind his door.

"What can I say?" He grinned at her. "I'm a great guy."

"And so modest, too."

The black linen suit and white sleeveless blouse with the scoop neck did little to boost her wobbly confidence. Her insides felt like an enormous bowl of mush.

Greg slid his hands into the pockets of his trousers,

perched on the edge of his desk and slowly examined her. Admiration danced from his eyes and made her feel uncomfortable.

"Honestly, I'm glad this day is finally here," she fidgeted with the handle of her black leather briefcase. At least she thought she was. "But I must confess, last night I had nightmares of Jayla and me, living on the street with signs that read, 'Will work for food.' "

Greg's hearty laughter rang out in the room. "Put your fears to rest. You won't end up on the streets. Besides, your grandmother wouldn't allow it." His tangy cologne tickled her nose as he stood, then moved behind the desk to his chair. "I think we're in pretty good shape. Everything's in order. You've never had a complaint before. That should work to our advantage."

"Can I have that in writing?"

He shrugged regretfully. "If I could, I would."

"Yeah, yeah, yeah," she smiled, waving away his pitiful excuse for an answer. "Tell me anything." Her grip tightened on the briefcase handle as the gravity of the situation brought her back to earth. "Really, I'll be glad when all of this is over. The complaint has been hanging over my head for months. It's time to finish it."

Greg eased into his black executive chair. A speculative glint filled his eyes.

"What?" she asked.

"Relax," he cautioned in his best attorney/client voice, smoothing his multi-colored striped tie against his cream shirt. "At this rate you won't make it through the afternoon. We've done everything possible to make this turn our way. Your business files are in order. The school and day care are in tip-top physical shape and the employees are prepped for their interviews. Pull yourself together and show me and the inspector the business professionalism that's your trademark."

A half smile touched her lips. Marek had given her pretty much the same advice earlier that morning, along with an offer to attend the hearing. His thoughtfulness made her love him more as he supported her though this ordeal. But it wasn't meant to be. Seconds later, his pager had gone off and out the door he went to the hospital.

Staring at the tops of her black pumps, she confessed, "My confidence level is pretty low today."

"It'll pass. You'll be fine."

Her gaze darted to the clock on his desk as she counted down the minutes like a military man waiting for his discharge papers. The band around her heart tightened a fraction, as the clock's second hand moved closer and closer to the eleven.

Fretting, she wandered around the office. Stopping at the window, she envied the shoppers going about their business on the downtown city street. She wished she could be out there with them, instead of going through this.

"Do you remember your prepping?" Greg broke into her private reverie. "Specifically, the way I want you to answer questions?"

Cameron nodded, glancing at the clock an additional time. "Short, simple." Seven more minutes. "Don't elaborate. If I'm unsure, take my cues from you."

Nodding, "Good girl." He leaned back in his chair. "Things are going to be fine. We're going to get through this."

"I know." She drew in an unsteady breath. "But so much of my life is up in the air until the complaint is resolved."

"Just think of things this way," Greg soothed. "Once it's over, you can move ahead."

"Since you brought it up, I've got a couple of questions for you." Cameron reached inside the pocket of her skirt and removed several scraps of paper. "Greg," she read from the first sheet. "After today, how long will it take before we know something?"

"I'm not sure." He tented his fingers together. "Once the team arrives, I'll ask."

She twisted the scrap into a ball and tossed it into the wastepaper basket, then glanced at the second bit of paper. "While you're at it," her tongue darted out and moistened her lips. "Ask them about their appeal process." This piece of paper followed the first.

"No, I won't. I don't like that fatalistic attitude and I won't present it. Once the state makes its determination, we'll consider our options. If, and that's a big if, it's necessary. You're going to beat these charges and get your license for the school."

"I know." She shrugged. "I'm just considering the worst-case scenario."

"Well, don't." He nodded at the sofa. "Conserve your energy. Come over here and have a seat. They should be here any minute." On cue, Greg's intercom buzzed. He gave Cameron a "told-you-so" look before answering the telephone. "Yes? Okay, give us a minute, then we'll be out."

Greg dropped the phone in its cradle, grabbed his bronze jacket from the hanger on the coat rack behind his desk and shrugged into it. "They're here," he announced unnecessarily. Buttoning the jacket, he made his way around the desk, caught Cameron's arm and led her toward the door. "Come on, it's time."

"Oh, Lord!" Heat surged up her neck. Getting a glimpse of herself, she halted in her tracks. Wide-eyed and trembling, she looked like a scared chicken.

Pull yourself together. Greg was right. No one would listen to her if she continued to play the role of the Cowardly Lion.

This was her business, her livelihood. What kind of person

would she be if she just laid down and let Tara bulldoze over her? She squared her shoulders and slipped into her professional mode, wrapping it around her like an expensive fur coat. With her head held high, she followed Greg to the door.

She wasn't going down without a fight. Tara's plans to destroy her business were about to be crushed.

The door swung open and Greg stepped into the reception area. The outer office reeked of Old Spice aftershave.

"Hello, I'm Gregory Hunter." He ushered a stout, broad-shouldered man into the office.

"Henry Kelling," the man responded and shook Greg's hand.

Cameron blinked and fought the urge to laugh. Henry Kelling was far from the image of a state investigator. Instead, his mixed blond and gray brush cut, vivid blue eyes and cagey features gave the impression of a football coach. In contrast, his high-pitched voice sounded like a twelve-year-old boy.

Greg placed a hand in the small of her back and propelled her forward. "This is Cameron Butler, the owner of Little Darlings Day Care Center."

Cameron forced a smile of welcome to her lips and shook his red, beefy hand.

"I'm Henry Kelling, from the State of Michigan."

Her eyes focused on the laminated color photo ID badge conspicuously clipped to the lapel of his navy blue sports jacket.

"Have a seat." Greg patted the back of the chair on his way around the desk. "I'm sure you've been on the road for a bit. How about a cup of coffee?"

"Thanks. I'd appreciate that." Mr. Kelling sat on the edge of his chair and arranged his jacket around his bulky frame.

AS LONG AS THERE IS LOVE 279

Tense, she took the chair next to Mr. Kelling and waited with her hands linked together in her lap.

Picking up the telephone, Greg tapped a button. "Liz, would you please bring in coffee?"

"If you don't mind, Mr. Hunter," Mr. Kelling braced his battered briefcase on his knee and folded his thick hands over the handle. A large angry scratch scarred the side of the brown case. "I'd like to get started as soon as possible. This is an extensive process, and I'd like to move through it as quickly and efficiently as possible."

"That's fine." Greg leaned farther into his chair. "But I do have several questions before you get started."

"Ask away."

With pen in hand, Greg pulled a yellow legal pad from his desk drawer. "How does this process work, Mr. Kelling?"

"We don't have to be so formal." He smiled broadly. "Call me Hank."

"Okay." Greg's eyebrows rose. "Hank."

Placing the briefcase on the floor, Mr. Kelling settled deeper into his chair. "The process is straightforward. Everyone involved will be interviewed. Ms. Butler," he smiled at Cameron, "her staff, Mrs. O'Rourke and Justin. After that's completed, we'll inspect the property."

"Isn't that a great deal of work for one person?" Greg twirled his gold Cross pen between his fingers.

"It can be."

"To be honest," Greg placed the pen next to a yellow notepad, "I expected as least one additional person, maybe more."

There was a tap on the door and Liz entered the room. "Excuse me," she said, carrying a black carafe in one hand and a tray of doughnuts in the other. "Coffee?" The strong aroma of brewed coffee filled the air. Conversation ceased while Liz poured coffee and distributed the refreshments.

"Thank you." Mr. Kelling nodded at Liz and took a

steaming mug. "Getting back to your question. We generally work in teams to cut down on the amount of time we're away from the office," he explained. "My coworker, Mrs. Williams, will arrive tomorrow."

"Hmmm."

"Today, I'd like—" he took a swallow of coffee, "to get the process going by working on the interviews. Once they're completed, we can get to the inspection, check your books and in general, wrap things up."

Greg scribbled on his notepad. "How long do you expect the complete process to take?"

"Normally, it takes two to three days. If we're lucky, we'll get done late Thursday or Friday morning." Mr. Kelling bit into a powdered sugar doughnut. "It'll take a day, day and a half to get through the interviews."

"Will we get a determination before you leave?" Greg asked.

"No." Mr. Kelling shook his head, brushing donut crumbs from his slacks. "We're the information gatherers. The State of Michigan uses a point system that determines your overall score and then you'll be notified."

"That's fine. How long before we get the results?"

"A few weeks."

"Good." Greg nodded.

"Mr. Hunter," Mr. Kelling replaced the empty mug on the tray. "I need a central place to work. Do you have an office I can use for the next couple of days?"

"Sure. Why don't you use my conference room?" Greg stood and led Mr. Kelling toward the door. "It's large and gives you plenty of space to spread out. In addition, you'll have access to a telephone."

"Thank you." Henry Kelling tossed the remains of his donut in his mouth. "I really appreciate your help."

"No problem." Opening the door, Greg turned to his

administrative assistant. "Liz, will you show Hank the conference room?"

The moment the door shut behind them, Greg moved to Cameron's chair and placed his hand on her shoulder. "What do you think?"

"He seems nice enough."

"True." His brows drew together over the bridge of his nose. "We haven't seen him in action yet. I suspect he'll be a pistol. Prepare yourself," he advised, striding toward the door. "You'll probably be the first person he interviews."

She nodded and retrieved her briefcase. "Give me a minute."

Cameron's hands shook as she checked her makeup in the rest room mirror. There was a little shine on her nose and she needed lipstick. She searched through her purse for her compact and tube of lipstick.

It surprised her to find that only part of the team had arrived. She felt less confident without meeting everyone involved. Tomorrow, she'd have a chance to size up Mrs. Williams.

The cherry lipstick slid over her lips. She stopped, picked up a tissue and blotted away the excess color.

The first meeting with Mr. Kelling had gone as she expected. He seemed like a decent guy. His voice still made her chuckle. That was an unexpected contradiction. Still, caution seemed the best approach, until she learned his game plan.

A positive attitude would help them through the inspection process. The more helpful she was, the sooner the inspection would be over. Then all she needed to do was cross her fingers and wait for the results to arrive in the mail.

Fluffing the ends of her hair, she gave herself a final

check. Butterflies danced in her belly each time she thought of what was ahead, but she'd make it through.

For the first time since Justin's accident, she felt a measure of confidence about the outcome. Whatever happened, it was time to make her stand. She smiled at her reflection and brushed away a speck from her jacket.

She was ready, slipping through the door and moving effortlessly toward the conference room.

Chapter Thirty-one

Several hours later, Cameron revised her initial impression of Mr. Kelling. She shifted on the cushioned chair and glanced at her watch. During the tedious hours they'd been in the conference room, he had plowed through an ocean of questions.

She lifted her mug to her lips, watching him under lowered lashes. Contrary to his frumpy appearance, he exhibited the talent of a skilled interrogator. The last drops of her tea slid down her throat. She grimaced. It was cold.

The clock on the wall read 1:48 P.M. Cameron moaned silently. How much longer did he plan to continue before calling it a day?

With each break, she and Greg huddled together, analyzing Kelling's questions and her answers. So far, Greg seemed pleased with her responses. Then they'd strategized about where he might go with his next set of questions.

But this phase of the process was far from complete. Once Kelling finished with her, he needed to interview the day care center's staff, plus Tara and Justin. After that, he'd move to the physical inspection of the property.

Making a clucking sound with his tongue, Mr. Kelling shuffled through his pages of questions. "It doesn't look as if I'm going to finish with everyone today." He glanced at his watch and counted the pages in his hands a second time. "Let's go over a few more things, then we'll take a break."

Cameron massaged the tight muscles at the back of her neck. Good. She needed a few minutes to herself. "How do you want to schedule things tomorrow?"

Tapping the pages with his pen, his brows furrowed over blue eyes. "I still have your staff, Mrs. O'Rourke, and Justin to interview. Generally, my associate conducts the site reviews. Why don't I have Mrs. Williams meet you at Little Darlings?"

"That'll be fine." She shoved the mug toward the center of the table. "What time should I expect her?"

"When we take our next break, I'll call and find out how she plans to work you into her schedule."

"Thank you."

Moving around the table, Mr. Kelling refilled his coffee mug. "Now, let's finish this portion, then take a break. How many fire and emergency drills do you conduct each year?"

"Minimum, one a month," she answered. "Two, if our schedule permits. I like to conduct at least one a month without the children."

"Mmm." He drew a line across the page. "In the event of an accident involving a child, what's your procedure?"

"Actually," Cameron fidgeted with her nails under the table, then began, "we—"

"Do you notify parents? Staff? What timeframe have you established when you can't reach a parent during a crisis? Do you have written medical authorization on file for each child in the case of an emergency?"

Running her hand over her face, Mr. Kelling's fast-fired questions made her uncomfortable. "The staff—"

"Before you answer that question, do you have a standard procedure in case an employee leaves the premises in the event there's an emergency involving a child?"

"Is this procedure profiled in a conspicuous location for all your employees to see? Do you have drills? Checklists? Are there periodic in-services to update your staff on changes to the state's guidelines?" He scratched his head with the blue cap of his pen. "Does your staff have assigned duties during an emergency? Are records kept up to date with date, time and results of your drills?"

It was time to put an end to this. "You know, umm, Mr. Kelling, that data is located at Little Darlings. If it would move things along I can assemble everything and give it to the inspector tomorrow." She ripped a small corner from the legal pad available on the table and scribbled a few notes. "Just tell me what you need and I'll make sure you have it," she said with her pen posed for more notes. "Anything else?"

Mr. Kelling folded the yellow sheets in half and tossed them inside his briefcase, then removed another yellow pad. "Yes, now, I'd like you to summarize any other accidents at Little Darlings involving children."

"Accidents?" Her face scrunched up. *What accidents? Where did he get an idea like that?* "There was only one accident."

"What accidents?" Greg moved around the edge of the table. His passive expression had been replaced by a sharp gleam of inquiry.

"Well," Mr. Kelling cleared his voice, "there have been additional allegations brought against your facility."

Cameron felt as if someone had just squeezed the air from her lungs. Her hands began to shake. "Allegations?"

"Yes." His blue eyes focused on her. "We recently received a letter detailing additional problems."

"Letter?" She blinked back at Mr. Kelling owlishly. "From who?"

"By whom?" Greg jumped in. "Why weren't we informed of this development?"

"From Mrs. O'Rourke." Mr. Kelling turned to Greg and added, "A letter dated last week was sent to you."

Cameron threw up her hands. "Of course," she muttered to no one in particular. Now Tara was fabricating incidents. Would there ever be a time when Tara left her the hell alone?

"Mr. Kelling," she began, "there's been only one accident in the three years I've operated Little Darlings. And that accident involved Justin O'Rourke. Don't you think these new allegations are a bit coincidental?"

"Well," his brows wrinkled as he spoke, "according to Mrs. O'Rourke, you've been covering up for years." He presented an ivory envelope from his briefcase, unfolded a sheet and began to read from it. "She states here that these customers left after confronting your staff with negligence of duty and you refused to investigate. No inspection, no inquiry, nothing."

"Excuse me," Greg broke into the discussion. "I think I need to see that document."

"Certainly." Mr. Kelling handed the letter to Greg.

The silence stretched before them, filling the room with quiet menace. Greg's expression grew dark. He handed the letter back to Kelling. "I need a few minutes with Ms. Butler. Can we break now?"

"Fine." Mr. Kelling swept the page from Greg's hand.

"Wait a minute." Cameron raised a hand to stop them, demanding, "Which children? Give me their names."

"Alexander Stein," Mr. Kelling stated, "Shirley Walker and Lynn Edwards."

She nodded, then began, "Alexander Stein left when his mother got a promotion and they moved to Chicago. There wasn't any accident or injury," she explained, then ran her tongue over her lips. "Shirley Walker tripped over her untied shoelaces *at home*. When her mother brought her in that morning, her chin was still bleeding. And like any kid, she cried."

"Cameron," Greg cautioned, touching her shoulders. "Let's talk before you say anything more."

"Greg, it's all right." She waved away his objection, turned back to Mr. Kelling, and continued, "I want to explain this part. We put a Band-Aid on Shirley's chin and off she went to play with the other children."

"Nothing happened to Lynn, at least not at Little Darlings. She was playing Xena Warrior Princess with her sister at home and tried to jump over the fence and cut her leg on a bottle. Again, none of it had anything to do with Little Darlings. We just took care of her when she returned." She shook her head. "I don't understand how Tara could tell such lies."

"Do you have addresses or telephone numbers for these families?" Mr. Kelling flipped to a clean page of his notepad. "I'll need statements from you and them."

"Deborah Stein's in Chicago. I have an address for her, but I'm not sure she's still at the same place." Cameron reached for the notepad and began to write. "That was more than a year ago. The other two families are still in town. I have telephone numbers for both." Shaking her head at this turn of events, she said, "Mr. Kelling, these allegations are totally off the mark. I don't understand why Tara would provide you with such misleading information."

"Regardless, we have to investigate." His mouth crimped into a line of annoyance. "No two ways about it. If an allegation is lodged, we have to follow up."

"We will need copies of all correspondence," Greg piped in.

"No problem." Mr. Kelling dropped everything inside his briefcase. He studied his watch for half a beat. "Let's meet back here in fifteen minutes."

"Sure. Will you finish with me tonight?"

"I'm planning to, Ms. Butler. If you're up to it. Tomorrow, you can send your staff over one by one and minimize the loss of employees to your operation."

"That sounds good." Fidgeting with the handle of her mug, Cameron smiled weakly at Mr. Kelling. "Thanks for considering Little Darlings."

"Hank, Ms. Butler and I are going to stretch our legs for a few minutes." Greg cupped Cameron's elbow. "We'll be back in fifteen."

Mr. Kelling nodded and reached for the telephone. "I'm going to try to reach Mrs. Williams."

Outside the conference room, Cameron ranted, "I don't believe that woman!"

"It's okay." He patted her shoulder. "We'll get past it."

"But how?" she cried.

"We're far from defeated." Greg glanced at his watch. "We'll ask for more time to review the new allegations. Then present our own case. Relax," he suggested, massaging the tight muscles in her shoulders. "You're doing great," he praised. "Keep up the good work. But I must say, Hank is quite a character."

"That he is," she responded with a weak smile.

Greg glanced at his watch and said, "Give me a few minutes." He started down the hallway. "I'm going to check my messages. I'll be right back."

Cameron waited outside the conference room. What else had Tara done? The ugliness kept coming and coming.

Fifteen minutes later, she and Greg returned to the conference room. Mr. Kelling dropped the telephone in its cradle

AS LONG AS THERE IS LOVE

as they approached. "That was Mrs. Williams. She'll arrive around ten tomorrow morning." He tore off several sheets from his yellow legal pad and tossed them inside his open briefcase. "How does that work for you?"

"Fine," she answered.

"How much longer do you plan to continue today?" Greg asked from the opposite end of the table. "Don't forget I need a copy of Mrs. O'Rourke's letter before you leave. Just give it to Liz."

Mr. Kelling glanced at his watch. "Hmmm, it's a little after two." He clucked his tongue. "I'll tell you what. Let's finish with Ms. Butler and then break for lunch. Then I'll start fresh Wednesday morning with Mrs. O'Rourke," turning to Cameron, he asked, "Is that all right with you?"

She sank into the chair, answering, "Yes. Fine. I definitely want to get my part done tonight."

"Let's do it," Greg took his place across from Cameron.

Mr. Kelling ran his fingers over his brush cut and said, "Okay, just a few more questions."

Cameron's eyes locked on the papers in his hands, counting along with him as his hands shuffled through the sheets. A few more. Cameron mentally shouted. Yeah right. Ten more. But she could handle it.

Greg threw his hands into the air and surrendered to Cameron's plan. "She's the boss."

Chapter Thirty-two

"Hold on." Cameron hurried down the hallway and glanced at the three items left on her list. She shoved the strip of paper into the pocket of her skirt and checked her wristwatch. Nine-eighteen. It couldn't be Mrs. Williams, could it? Mr. Kelling had said ten o'clock.

Whoever stood on the other side of the door must go. She'd earmarked every precious moment to complete her tasks before Mrs. Williams's arrival.

"If you're happy and you know it, clap your hands," rang out, followed by the rolling thunder of clapping. Cameron grinned at the sound of the enthusiastic and often off-key voices of the kids. By day's end, she hoped to have something to clap about herself.

She flung the door open and stood there, amazed. Oh, Lord. Her stomach muscles twisted into tight knots. Nikki Anderson.

Her eyes squeezed shut against the impossible sight. When she opened her eyes seconds later, she zeroed in on the badge that hung on a chain around Nikki's neck. It read "Nikki Williams, state of Michigan."

A strangled cry escaped before she bit it back. *Please God, don't let it be true,* she begged. But her deepest instincts told her it was. Oh, Lord. *This can't be happening.*

A calm mask shielded Nikki's expression as she held the handle of her briefcase in a death grip with one hand and stroked a piece of jewelry pinned to her lapel with the other. Her brown-green eyes were focused on Cameron's face.

Recovering from her initial shock, Cameron took a closer look at Nikki. The years hadn't been kind.

Her calf-length black skirt hid nothing from Cameron's sharp inspection, not to mention the thirty-odd extra pounds spread over her once-slender frame. A gold pin declaring "Jesus Saves" decorated the lapel of Nikki's black jacket. The pin seemed out of place on a woman who Cameron remembered loved to party the weekend away. Her once-beautiful amber hair lacked its usual luster and style. Today it was pulled into a ponytail at the back of her neck.

A pitiful excuse for a smile fluttered and died away on Nikki's lips. "Hi Ca—mm—eron." She switched her briefcase to her left hand and offered the right hand.

Cameron cringed. Her fingers curled into a protective fist against her breast, refusing to offer this woman any sign of encouragement.

Red stain added color to Nikki's mole-dotted cocoa cheeks. She chewed on the corner of her bottom lip as her hand returned to her lapel and stroked the pin. "May I come in?"

"Are you here for the inspection?" Cameron countered.

"Yes."

She gazed at her wristwatch, then back at Nikki. "You're a little early."

"I know." Nikki's eyes pled for understanding. "I wanted to have a few minutes with you before we proceeded."

Cameron's heart slammed against her chest and palpitated. "Ohh? About?"

"May I come in?" Nikki's brow wrinkled as she glanced at the house to the left, then right. "I don't want to discuss our private business on your front porch."

Okay, she'd bite. For at least a few minutes, Nikki commanded center stage.

"We don't have any private business." Cameron pivoted away from the door. Goosebumps pricked her skin as the protective coolness of the house welcomed her.

Why was Nikki here? hummed in her head like a litany. Cameron started down the hall, not concerned if Nikki followed. They hadn't spoken in years. Why now? When her life was back together. Why was she here?

"Thank you, Lord, for bringing me here," Nikki muttered to Cameron's back. "I wasn't sure it was you," Nikki began, in a stiff voice. "Our department conducts weekly staff meetings. They're more or less a way to distribute new cases," she babbled to Cameron's back. "When my manager started discussing this case, there were too many coincidences."

"Mmmm," Cameron mumbled, turning into the living room. She lifted a hand to her throbbing temple and tried to massage the pain away. Right now, she'd pay good money to get Nikki to shut up and give her a chance to think.

"I wasn't positive." Nikki placed her briefcase next to the sofa and looked around the room as she spoke, "I remembered your grandmother lived in Holland. My coworker made me trade two of her cases to get this one." A smile touched Nikki's lips through her mask of uncertainty. "It was worth it to get here."

"Oh," Cameron answered. "Why did you go to so much trouble?"

Jayla burst through the door. "Daddy?" Her Honeybunny

AS LONG AS THERE IS LOVE 293

stopped short inside the entrance and stared from one woman to the other. "Honey? Where's my daddy?"

Nikki gave a startled cry. All color drained from her face. With guilt-filled eyes, she studied Jayla.

Cameron's protective instincts kicked in and she raced to Jayla. With her back to Nikki, she settled Jayla on her hip and headed to the door.

"Hi," Nikki's greeted softly.

Cameron struggled for a moment with her need to protect her daughter. Jayla hadn't been raised to be disrespectful to adults, even if the adult was her mother's enemy.

"Honeybunny, where's your manners?" Cameron reminded. "Say hello to Mrs. Williams."

"Hello," Jayla responded with an up and down motion of her hand.

"Good girl. Your daddy isn't here yet. I want you to go back to the kitchen and keep Granny company until he gets here. Okay?"

"Okay."

"Kiss?" Cameron requested.

Jayla kissed her mother's lips, than wriggled off her hip.

"Thank you," she called after her baby.

"You welcome."

Tears clung to Nikki's lashes when she turned to the other woman. Cameron hardened her heart against Nikki's bid for sympathy. Each time Nikki got caught doing wrong, she broke out in tears. This time Cameron refused to buy Nikki's sob story.

"I'm so sorry," Nikki mopped away her tears with a tissue. "So sorry."

"Sorry." Disgusted, Cameron shook her head. "It's too late for that."

Eyes shut, Nikki bowed her head. "Lord give me the strength to make things right," she prayed. "I had no idea you'd had a child. I can't believe how much she looks like

Marek. His eyes and hair." Wonder filled her voice. "It's amazing."

"Leave my family out of this," Cameron stiffened. She hated Nikki's reference to her relationship with Marek. "They're none of your business."

"I didn't mean to upset you," Nikki raised a hand as if to touch Cameron. "Seeing your daughter brought it all back to me. But, we have business to discuss. Things to finish."

"Finish?" Cameron snorted, stepping away from the other woman's outstretched hand. "We said everything four years ago."

"No." Nikki shook her head. "Four years ago I deliberately set out to hurt you. It's time to talk about everything and put an end to it all."

"I don't think so," Cameron denied forcefully. "The only thing we have to discuss is the inspection. End of story."

"That can't be the end of things. Now that I've seen your daughter, I'm more certain than ever this was the right thing to do." Her words rushed forth like a roller coaster at high speed. "We must talk! Now! Today!"

Now they needed to talk. Cameron thought. If they'd talked four years ago, maybe things would have been different.

"Nikki, I'm saying this for the last time, there's nothing to discuss."

"Maybe you don't have anything to say, but I do," Nikki's voice broke, and she looked away. "You were my closest friend and I betrayed you," she grimaced. "Hurt you. It's important that you understand how confused I was back then."

Cameron ran her hand over her face. Why hadn't that friendship meant enough to keep Nikki away from Marek?

"Your explanation won't change anything." Cameron

shoved her hands inside her skirt pockets. "What good does it do for you to come here and stir up trouble? What are you gaining?"

"The look on your face when you caught Marek and me stayed with me all these years," she whispered. "Oh, Cameron, it haunted me."

Cameron felt uneasiness take root inside her. Her feelings about that incident were so raw. Now she felt as if she were reliving that pain a second time. From the determined set of Nikki's chin, she was going to have her say.

"Go ahead. Unburden yourself. That's what this is all about." Cameron folded her arms across her chest. 'It's obvious you're not going to leave until you've had your say. But, I'm warning you, don't expect me to buy anything you say."

"Just listen with an open mind, that's all I'm asking," Nikki asked and swallowed hard. "First, I never slept with Marek," she stated with quiet but determined intensity. "We never had sex. Ever! We never held hands, whispered sweet nothings in each other's ears, nothing. Whenever Marek came to see you, he treated me politely, but kept his distance. That was it."

Nikki gazed steadily back at her. The truth of her words was visible in her face, voice. It shimmered over Cameron and filled her with joy. She turned aside, savoring Nikki's confession. After a moment, she faced Nikki, braced for more revelations.

"That night he was waiting for you to get home. He told me that he'd been on call and felt dead on his feet." She twisted the pin in her lapel. "I encouraged him to go lie down in your room."

Nikki began to pace. "I had always wanted to be with Marek. When I set up your tutoring sessions, I hoped for more time alone with him. I never considered you a rival." A sharp, bitter cackle exploded from her lips. "Boy, was I wrong. Within days you two were tight, a couple, the little virgin and that hot doctor."

Something ugly smoldered in Nikki's eyes. Cameron's stomach muscles twisted and she took a step back.

"Marek and I were friends way before you came into the picture. You know we worked at the hospital together. But once you got with him, he shut me out. I felt like an outsider in my own home."

Cameron's face burned when she remembered how engrossed she and Marek had been with one another. Nothing else mattered. She acknowledged the truth of Nikki's comment. Maybe she'd fallen down on her job as a friend.

"You had everything. Marek. Parents. My life was so different." She flapped her arms aimlessly, than dropped them to her side. "My parents never wanted children and wanted me on my own as soon as possible. Do you remember how many times they came to visit?" She lifted a finger, than answered her own question. "Beginning of the school year to drop me off," then added a second finger. "And the end, to pick me up."

Cameron shuffled through her memories for one occasion when the Andersons had visited. They never came. No birthdays, holidays, nothing. Although she fought it, sympathy for Nikki began to blossom within her.

While she and her parents had disagreements, Cameron had no doubt they would support her if she needed them.

Eyes sparkling with determination, Nikki pressed on, "I'm not looking for your sympathy."

Cameron raised a hand to stop her. "Look—"

"No. Please. Let me finish." Nikki wrung her hands together. "I was jealous. I wanted some of that perfect life you claimed as if it were your due."

"Nikki, I don't want to hear any more." Cameron shut her eyes against the expression in Nikki's eyes. "Let it be."

"I can't," Nikki cried. "Until this is done, I won't have

any peace. God sent me here. And I'm not leaving until I've explained everything."

If she refused to listen, Nikki could quite possibly show up on her doorstep again. Cameron wanted to avoid that at all costs. "Go ahead."

Breathing a sigh of relief, "Thank you. Right before graduation, I realized it was my last chance to show Marek how I felt about him," she met Cameron's gaze with steady force. "I'm sorry, you weren't a consideration. If I eliminated you from the mix, he'd be mine. And that's how I planned it. All I knew was I wanted Marek and somehow I had to get rid of you."

Strains of scarlet added color to Nikki's cheeks. "When I heard your whoopzie pull into the drive, I ran to your room and snuggled down beside Marek. He was out for the count."

Bile inched its way up Cameron's throat as the image of Nikki with Marek in her bed flashed in her mind. She stiffened her spine and prepared to hear the rest of the tale. Anything, to have it done and this woman out of their lives.

"He was oblivious to my plans. Marek told the truth when he said he had no idea how I got in your bed."

Poor Marek. He hadn't seen any of this coming before it hit them. Neither had she.

"Being roomies taught me a lot about you. For instance, you always made up your mind about a situation and that was it. More importantly, if things got too hot, you aways split. I think that came from being the pampered baby of your family. Don't deal with the problem, just run away. And I was banking on that." Nikki's fingers did a nervous rat-a-tat-tat on her thigh as she continued speaking, "You ran out before Marek had a chance to explain. That was your usual M.O." She shrugged, an apologetic smile curved her lips. "You didn't disappoint me."

In her mind's eye, Cameron saw herself, trusting and

naïve, while Nikki manipulated her. What an idiot she'd been! A gullible, predictable fool.

"But take heart, nothing worked out my way. Marek didn't want me," Nikki lowered her head and whispered, "He never wanted me. Once you left, he told me so in some pretty colorful language. After that, I'd see him at work, looking haunted and alone. But I stayed away, because he made it clear I wasn't welcome."

Cameron believed she'd been prepared for Nikki's confession. She was wrong. Nikki's level of deviousness shocked her. The one shining element in her confession was the fact that Marek hadn't betrayed her. He'd loved her then, and did now. She held that thought close to her heart. It shielded her against Nikki's harsh words.

"I always envied Marek's love for you. For him, there wasn't anyone else. Believe me, I saw women try to get next to him. They just didn't interest him. Just like I didn't."

Everything Nikki said sounded genuine. But there were still missing pieces, and Cameron needed one question answered. "Nikki, what are you getting out of this? Why now? What do you want from me?"

"Peace," Nikki sighed reverently. "Peace. You can't imagine how this has preyed on my mind over the years." Tears quivered on the edge of Nikki's lashes. "But with God's help, I realized what I had to do. I had to find you and ask for your forgiveness."

Don't do this, hands balled into fist, Cameron cried. *Don't push religion at me.*

"I quit school and wandered through life for a couple of years, lost and confused, before I started to work for the state. I'm so blessed. That's where my husband, Isiah, found me and taught me that I was worthy of God and his love." Her face was transformed when she mentioned her man. "Now I have my own family."

"It's not that simple," Cameron broke in. "I can't just

forgive and forget the pain and trouble you caused me."
The doorbell rang as she ran her fingers through her hair. Nikki's trip down memory lane had gotten to her. "Excuse me," she hurried from the room, her nerves throbbing under the pressure.

Cameron flung the door open.

"Hey," Marek greeted, kissing her lips.

As always, his presence warmed her heart. She wrapped her arms around his waist, held him close and burrowed her face into his neck. He was so dear to her.

He set her a step away, examining her face. "This is nice. But I'm here to pick up Jayla." His eyebrows did a significant double lift. "Maybe we can follow up on things after Jayla goes to bed this evening."

Laughing, she playfully hit his arm. "Oh, you!"

Marek's gaze ran over her. His pleasant smile changed to concern. "What's wrong?"

"We've got some unexpected company."

"Company?"

She nodded. "Follow me." Cameron crooked a finger toward the living room. "I've got something to show you."

Eyebrows drawn into a straight line above his eyes, Marek strode along beside her. A tight suspicious expression quickly replaced his curious gaze.

"Nikki," he nodded at the other woman, then moved closer to Cameron's side and placed a protective arm around her shoulders. "What brings you here?"

"She's the inspector on my case," Cameron explained.

"Is that right?" His lips thinned.

Hesitantly, Nikki moved closer to the pair. "Marek, I'm glad to see you here. It shows me that things worked out, despite everything." Sorrow peppered her next words. "Whether you believe it or not, I'm sorry." She faced Marek, adding, "You guys deserved better."

"You're right. We did," Marek agreed. The expression

in his eyes turned glacier. "I've missed the first three years of my daughter's life because of you. No one can replace that time. It's gone."

Cameron watched Marek under lowered lashes. If it had been anyone else, she might have tried to intervene. But not Nikki. She didn't deserve help.

"I'm sorry," Nikki stiffened, but maintained her vigil. "I truly mean it. I know the words are inadequate." She bit down on her bottom lip and gazed at the carpet. "But that's all I have. If it were possible to change things, I would."

"If you had wanted to change things, why didn't you go to Cameron and tell her the truth after this crap happened?" Anger seethed from his voice. "Suddenly, after four years, you've had a change of heart? I don't buy it."

"Marek, please," Nikki begged, raising a hand to touch him. "Things got out of hand. I don't know what I was thinking. I just wanted someone to love me."

"Nikki," he stepped away from her touch. "I stayed on campus for weeks after Cameron left. Why didn't you say anything *then?*"

"Because I wanted you to see me. Me! Me!" She hit her chest, crying, "Instead of her." She jabbed at Cameron. "I was jealous and I reacted like a child. I'm sorry."

"Are you expecting us to offer you absolution?" His harsh chuckle made Cameron's skin crawl. "If so, you've come a long way for nothing."

"I didn't know where you lived. I worked hard to get this case, so I could talk to you both."

"Half of your wish has come true. You have talked to us." He stepped closer. "But there won't be any forgiveness, at least not from me. Instead, let me offer you a piece of advice. Don't fu—"

Cameron gasped, shocked at his use of profanity. "Marek!" She warned, grasping his arm, "Remember Jayla."

AS LONG AS THERE IS LOVE 301

Shutting his eyes, he drew in a deep breath. His fingers unclenched as he opened his eyes and focused on Nikki with a frosty glare of warning.

The look on his face made the blood freeze in Cameron's veins. Boy, even in their worst times, she'd never seen him like this. It frightened and fascinated her all at once.

"I can't forgive you. Let me be a bit more honest. I don't want to forgive you. If your conscience refuses to let you rest, I say," he saluted her, "good."

Nikki stood mute, like a chastised child and took the verbal assault Marek heaped upon her.

Ignoring her dejected stance, he turned to Cameron. "Is Jayla ready?"

"Yes," Cameron nodded toward the hallway. "She's in the kitchen with Granny."

"We'll be back in a minute," he took Cameron's arm and led her from the room.

"You okay?" he asked.

Cameron nodded.

"I can stick around if you need me."

"No. I'm fine."

"Sure?"

"Sure."

"I'm going for Jayla and I'll see you later. Call me if you need me."

"Marek, how do you plan to get any work done with Jayla in your office?"

"Ahhh," he dismissed. "She won't be that hard to manage. Besides, Diane's in today. She'll help," he explained and stole a kiss. "You're got a busy day ahead. Plus, an unexpected problem," he tipped his head toward the living room. "I want to make things easier for you. Besides, it never fails—when you want to impress someone, your child cuts up. She'll be fine with me."

"If you're sure?"

"I'm sure." He hugged her close. "Everything's going to be fine," he promised, releasing her and starting toward the kitchen.

Re-entering the living room, Cameron hardened her heart against the hope gleaming in Nikki's eyes.

"Cameron," Nikki's tongue brushed across her lips, "can you understand what I'm saying?"

"No. I can't," Cameron said. "You walk into my home after years of silence and tell me how sorry you are and how your life has changed. Guess what? Mine changed, too. And not everything has been good."

"Cameron, please. Don't discount my words. Take a good, hard look at the facts. We all need closure to that incident."

"You're going to have to leave today without it. I can't give you the answer you're seeking." Cameron shook her head. "I don't have forgiveness in me."

"The Lord led me here today. I've tried to make you see." Sadness filled Nikki's eyes. Resignation followed. "I understand." She glanced around the room. Retrieving her briefcase, she fumbled inside and withdrew a pen, notebook and manila folder. "Why don't we get this inspection going?"

"I think that's a good idea." Silence settled between them.

"Cameron, don't worry. I'll be fair. Whatever I see wrong, I'll comment on. But I won't use this against you."

"I hope I can believe you."

I must be jinxed, Cameron thought, as she led Nikki through the house to Little Darlings.

This situation just kept getting worse and worse. First, Mr. Kelling presented her with a list of new alleged injuries that supposedly had occurred at Little Darlings. And, today, when she opened the door, the last person she expected to find was Nikki Anderson.

As Nikki poked and prodded around the toddler's nap room, Cameron admired her level of professionalism. Cameron hoped that professionalism extended past their differences.

This was the second time Nikki had entered her life with the potential to destroy everything she'd worked for. But this time, things were going to be different. Cameron was a grown woman with a family to support. She wouldn't run from this fight. Too much money, time and energy had gone into this business. And she'd fight Nikki with everything she had to keep the things that mattered to her.

Chapter Thirty-three

"No candy," Cameron called after Jayla. "Ask Granny for a piece of fruit."

"Okay," Jayla sang and headed toward the kitchen. She stopped, U-turned and hugged Cameron around the knees before she took off again.

Marek gazed intently into Cameron's eyes. With gentle fingers, he smoothed the frown that marred her forehead and eased her body into the crook of his arm.

"Is Nikki gone?" his husky voice questioned.

Cameron nodded and managed a smile. "Yep," she soaked up some of his solid, quiet strength.

"How did it go?"

How had it gone? Hunching her shoulders, she gazed up at him. Good question. Slipping her hand in his, they started down the hall. The whole situation disturbed and confused her. One thing she did know: if it hadn't gone well, she'd find out pretty soon.

Marek's mouth thinned. "For her sake, she had better be

fair," he warned. "If she's not," his voice held an edge of cold steel, "we'll be filing a complaint against her."

Granny looked up from peeling an orange. Handing the fruit and napkin to Jayla, "You can watch Rugrats," she said, tucking a second napkin into Jayla's palm. "Be careful of the seeds."

"Okay." Jayla hurried from the room. "Thank you."

"Did you wash your hands?" Cameron called after her.

"Yesss."

Granny busied herself at the sink. "Hi, you two."

"Hey, Granny," Cameron crossed the kitchen floor and kissed the old girl. She nestled close, drawing comfort from Granny's quiet strength.

Marek moved to the breakfast nook table. "How are you, Alice?"

"Doin' just fine. Just fine," Granny reached inside the cabinet for teabags. "Want some tea?"

"Sounds good," Cameron opened the cupboard door, "I'll help."

Granny shooed her away. "Go sit down," she plucked spoons from the drawer and placed them next to the mugs. "I can handle this."

"Okay," Cameron conceded. "I'll take these." She scooped up three mugs and spoons from the countertop, moved to the breakfast nook and slipped into a chair opposite Marek.

Granny followed with the teapot. "Marek, how did you and Jayla get along today?"

"She had a ball." He grinned, then admitted a little sheepishly. "So did I."

"Good." Granny nodded. "She needs to know about her daddy's work." Turning to Cameron, she asked, "Speaking of work, Sweet Peaches, did I see your college roommate putterin' around here today?"

Cameron's eyes widened. Wow! Nothing got by Granny.

"How did you know?" The old girl never ceased to amaze her. Granny had seen Nikki a half a dozen times four years ago in the hub of her college years, yet she had recognized Nikki.

"I pay good money to keep my eyeballs workin'." The old girl winked at Cameron. "That gal's put on a few pounds, hasn't she?"

"That she has," Cameron agreed. "Nikki works for the state now as an inspector."

"Mmmm, hmmm. Marek, hold up your cup." Granny poured tea with both hands on the teapot. "If I remember correctly, wasn't she the one who caused all that trouble between you two?"

"Yes," Cameron answered, shooting the old girl an off-limits warning.

"Mmmm, hmmm." A thoughtful expression clouded her face. "What did she want?"

"How do you know she wanted anything?" Cameron challenged. "She was here for the inspection."

Granny slipped into the chair opposite Cameron, picked up her spoon and stirred her tea. "I saw it in her eyes."

It took the old girl to see beyond the obvious. She might as well tell Granny, because she wouldn't let the issue drop. Cameron said, "She wanted me to forgive her."

"Mmmm, hmmm." Granny's brows knitted together. "And what did you say?"

"What do you think?" Cameron squeaked, more than a little surprised by her question. "I didn't feel real charity, and I told her so." Cameron lips thinned. "Too much has happened between us."

Eyes narrowing, Granny turned to Marek and asked, "What about you?"

A dark, amber fire blazed from his eyes. This side of him was so foreign to Cameron. It frightened her a little.

Marek's face flushed with indignation. "I don't trust her.

She deliberately set out to hurt us and she succeeded. I have a problem with her showing up here, wanting us to clear her conscience," Marek explained further, lifting his mug to his lips. "I think she needs to take responsibility for the things she's done."

"Mmmm, hmmm." Granny lifted her cup and sipped her tea for several minutes. "Sometimes the best way to get past a painful memory is to forgive."

Granny's words hung in the air. Marek's mouth tightened into a stubborn line, making Cameron's insides knot.

He placed his mug on the table. "That woman almost destroyed my family. I don't have a lot of compassion for her."

The old girl shook her head. "Didn't say you had to," she wagged a red manicured finger in his direction. "But in order to move on, you have to put an end to this."

"I don't know if I have it in me."

Smiling reassuringly, "Sure you do," she patted his hand and jabbed a finger in Cameron's direction. "You forgave Sweet Peaches for not tellin' you about Jayla. And that's all been good."

"That's different," he rejected. "Ronnie didn't deliberately keep Jayla from me. That's something else we can thank Nikki for."

"Mmmm, hmmm," Granny mumbled. "But you did forgive her. Even if she had deliberately misled you, you'd still forgive her, I think. You know why? Because you wanted to move on and have more with Sweet Peaches." She winked at them. "To do that, the problems between you two needed an ending."

He opened his mouth to add something, but Granny cut him off. "You two can't live like this." Granny glared at him, then at Cameron and back again. "That roommate deserves at least the minimum consideration. Think about how hard it was for her to come all this way and stand in front of you. It wasn't easy. Chances are, it was damn hard. But she did it."

Cameron's head swirled with doubts. "Granny, how can I forgive her?" Agitated, she ran her hand over her face. "I thought Nikki was my friend. All the while she was plotting to take Marek from me. How can I trust a dirty dog like that?"

"Sweet Peaches, nobody said you have to trust her. She doesn't live here. She's not part of your life now," Granny persuaded. "All you got to do is forgive her and let it go. I know you can do that."

Baffled, "Why?" Cameron cried. "Why is it so important that we do this? I didn't expect this from you. I thought you understood my feelings."

"I do, Sweet Peaches. I do," she patted Cameron's hand. "But I also know you can't live with these feelings in your heart. Things like this can take root and grow. If you hold that hatred, Nikki will still have an important place in your life. Let it go and let her go. God's been too good to you to have you hold a grudge. Marek's part of you and you're part of him. Don't let something so small and petty hold you captive. Forgive! Put her and what she did behind you."

"And if I do, then what? Do I open myself up for another attack from her?"

"No!" she vetoed. "I didn't say to be stupid. You'll never have to put your head in that particular lion's mouth a second time. But you must forgive. Don't forget. Always learn from your mistake. If you don't, it'll poison everything you hold dear. Don't let her sour your happiness."

"I don't know," Cameron answered honestly.

Granny watched her steadily. "Have I ever steered you wrong?"

"No."

"Then trust me. Look into your heart and forgive. Remember, the things you do have. Marek's love, your child and family, plus me. Then cautiously back away from the lion."

"And you," Granny glared a Marek, "do the same. Look at everything you have together and realize that regardless of that gal's sneakiness, you and Sweet Peaches are strong and good."

Cameron and Marek exchanged uncertain looks. Their hands crept toward each other and intertwined.

"Now," Granny stood, took her mug to the sink and rinsed it. "I'm going upstairs to see Jayla. I haven't had a chance to talk with my great-grandbaby, to see how she liked being in her daddy's office. While I'm gone, you two think about what I've said."

The wisdom of Granny's words hung in the air. As the old girl strolled from the room, Cameron glanced at Marek and found his eyes on her. The old girl only wanted the best for them and Cameron knew it.

This wasn't the first time Granny offered advice that proved helpful. But offering Nikki forgiveness wasn't Cameron's thing.

Marek was the first to speak. "Well, what do you think?"

She circled the rim of her mug with a finger. "She's got a point."

"Ronnie, how do you really feel about Nikki?" He held her hands within both of his. "Can you truly forgive her?"

"I don't know," she answered. "Seeing her today has dulled some of my anger. How about you? Do you feel any better?"

Marek's eyes narrowed to thin slits, admitted, "A little. I don't know if it's enough to forgive her."

"Granny's never steered me wrong. If she hadn't insisted I work out things with you, we'd still be feuding over foolishness," Cameron reminded. "The old girl moved us together.

Plus, my parents are coming around. Granted, it's a slow process, but it's happening. I don't want the sense of incompleteness hanging over us. Maybe it is time to move on."

Marek ran his fingers through his hair, offering her a resigned smile. "Let's give it a week. If Alice lets us. Then, if we feel differently, we can leave a message on Nikki's voice mail saying we forgive her. What do you think?"

"It sounds good." Cameron rounded the table, sat on Marek's lap and wrapped her arms around his neck. "You know Granny's not going to leave us alone until we resolve this?"

"I know," he ran his knuckle across her cheek. "But I want to pretend it's my decision."

Laughing, she whispered, "I love you," then lowered her lips a breath away from his.

"Ditto!"

Chapter Thirty-four

Cameron flipped through the pages of her Franklin Planner and sighed. The school opened in little more than a month and she still hadn't received the license. Frustrated, she slammed the book shut and tapped the edge of it with her fingers.

"Three weeks," Cameron mumbled aloud, counting the weeks since the inspection. "All I can do is wait," she muttered. There was plenty to do before the September grand opening. She took a yellow legal pad and a pencil from her desk and jotted down her ideas for the student orientation day.

Cameron shifted in her grandpa's wooden chair, remembering the day Granny gave it to her. "It'll bring you luck," Granny predicted as she supervised Marek's efforts to get the chair moved to the new location for the school.

It looks as if the old girl knew her stuff, she thought reviewing the student enrollment list. If her accountant's projections were correct, there were more than enough students to cover the school's operating expenses.

Outside her office, the front door slammed. One fluid motion brought Cameron across her room, as she smoothed her T-shirt over her jeans. If a prospective parent had dropped in for a look-see, she wanted to intercept them before they wandered deep into the school's interior.

Heading out the door, Cameron came to an abrupt stop inside the main office. Oh, Lord. Her heart jumped in her chest. Tara O'Rourke. *What did she want?*

"Good afternoon, Tara," she greeted stiffly. Uneasiness pricked like a needle on her skin. "What can I do for you?"

"Cameron," she returned evenly. "So this is your new place." Tara sauntered further into the room and ran a finger across the new workstation. "Nice. Real nice."

"Thank you." Suspicion made her cautious, as Cameron waited for Tara to reveal the true reason for her visit. Something was up. Tara's superior attitude guaranteed that.

"How's Justin?" She blurted out, hating the need to ask Tara for information about Justin. The redhead took such pleasure in doling out tidbits as she saw fit.

"Doing well in his new school."

"And his arm?" She persisted. "Is everything all right?"

"He's safe now."

Damn her! Cameron bit down hard on her bottom lip. Tara never missed an opportunity to place blame on her head.

"Good." She brushed away a drop of blood from her lip and said, "Jayla and I really miss him."

"I bet you do."

"I assume this isn't a social call," Cameron matched the other woman's casual tone, leaning her hip against the workstation. "What do you want, Tara?"

"Oh, nothing in particular." Shrugging, her green eyes

sparked with malice. "I just wanted to see your little operation before the state shuts the doors. That's all."

Cameron's heart galloped. What did Tara know that she didn't? Had the state contacted her? "That's not going to happen."

"Oh, really?" Tara's smile grew broader, tapping a finger against her lips. "Let me think. You've received your license, right?"

The heat of discovery rushed up Cameron's neck. Score one for Tara. *You're not getting to score any more points off me today.*

"I don't have time to play games with you. I've got work to do." She gave Tara a curt nod of dismissal, and turned toward her office. "Good-bye."

Tara's tee-hee stopped Cameron. "You didn't get it, did you?"

"My attorney thinks it'll happen any day."

"Sure he does." Tara laughed. "For my part, it doesn't matter if you do get it," her voice hardened and a sullen expression appeared on her face. "That piece of paper won't do you any good. I'm going to sue you and put your ass on the street. It'll be fun to see you scuffle for a way to feed your child."

I'm sick of you, Cameron thought as anger rocketed through her. Hands clenched and unclenched at her sides as she fought the urge to wrap her fingers around Tara's neck. Just as she was about to lose her mind, bits of her last conversation with Greg soothed her. 'She won't have a leg to stand on,' Greg promised that day. 'Without the validation of the state, there's nothing to back up her claim.' A sense of peace shimmered over her like a spring rain.

"Tara, file as many lawsuits as you want," Cameron smiled confidently. "It won't change my plans."

Cheeks spiked with red color, Tara accused, "You think

you're so slick. Living the good life, having everything you want. It's time somebody knocked you off your high horse."

"That's enough," Cameron snapped and moved to the door. "I've tried to be understanding because Justin's accident happened on my property. But it was just that, an accident. Your persistence in keeping the animosity brewing between us ends now. If you want to spend your life playing games, that's fine. Don't come here with that crap."

"What do you think you're doing? Dismissing me?" Tara placed her hands on her hips and sashayed around the room. "I don't think so."

"You've got the great career, the doctor boyfriend and a supportive family while I've got nothing. Nothing!" Tara cried. Eyes blazed and her nostrils flared. "You've stolen everything I wanted. I have to fight every day to feed my child. It's not fair," she stamped her foot like a spoiled child. "Why are you the one entitled to the golden life?"

Cameron wavered in the doorway, shocked by Tara's raving. What golden life? She had problems like everyone else, and Tara was a major contributor. "My life isn't perfect. I've never taken anything from you."

"That's where you're wrong." Tara sneered. She propped her hip on the edge of a workstation. "Think back about nine months. The Vanderhauf scholarship? How you got it and I didn't?"

"You applied for the Vanderhauf?"

"I applied." Tara lips thinned into a straight line. "Little good it did me."

"Let me get this straight," Cameron spoke slowly, putting all of her facts together in her head. "You caused all this trouble because I won the Vanderhauf scholarship?"

"Hell yeah."

Cameron's pulse spun out of control. She stumbled over her next question. "Jus—Jus Justin's accident? The complaint and the second letter was a set-up, to get back at me?''

"You got it in one. The Ed department taught you well," Tara's triumphant grin further increased Cameron's galloping pulse.

"That is the most petty, childish excuse I've ever heard. Do you realize what you've done?" Cameron shook her head, slamming her palm against the tabletop. The sound vibrated through the room. "What you've put my family through? Your own son? Over some money that wasn't yours to start with?"

"But not just any money. The Vanderhauf," Tara replied with reverence. "You got $50,000, prestige and first shot at every good teaching job in the statewide system." A look of unparalleled envy covered her white face. "There's not a student in the Ed department that doesn't covet that scholarship."

"Didn't you read the entry form?" Cameron stared back at Tara. "The judging was based on merit." She struggled to explain. "Don't you understand the rules of competition? Anyone could have won that scholarship. Anyone! I got lucky."

"Oh, come on, Cameron. It wasn't just *luck*. You kissed up to everyone in the department. You were their golden child. The rest of us didn't have a chance."

"You're wrong," Cameron repeated. "I got that scholarship through hard work, GPA and letters of recommendation."

"Justin and I are alone. With that scholarship I could have quit my job and taken the next year off to finish my degree." Tears of failure filled Tara's eyes. "The way things look now, I'll have to work a second job to save enough money for tuition. I hate spending so much time away from Justin." She wiped away a tear. "The last thing I want is to miss his childhood. Each day my dreams seem more and more remote. When will it be my turn?"

The tears in Tara's eyes were beginning to get to her. Cameron found herself swayed by the other woman's desperation.

"Tara, there has to be another way," Cameron insisted, stepping closer. "People go to school and work all the time. Why didn't you apply for another scholarship? Loans? Or grants?"

The hopeless expression in Tara's eyes mirrored the fright and despair Cameron felt when she realized she was pregnant. Oh, Lord. Those were such horrible, painful times. And Granny had been her salvation. She understood Tara's desperation. But not the reason for her accusations.

"I poured everything I had into getting that scholarship." Tara's eyes flashed with angry flints. "I lost pay, studied all night and took Saturday and Sunday classes. But in the end, you waltzed out with the money and opened up this place," she gave the room a disparaging once-over. "If I have to, I'll make it my life's work to close you down. God, how I hate you. You don't deserve all of this."

Appalled, Cameron retorted, "I didn't open this school with the Vanderhauf. There were specific guidelines. I had to adhere to each and every one of them."

"Yeah. At least you had the money. I don't have any help. Justin's dad isn't a doctor. Ralph would rather quit his job than pay child support. Hell, we haven't heard from him in years," Tara ranted, hands flying in the air. "And my parents are a lost cause. They told me not to look for anything from them when I kept Justin." She beat her fist against her chest. "I only have me."

Despair drove Tara, and Cameron felt it. It buzzed around the room like an annoying fly. But she wasn't responsible for the place Tara found herself.

"There was a time I believed we had things in common,"

AS LONG AS THERE IS LOVE

Tara continued. "Maybe we could have been friends. But life is so easy for you. Dr. Redding came along and gave your daughter a father. Justin wants a daddy so much," her voice broke. "Ralph certainly isn't it. And I can't give him one." She stamped her foot like a small child. "It's not fair."

"Tara," Cameron raised a comforting hand toward her.

"Don't come near me," she smacked Cameron's hand away.

"I'm sorry you banked all your hopes on that scholarship," Cameron said. "But I'm not responsible for your problems. It was a competition with a lot of applicants. Anyone with a better GPA and recommendation letters could have wiped me out of the box."

The rage etched into Tara's face, the anger in her voice, and the way her hands were balled into fists made Cameron feel exposed and vulnerable. A twinge of fear raced up her spine. Although she didn't think Tara would harm her, she didn't want to test that theory.

"Tara, I'm one of your resources. Why didn't you come to me?" Cameron inched her way to the door. "I might have been able to help you."

"And just how would you have done that?"

"I know people who could have offered you a job. They could have worked around your school schedule. Maybe even helped you find tuition money. I still can. If you want my help."

"No. You're not going to appease your conscience that easily."

"I'm just trying to help you."

Tara eyed her. "I won't take anything from you."

"Your choice," Cameron shrugged. "But I do suggest you contact your school advisor."

The front door slammed and this time both women turned

toward the sound. Briefcase in hand, Greg strolled into the main office.

"Hi," he greeted. His sharp gaze slid over each woman as he assessed the situation.

"Hey, yourself." Cameron moved closer to him.

He offered Tara his hand. "How are you, Mrs. O'Rourke?"

"Okay," Tara muttered, dropping his hand.

He nodded. "Glad to hear it."

"Excuse me," she pushed passed them. "It's time to pick up Justin." She stopped at the door to fire a final venomous gaze in Cameron's direction than hurried away.

Cameron's shoulders sagged.

"So what was that about?" Greg watched the empty doorway for a beat longer. "I'm surprised to find you two in the same room without bloodshed."

"Cute," she responded. "What brings you here? Wait," she raised a hand. "Give me a minute to lock the door."

Cameron considered Tara's confession as she returned to her office. It seemed incredible that her animosity stemmed from money.

The accusation about the Vanderhauf scholarship really stung. Hard work, her GPA and recommendation letters contributed to her being awarded the scholarship.

If only Tara had put the foolishness aside, come to her and talked about her situation. There might have been something she could have done. Maybe one of her colleagues could have offered Tara a position with flexible hours. Although the professors were sticklers about many things, they did understand the stress working adult students faced and usually tried to offer support and guidance.

Now, there wasn't much she could do. Tara's boisterous, continual complaints made it almost impossible for Cameron's colleagues to trust or hire her.

AS LONG AS THERE IS LOVE

Greg's appearance was a surprise. She rarely caught him away from his office or courtroom, in the middle of the day. Maybe he had news about the inspection. She really needed something to boost her tepid spirits.

Chapter Thirty-five

"Boy, am I glad you showed up," Cameron said in a tight voice. "Tara was getting a tad intense."

"Intense?" Frowning, Greg glanced back at the door. "How? Why?"

Despite the warmth of the day, goosebumps rose on Cameron's skin. "She finally revealed why she hates me so much," she rubbed her hands up and down her arms. "The lady has some serious emotional problems."

"How so?" Greg placed his briefcase on the floor and perched on the edge of her desk, a curious expression on his face. "What did she say?"

"Her reasoning." Cameron sank into her chair, turned to face him. "I won a scholarship she believed was earmarked for her."

Greg shook his head. "That's sad."

"Sure is."

"I assume you weren't the only person to apply for that money," he stated.

"You assume right."

"Did anyone ever tell Mrs. O'Rourke when you apply for a scholarship it means competing against your peers?" He shook his head again, rose and settled into the chair opposite her desk. "Other qualified applicants?"

"The Vanderhauf is the biggest scholarship offered each year. There are two categories in which graduates and undergrads compete. Unfortunately, that didn't register with Tara," Cameron sighed. Pity tugged at her heart. "She caused all this trouble over something that was out of my hands from the get-go."

"Now we know." Greg stretched his legs in front of him and studied her for several silent seconds. Seconds that seemed to stretch into hours. His brow wrinkled as he ran a finger back and forth across his chin. "What else?"

Embarrassed, her cheeks flushed. "I feel bad for her," she admitted.

"Why? The woman nearly destroyed your business. And you feel sorry for her?" A spasm of irritation crossed his face. "I don't believe you."

How was she supposed to explain this when she didn't understand herself? All she knew was that the hopeless, fed-up expression in Tara's eyes touched something within her.

"It's hard raising a child alone," Cameron answered. "My parents and Granny are my backup. But Tara's alone. And that's pretty scary. I've always believed single parents should try to form a network to help each other. Somewhere along the line, I didn't get that across to Tara. If she'd just trusted me a little, maybe things would have been different for her. I know people who could have helped her," she shook her head remorsefully. "Nobody will touch her now. I can't help her. Granny would say Tara cut off her nose to spite her face."

He eyed her uncertainly. "You're not planning to get involved with her again? Are you?"

"I don't know."

"You could be setting yourself up for more grief. Do you think that's wise?" A dubious expression marred his features. "Your emotions are in an uproar. Take a step back, think things through."

Cameron knew that. But she didn't plan to concede anything just yet. She drummed her fingers on her desktop, then added, "I don't know if I can or should help her. All I'm saying is I'm a single mother just like her and I sympathize with the place she's at in her life."

"I'm sorry Mrs. O'Rourke is not where she wants to be. But I didn't put her there. Neither did you." He strummed a finger at her. "Listen to me and listen good. You can't save the world, Cameron."

"I'm not trying to save the world," she denied, then forced down an egg-sized lump in her throat. "I know it sounds crazy after everything that's happened and I'm still pissed off about that crap. What I mean is, I understand the position she's in. Not what she did. I understand the desperation that drove her."

Greg threw up a hand in defeat. "I can't stop you. But," he stated in his most formidable voice, "as your attorney, I recommend that you think long and hard about this before putting yourself in the middle. And please, contact me before you make a move."

"I won't do anything without talking to you first," she promised. "Okay?"

"Good." He settled back into his chair. "Did she say anything else?"

"Yes," Cameron answered sheepishly. Greg was going to think she'd lost her mind when he heard this. "She going to sue me in civil court."

"Mrs. O'Rourke doesn't have a leg to stand on," he stated firmly and plucked an invisible bit of lint from his Ralph Lauren jacket.

"Right," she responded. "That's if the state finds her complaint unwarranted."

"Mrs. O'Rourke," he laced his fingers together and placed them in his lap, saying, "doesn't have a leg to stand on."

She straightened in her chair, scrutinizing Greg's passive expression for clues. A kernel of suspicion bloomed inside her. "You're awfully confident."

"I am."

"Why?"

"I got the letter today," he revealed, placing his briefcase on the edge of her desk and opening it. An official-looking white envelope lay on the top of his files. "Congratulations!" Grinning, he handed her the envelope. "You've been cleared of all neglect charges. There's some violations regarding the physical plant that you need to address within ninety days, and you need to have a few more fire drills each year. But everything else is in order."

Elated, Cameron hesitated, afraid to voice her other concerns. "W—what about the license for the school?" she stammered. "I need it ASAP."

Greg dug into his briefcase a second time and produced a second envelope. "You mean this?"

Cameron sprang from her chair and raced around the desk, snatched the envelope from Greg's hands and sent a silent 'thank you' heavenward, before removing the document from the envelope with shaky hands.

Finally, after all the stress of wondering and worrying, she had her license. Tears swam in her eyes as she examined the precious document.

Perching on the edge of her desk, Cameron struggled to control the trembling note in her voice. "Greg, does this mean I'm done with the State?"

"Almost. You have to fix those violations before they send someone to do a second check." He closed, locked his briefcase and set it on the floor next to his chair. "Once that's completed, the only time you'll need to deal with them is to renew your license."

"Thank God!" Peace cocooned her. "And thank you," she squeezed his hand. "I really appreciate all of your help."

"I told you we'd beat this." His thumb brushed sensuously across the back of her hand. "You didn't deserve the bad rep Tara's been passing around town. Especially now that we know what motivated her."

"True. But it's all behind me now," Cameron tugged her hand away and rubbed it against her jeans. She felt a tight, uncomfortable flutter in the pit of her stomach. "I was afraid the State was holding the license until after the inspection. It looks as if I was right. Wait a minute. If we got a letter. That means Tara must have one, too. Maybe that's why she paid me this nice-nasty visit."

"Could be," he said. "Although I don't see the point. What good would it do?"

"I don't know." She shrugged. "Personal gratification? Or one final stab at me. An opportunity to dig for more info? Who knows."

"I'll say it for the third and final time. She doesn't have a leg to stand on. So now that this case has been officially and successfully concluded, let's celebrate." The sensuous flame in Greg's eyes made her pulse race. "What are you doing this evening? How about dinner?"

She planned to celebrate, but with Marek. The time had come to clear the air, she couldn't avoid it anymore.

"Greg?" she began. He was so dear to her. The last thing she wanted to do was hurt him, but this talk was inevitable. "I can't do dinner."

"Why not?" He lifted a brow. "Doesn't Mrs. Butler have Jayla?"

"Yes," she answered, searching for the right words.

"So, what's up?"

"I've already got dinner plans."

"I see." His eyes narrowed. "With Marek?"

Cameron eyes widened in surprise. He was more in tune with her life than she had suspected. "Yes." Dropping the license on her desk, she faced him. "We're working things out." She brushed her damp palms along the side of her jeans.

"I see," he answered, evenly.

"Do you?" She shifted from one leg to the other.

Greg stepped close and placed a hand on her shoulder. "I didn't know things had gone that far," he remarked. "Are you guys talking about marriage?"

Heat raced up her neck. What was the deal? Everyone kept asking if they were getting married. "The subject hasn't come up."

"Then you're still free," he pressed.

"No," she paused. "I'm not."

Silence reigned for several tension-filled seconds as new parameters for their relationship shifted and were quietly accepted.

After several moments, he stated, "I see."

"Do you really?"

"Yes." Greg nodded and glanced at the toes of his highly polished wingtips. "I can't deny that I had hoped for something more." He lifted his head and his eyes darkened with sadness. "Especially after this case was settled. I thought you might feel free to explore the possibilities."

"I'm sorry. I've always loved Marek," she whispered. "I can't change my feelings. Believe me, I've tried. There isn't anyone else for me."

He picked up his briefcase and stood stiffly before her. Disappointment had extinguished the sensual fire in his eyes. "There's not much more to say, is there?"

"No." She raised a hand toward him. "Greg, you're a good friend—"

"Stop!" He clamped his eyes shut. "Save it," he shot back, opening his eyes. "I don't want to hear it."

Her hand dropped to her side. "I'm sorry."

Cameron trailed Greg to the front door and stopped, hoping some words of comfort would overtake her. There weren't any words to console him. She felt so guilty. What could she say? As Greg stepped into the bright afternoon sun, regret pierced her heart. Why did people have to get hurt?

When they had first discussed dating, she had been up front with Greg and warned him against expecting too much from her. But he had proceeded to make his own plans. And now they both were suffering because of it.

Giving herself a mental shake, *Come on, Cameron,* she coaxed. There wasn't anything more she could do for Greg. It was time to think about the positive things.

She had the license.

Returning to her office, Cameron straightened her desk and gathered her purse. She snatched the license from the desk and strolled from the office. Since Granny had Jayla, this was a perfect opportunity to drop by Marek's and tell him the good news.

If her luck held out, she'd get to his condo with a little time to spare for a private celebration. Maybe they'd share a little afternoon delight before she returned home. Humming, Cameron locked the front door and hurried to her car. She couldn't wait.

Chapter Thirty-six

Excitement bubbled up inside Cameron as she raced to Marek's door. She stabbed the doorbell and waited with the school license clenched in her hands.

"Come on, Marek." She punched the button a second time and muttered, "I've got something to tell you."

The door flew open and Marek filled the entrance in a pair of faded jeans, a blue T-shirt, bare feet and the portable telephone attached to his ear. His eyes slid along her body, sparkling with welcoming fire.

Her skin tingled everywhere his eyes touched. He leaned forward and tasted her lips, lingered for a pulse. The sweet tenderness of his kiss made her quiver.

Marek broke the spell when he spoke into the telephone. "No, Dad." He motioned with a tip of his head for her to follow him. "There's a better way."

She traipsed behind him. He placed a hand over the telephone mouthpiece and whispered, "Be with you in a minute."

Nodding, she followed him into the kitchen.

"There's a couple of hotels in the area. The Holiday Inn or Best Western are pretty good." Opening the refrigerator door, he removed a Pepsi and tipped the can in her direction.

She scrunched up her face, shaking her head. "No."

"They're comfortable," he spoke into the phone and popped the tab on the can. "I would recommend them."

Cameron left him to his call, making her way to the living room. "Come on, Marek. Get off the phone," she muttered, peeved. "I've got something to tell you."

All My Children's Erica Kane's animated face graced the television screen in Marek's living room. Cameron went hot all over when she remembered the last time he convinced her to join him on the sofa to watch their soap. At least that's what he called it. But the tape rewound several times before they actually saw the perils and heartaches of the residents living in Pine Valley.

From the center of the room, she looked around and spied the curio. "Hey, the lights are out." She moved closer for a look-see and flipped the light switch. It filled with muted light.

"What in the world!" She snatched open the door. The curio shelves were empty. Hmm, she stroked her chin. Maybe the housekeeper removed them.

I'll ask Marek, she decided, hurrying to Marek's bedroom and stopped outside his door. With his back to her, he stood over the bed with the telephone still glued to his ear. Over his shoulder, she recognized the curio's photographs strewed across the bed.

"What time do you think you'll get here?" He asked, shoving photograph after photograph into a manila folder. "Dad, why don't you and mother stay here?"

Outlaws? Her stomach tangled into a thousand knots. Mr. and Mrs. Redding were headed to Holland. Why hadn't Marek told her?

She wavered in the doorway. Her head swirled with questions and doubts. What was he up to?

Suddenly, everything jelled. The photographs. His secrecy. Marek didn't want his parents to know about her and Jayla? Hurt threaded its way through her heart. Could Marek be that devious?

With this newfound deduction, she stumbled back down the hallway on a cloud of uncertainty and turned a critical eye to the living room. Jayla's rocking chair was gone. She grimaced, as if she'd just taken a blow to the chest. Marek bought that chair on one of their first days together. The toy chest that sat next to the patio door was conspicuously missing. Each discovery shoved a stake of betrayal further into her heart. How could he do this to them?

NO! Marek wouldn't. This must be a mistake. He loves us. Or did he?

Her gaze returned to the curio's empty shelves. *I'm going to be sick,* she gripped her stomach.

How could she have been so stupid? Such a fool? Why had she believed he loved them when it looked as if he used them for his own sick reason? Her father was right. Actions always spoke louder than words.

Tears ran down her cheeks. But her resolve remained firm. Things were just fine before Marek barged into their lives. They'd be fine once he was gone.

It was time to head for the mountains, she decided. Cameron gathered the license from the sofa and tore down the hallway and out the front door.

This ended their relationship. Tears blinded her as she tripped down the stairs and caught herself seconds before she hit the ground.

At the base of the steps she glanced over her shoulder, staring at Marek's condo through a haze of tears. Bitter waves of betrayal ate into her soul. Turning away, she rushed to her car.

Cameron shoved the key into the lock and opened the door. Once more she glanced at Marek's house, then at the keys in her hand. A wave of uncertainty attacked her as she speculated on the last time she'd raced away without talking with Marek.

That time cost her dearly. Now, there was even more to lose. Was she willing to take that risk a second time without confronting Marek?

Like a nagging wife, Nikki Anderson's smug declaration filled Cameron's thoughts and confused her a little more. 'You don't know how to trust. Every time things get too difficult you always follow the same M.O. Run away without asking for the truth.'

What had the whole Nikki incident taught her? Hadn't she been wrong that time? Who's to say she's wasn't wrong this time? Didn't Marek deserve the benefit of the doubt?

Tapping the key against the palm of her hand, she considered everything. Maybe she hadn't known how to trust, but it was time for her to figure it all out. How difficult would it be to ask, "What's going on?" After all, Jayla's happiness was on the line. As well as her own.

I laid in his arms and promised to trust him, she thought, remembering her first visit to his condo. Now, she was on the threshold of breaking all her promises.

If she left now, she'd never get to the bottom of things. Or learn the whole truth.

Trust must start now, Cameron decided, slamming her car door. She couldn't leave. They'd come too far to let everything disintegrate without a word or explanation.

Slowly, she climbed the steps, rang the doorbell and placed a calming hand over her queasy stomach. When she returned to her car, all of her questions would be answered.

The door swung open and Marek looked down at her with a puzzled expression on his face. "Did you lock yourself out?"

AS LONG AS THERE IS LOVE

She shook her head unable to speak.

He stepped aside. Cameron moved past him back to the living room, feeling very much like "dead man walking." Totally afraid. For a second, her resolve faltered. She considered escaping without asking a question. No. This time she needed the truth.

"Are you done with your phone call?" she asked softly.

"Mmm, hmm." Marek dropped his running shoes on the floor in front of him. "That was my Dad."

"Oh?"

"My parents want to come for a visit this weekend." He watched her very closely.

Cameron stiffened at the mention of his parents' visit. She still hadn't forgotten his family's role in their separation.

"Mmm," she responded as the band around her heart tightened a bit.

"How do you feel about that?" he asked.

Shrugging, she answered in a even, noncommittal tone, "They're your parents."

"True," he returned in the same tone. "But you're my family, too."

"When are they due?" she asked.

"Saturday afternoon."

Cameron nodded. This was the moment of truth. She had to let it go or ask what was going on. Swallowing hard, she realized she couldn't let it go. "Marek?" She ran her fingers though her loose hair, hesitating. A part of her needed proof, wanted the reassurance of comforting words. But that wasn't trust. Maybe it was time to let it go.

"You need something?" he asked, brows wrinkled above his eyes.

I promised to trust, to stand with you. She shook her head. *Let it go.*

Marek slipped his sock covered feet inside his shoes,

dropped to one knee and tied them. He glanced up at her and asked. "Are you okay?"

"Umm, hmm."

"Good," Marek smiled. "Do you have time to run to the mall with me?" He stood and grabbed the manila envelope off the coffee table.

Her heart did a rat-a-tat-tat in her chest when she saw the envelope. "How long do you think you'll be?"

"Long enough to drop these pictures at the framing shop."

"Pictures?" She parroted. "Frame shop?"

"The pictures from the curio. I'm having them professionally framed."

Her mistrust eased. "What prompted that?"

"I'm tired of them slipping between the shelves. Plus, I'm always afraid they'll get torn beyond repair."

Guiltily, he looked away, than turned back to her. "I can't lie to you," he watched her with a steady gaze. "You know my parents. They aren't going to be real happy about what's going on," he drew his fingers through his already tousled hair. "But that's their problem, not mine," he stated flatly. "I just felt Jayla deserves all the benefits that come with having both sets of grandparents. So, I'm trying to give my parents an opportunity to rise to the occasion. Accept it and allow them time to understand how important their contribution as grandparents can be."

Cameron heard the uncertainty in his voice. She wanted to go to him and hold him, promise him things would work out. But she couldn't guarantee it.

"To be fair, I wanted to bring them here on even ground. They don't know anything about Jayla and I wanted to be the person to tell them," he paced back and forth in front of the television. "Having pictures of us proudly displayed would pretty much steal my thunder and give them a chance to secure their masks in place. I want the real deal. No polite lies. The truth. Then I'll know how to work with them. No

AS LONG AS THERE IS LOVE

matter what they say, you, me and Jayla are a family. And we're going to stay that way."

"Marek," she wanted to make things easier for him, offering, "this doesn't have to be done right now."

"You're wrong," Pain skirted across his face and vanished. "Now is exactly the time to get this done."

But she also heard the jiggle of coins in his pocket, noticed his stiff posture. Poor baby! This was more important to him than he'd let on.

"Family is important. We can chose just about everything else, but not our family. I went through enough with my own. Are you sure you're ready to go fifteen rounds? If things don't work out, you could end up further adrift than you are now. I don't want to see that happen."

"It won't," he answered firmly, without hesitation. "Things will work out. Just remember, you and Jayla come first."

"Why can't you have them both?" she asked. "With a little finesse, you can do this."

"Ronnie, don't be disappointed if it doesn't work out the way you'd like," he warned, cupping her cheek. "My family isn't close like yours. They need to know where I stand. That's why I'm doing this."

"Please think long and hard before you make any decision."

"You'll be involved in any decision I make," he promised and drew her into his arms.

"Marek, do you love me?" Cameron asked than kissed his lips.

"Yes. I love you," he nuzzled her neck. "What kind of question is that?"

"How about proving it?" Now that she'd started this, she wasn't sure she had the guts to finish things. Taking a deep breath, she plunged ahead. "Are you willing to make a change in your life? I'm tired of being in your place or my place." She waved a hand around the room. "I want to be in our place."

"What's your suggestion?"

"Do you love me enough to marry me?" she asked, momentarily stunned by her boldness.

"Ronnie, are you proposing?"

Oh, Lord. She'd actually did it. *Way to go, Cam!* First you don't trust him. Now you propose marriage. She had it all going on today.

This wasn't the time to back down. "Yes," she answered. "I am. Will you marry me?"

Laughing, Marek grabbed her hand and dragged her down the hallway to his bedroom.

"What have you got in mind?" she asked with a saucy wink. "A little afternoon delight?"

Marek swirled her around so that the back of her legs leaned against the bed. "You always upstage me." He gave her a tiny shove and she landed on the bed.

"Hey!"

Marek followed her down onto the comforter and rolled onto his side. He dug inside his nightstand and produced a small black velvet box. Her heart fluttered in her chest when she realized its significance.

"Alice and I had it all planned. She'd keep Jayla. I was going to wine and dine you. Impress you with my charm and wit." Marek's large frame settled next to hers and he took her left hand. "After dinner we'd stroll downtown, enjoying the evening sights. Then I was going to bring you back here for a night of long, persuasive lovemaking." Marek's kiss offered a promise of things to come. "Saturday, when my parents showed up I'd present you as my fiancée. But," he stated, "you insist on being one step ahead of me. So I'll say yes. I will marry you."

He opened the velvet box and presented her with the most

beautiful pear-shaped yellow diamond ring set in gold. "I have one condition."

She gazed longingly at the ring. "What's that?"

"You can propose." He slipped the ring on her third finger and added, "and I'll even accept. But, I choose the ring."

Happiness welled inside her. "Oh, Marek!" She threw her arms around him. "I can live with that."

He grinned at her. "Cameron Butler, I love you." He smiled down at her. "Now," he kissed her lips, "how about that afternoon delight?"

ABOUT THE AUTHOR

As Long As There's Love is Karen White-Owens debut novel. Ms. White-Owens was born in Detroit, Michigan and resides in the Motor City. She holds a bachelors degree in Sociology from Wayne State University and is currently working toward a master's in Library and Information Science.

In addition to writing, she is a librarian at Loyola High School and devotes her free time to editing manuscripts for aspiring authors and teaching the fundamentals of creative writing to the students of the Detroit Writers Guild Young Authors Program.

Her husband of twelve years is her biggest fan.